BEATING HEART
BABY

BEATING HEART BABY

LIO MIN

FLATIRON
BOOKS
NEW YORK

BEATING HEART BABY. Copyright © 2022 by Lio Min. All rights reserved. Printed in the United States of America. For information, address Flatiron Books, 120 Broadway, New York, NY 10271.

www.flatironbooks.com

Library of Congress Cataloging-in-Publication Data

Names: Min, Lio, author.
Title: Beating Heart Baby / Lio Min.
Description: First edition. | New York : Flatiron Books, 2022. | Audience: Ages 14–18.
Identifiers: LCCN 2021056812 | ISBN 9781250819093 (hardcover) | ISBN 9781250819109 (ebook)
Subjects: CYAC: Musicians—Fiction. | Sexual orientation—Fiction. | Transgender people—Fiction. | Dating (Social customs)—Fiction. | Asian Americans—Fiction. | Los Angeles (Calif.)—Fiction. | LCGFT: Novels.
Classification: LCC PZ7.1.M638 Be 2022 | DDC [Fic]—dc23
LC record available at https://lccn.loc.gov/2021056812

Our books may be purchased in bulk for promotional, educational, or business use. Please contact your local bookseller or the Macmillan Corporate and Premium Sales Department at 1-800-221-7945, extension 5442, or by email at MacmillanSpecialMarkets@macmillan.com.

First Edition: 2022

10 9 8 7 6 5 4 3 2 1

To my boy best friend

I think that I'm bigger than the sound!

—"CHEATED HEARTS," YEAH YEAH YEAHS

Regardless of warnings,

the future doesn't scare me at all.

Nothing's like before.

—"SIMPLE AND CLEAN," UTADA HIKARU

SIDE A

The Sunshower Sessions

Track 1

I glance at the billboard—an ad for college-prep tutors—as it passes by before bringing my gaze down to street level. While Aya navigates traffic, Los Angeles taunts me through my open window: giant succulents chewing up whole squares of sidewalk; palm trees shooting up into the sky like leafy rockets; corner stores blasting snippets of reggaetón and K-pop and Top 40 and rancheras. A city of a thousand cities, the signs on storefronts changing languages and styles every few blocks.

At the red, the car next to us collectively shrieks, "This is my *jaaam*!" The bass of Cola Carter's new single shakes the Agumon bobblehead stuck to our dashboard. I wince. Obviously Cola Carter didn't become a pop star just to get at me. But it's impossible for me to hear her music and not think about Memo's song. The soundtrack of the best and then worst moment of my life.

When I close my eyes against the harsh sun, the billboard's afterimage flashes behind my lids. *Now what?*

Aya tilts her head toward the other car. Of course she's going to make a comment about Cola's track. "You listen to any of her stuff?"

I shrug and mumble, "I guess," twisting deeper in my seat both to get a clearer look at the city unfurling around us and to avoid the weight of her eyes scanning over me, searching for an opening. When I refuse to give, Aya sighs and cranks up the stereo. We roll down Alvarado as Vince Staples and Kilo Kish call and respond over a cold beat.

We only got to LA a couple of days ago, but so much of this city is already familiar. Not because of movies or music videos or social media. But because of Memo. It's the place they grew up, where they maybe still live. And all these things I've only ever imagined, impressions of a sun-soaked life pieced together from our chats, are now streaming past my window.

I spent years dreaming of visiting them here, of finally meeting them in person. But I never got the chance. And then they were gone.

I've heard that it should take you as long as a relationship lasted to get over it. For three years, Memo was the first person I talked to in the morning and the last person I talked to at night. After they ghosted me, I kept up the routine, checking my phone and waiting for their username to blink back online, for their chat window to pop up with a "Hey" or even "I hate you," taking whatever they gave me if it meant an end to the radio silence. But for three years, I've been in what Aya generously calls "a bad place," spiraling out in school, getting in fights and cutting classes like they didn't matter, because they didn't. Because nothing did.

Now, I should finally be free. Instead, I've landed right in the middle of the city that reminds me of Memo the most.

The thing is, I wouldn't recognize their face if we drove past them. I don't know their real name or what their voice would sound like if they called out mine. But for a long time, Memo was my only real friend. My best friend. They'd understood me in a way no one ever had before or has since, but I don't think I ever told them that. And I'll never have the chance.

Aya honks and curses as the car ahead of her changes lanes without signaling. After a few more minutes of tense driving, she pulls over to the curb and clears her throat. Her long black ponytail makes a swishing sound against her headrest when she turns to me. I steel myself for the usual talk about the future, but Aya surprises me when she takes a sharp breath and sighs, "Santi. I know it's been hard, and I've been hard on you. But I'm also proud of you. You've been through so much and . . . I know your mami would be proud of you, too. We're home now, okay?"

I can't help it—tears spring to my eyes. I grit my teeth to keep them from growing. According to Aya, Inay had been an easy crier, too. Out of all the things I could've inherited from her, of course I got the tears.

Most of what I know about Inay is secondhand, recollected through Aya, or discovered by accident. It's like after her death, I couldn't hold on to any of our actual memories together. But Aya keeps her alive. The only furniture we've always moved with is the folding table where Aya and Inay used to do their homework and share meals together as kids. Wherever we live, it serves the same purpose: to hold a framed photo of the three of us together, mango studding our wide smiles, and a program from the funeral. MERCEDES ARBOLEDA: FOREVER IN OUR HEARTS.

By reflex, I touch the small golden cross around my neck. It'd been Inay's, given to her by her parents when she got married.

She and Aya had grown up together in the same tight-knit community a few hours north of LA. The kind of place where the girls become wives before they graduate high school—which is what happened with Inay.

In the end, Inay moved south to start a family while Aya saved money and faked interest in the guys her parents brought around. They didn't talk for years and Aya moved east, chasing record deals that always fell through and playing tours with bands that a lot of times treated her like a live-in maid, based on her stories. But when Inay showed up at Aya's door with a suitcase, that folded-up table, and a baby from a man who wasn't her husband, Aya took us both into her life like we'd been there all along.

I want to ask Aya what it feels like to come home without Inay. If she misses her parents, who cut off contact both because of Aya's girlfriends and because she didn't turn her best friend away. If there's any chance my grandparents will ever forgive their daughter for living her own life, or want to meet me. But I swallow these thoughts and fix my watery gaze at the next place I'm supposed to start fresh again.

De Longpre High is nothing like my last school, or the school before, or maybe any school not in LA. For one, it actually looks kinda nice. Arched open-air hallways. Solar panels on the roof. Floor-to-ceiling windows in the library. A large banner that reads WELCOME, SUNSHOWERS! stretches across a tiled courtyard. It's too wholesome, too Hollywood perfect. But then a sign of life: a lush camellia fails to cover someone's tag, CLOWDY BOYS 666, which a chain-smoking custodian tries in vain to wash off.

A line of kids snakes out of the courtyard. More mill around in small groups, catching up and taking videos and pictures. Almost everyone's holding an instrument case or a flag. They all look at ease. I haven't been around this many brown people since we lived in New York.

We're home now.

Aya's quiet cough takes me out of my head. When I blink again, the light's a little dimmer, and the people look less like a casting call and more like a bunch of kids who are willingly at school on a Sunday afternoon for the first day of the Sunshowers marching-band camp. Aya sucks in her cheeks and searches for the right words, the ones that'll get me through my second attempt at junior year without any suspensions or late-night phone calls wondering where I am. Before she can say anything, I mutter, "What if I can't do this?"

"This" is marching band, but also De Longpre High and LA. "This" is the promise of stability, which both of us know isn't guaranteed. Aya reaches over and lightly cuffs my shoulder. Her voice drops in annoyance but also weariness. "Just try. Not for me, but for yourself. Please. Oh, and don't forget, I'll be at a session so take the bus home."

The part of me that cared about trying, that thought about the future and wanted something from it, disappeared when Memo did. But Aya has that look in her eyes, like she's the one who failed me and not the other way around.

I grunt in response, grab my trumpet case from the back seat, and duck out of the car.

De Longpre High has never had much of a football team, but over the past decade, the school's marching-band program has become "a force to be reckoned with in the Southern California band circuit," according to a local news video I found online. Behind the reckoning: Kai Kahalehoe, a.k.a. "Cap." Ever since he brought his Marine Band–trained direction to De Longpre a decade ago, the Sunshowers marching band became one of the best in the state. Its reputation was big enough to attract the attention of a documentary crew a while back, but something fell through and it didn't happen.

More seniors who do marching band graduate than from any other De Longpre school group. This is part of the reason why, at the beginning of the summer, Aya sat me down, put on *Drumline*, and said coolly, "Santi, you better start practicing trumpet again."

The other part is because of Cap. Because he was Aya's high school marching band director, once upon a time. Because he's the one who brought her back to LA. And because she's counting on him to perform a miracle.

My palms start to sweat. I grip onto my case tighter. Am I nervous? Why would I be nervous? None of these kids look like they'd be able to take me in a fight. And what's stopping me from turning around and walking away? It's LA, it's summer, and I'm in the middle of the city instead of dipping my toes into the Pacific for the first time.

I could tell Aya I didn't fit in. No, too vague. How about, they made us play at orientation and my section leaders cut me? But then she'll ask Cap. . . . I scratch my cheek and try to think of another out. Okay. I have until the end of the week of band camp to figure out why I can't stay. Otherwise, I'll commit. It's the least I owe Aya for going to bat for me now and so many other times. If nothing else, maybe I'll make some friends.

The line moves forward. I pull out my phone and scroll aimlessly, artist artist thirst trap ad thirst thirst tattoos anime ad ad anime anime ad—

"Oh my god, Prof!!!"

I fumble my phone as the girl in front of me stops abruptly and I get a faceful of curly dark green, almost black hair. Green waves her phone at the lanky boy next to her. His long black braids slide over his shoulders and form a curtain as he bends down to look at her screen. "Wow. Of course Suwa drops the biggest news of his life as a line in the group chat."

Just as suddenly, Green turns around. "My bad, I'm all up in your—" She freezes and peers at me. "I don't know you, but I know you . . . the junior-senior-freshman! Wow, huh, you're way cuter in person." My eyebrows shoot up in surprise as she loops an arm with mine, chattering, "I'm Mira, this is Octavian. Your name's Santiago, yeah? An alto—no, right, you're a *trumpet*."

Octavian unravels Mira's arm from mine and cuts in dryly, "Welcome to the Sunshowers, Santiago. Mira, back it up."

They seem friendly. More touchy-feely than I'm used to, but maybe that's an LA thing. I flash a peace sign and a smile. "Santi. Nice to meet you."

They exchange looks. Octavian pretends to sniffle. "A sweetheart."

Mira grins. "Oh, you're ours, baby boy."

I don't mean to laugh but one escapes, too loud.

They exchange another look. Mira pouts. "We have to keep him."

Octavian rolls his eyes. "For someone who's not into guys, you're coming on strong."

Mira waves him away. "All right, Santi 101, let's go. Favorite song?"

My heart stops. Out of all the questions she could've asked. I try to be chill about answering so of course I start rambling, "Well, uh, it's pretty basic if you're like, into music, and we're at band camp, so, you must be . . . into it. But, um, it's 'Exit Music.' That mystery song that dropped a few years back and it's . . . It means a lot to me. Personally." At some point my voice drops to a whisper. I hadn't meant to sound so wounded.

"Exit Music." Memo's song. The one they shared with me in confidence and that I leaked by accident, setting off a chain of events that ended in Memo disappearing from the world. The mistake that's haunted me for three impossibly long years.

Octavian's expression shifts but Mira doesn't catch my tone. She laughs, "Real. Some songs just hit different," then asks me a few more rapid-fire questions—"What kind of food do you like?" "You dance? You look like you got moves"—as we sign in and head over to the football field.

This time Octavian's the one who pulls me in toward the center of the crowd that's assembled in front of a set of beat-up bleachers. Mira immediately gets swept into a group hug while Octavian starts catching up with a girl with shaggy white-blond hair. I step aside as someone wearing a rainbow tie-dye hoodie pushes past me to join Mira's hug circle, and self-consciously hold my case closer to my side.

Right. Despite the warm welcome, I'm still the new kid. I make eye contact with a crow perched on the surrounding fence. It stares beadily at me but flies off when a cheer erupts from the crowd. Everyone around me has stopped what they were doing and turned toward the bleachers, faces rapt with excitement.

A deep, spine-tinglingly loud voice booms, "Good morning, Sunshowers! Shall we?" And I finally get my first IRL look at Cap: a broad, beaming man wearing golden aviators and a white polo, its short sleeves straining around his biceps. In photos, he looks like he could pass for his fifties, but according to Aya, he's pushing seventy. I wonder how he keeps up with a bunch of kids until I watch him walk over to a raised platform, bypassing the stairs, and hoist himself onto it before hopping to his feet.

"WE SHALL!" I shiver as everybody but me shouts back. When Cap calls out, "Section leaders, assemble," Mira and Octavian straighten their postures and drop their smiles as they line up behind him.

I listen closely to Cap's introductions. Felipe Morales, the drum major, stands apart from the rest of the group. Mira Ortiz-Walker, with the sousas. Octavian Williams, trombone.

Cap gets to my section last. "Lucía Hernandez, trumpet." Their white-blond friend steps up. "And Suwa Moon, trumpet."

I crane my neck to get a better view of Suwa. His name popped up a few times in articles about the Sunshowers. One of the best trumpet players in the entire state. And unless there's another Suwa at this school, he's also the one Mira and Octavian were talking about before.

I'm not trying to stare, but unlike everyone else wearing T-shirts and soft shorts and sneakers, Suwa's wearing ripped black jeans, black velvet creepers, and that rainbow tie-dye hoodie. The ends of his inky black hair cling to his cheeks. He'd seemed smaller when he walked past me, but his presence overwhelms everyone else's: a flower in a field of grass.

I study his face. He looks a little bored, eyes roaming beneath curling bangs. But when they land on me, his face changes into a scowl. I break out into goosebumps and look away.

"Hey, freshman, some advice." The girl standing next to me taps my shoulder. "Don't stare at Suwa. He'll bite before he barks, you get what I'm sayin'?"

I laugh nervously but I can't help it. Like a moth to a flame, I look back at Suwa. Our eyes connect again. His dart away and I twitch at the sudden jolt in my chest.

After an hour of inside jokes, Sunshower history, and reviewing basic drills and commands, Cap calls a quick time-out before we break for section intros. I step into the bathroom for a breather after I drop off my case and think about what Aya said, about me really trying. I psych myself up: *Maybe this will be the year I turn it around.*

Then the bathroom door creaks, and I watch a pair of familiar creepers cross the floor. I pull up my phone camera to quickly check how I look before opening the stall door.

Suwa's at the sink, one hand pushing up his bangs while holding the corner of his eye. The other smudges a black pencil into his lash line. He ignores me as I take the sink two down from him, but I can't stop myself from trying to catch his gaze in the mirror.

"What're you staring at, freshman?" Suwa's voice isn't what I expected—scratchy and low.

Why does everyone keep calling me that? "I'm not a freshman," I say automatically, then cringe. I'd been aiming for friendly and landed on awkwardly defensive.

He's still only looking at my reflection. I pick at my outfit:

an oversized T-shirt and jean shorts, both from the Goodwill we lived next to in Nashville. Suwa obviously cares about fashion more than I do or can afford to. His cheekbones glow—is that highlighter, or some supernatural dewiness? I want to ask him how he isn't sweating in the heat but what comes out of my mouth is "You wear makeup?"

Suwa puts down his pencil and finally faces me. I was right, he's pretty short. I smile, another defensive reflex, as his eyes turn up to meet mine.

"Do we have a problem, *freshman*?"

I wince at the venom in his tone, the way the words curl in his mouth. I'd only wanted to comment on how put-together he looks compared to everyone else, but I suddenly remember something else Aya'd told me about Cap: "Back in the day, he was one of the only people who looked out for us."

"Us": a universe in a word. I know what she meant because I'm one of "us," too, though the definition shifted depending on where I lived. In New York, it meant I cried a little too easily. And then I started kissing boys. Around Nashville and then Jacksonville, it meant all that, plus I was the only person in my class darker than blond.

I stumble over myself as I take a step back. "No, I uh—that's cool, makeup's cool, I mean, you look like *that*." I start to nervously laugh when Suwa's eyes, one rimmed in black and one bare, narrow, but I bite it back, my teeth cutting into my bottom lip hard enough to almost draw blood.

Neither of us says anything for what feels like forever. I'm frozen in embarrassment, but I can't read Suwa's reaction. Should I tell him I like everyone? I linger on the twitch of his bare eye, then the slight tremor of his fingers, and finally the rise and fall of his chest, a motion that picks up as he realizes where I'm looking.

And something dawns on me. One of Aya's best friends is a trans guy and he once talked to me a little about what he looked like, how he carried himself, before he got top surgery. I open my mouth to tell Suwa if that's what's up, I didn't mean to stare and I'm not normally this awkward, for real.

I take a pause to actually gather my thoughts instead of blurting that out, but it's too late. Suwa swipes his eyeliner off the edge of the sink and, as he finishes his other eye, announces frostily, "You don't belong here." A chill runs down my body as he continues, "I listened to the recording you sent of your playing. I don't know how you finessed your way into the band, but this is my turf. My family. But since Cap's asked me to watch out for you, I will be."

Suwa caps his eyeliner and slips it into his pocket. Every step he takes toward me echoes in my ears. When we're shoulder to shoulder he tilts his head and murmurs, "Whatever you're thinking of saying, don't. Luckily for you, I'm only around for your freshman season, but you better not fuck things up for the rest of us." He laughs, acid in the sound. "Have fun with junior year again. You're off to a great start."

Suwa breezes past me. I catch the backdraft scent of smoke. Some bite.

Track 2

I pace outside the auditorium doors. I want to tell Suwa this is a big misunderstanding. Actually, no, I don't want to tell him shit. When I replay his little speech in my head, anger thunderclaps through my body. But it's also self-directed. He'd reacted to what he saw and heard in front of him: At best, I was an asshole, and at worst, I might be someone who'd want to hurt him. God, and the day had been going pretty well up until then.

I push a little too hard on the auditorium doors. The rest of the trumpet section whips their heads around as the doors bang open, then shut.

There are nineteen of us—four new kids, including me. The other trumpet section leader, Lucía, leans against the edge of the stage. A name tag on her chest reads *Lucía, she/her*. She'd startled at my entrance but has since remained in the same position, checking her phone and pursing her lips while the rest of the section catches up.

Then a door slams from the back of the stage. Lucía shakes her head but grins as she calls out, "Always so dramatic."

Suwa slips through the curtains and leaps down into a slouch next to her. Like Lucía, he's now wearing a name tag: *Suwa, he/him*. He slides his hands into his hoodie pocket and surveys the room. I don't think I imagine the way he purposely avoids looking at me.

Fine. The feeling's mutual.

I shift in my seat so I'm facing Lucía, who runs a hand through her hair. A flash of black roots underneath the white-blond. "Hi. I'm Lucía, one of the trumpet section leaders."

She turns to Suwa. "Suwa's the other. If you're doing concert band, too, chair auditions can be kind of cutthroat. But within the Sunshowers, Cap likes to say that we're a family. Think of me and Suwa as your parents." Suwa raises an eyebrow. I hear giggling in the back. "You can come to us if you have any problems with the music or the charts."

Lucía goes over the highlights of the football schedule: homecoming, a "rivalry" game with another local high school. "Hey, maybe we'll make the playoffs this year." Suwa cracks a small smile at that, then outright laughs when she starts doing a spirited Cap impression. He fiddles with his hoodie strings, blows his bangs out of his eyes, laughs again at something one of the other trumpets shouts out, stretches his shoulder and makes a face, takes a pull from Lucía's water bottle—

I jump when Lucía claps her hands and says, "Floor is yours, Suwa," and realize I've missed everything she's said for the past few minutes. I mentally pinch myself for not paying more attention to her. She seems nice; Mira and Octavian were warm and funny. Why am I fixated on the one person in the Sunshowers who's gone out of his way to be mean?

"Okay, so." A few people whispered through Lucía's intro, but they hush when Suwa takes over. "On top of the football games, we play in the Southern California Band Association awards circuit. We don't care if you screw around during the games, but the competitions are the real deal. We start with the Empress Eyes Gala, held at St. Ofelia's in Malibu. Then the Silversun Cup, held at El Diamante in Ladera Heights. And finally, the Angel City Festival of Music, held at the Rose Bowl.

"Freshmen," he continues, and dips his head to look me in the eyes, "all the band first-years. You'll be assigned reserve spots, but no one marches in the shows until they're up to our standard."

I want to yell back at him: *Message received.*

Suwa checks his phone. "Lunch is from now until one. There's a spread on the field. There'll also be name tags there, for your preferred names and pronouns. Get to know each other. Squad leaders, hang tight, we're doing the leadership meeting now."

As the rest of the section leaves, the other band leadership files into the auditorium. Mira's talking at Octavian, her arms waving wildly as his expression gets more and more pinched in confusion. *Mira, she/her; Octavian, he/they.* Then Mira spots Suwa. Her eyes light up and she yells, "How's my best boy doing?" When he grins and flips her off, she laughs and blows him a kiss.

Suwa's gaze flickers to me and his grin turns into a cold glare. I turn around so quickly that I almost body-check one of the percussion section leaders, who'd also been in Mira's huddle earlier. *Ariso Ng, they/them.* Their hair, streaked with all different shades of purples, hangs just past their ears. Considering the dead-eyed look on their face, the multicolored hearts doodled around their name are someone else's addition.

They look me over. "So you're the one Mira keeps bringing up. Not that she's the only one." Ariso makes a face that's either a smirk or a grimace.

I don't have the energy to figure out what they mean so I say, "Sorry, I gotta . . . hungry," and dip past them.

Every other school I've been at, it took a few days for people to acknowledge me. What's the deal with De Longpre High?

I pull on the door leading to the practice field and barrel straight into Felipe (*Feli, he/him!*). He flashes me a good-natured smile and claps me on the shoulder so hard that my teeth rattle. "Keep that energy!" As Felipe walks away, I watch his back muscles shift under his tank top. Should I start working out? How physical is marching band, anyway? Not that I'll be doing any marching, if Suwa has his way.

I'm still dazed as I make my way onto the field. One of the trumpet freshmen waves me over to the food line. I don't want to cut but she keeps waving; I try to look apologetic as I slip in the line behind her.

"I'm Laurel. Santiago, right?" Laurel hands me a "bulgogi burrito," which looks promising. She opens her mouth, closes it, then opens it again to ask, "Um, I'm not trying to be rude, but the rest of us were wondering, are you . . . ?" She gestures toward her face.

I guess LA isn't that different from the rest of the country. I mull over my answer as I take a bite, and *wow, that's good*. "Call me Santi. And my in—my mom . . . is Filipino but I'm mixed—"

"No, I mean like, are you on TikTok or Twitch or . . . ?" Laurel pauses before blurting out, "Did you move to LA for acting?"

My eyebrows shoot up in surprise. That's a first. I'm used to being asked about my appearance but always "What *are* you?" in a tone that makes me feel like an exotic animal. I'm both flattered and confused by Laurel's question. "Um. No?"

I take it back, LA's *different* different.

We're settling into our seats with the other new trumpets when Cap's voice cuts through from behind me: "Trompetistas! Good afternoon!" He laughs—another close-quarters sonic boom—and wedges himself between two of the other kids. "Marcus, amazing glasses. Tiffany, how's your brother doing at Michigan?"

I tune out their chatter as I finish my burrito, racking my brain for everything Aya's told me about her old band director. Scar on his left eyebrow from a motorcycle accident. Played a gig with Prince and got his autograph tattooed on his shoulder. Once pretended to be Aya's dad so she could go to LA for a summer music camp while her parents thought she was doing some church youth retreat.

I wonder if he knew Inay. I wonder if there's any way to ask him about her.

As if he read my mind, Cap gets up, lays a hand on my shoulder, and drops his voice. "Santiago, find me after orientation. Just to check in." Then he cups his hand over his mouth and shouts, "Five-minute warning!"

After lunch, the full band gathers in the auditorium. We spend the rest of the afternoon listening to a recording of the show "performed by our wonderful leadership!" and taking care of paperwork. By the time Cap dismisses the band with another call-and-response "Shall we?" "We shall!" my head's throbbing. The sheet music looks like nothing I've ever played. I squint at the drill charts but my eyes keep blurring as I try to keep track of the numbers and arrows and overlapping Xs.

And it finally hits me: I'm way out of my league here. Do I really want to spend the next few months playing catch-up and getting picked on by my section leader? I told myself I'd stick with this for at least the week, but I honestly don't know if I'll even last that long.

I wait around the band office for Cap. In videos of Sunshower performances, he's all stern brows and orders, so it's disorienting watching him ham it up. He has personalized send-offs for everyone, even the new kids. But when everybody's gone, he sighs. In the glow of the golden hour, the white in his hair burns and I finally see how deep the wrinkles around his eyes are.

"All right, Santi. May I call you Santi?" He holds the door open for me and I nod as I pass through before walking straight into a rolling rack of uniforms.

"Careful!" Cap laughs sheepishly as we weave through a maze of instrument cases and other band equipment. He lifts an overstuffed folder of sheet music off of a chair and gestures for me to take a seat. His desk is covered in framed photographs; generations of band kids, beaming through the decades.

Cap takes a deep breath and carefully chooses his words. "How's the move? Settled in yet?"

"Yeah, we're mostly unpacked, still getting to know the city. Thank you for all your help, sir."

The corners of Cap's eyes crinkle when I say "sir." He steeples his hands and pulls one side of his mouth up in a sloping smile. "No need to be formal. Aya's practically family, which means you are, too."

After she found out that I'd failed my junior year, Aya started bringing me to church, which was how I knew that shit had really hit the fan. But then, a sign: Cap rang her up out of nowhere and asked if she was free to gig for a friend who handled a lot of film and TV contracts. She jumped at the chance for a clean start, so she packed up our life again and headed back to the state she'd once run from.

"I've been trying to set aside some time for us to meet but my schedule's tight through the season, and she's already working like mad, squeezing my buddy for more gigs. A ballbuster, then and now." I make a startled noise and Cap laughs, this time quietly. "She's always been a hard worker. And loyal, too. To what she loves, and who."

I try not to melt into the chair as Cap continues, "I met her a few times. Your mother. She'd come to practices and draw the players. Had quite the talent, but most of the kids back then didn't have the time for dreams. Or the support." Something shifts in his eyes. "Santi, I . . . I'm so sorry about your loss. Aya called me after the accident, and . . ."

I cut the pause by saying a little too loudly, "I appreciate that, sir. And thank you again for the welcome, though honestly, I don't think I'm good enough to be here."

Cap shakes his head. "Everybody starts somewhere. All you gotta do is keep showing up. Your section leaders are two of the best kids I've ever taught and they'll help you out. You'll be on the field soon enough." I don't have the heart to tell him that one of his favorites would probably rather drink bleach than give me the time of day.

"Well then, my boy." Cap gets up so I do, too. As he holds the door for me again, he whistles. "It's gonna be an interesting season."

Since my bus is still twenty minutes away, I take my time roaming around the empty school. A few other clubs meet before the semester starts and I take note of their calling cards: someone's uniform abandoned in the locker room, a ring light left on outside a door marked YEARBOOK in collaged letters. I turn the light off before heading out into one of the open hallways. Close my eyes, take a deep breath.

Then someone barks, "Who's there?" I tense up and turn around to face Suwa, because of course. We stare each other down like that Spider-Man meme. I'm pretty sure my expression is a mirror of his, a mix of genuine surprise and annoyance. What's *he* still doing here?

Suwa clears his throat, looks down, and drags one shoe along the ground, the sole kicking up little bits of rock and sand. Then he raises his head, looks me dead in the eye, and asks, "Coming back tomorrow?"

What is his deal? I try to get through to him. "Hey, I'm sorry, okay? For before, in the bath—"

He cuts me off and takes a step forward. "My friends are tripping over you, but I'm not as easy as they are. Once the 'Ooh, pretty new kid' thing wears off, you'll have to prove yourself on the field like the rest of us. Which, good luck with that."

My face flushes. If his opinion of me is already at rock bottom, I might as well grab a shovel and dig. "You think I'm pretty?"

Suwa's jaw drops. Before I can savor my "got 'em," I notice a flake of eyeliner on his cheekbone and impulsively swipe my thumb on his face. The flake falls, leaving a smudge. My thumb stays. Our point of contact buzzes like a cicada summer.

I jerk my hand back, but the damage has been done. Now Suwa's the one blushing but his voice sounds strained when he spits, "Save the jokes for when you've learned the show, freshman. Despite what Lucía said, I'm not responsible for you. When you need hand-holding, go to her."

I think back on all the times we've collided today. Is it weird that I'm now finding Suwa's prickly-pear thing kind of funny? His put-downs are kindling for the fire he's lit under me. I still don't know what I'm doing here, but I'm not going anywhere. And I want to prove that he's wrong about me.

Instead of declaring any of that, my brain latches on to what Lucía had said—*Think of me and Suwa as your parents*—and I blurt out, "You got it, Dad!"

Before he has time to react, I sprint for the bus stop, my cheeks burning as I run toward home.

Track 3

I learn a lot about marching band in the weeks before our first competition, but only one thing about Suwa: He's trying to kill me.

The only times he talks to me directly—always preceded or followed with a mocking *"freshman"*—are when he's yelling at me for stepping in the hole and ordering me to run laps as punishment. It's embarrassing how often I find myself running, but one time, I catch him staring as I wipe the sweat off my face with my shirt. His expression when he sees that I've noticed is almost worth all the humiliation he's put me through.

Suwa was right, though, even if he was a dick about it. Despite Lucía's constant corrections and Felipe's occasional motivational back-slaps, I'm just not as good as everyone else. And if I'm being honest, without Suwa on my ass from the beginning, I might not have "applied myself," as my old guidance counselors used to stress.

For the first time in years, I go straight home after practices to work on the show music. (The first night I did this, every neighbor in the building stopped by our door to introduce themselves and politely ask me to "stop that shit." Aya and I stayed up until midnight soundproofing my room as best as we could.) On the weekends, I explore LA alone while she works, only meeting up for dinner. I start running regularly again, first one panting mile, then three, then five, following single streets through the city before turning around.

School's tougher. I'm one of the only band kids who doesn't also do concert band or wind ensemble so my schedule is totally different from most of theirs. I spend my lunch listening to music at a table with a bunch of other loners. I sketch a little or use the time to study the drill charts. I actually pay attention in class. My first tests all come back as Bs and even one A, which I leave in Aya's gig bag tucked in with her mallets.

During practices, the kids in my section are friendly enough but everyone else sidesteps me, especially since I have a habit of marching into other people. Sometimes I hang around Mira and her crew before the football games, though if Suwa's with them, I steer clear. Mira gives me her phone number and we text about hanging out. I never follow through, not because I don't want friends, but because I'm so busy working on . . . myself, I guess.

Then the night before the Empress Eyes gala, two games into the season, Aya drags me out to dinner after practice. After a suspiciously silent start to the meal, she kicks my shin under the shimmering grill table, which is covered with about fifteen plates of banchan and marinated meats.

"Santi."

"Huh?" I snag the last chunk of candied sweet potato. "Aya, that hurt."

"You should be hanging out with people your own age."

I devour a lettuce wrap and answer with my mouth full, "I

don't mind hanging out with old—" I freeze. Aya isn't strict about much, but she does have rules, and rule number one is: Never say anything about her age, even if she brings it up.

Aya reaches across the table and pinches my cheek. "So relaxed, huh? Like a frog thinking it's in a warm bath when it's slowly being boiled alive." She releases me, perches her elbows on the table, and stabs a chopstick in my direction.

"You"—*STAB STAB*—"need to fess up about whatever's going on"—*STAB*—"because all you do is practice and run and cook with me. Don't get me wrong, I love it, but you're seventeen. I know I told you I don't want you working this year, but that doesn't mean you gotta spend this much time alone and at home."

I rub my cheek as I work out what to tell Aya. She's right, most kids wouldn't be actively trying to hang out with their parents. Parental figures. "I'm trying to make up for all the years I gave you trouble."

Aya sighs in exasperation before putting me on blast: "Or you have no friends, Santi." Even with K-pop blaring from the speakers and the drone of sizzling meat coming from every table in the packed dining room, half of the diners turn their heads in our direction.

I shift uncomfortably in my seat. That's not true, exactly. There's Mira and Octavian and Felipe, kind of. Ariso's hard to read, but Reva, their girlfriend and one of the color guard captains, is pretty funny and really chatty; she seems to know everyone in band's personal business. Una chismosa for sure. Lucía would probably be a friend if I wasn't such a pain in her ass.

Sure, most kids manage school and other stuff around their social life, but maybe I've got a chip on my shoulder because I'm repeating a grade. And, a dark thought: I spent years trying to fit in places that didn't want me, so I got used to going out of my way to be liked. What if I'm having trouble adjusting to being normal, instead of always being the odd one out?

Rather than explain any of that to Aya, I roll my eyes and focus on loading the last piece of seafood pancake onto my plate.

Aya pins it with a chopstick. "Don't roll your eyes at me. Santi"—*STAB STAB STAB*, now with the other one—"I brought you out here to have a life. Live."

Now I'm the one who makes heads turn with an incredulous laugh. "You brought me here to get it together. I'm here. I'm together." I eye the pancake piece. "Ask Cap if you want. I'm fine."

"Oh, bueno." Aya pulls out her chopstick, only to pluck the piece off of my plate. Between chews she says, "I'm gonna give you a green light. The next time you can go out, go. No questions, no strings. It doesn't have to be all-or-nothing. I know you know this."

I sit back in my chair and look, really look, at Aya. Even before Inay died, Aya was one of the only constants in my life. I never knew my dad; I have trouble remembering Inay's face without a photograph in front of me. How many times has Aya insisted that I can be and do better? That I'm worth the effort she puts into our lives?

"Okay."

Aya blinks slowly at me, then cracks a smile. "Thought so. Ay!" She waves down a waiter. "Santi, order whatever you want."

When the sun rises on Saturday, I drag my feet getting up until Aya literally pulls me out of bed. On the drive over to the school

I tap out my fingerings on the dashboard, practicing even though I know I'm not going to be playing.

A fleet of buses awaits to bring us to St. Ofelia's for my first marching band competition. I sit in the front of the bus with the other first-years. We trail after the rest of our section as the Sunshowers make camp under a large tent by the football field. I didn't think I'd be nervous, but somehow just being around that many people who are hardcore about band makes me take the whole thing more seriously.

After our warm-up, I search for a spot to chill before our call time. I wander the halls—these West Coast schools and their open campuses—before stumbling into a secluded courtyard. And then I hear a familiar voice: "So this is how it goes? We're right back where we started?"

Suwa steps out from behind a column. He's arguing with someone over the phone. "I'm not going to pretend I'm someone I'm not. Not anymore. Never again." He paces in tight circles, his eyes down. I search for an escape route but he keeps moving until he sputters, "Well, she's not here. Look, I'm about to play for a thousand people. Because I like this. I'm good at this. And I want to be *seen*." He spits out something in Korean; Aya's hooked on K-dramas, so I think I get the gist of what he said.

Suwa hangs up, flings his phone away from him, and howls. There's no other word to describe the sound. The echo's still going when his phone skids to a halt right in front of me. I pick it up and hold it out, racking my brain for an excuse for eavesdropping. "I, uh, I was grabbing some air."

Suwa doesn't move so I walk toward him, careful to keep my head down so he doesn't see any pity on my face. He'd said "Dad" for sure, then something about love with a voice that cracked with pain. I've learned more about Suwa in thirty seconds of accidental eavesdropping than I have in weeks of being around him.

When he makes no move to take his phone back, I look up.

Suwa's crying. Based on the way he's clenching his jaw, he's trying hard not to, but the tears pool at his chin. His hand shakes when he finally reaches for his phone and he mumbles, "Don't be late for call time, freshman." For once, no fire behind his words.

If he doesn't want to talk about it, I get it. But I'm only halfway down the hall when I hear his phone clatter onto the ground again. I turn back and watch Suwa's knees buckle before he collapses, wheezing. I run over to him. His gasps are coming out ragged and his hands are frozen into claws except when his fingers twitch jerkily into painful-looking fists.

I know what this is. The first few months after Inay died, I'd have night terrors and wake up in the middle of a panic attack. When Aya learned they were happening, she'd taught me how to keep from falling apart.

I crouch down but pause before reaching out to him. Suwa's made it clear that he doesn't like me. If our roles were reversed, would he help me? I mentally knock myself on the head. I can't think like that, not when he's sipping on air, wide eyes fixed on the floor.

I unfurl his fingers and hold his hands. "Hey, man, you're—you're gonna be fine; you just have to breathe. Follow my lead." I let out a half laugh. Like he needs help with breathing exercises; Suwa can maybe hold a note longer than it takes me to run a lap around the practice field. "You've probably got the best lungs in the band. Now." I lift my head and our arms. I breathe in through my nose, then let the air whoosh through my mouth.

When he mirrors me, he whistles. We both smile, mine wide and his weak. "Okay, we're gonna do that again."

I don't know how long we spend together on the ground but eventually Suwa starts breathing normally again. I clear my throat as I get up. "How—how're you feeling?"

Suwa sits with his palms up on his thighs. He isn't returning my gaze. I shift between my feet. I don't expect him to suddenly change his mind about me, but not even a "Thanks"? But this isn't about me. I should get his friends.

As I'm about to walk away: "I—could you help me up?" Suwa clenches his hands as he says this, eyes cast to the side. I reach a hand down and after some hesitation, he takes it. I hover my other hand over his shoulder. When he nods, I hold on to him and pull him up.

We stand like that for a beat before I spring back. I take a deep, shuddering breath, and when Suwa does, too, I feel a sudden charge in the air.

I start, "Sorry," but he whispers, "Thank you." It's the gentlest I've ever heard him speak.

A roar ripples out of the stadium. When the announcer calls out the name of the band going on before us, Suwa picks his phone off of the ground and starts walking. I trail a few paces behind, shoving my hands in my pockets, watching the swing of his uniform tassels as we return back to the Sunshowers camp. I want to ask about what just happened, but there's too much else going on right now.

When we regroup with the trumpets, Lucía runs up to Suwa. She says, her voice spiking with panic, "Chloe tripped and landed weird on her ankle. She's getting checked out at the med tent, but—" She notices me behind Suwa. "Santi. Can you march her spot?"

I glance over to the group of people who aren't playing, lining up to join the Sunshowers' friends and family cheer squad from the stands. I think about the hours of practice I've drummed into my head, my body. My fingers tingle and for whatever reason, I think of the fluttering heartbeat I'd felt through Suwa's skin. "Sure. Yeah. I can."

As we assemble in the tunnel, Mira catches me in the lineup. She mouths, *Oh my god!* and gives me a big grin and a thumbs-up. Ariso raises an eyebrow as they coax the snares into formation. When Lucía brings her squad past me, she grabs my elbow. "You got this. Just follow the music. Suwa's your marker: As long as you can see him, you're not too far off."

When Suwa lines up next to me, I almost don't hear him shout, "You're going to be fine!" above the din of the tunnel. And as the announcer's voice booms out, "Last but not least, the De Longpre Sunshowers!" I watch his lips pull into a wry smile, then read their command: *Breathe.*

For the first time all season, from the top of the chart to the final bow, I hit every note.

The Sunshowers place first. Suwa receives a soloist honor. As he collects the trophy, he flashes our section a smile so wide and radiant, I almost drop my trumpet. Then it's back on to the buses, where I promptly fall asleep, crashing from the day's adrenaline high.

As we're unloading at school, I spy Mira struggling to pry her sousa case out from under a mountain of gig bags. I lend her a hand and almost strain my shoulder; how does she march with this giant thing around her?

"Great job out there!" She winks and whispers, "See you tonight!" before skipping away.

She's out of earshot when it hits. *Tonight?*

Aya drives me home. I eventually forget about what Mira said and fall into my regular nighttime routine. Go on a run. Wolf down dinner. Watch some TV with Aya. I'm shaving after my shower when my phone buzzes.

Second buzz. I frown at the mirror. I almost don't recognize my own reflection; this is the longest my hair's ever been, curls starting to sprout off in alarming directions.

Third buzz. I grab my phone off of the sink and find that I'm now in a group chat with Mira and a few unknown numbers.

SANTI U CAN'T GET OUT OF THIS ONE
Whatup dude it's Octavian
Feli In Da Chat !!!
DO U KNO HOW TO GET OUTTA YR PLACE YET

I pause before sending, like can i leave? ya. Aya will probably push me out the door.

A flurry of messages buzz in response. A party at the place of someone named "Pocky," which should be memorable but I draw a blank. TTALLY MAND AATORY, according to Mira.

I look up the bus schedule. Next one's in twenty, but no transfers. I type back:

taking bus. eta 30-ish

Another flurry of buzzes almost immediately:

Cool seeyou soon
Y ARE ALL THE BOYS O BUSES
NO MRE DRIVERS IN LA??????
SANTI HURY LAAATE LT SWAA !

I snort at Mira's devolving messages. All right, I've missed
parties. And I guess I kinda want to see the super-serious Sunshowers after dark. I pad over to Aya's door and knock. Based
on the smell seeping out, she's lit some incense. When I press my
ear to the door, I hear Kelis cooing.

"Hm?" She cracks open the door and pokes her head out. I
do a double-take at her sheet mask.

"I think . . . I've got plans. I'll make my own way there."

"Oh. OH!" She gently smacks the side of my head. "Look at
you, with your *plans*. Hey, if you can't get a ride back, I'll probably be up. Let me know and I'll grab you. Be safe. Have *fun*."

She shuts the door with a click.

I look down at my bare chest, boxers, and slippers. I should
probably change.

I pace the sidewalk as I wait for the bus. I'm not used to wearing
flashy clothes but I'm trying to make an impression tonight. On
top of black jeans and an Odd Future shirt from one of my not-
exes, a silver motorcycle jacket that's actually Aya's. I'm hoping
it'll help get my message across: *I'm here to make friends.* My pink
Vans are covered in clouds, from when I used to draw on everything I touched.

The bus is packed. I grab a standing bar and zone out, caught in the crush of bodies. A few stops later a bunch of people leave. I slip into a newly vacated seat and apologize to the person next to me for bumping into them. "My bad."

It's Suwa.

He has headphones on but he slowly takes them off, resting them loosely around his neck. He looks shocked, and when I peek at my reflection in the window, I have the same look on my face.

"...Hi?" He breaks the silence first, shock giving way to confusion.

I gulp and croak back, "Sup," then wave weakly. I leave my hand up for an uncomfortable beat before abruptly dropping it.

Suwa makes a sound like a muffled laugh. His eyes flick over my outfit, or maybe it's just a trick of the flashing lights on the bus.

"I thought you drove." I almost don't hear him, thanks to a chorus of shouting from a few drunks in the back. He clears his throat before continuing, "You always pull up to games in that old Toyota."

"Oh, that's my, uh, guardian's car." God, I hope he didn't notice it the night I spent ten minutes in the parking lot trying to get the engine to start. "She lets me borrow it for the games but I figured it probably wasn't a good idea to drive tonight, to a party. Since it's ... a real party, right?" Wait, what if this is some wholesome team-bonding thing?

Except Suwa's not dressed for trust falls and campfire stories. My breath hitches in my throat: he's wearing a cropped black-and-white striped sweater over a different pair of ripped black jeans. Visible through the rips, fishnets. Suwa tucks his headphones into a small black backpack and brings his feet up behind the wheel well. Those damn creepers.

When I look back at Suwa's face, he seems amused. "It's a real party." His phone pings; he starts typing rapidly in response to a seemingly endless series of messages.

He's got a *Paranoia Agent* phone case. Okay, he's not a casual. "You like Satoshi Kon?"

Suwa slowly turns his head before cautiously replying, "Yeah. You watch anime?" He sounds surprised.

"Some." We're not friendly enough for me to let him know how deep it goes. "But not any of his stuff."

Suwa puts his phone in his pocket and opens his mouth, but doesn't say anything. Then he leans toward me and asks, in a low voice that makes my stomach twist, "How . . . did you do that? At the competition."

Oh. Can he really not believe that I made it through the show without messing up? "Uh, well, Chloe's my squad leader, and I've been practicing a lot, on my own."

Suwa bites his lip. His tone is apologetic when he says, "No, inside the school. When you . . . you saw me, and you knew what to do." He pauses before blurting out, "How did you know?"

I crack my thumbs; it's a nervous tic I'm pretty sure I picked up from Aya. I don't know why, but I answer honestly. "I used to have panic attacks all the time. It's easier to deal with them when someone's there. Like, guiding you through the process. But, y'know, if you're stuck in a spot where you have to deal with one alone, you can kind of train yourself to redirect that energy. Like . . ." *Am I rambling?* "I used to keep a notebook on me and draw, to distract myself. It's hard to think in the moment but if you get them regularly, it's helpful to build a practice. An . . . an escape route, kind of."

Suwa laughs. The hair on the back of my neck stands up when he says, "An escape route, huh? An exit."

The PA system calls out, "Las Palmas. Las Palmas."

Maybe Suwa's only being nice now because I've proven that I'm not totally useless. And it's not like I've forgotten how he's treated me since I first got here. I tell myself that's why when the bus pulls up to our stop, I bolt, following the sound of blasting music as I walk into the party alone.

"Who the hell is Pocky?" I shout at Mira as she fiddles with her phone, queuing up songs that make everybody go, "Oh my godddd, I forgot about this."

In sharp contrast to every other high school party I've been to, not everyone's drinking. There are a few vats of ominously bright blue liquid and cases upon cases of beer, but Ariso and Reva are only passing out drinks to upperclassmen; I guess I make the cut, despite my "freshman" status in the band. Other kids knock back Jarritos and aguas frescas. The smell of pizza makes my stomach growl. Cups litter the table, some of them with scrawled-on names. "Blondie"? "Supe"?

Who *are* these people? I guess my inner thought came out, because Mira shouts, "You'll find out soon enough, bud! Wow, I'm done with this, if you want the rest," giggling as she passes me her cup. Hers is labeled "GG."

I stack it on top of mine and drain it. The music swirls around me and the sickly taste of cheap alcohol gives way to a kind of honey-sweet euphoria. All the songs she's put on are pleasantly nostalgic, until a too-familiar intro starts playing through the speakers.

"Oh, *this* is a throwback!" Reva detaches herself from Ariso and shouts out, "Mira, turn it up!"

And suddenly, I hear "Exit Music." My good mood collapses. Of course everyone here knows it, loves it. Mira sings along to the opening chorus, then shouts, "It's your number one, yeah?"

She's trying to do me a favor but I feel like I'm standing at the edge of a rabbit hole, my chest tightening as Memo's song blasts around me. Before my body starts to full-on freak-out, Ariso cups their hands around their mouth and hollers, "FRESH-MEN, ASSEMBLE."

The music stops abruptly. I shake my shoulders out. It's okay. I'm okay.

"C'mon, now." Lucía, appearing from nowhere, motions toward the front. I point to myself, swaying a little, and protest, "Wait, are you serious—"

"Step to it, freshman!" She cuts me off and pushes me toward the front. All the first-years are holding hands. Laurel reaches her free hand out to me; I grab it and almost take her down when I stumble.

Then, "Sunshower freshmen!" Felipe—Feli—has the tenor of a coach, or a cult leader, addressing the party from his perch on the bar table. "Congrats on making it through the first competition!"

"As you can tell," he continues, "we take marching band pretty damn seriously. In Sunshower band tradition, it's finally time to bestow you with a special initiation gift: band names. For the rest of your first year, this is what you'll answer to."

Feli hops off of the table. "Some of y'all might've been told that tonight we're meeting at Pocky's place. That's our lovely and gracious host Reva, the literal model captain of the color guard." Reva waves daintily from the front.

"What's your name, Reva Yu?"

"My name is Pocky Monster, because I love chocolate cookie snacks and I know y'all wanna catch *all* of this." She blows Feli a kiss and giggles as wolf whistles pierce the air, before returning the question. "What's your name, Felipe Morales?"

"My name," Feli says as he grins and rolls up a sleeve, "is Super Smasher, a.k.a. Supe, which is definitely only because I love video games." He flexes and kisses his bicep. Reva pretends to swoon as the crowd erupts rowdily again.

From the corner of my eye, I spy Suwa slinking into the patio area. Since leaving him on the bus, I haven't spotted him again until now. He'd been typing on his phone but he puts it away and visibly reorients himself. I realize the blue might be hitting me hard as my eyes hazily drag up his legs, catching on the parts where his skin flashes through the rips in his jeans.

"Section leaders! You know what to do." Feli tips over into a deep bow before striding over to Suwa, who scowls but also blushes when Feli slings an arm around his shoulders and whispers in his ear. Suwa removes Feli's arm but smirks at what he says. I have to tear my gaze away from the nonexistent space between them, mentally throwing cold water on myself before joining the rest of my section, huddled up by a hanging wall of ferns.

Lucía smiles widely. "Freshmen, *steeee-ehp* forward. Suw*aaa*, get over here." She pouts as Suwa approaches. He pokes her cheek before threading his arm around hers.

Around me, the other upperclassmen link arms. And then

Laurel loops her arm around mine, shooting me a smile that I think is supposed to be reassuring.

"These names, freshmen, arise from a combination of careful observation and research." I can't tell if Suwa's being sarcastic or not until he adds, "But if you have a genuine problem with yours, let us know. We can be wrong. And after this year, if you feel whatever about it, you never have to use it again. Clearly, Feli likes responding to his. I didn't."

"Disclaimer over." Lucía giggles. "Think of this as like, your official 'Hi, you're one of us.' Laurel, come up, come up, come *up*." Laurel skips over to Suwa and Lucía, who envelop her in a hug and whisper into her ears. When Laurel steps away, her eyes are sparkling. Someone shouts, "What's your name, Laurel Mendoza?"

Laurel belts out, "My name is Princess Peachy because I'm a goddamn princess and I have a great attitude!" The section breaks out in applause and she curtsies before taking a spot next to her squad leader. This is kinda corny but her smile's about to swallow her face. Clearly this means something, and as the new-bie, I can roll my eyes at this tradition or be game. I can be game.

I fidget from foot to foot as the other freshmen call back their names. And then I step up and am so, so close to Lucía, and Suwa, who smells like smoke and something sweetly floral. Honeysuckle, maybe. I lean forward and steady myself against his shoulder to keep from turning my face into his hair.

"Santi, there was a *lot* of debate about your name." Lucía's the one whispering but it's Suwa's breath that's hot against the side of my neck.

"Mira told us that you love 'Exit Music,' so your name's a lil' tribute to *BEATING HEART* and their 'Freshman Feature.' We know you've been grinding, keeping your head down, but trust me when I say our class has been talking about *you* since before you got here." Then she whispers my new band name.

Suwa doesn't say a word during the entire exchange. After we break, he looks everywhere but at me. I clear my throat and turn around. Someone calls out, "What's your name, Santiago Arboleda?"

I take a deep breath and answer:

"My name is Beating Heart Baby because I've got good taste in music, I'm a fake freshman, and, um, I'm single, if anyone wants to change that."

My face reddens as people actually whistle and cheer for me.

When I turn back around, Suwa's gone.

It's my own fault for mentioning "Exit Music" back at band camp.

I'm a band freshman. "Exit Music" became famous because of the music magazine *BEATING HEART*'s "Freshman Feature" special issue. The kind of press that, even these days, can still put a song or an artist on the map overnight. Which is what happened to Memo. Only, that's not what they wanted.

I bite the lip of my cup. What is it about LA that's got me constantly in my feelings? No, that's missing the point. What's up with *me* that every vague reminder of someone I haven't talked to in years sucks the air out of my lungs?

I let Mira pull me into a circle with Octavian and Feli to "welcome our lil' Beating Heart Baby for real," and they reminisce about their own freshman-year initiation ceremony. At some point Ariso and Reva join in, but I just can't stop thinking about Memo. I excuse myself and step away from the group, my head swimming from sugar and booze and old, sad memories.

I put my drink down and slip out of the patio to wander the grounds. There are *grounds*. Aya and I only ever lived in apartments or shared houses. De Longpre High isn't like, Beverly Hills, but it's glossy in a way that I hadn't expected. I'm reminded of what some of my Florida friends joked about when I told them I was going to LA: a lot of gangland; metal detectors at the gates; "You'll finally be with your people" jokes. Which, reflecting on it now, was definitely racist. I wrinkle my nose.

Then I stop. Sniff. Smoke. I follow the scent to an alcove deeper inside the garden.

It's coming from Suwa, who's leaning up on one leg against a super-dramatic statue of an angel. He's got a lit cigarette in his hand but he doesn't make any move to smoke it. A sliver of moonlight ripples against his hair. When his closed eyes flutter open, Suwa growls, "Who's th—" But his face relaxes into surprise when I step into the light. "Oh."

Cute.

Of course I've seen him before but I take a moment to really look at him. His eyes are dark brown, almost black. His lips, not quite closed. And my fingertips still remember how soft his skin is.

I square my shoulders. "Me again."

Suwa mumbles something to himself before he stubs the cigarette out against his shoe and slips it into his pocket. "You should be celebrating."

"I did. That blue stuff is, whew." I clear my throat. He isn't walking away or telling me to shut up. Am I imagining it, or is Suwa giving me an opening? Where do I even begin? *Do you*

*hate me for leaving you on the bus? Do you still think I'm an asshole
from our first encounter? Are you actually okay? What's the deal
with your dad? And, why* do *we keep bumping into each other like
this?* I guess I could start with the obvious. "I don't mean to be
that guy, but smoking is like, terrible for your playing. Lungs.
And your regular lungs."

He stretches. The hem of his sweater rises, revealing a crescent of belly. Then he steps toward me. I gulp.

"I don't smoke."

I look at his pocket, then his face, then his hand, then back to
his face again. ". . . Right."

Suwa shrugs. "The smell . . . reminds me of someone." Then
he smirks and changes the subject. "What the hell does that
mean? 'Best lungs in the band'?"

Out of all the things he could bring up. I blush so hard I'm
surprised I don't explode into flames and exclaim a little too
loudly, "I don't know, I was running my mouth!" Then quieter,
"I'm sorry. For ditching you on the bus. How . . . how're you
doing?"

Suwa lets out a long sigh and takes a seat at the base of the
statue. My body moves before I have time to think about it and
I slide into the space next to him. And it appears again—that
buzzing charge I'd felt after I helped him through his panic attack. I instantly visualize this feeling as lightning. If I touched
Suwa's skin, would he have goosebumps, too?

What am I *doing*, thinking about touching him again?

Suwa grimaces. "*I'm* sorry, for being such a dick from the
beginning of the season to, um, now." He sullenly traces a spiral
in the dirt between us. "My class, specifically me and my best

friends, went through a lot of shit when we were freshmen. We really only had each other in school for a long time. So when they immediately claimed this new kid, wanted to fold you into our family . . . I rejected it." His voice fades into a whisper. "But you looked out for me, even though you had every reason not to. Why?"

I turn my head up toward the sky. *Why?* Even yesterday I would've gone on record saying Suwa despises me. I don't want to think about it as catching him in a moment of weakness. He was in trouble and I happened to know what to do. Maybe that's what made him change his mind about me, and lower his guard.

Unsure where to start, I stammer, "You—you have every right to be, um . . . careful. About who you want to let into your life. It's not the same, but—I, uh, I get it. I was bullied a lot growing up. People picked on me for being the only not-white kid in class and not having, like, 'real' parents."

I hesitate, waiting for Suwa to say one of the usual things: "I'm so sorry," or "I can't imagine what that's like." But instead he tilts his head. I realize he's waiting for me to continue. "Mira and everyone have been so cool here, but trust, I know what it's like to be different. Y'know, because I'm the worst player in the band." Suwa snorts at the joke. "Seriously, though, I'm like, a baseline-decent human being. I'm really sorry if I did anything to suggest otherwise when I got here."

Suwa's voice is shaky when he responds, "So you . . . know. That I'm not . . . that I'm not like you."

I shouldn't stare at him, but I can't look away. God, I must've set off so many alarm bells when I started asking what, in hindsight, were pointed questions in the bathroom that first day.

I've betrayed this kind of trust before, by being careless. I won't do that again.

I can barely hear myself say, "I don't mean to pull the whole, like, 'I know someone who's . . . who's trans,' but, I did. And my guardian has a bunch of friends who identify along the whole gender spectrum. Thing." *Real smooth, Santi.* Suwa scoffs but doesn't correct me so I continue, "I don't know how many people in your life have turned the other way when you were in trouble, but that ain't me."

I pause. He'll either believe me or he won't.

Suwa looks at me for a long time before whispering, "You didn't. Turn away."

I feel like I have to wait for him to keep talking but we stay in a tense silence. I'm wondering if I've overstayed my welcome when Suwa starts speaking like he's burning, his voice flaring erratically: "I knew I wanted to transition before high school but . . . it finally happened, freshman year. Now most people think I'm really gay, which, I mean I am, too, so. Which can still sometimes be a 'problem' but it's a lot easier to deal with now." He laughs but it's a bitter sound. "It's been a while since I've been clocked."

Suwa shivers and buries his head into his knees. His voice is muffled when he says, "Are you a hypnotist or something? I normally don't, like, talk about myself."

"Nah, I just know when to shut up. Thanks for sharing all that." Suwa keeps shivering so I do the thing that comes naturally. I stand up, face him, slip off Aya's jacket, and slide it over his shoulders. When my fingers brush against his neck, Suwa whips his head up and slams his forehead into my nose.

"Fuck!" He scrambles to his feet. "Santi, I'm so sorry, I—"

Neither of us expects the triumphant laugh that leaps out of my mouth. Suwa stares slack-jawed at me so I try to explain, pretending that my nose isn't a fountain of blood, "I swore I'd only ever hear—" I press my palm to my face, then pull my mouth into a frown and try to mimic his voice. "'Don't think I didn't hear you miss that run, *freshman*. Having trouble keeping your horn up? Ten push-ups should help, *freshman*.'"

And at this, Suwa laughs. Really laughs, doubling over and clutching the arms of Aya's jacket, the sound ricocheting like bells. When he looks up, his eyes sparkle with a light I've never seen directed at me. "Oh my god. You think you're funny, Baby?"

My palms are suddenly slick with sweat. He called me "Baby"—without a second thought. Like he'd been rolling the word around in his mouth this entire time. I'm riding high on my newfound "Someone smashed their head into my head" courage. "Were you the one who gave me my name?"

Suwa coolly says, "Everyone in leadership throws out suggestions." But I watch his face tint red. *Got 'em.*

I step forward and ask the question that'd been in the back of my mind ever since Feli first introduced the idea of band names tonight. "What's *your* name, Suwa Moon?"

His eyes widen and his smile curves, sharp and bright. "Sorry, freshman, you don't get to know that."

Fair enough. I laugh and taste the sting of salty iron. I should take care of my nose. But I don't want to leave this suspended moment.

In the distance, "Exit Music" starts up again. Okay, that's my cue to go. Then Suwa looks up at the moon and softly recites something that makes my heart stop: "The worst thing about music is that other people get to hear it."

That's a line from *Mugen Glider*.

The worst thing about music is that other people get to hear it—

Track 4

This is the story of me and *Mugen Glider*. Me and Memo. Me and the only person I've ever called my best friend. Which is also, at least partly, the story of how I lost Inay.

I know her by her presence. The way light pulses like a heartbeat around her and makes her hair, long and braided down her back, gleam, a contrast to Aya's, which used to always be cropped at the chin. For almost ten years, the three of us live in Queens. More accurately, Inay and I hold down Aya's apartment while she gigs and tours. I don't know how many jobs Inay works but between the two of them, we live tightly but comfortably.

Life's okay; I have some friends, and so does Inay, but we mostly keep to ourselves when Aya's not home. Around the time I turn seven, the other boys start to treat me differently. Saying I'm not wearing the right clothes, I don't walk right, pushing me around. I'm a small kid but I get by because I'm fast, booking it as soon as the bell rings so I can get home without being intercepted.

We're on some school field trip at a museum when a few guys steal my backpack. I chase them but get myself way lost in the process. By the time I realize I've lost track of time, my school group's gone.

A docent helps me look for it. We find it in a trash can by the café underneath a pile of half-eaten sandwiches. All of my money's gone but my emergency flip phone is still there, too old to steal. I call Inay, begging her to pick me up. She's in the middle of a receptionist shift at a salon but promises she'll come get me as soon as she can.

She never arrives. But Aya does, hours later, collapsing into me as she delivers news I hear but don't process until I'm in my room, staring at the bed Inay made for me every day because I never bothered. A traffic accident; a drunk driver with a suspended license. The police almost take me away from Aya when they learn we're not related and want to know if there's any other family I should contact. A social worker tells me a few days later that Aya's my new guardian, per Inay's will. My school guidance counselor gives me some books about grief, which pile up in a corner in my room. The other boys lay off.

Then I start fifth grade. Shit gets bad again so I start training like the boys in my favorite comics. I lose my first few fights but after I bust someone's lip, the kids at school stop bothering me.

I turn eleven. My first kiss is with Maria Reyes, a chaste peck after her grand confession. But a few days later, Benito Ortega kisses me in the alley behind the bodega his family runs, and I kiss him back. The whole school finds out. Benito transfers; I narrowly escape being jumped in the locker room. And then I start racking up detentions for "delinquent behavior" because I always fight back.

Of course Aya notices. And even though she'd spent her whole life railing against the corporate music industry, she gets a full-time job in Nashville scouting talent for a label that trots her out for endless diversity panels. For the first time in my life

I'm called not Santi but Santiago, pronounced with pinched *A*s and usually followed with some comment about how the Mexican food around here is fan*ta*stic, actually. Sometimes days pass before I talk to another person besides Aya, who's so tired and sad all the time that she doesn't say anything about my falling grades. I crawl further and further into myself.

During one of my lowest moments, I literally stumble onto *Mugen Glider*, almost tripping over a set of DVDs by our building's dumpster. The kitschy anime box art catches my attention and the show hooks me: a surreal and kind of messed-up story about a woman who becomes convinced that the love of her life, a musician who'd supposedly perished in a plane crash years ago, had actually become the ruler of a secret kingdom in the clouds. Marigold—the main character—obsesses over a design that appears in her dreams of a glider that's attuned to the magical otherworld existing inside and around our reality.

For months, the first thing I do when I come home from school is watch *Mugen Glider*. At the beginning of the show, Marigold cries and screams and runs through the streets, desperate to find anyone who'll listen to her. But as she settles into her constant, lonely grief, she channels it into building her dream glider.

When I feel down, I rewatch episodes and actually try to reflect on how I'm feeling, using her as a guide. Then I decide I need something like that. My own glider.

I'm mesmerized by the show's style, the swirling colors that bleed between background and foreground, natural and unnatural texture, sky into ocean into earth. I start to doodle clouds everywhere. Aya takes notice and right before I turn twelve, she gifts me some painting supplies and my own laptop, a dinosaur of a machine that takes minutes to boot up.

But it works. I look up *Mugen Glider* immediately and find almost nothing. Like three sold-out DVD listings on Japanese websites and a couple of bootleg shirts with terrible collage graphics. Some, uh, memorable fan art on Pixiv. A few typography designs of the only words Marigold's lover says, once in the first episode and echoed by Marigold in the finale: "The worst thing about music is that other people get to hear it."

There's only one website where people actually discuss the show: 80snoanime.net, a bare-bones forum board. Its mascot is a cartoon cat making an XD face.

The site doesn't look like it's been updated since the millennium but there's a single thread on *Mugen Glider*. Most of the posts are one-shot declarations: Luv this show ^^!! Wish we got a 2nd season; Underrated, def wouldn't be canceled if it aired now; Wish marigold was my waifu OTL. Except for a few of the most recent ones. Comments in the form of essays, delving into the show's exploration of isolation, obsession, and gender from an account named @EmoOcean.

I make an account (@bubblegum-crises, based on another popular show on the site) to respond to the last one of those essay posts: love this show and your thoughts on it. how do you think season two wouldve gone?

Less than an hour later, I get a bite in my inbox.

@EmoOcean: Another active person in this
   wasteland? Hi
@EmoOcean: I have a whole thing
@EmoOcean: You don't know what you just
   signed up for

This is how we meet. I talk to a few other people about the show but @EmoOcean is the only one I chat with regularly. Later, I join them on Tumblr. At first, @EmoOcean and I only discuss *Mugen Glider* and other anime, neither of us pushing on the unspoken boundary between our online and offline worlds. But the more we talk, the more convinced I am that we're around the same age, two kids who happened to bond over the same obscure show. And I'm really, really lonely.

I start dropping personal details. I live with my "mom." I make up school "friends." My "name" online is Canti, a typo of my real one. I don't even notice the mistake until Memo shares a trove of pirated shows labeled *For Canti*.

Unlike pretty much every other kid on the internet, @EmoOcean doesn't post anything about themselves. Not even a fake name. So I start calling them "Memo" as a placeholder, a nickname I land on after repeating "Emo emo emo" in my head.

The first time I use it for them, they don't respond for a long time.

@EmoOcean: . . . Memo. Is that . . . me?
@bubblegum-crises: yeah sorry i shouldve
  made clear lol
@bubblegum-crises: is that okay i know its
  kinda outta nowhere but no offense "emo
  ocean" is a lot for like a name to call
  your friend yknow
@EmoOcean: I get it, just
@EmoOcean: Wow. I love it. Thank you

The next time I log on, I'm talking to @m-emo.

After this, Memo starts slipping in details about their own life. They live on the West Coast. Based on the way they talk about their family, they don't really have a good relationship with them, but I don't press it.

They're in concert band but that's not the kind of music they're really into and want to make. Over the course of our first year, they scrape together enough money to buy a bass from someone off of Craigslist.

```
@m-emo: There's an actual place in my
  hometown called Stoner Park, we met there
@m-emo: I tucked the money into my shoe
  and brought a kitchen knife in a bag, but
  the seller ended up being an old woman
  who couldn't play anymore because of her
  arthritis
```

Memo asks me if I have any hobbies. I tell them I'm in band but I'm not as serious as they are about music. Besides talking to Memo, I spend most of my free time drawing, but I don't tell them this. Too self-conscious.

I get a "summer job" at a local plant nursery, mostly hauling dirt and keeping other kids from picking the flowers in exchange for petty cash and, occasionally, movie tickets at the local theater. In my downtime, I draw action sketches of the gardeners at work, all in the *Mugen Glider* style. I hoard what cash I don't immediately spend on art supplies or anime merch in a shoebox under my bed. Every now and then, I look up plane tickets to LA, based on the Stoner Park detail, and dream of the Hollywood sign and beach sunsets.

One thing I notice is that I can't really "read" Memo's gender. For a while I call them "bro" and "dude" but they never use it back for me, so I cut it out. I know Aya has trans and nonbinary friends, members of her artist crew in New York, so I bring up the situation in a roundabout way to her: "There's this kid at school . . ."

She gives me a long and tearful hug for, I guess, finally making a friend in Nashville. Then she sits me down. "Ask them for their pronouns. If the answer isn't what you expect, don't show surprise or question them or ask them for more than they volunteer. They might not have anyone else they can talk to."

So I ask. I watch Memo's typing bubbles pop up and disappear several times before they finally send, "I'm using they/them for now." I take note of the terms they use—"dysphoria," "FTM," "transmasc"—and look them up. And even though I don't understand what they describe, how they feel about their body, I know exactly what it's like to finally find someone who will listen to what you have to say.

I've just turned thirteen when Memo finally sends me their music. Our chat window pops up on my screen.

```
@m-emo: You have to promise, you can't tell
 anyone about it. No one. I mean it
@bubblegum-crises: duh
@bubblegum-crises: of course, memo. i
 promise. gimme the goods!!!
```

They send me a Soundcloud link: *Memo demo*. It starts off quiet. You can hear sirens going off behind multiple basslines, which dip and weave and build in seemingly random progressions before coming together into an instantly sticky hook. My heart skips a beat when they start singing—I've "talked" to Memo pretty much every day for a year and a half but this is my first time *hearing* them. Their voice is sweet and clear but when it dips into a growl, I get chills. They've mentioned that they wish their voice was deeper but it sounds perfect to me.

As the song fades out, the outro repeats like a mantra: *Talking in circles to no one / about nothing*.

```
@bubblegum-crises: memo
@m-emo: . . . ???
@bubblegum-crises: this is so good
@bubblegum-crises: [GIF of Chihiro from
  Spirited Away crying while eating a rice
  ball]
@m-emo: Don't be patronizing
@bubblegum-crises: im serious. dead
  serious. deadly serious
@m-emo: Shut up
@m-emo: You actually like it though?
@bubblegum-crises: [GIF of China from
  Ping Pong the Animation singing karaoke
  passionately]
@m-emo: Canti. Is that an affirmative or
@bubblegum-crises: yeah, memo. this bumps
@bubblegum-crises: i know what it means,
  for you to share it w me. really really.
  thank you. youve got a real gift for this
  a magic memo touch
```

```
@m-emo: Alright tone it down
@m-emo: You're making me blush
```

Then things change. Fast. Puberty hits me like a locker room towel and suddenly I'm getting a new sort of attention. I start getting invited over to play basketball or video games or swim in other people's pools. Apparently being able to draw makes me cool and I fill up a sketchbook with a lot of flattering portraits and some honest ones. At some point I realize that people will disappear from these gatherings in pairs and, with only a little shock, think that I wouldn't care who I went off with.

After some debate, I send Memo like a hundred messages in a row, trying to figure out—the memory of Benito's lips on mine—my feelings.

```
@m-emo: . . .
@bubblegum-crises: HELP
@m-emo: Well
@m-emo: You're definitely not straight
```

Well. What Memo says lingers. When I'm at school, I look—like, really *look*—at my classmates to try to see if there's a difference in my attraction based on gender. Then I, uh, go online and *test* those feelings.

The first person I come out to is Memo, who replies:

```
@m-emo: No shit
@m-emo: Sorry but, you literally wouldn't
  shut up about Haku after we watched Naruto
  so I figured like
```

@m-emo: Anyway, here's your formal welcome
 to the club
@m-emo: [GIF of Marceline from *Adventure*
 Time wiggling her eyebrows]

I come out to Aya, too. She's busier than ever but the night I tell her, she cries a bit, happy tears. The next day, she calls out from work, picks me up at school, and takes me to the movies, where we swap theaters until we've watched every film being screened. Later that week, I find a bin of books and DVDs, labeled with a rainbow flag sticker, outside my room, which is cute but also mortifying.

Life goes on. I start dating, kind of. What I mean is, I kiss a few people who like me and try other stuff with people who I like back. But nothing feels serious. I try to talk with Memo about this but it tends to be a one-sided conversation so I stop bringing it up. They start to chat less in general, disappearing for days sometimes. The moments when we talk like we used to when we first met, the summer before sixth grade, feel rarer. And as eighth grade begins, I start to wonder if Memo still thinks of me as often as I think about them.

All of a sudden, I'm fourteen. Aya gets me a real phone. And after almost a week of silence, Memo sends me a rework of their demo. It has a name now: "Exit Music." The giddy joy I feel when I press play fades into a mixture of awe and something else I can't pin down, a kind of relief that makes my chest feel like it's been flooded with steam.

The song is . . . darker. But better for it, crackling with this bass-heavy energy that makes me want to run. So I do; I let it loop and try to match its pace. When I get back home I'm panting, but the first thing I do is sketch out a scene from *Mugen Glider*, Memo's favorite still in the show, onto the largest canvas I have. I've never talked to Memo about my art before, but if they're making *this*, I can be bolder and more ambitious, too.

The next night, I come home from a "study session" (party) with some friends to a flurry of messages:

@m-emo: I want to die
@m-emo: I went to the boys bathroom because
  the nearest girls one was out of order and
@m-emo: These guys pushed me around and
  ripped my shirt. Tried to take off my
  binder
@m-emo: And now they're like, writing shit
  on my locker, screaming at me when they
  see me in the hallways
@m-emo: I hate school. I hate this place
@m-emo: And things have been getting worse
  at home, god, I knew it'd be bad, but this
  is just

The timestamp on their last message is from a few hours ago. I stare at the screen for a long time. Potential responses flutter in and out of my head but mostly I feel angry, at these jackasses but also myself. I knew something was up. I could've paid a little more attention.

@bubblegum-crises: im so sorry that
  happened to you
@bubblegum-crises: wish i could pop through

```
your screen, find these losers and make them
pay
@bubblegum-crises: i know that doesnt
change what happened but
@bubblegum-crises: wish you didnt have to
deal w things alone
@bubblegum-crises: like not alone, but
also, not not alone, idk. wish i could
actually be there instead of just "here"
```

Memo takes their time replying.

```
@m-emo: You'd visit me?
```

I catch my breath. I'd been saving up money for a dirt bike
but if that's an invitation, I'm taking it.

```
@bubblegum-crises: hell yeah
@bubblegum-crises: got some dosh, ill find a
real real job and make up the rest
@bubblegum-crises: get ready LA, canti and
memo taking over
@bubblegum-crises: not rn but soon. promise
@m-emo: :'( but also :')
@m-emo: It's a date
```

We start talking all the time again. I tell Memo about my drawing, how I'd love to one day paint murals so that anyone could
see my art. Meanwhile, I keep working on my painting for them.

Memo's favorite still in *Mugen Glider* is Marigold's first appearance as a boy. They're the one who points out the transition metaphor in the show, which we rewatch all the time. When Marigold gets locked up in a castle by their father, Marigold's twin brother, Norio, calls upon the magic of the world to change their places. Under the cover of night, the twins switch bodies, pressing palms through the castle portcullis as iridescent ribbons and clouds cover them. Marigold-as-Norio slips outside to work on the glider and Norio-as-Marigold meets up with his lover, one of the castle guards.

For Norio, the transformation is played off as a joke, which Memo once explained as "persistent transmisogyny even within queer spaces."

For Marigold, the transformation is treated differently. More tenderly. Like they were finally becoming who they were supposed to be, to do what they were supposed to do.

I start thinking of Marigold as "them." Because of Memo.

Eighth grade is almost over when the painting's finally done. I take a picture of the canvas and fire it off to Memo. I get antsy after thirty seconds pass by without a ping. Then I'm counting minutes, and eighteen minutes after I sent my photo, Memo responds.

```
@m-emo: Canti, I
@m-emo: This is so beautiful
@m-emo: [attachment upload]
```

They've sent a screenshot of their phone background. This is the first time I've *seen* anything of Memo's. My version of Marigold stares back at me as they offer a hidden reflection of Memo's life. Tumblr, LINE, Soundcloud, a few music editing apps.

Alone in my room, I beam at the screen.

———

Part of me wonders if bringing up moving to video chat or—a baby step—voice chat will actually ruin what I've got with Memo. So much of our friendship is about not being able to imagine the other person at all, filling in these details without ever drawing borders. But I know what at least one version of their voice sounds like; would they talk like they type? Deadpan with bursts of passion? Would they be surprised by my accent? Will they think I sound, like some of my friends say, stu—

I push the thought out of my head, and send.

@bubblegum-crises: hey. would you ever do
 like, voice or vid chat?
@bubblegum-crises: like i know yr singing
 voice but not like, your "real" real one
@bubblegum-crises: not cause theres anything
 wrong w this but its been years and
@bubblegum-crises: idk. you dont get
 curious?
@bubblegum-crises: i do

They don't respond for a day. I go over to a friend's house but leave before his brother comes back with high school girls and beer, jogging home to try to clear my mind. I definitely didn't say something weird. I didn't ruin my friendship with Memo. They'll respond to me.

I get home, shower, post up in my bed, and refresh. Refresh. Refresh.

Finally: a new message. I read it and immediately take a sharp breath.

```
@m-emo: I can't show myself like this
```

I stare at the text. Why does "like this" sound so ominous? Their icon's still online. I type as fast as I can.

```
@bubblegum-crises: dont know what you mean
  by that but feel like its not being fair
  to yourself
@bubblegum-crises: anyway its cool just
  three yr anniversary coming up haha
@bubblegum-crises: then off to high school.
  damn
```

Memo takes a long time to respond.

```
@m-emo: I don't know if I'm going to make
  it to high school
```

I frown, thumbs trembling above the glass. There must be another way to read this sentence but I'm coming up blank. My heart races as I type, this time slowly:

```
@bubblegum-crises: what does that mean
@bubblegum-crises: hey. memo. you there?
```

It's true that it's been a while since Memo talked about their school life or their family. I guess I'd assumed things got better, or at least not worse. Once again, I hadn't thought to ask about what was missing from our talks. But I've realized by now that Memo is extremely good at dividing and hiding away different parts of their life.

I've been working at a local diner since school ended but I'm still short for a plane ticket. Only one more double shift. I already came up with a cover for Aya, that I'm going camping with school friends.

```
@m-emo: Sorry. Being dramatic
@m-emo: I'd like to stick to chat for now
@m-emo: But here's more Memo voice. Finally
  okay with the song. I think you'll like it
```

I sit back against my headboard, heart racing. They're lying to me. Something was *wrong* and I wasn't there. I'd met Memo at the loneliest time of my life. Things are finally kind of okay for me but Memo is still suffering on their own.

They send a link to the song, titled "Exit Music (Memo final)," and then their icon blinks offline.

Aya's not home so I let myself into her room, which is her studio rig plus a fold-out futon. I shut the door, plug in my phone, play Memo's song over the speakers, and get swallowed up by the sound. This is *it*. The bass growls like a low-rider motor over a programmed beat that's massive, threaded with a guitar hook that coils between blistering runs. Their vocals are clearer and stronger, raw at the edges even when layered into chilling harmony, telling a story about two people caught in a cycle of near-miss encounters.

It's the kind of song that'd make me do a double-take if I

heard it coming out of a car or at a party. It makes my chest ache in a way I can't explain. It's a *hit*.

I've asked Aya to listen to my friends' music before and after the last rap-country mash-up about girls who don't text back, she told me to stop. But this—she could do something with this. Memo needs something good, and something good could happen now. A way out. An exit. In the morning, I'll ask Memo if I can play their song for Aya. If we can make their dreams come true.

My body buzzes with energy. I clean the apartment, clearing the sink and picking up the clothes I've left lying around. It's as I'm putting away a set of colorful striped blankets, which Inay had bought for Aya when we first moved in with her, that I find the sketchbooks. They're stacked neatly in a corner of the hall closet, not exactly hidden but clearly meant to be kept apart from everything else. I flip open one of the waxed-paper covers and catch my breath.

Mercedes. 10. Fall. Neat black script on the upper right corner. As I scan the pages, time and space collapse and I slip into Inay's life, taking in her high school memories through her drawings. Including ones of what look like people marching in formation, instruments shaded and highlighted to mimic sparkling in California sun. So many portraits of what has to be young Aya, arguing, laughing, and in one, staring at the sky, her mouth open in awe at something beyond the page.

At some point I hear Aya and a few other people come home from a potential signee's show. She's finally settled in at work and might even get promoted. I take the stack of notebooks and retreat to my room. Inay's art feels so intimate; I can practically hear her pencils scratching on the paper. While I guess I understand why Aya hadn't shown me these before, I have so many questions for her about this part of Inay's life, which has, over the past few years, become a part of mine.

Lost in my own world, I don't notice or remember that my phone's still in Aya's room. I fall asleep to the background hum of clinking glasses and muffled laughter.

When I wake up, Aya's at my bedside. I scramble to put away the sketchbooks but she ignores them as she grabs my hands and, voice trembling, whispers, "Santi, something's happened."

I hear what Aya says through a fog. She and her coworkers went into her studio to go through some other demos. One of them started playing the song off of my phone; it blew everyone away. And before Aya stopped to consider how I'd gotten hold of an unlisted link, someone shared it with Cola Carter, the journalist-slash-video-star at *BEATING HEART* magazine, and boom.

Suddenly, "Exit Music" is the hottest song on the internet. Its play count seems to double every time Aya refreshes the original page. She shows me a few videos of people reacting to the song or using it as a fancam soundtrack. It's already being covered and chopped up into remixes. There's even an #ExitMusicChallenge: You lip-synch longingly into the camera, standing "still" as you jump-cut between actual EXIT signs.

Her boss wants to schedule a meeting with Memo. Cola Carter wants to do an exclusive with Memo in time for the "Freshman Feature." Aya smiles hesitantly. "How did you find 'Exit Music'? There's nothing else about Memo online."

Her eyes get wider and wider as I share my secret life with

Memo to another person for the first time. When I'm done I'm breathless, caught in a whirlpool of conflicting emotions: I'm happy Memo's dream is going to come true, but I wish this wasn't happening without their knowledge.

Aya cracks her thumbs, then murmurs, "Okay. Can you get in touch with Memo? I'll hold the wolves back, but we have to act fast."

She hands me my phone. As soon as she leaves the room, I send off a flurry of messages to Memo, who's online.

> @bubblegum-crises: memo hi i have some stuff i gotta share w you
> @bubblegum-crises: my mom works in music discovery and
> @bubblegum-crises: i know i promised not to share your song but long story short shes heard exit music
> @bubblegum-crises: and so have um thousands of other people
> @bubblegum-crises: ok sorry i left my phone out and one of her coworkers shared it to cola carter i swear it was an accident but no one i mean no one thought it was gonna go crazy overnight
> @bubblegum-crises: her label wants to talk, beating heart wants to talk
> @bubblegum-crises: i know your fams gonna fight you but well be in your corner
> @m-emo: Stop. Please fucking stop

I'm taken aback by their message. I knew they might be mad at me, but Memo's said for years that they wanted to be a part of the music world. Isn't this what they want? A way in?

Then it hits me that Memo has probably been watching the count on "Exit Music" climb with no idea why or how it's happening.

```
@bubblegum-crises: sorry i didnt mean to
  dump that
@bubblegum-crises: it really was an honest
  accident but like
@bubblegum-crises: so many people have
  heard your song and want to work w you,
  support you and once they know your story
  like
```

I'm still typing when their messages start rolling in:

```
@m-emo: My story?
@m-emo: Canti, what do you actually know
  about me?
@m-emo: I can't
@m-emo: I can't believe this is all
  happening right now
@m-emo: You're right that I freaked the
  fuck out when the song I ONLY shared with
  you started BLOWING UP to the point where
  my phone crashed from the notifications
```

Memo never uses caps.

```
@m-emo: I'm starting to realize that how
  you think about me and how I think about
  you are different
@m-emo: In ways that I thought didn't
  matter but clearly do
@m-emo: Honestly a lot of this is my own
  fault. I should've just told you
@m-emo: Actually, no. You made a promise.
  And you broke it
```

I rub the cross around my neck and blink furiously at my screen. If I could go back to last night. If I could leave my room to say hi to Aya and grab my phone before going to bed. If if if if if.

```
@m-emo: I didn't make "Exit Music" for the
  masses. I made it for you.
@m-emo: You've actually been a really great
  friend, but I think we both need to move
  on with our real lives. Because in my real
  life, I can't do this.
```

My stomach drops. We were going to meet up this summer. We were finally going to turn three years of memes and late-night spirals and shared dreams into something real. *"Our real lives?"* I don't know what my life looks like without Memo in it.

```
@bubblegum-crises: memo im sorry please
  talk to me
@bubblegum-crises: memo
@bubblegum-crises: MEMO
```

————

Cola Carter dedicates three episodes of her *BEATING HEART* show to finding Memo, "the mystery voice behind the song of the summer." The internet explodes with conspiracy theories linking "Memo" to a bunch of other people. Almost everyone refers to Memo as a girl—"her" vocals; there's no way "she" plays anything on the track, too; who's the actual brains behind the song? I spend way too much time scrolling through threads about Memo's identity in a desperate bid to see if anyone's found a lead. I keep checking flights to LA, and even write Memo a letter hoping to hand-deliver it. But I know it's a lost cause.

When Aya tells her boss that I just stumbled on to "Exit Music" but otherwise have no special connection to it, he starts removing her from all of her projects. She doesn't get that promotion. The day I turn sixteen, she loses her job. One of her friends offers her contract work at a casino in Florida and she takes it; we move over winter break. She juggles a few other jobs on the side: substitute teacher, club hostess, barback, whatever keeps the lights on. I work the line at Waffle House, avoiding eye contact with the kids from school when they come through.

I stop drawing. I stop going to most of my classes, instead spending time with the other burnouts drinking, smoking, and screwing around. Aya sits me down a few times but we both know that she can't stop me. I have to want to change and all I want is an escape from a world in which I've lost two of the most important people in my life.

"Exit Music" becomes one of those cult songs kids use as a

secret handshake: under the radar of radio airplay and official charts but inescapable online, discussed in rambling posts and shared in ship playlists. When it plays at parties, I leave. Someone at school scratches the lyrics into the wall of a bathroom stall. For the first time in years, I burst into tears.

I never hear from Memo again.

Track 5

The worst thing about music is that other people get to hear it.

Suwa and I take a deep breath at the same time. He releases his first and then smiles at me, a small but bright silvery sickle, and I suddenly feel like I'm being smothered.

"Santi—"

"I gotta, uh, my nose is actually pretty messed up. I'll see you at practice!"

For a split second, Suwa's face falls, but he gathers himself quickly. "Right, um. The bathroom is the first left out of the kitchen."

The universe is playing a trick on me. That's what I tell myself as I splash my face with cold water, leaving pale-pink stains on the Yus' bathroom sink. I lie to Aya when I call her and say I ate shit while dancing. She spends the car ride home telling me her own wild party stories; I half listen to her, my eyes fixed on the slice of moon in the sky and my mind fixed on Suwa's *Mugen Glider* quote and the way he'd called me "Baby."

At home, I examine my nose again in the bathroom mirror. What if Suwa thinks I freaked out because of his disclosures instead of my own nostalgic recoil? I kick myself for slamming the door on him. And just when I thought we were getting some-where.

My phone buzzes. It's the group chat. When I slide the no-tification open, I'm treated to a blurry photo of Mira, Octavian, Lucía, and Suwa crammed onto a bed together. Everyone but Suwa is posing for the camera. His eyes are frozen mid-roll but one of the corners of his mouth pulls upward.

He's still wearing the jacket. My—well, Aya's jacket. I imme-diately save the photo, then delete it. As I'm trailing off to sleep, I grab my phone and restore it.

When I unlock my phone in the morning, the first thing I see is the close crop of his face from where I'd zoomed in.

After initiation, I start hanging out with the seniors all the time. On weekends we'll post up at the bubble tea shop where Octa-vian works or play video games at Lucía's place. A few of them skate, including Suwa, which explains his collection of torn-up jeans. Ariso's teaching Reva, who I suspect is only learning so she has an excuse to fall into their arms, and Ariso offers to teach me, too. I end up borrowing a board and shakily glide around the perimeter of the skate park before deciding, *Not my thing*.

Unlike the friends I made at other schools, the Sunshowers are good for me. I go to the study group that Octavian runs on the days we don't have practice. Mira and I take the same bus home; she tells me about her sisters and brothers and pries a few more personal details out of me. After I bump into Feli while running in the neighborhood, we start going to the school gym together during my lunch.

Everything's great. Except that I don't have the chance to get through to Suwa.

I try to speak to him more during group hangs but it's like he purposefully keeps his distance, always excusing himself right as I make moves to talk to him one-on-one. The night of the homecoming dance, we go out to karaoke instead. Suwa's nursing a sore throat so he stays away from the mic but even though he hugs everyone else good night, he only waves goodbye to me.

I get it. We're barely friends. Still, I feel a familiar flicker of disappointment when I show up to Echo Park lake one Sunday afternoon and only Mira, Ariso, Reva, and Feli are gathered in the shadow of the fountain's spray to welcome me.

Feli waves me over to their blanket. A speaker's playing lo-fi hip-hop beats. He cracks open the cooler and tosses me a can of Milo. "What's good? Los Angeles is treating you right, bro. You look great."

"Thanks?" I take a seat next to Reva after she taps the space next to her. She passes me a box of Cuban pastries and I switch between sips of chocolate and bites of cream. LA's giving me a sweet tooth.

"Baby, got a question for you. Do you have a thing with Suwa?"

I choke on my cheese roll and croak, "Excuse me?"

Reva bats her eyelashes at me and repeats, "Do you have a thing? With Suwa?"

I start to sweat. It should be easy to tell the truth—no— except, well, I do. It's just not the kind of "thing" she's talking about. "He's . . . he's cool. I don't know, we all hang out together, yeah?"

"Right, 'cept"—Feli pulls from a vape and blows the cloud

skyward—"you look at him the way Ari looks at goth shit on Depop." I send him a look that I hope communicates *Why?* while also not quite stifling a laugh. The only non-all-black outfit I've ever seen Ariso wear is their band uniform.

Reva giggles, "Sorry, babe, it's true," and plants a kiss on Ariso's cheek as they side-eye me and flip Feli off.

Okay, I guess I've been a little more obvious about my curiosity than I thought. But before I can defend myself, Feli continues, "Just so you know, pretty sure the feeling's mutual. He wears your jacket all the time."

My brain short-circuits. Suwa's been wearing the jacket? I've thought about it in the weeks since initiation but it didn't feel right to bring it up. Aya hasn't asked about it, and a gift is a gift.

I glance at everyone else. Mira's eyes gleam as she grins widely; Reva winks. And it hits me: If they're interrogating me like this, does that mean that they've talked to—?

Ariso looks past me and laughs. "Perfect timing."

Suddenly, Suwa. Skateboard tucked under his arm. His other arm brushes against mine as he sits in the only free space. A holographic bandage trying but failing to cover a nasty scrape on his shin catches the light, and I'm sunstruck.

He's wearing the jacket. I've never felt more at the mercy of God's plan.

"Hit the park early?" Feli throws Suwa a can from the cooler.

Suwa snatches it out of transit and takes a long, languid gulp before retorting, "Some of us wake up before noon on the weekends." Then he so, so casually turns to me. "Hey." His lips twitch upward in a small smile.

"Hey." I pretend I can't feel everyone else's eyes on us. "Nice threads."

A blush crashes down Suwa's face like a broken blind. "I—sorry, I've been, I keep meaning to give it back to you."

He starts to shrug it off, but I stop him. "It's cool. It looks better on you, anyway." *What am I saying? It's not even my jacket.* Suwa hesitates before sliding his arms back into the sleeves. I did mean it. The silver suits him.

"Oh, shit." Mira looks at her bare wrist. "I gotta jet. Supe, gimme a ride?" She pulls Feli up by the elbow and scoops the cooler with her other hand. "See you tomorrow!"

Reva picks up her phone and frowns at the screen. "Whoops, I think I have an essay due tonight. All yours!" She hands the pastry box to me and drags Ariso away, throwing "Sorry!" over her shoulder.

And then it's just me and Suwa. The speaker's connected to someone else's phone so the music sputters, then eventually dies.

I swallow hard. I wanted a chance to learn more about Suwa. Here it is.

". . . I guess I'll go—"

"You hungry?"

Suwa blinks owlishly. "Huh?"

I clear my throat and open the box. "You hungry? There's nothing left, and I kinda want some real food. I have my guardian's car, so we can go anywhere."

Suwa hesitates before saying, "I could eat." He pulls on the jacket sleeves. "I can also bus on my own, it's no big deal—"

"Naw, I'm trying to explore around here more." I flash what I hope is a winning smile. "Show me your world."

Suwa gives me a look I can't decipher before saying, "I know a place. Take Sunset a few blocks west." He starts walking in the direction of Aya's car. It takes me a moment to follow him, collecting everything the others left behind after they sprang their ambush.

I should've cleaned the car. I toss a few sweatshirts, the book I'm reading in English class, and a lukewarm bottle of grass jelly drink out of the passenger seat into the back. "Um, aux cord's yours."

Suwa plugs his phone in—his wallpaper looks like an anime background, but I can't tell exactly what—and something with a scuzzy guitar starts playing. As I pull out of my spot, he pokes Agumon on the dash. "Wow. I haven't thought about *Digimon* in years."

I wince; how many cool kids are out here with little orange dinosaurs stuck to their dashboards? He probably thinks it's childish, which, this was literally an ancient Happy Meal toy. But I'm surprised when he says, "Of course. You're such a Tai."

I work overtime in my brain to figure out what he might mean by that. What comes out is "*Digimon* holds up. Like, the themes and stuff." Wow, not cool at all.

But Suwa responds with, "Anything that's made for the explicit purpose of selling toys is an op. The OG *Digimon* theme is a banger, though."

We both start singing it under our breaths, then burst out into embarrassed laughter. Suwa shakes his head. "God, I don't remember the stuff on last week's calc test, but this? Stuck forever."

"What other anime are you into?" I pretend to adjust my rearview and sneak a long glance at him. He drums his fingers on his skateboard and chews his lip thoughtfully. He's really thinking about this.

"Mm. I like anything that's bittersweet and a little fucked-up."
Suwa's cheeks tinge pink as we pass a truck carrying huge panes
of rose-colored glass. "Let me guess, you're into *Shonen Jump*
stuff. Oh, it's that place over there."

"Ha-ha, you got me." I mentally cross myself before I try to
parallel park. I only have to start over twice. "I know a few older
series, too. Back at initiation. That was a line from *Mugen Glider*,
yeah?"

Suwa's eyes light up. "So you're a man of culture, as well." He
blinks quickly, like he hadn't meant to say that, then steps out of
the car and makes a beeline for the restaurant.

I do a double-take when we enter the space. The menu looks
legit; I haven't had sisig since Inay passed, so I order that. Suwa
gets chicken adobo and two cans of flavored sparkling water. He
places one in front of me when he joins me at a table on the patio.

"Thanks. You choose this place because of me?"

I'm half joking but I'm weirdly touched when he murmurs,
"You said you haven't had Pinoy food in ages."

I'd made a throwaway comment to Feli a few days ago when
we were at the skate park. I take a sip of calamansi bubbly and
hide my smile behind the can.

"What?" Suwa peers at me.

I shake my head. "Nothing, just—I guess you never had that
problem since you're Korean and LA's like, kind of a colony."

Suwa bristles. "Yeah, that's . . . definitely good for some
things. But not everything." I kick myself for what now comes
off as a glib comment. I know he's got some shit with his dad
and based on my convos with Aya about her K-dramas, being
"different" is still pretty stigmatized in the culture.

"I'm not all Korean." He quickly adds, "I know, 'Moon.' But my mother's Japanese. 'Suwa' was actually her maiden name."

"How does she feel about your . . . ?" I falter, unprepared for Suwa's sudden willingness to talk today.

I fight to keep my face neutral when he continues, "She died when I was pretty young. She . . . was dealing with a lot, even before she got sick, because my entire Korean side actively hates everything Japanese. None of them came to her funeral. And after she passed, my father . . ."

I'm trying to follow him but I guess my confusion is obvious. Suwa sighs. "Uh, looong story short, there's a lot of spilled blood between Japan and Korea. And even now, the way the Japanese government talks about its occupation of Korea, and a bunch of other countries, including the Philippines, is . . . I honestly get how my father's family feels. I do. Anyone who's lived through history instead of learning about it carries that knowledge differently. But I also have to live as who I am. Which—that applies to a lot of things. For me."

He blows his bangs out of his face and says, "Damn, what's your deal? I truly don't talk about this stuff at all, even to the rest of them."

I so don't know my history. And how do you follow that up? But Suwa's starting to look a little uneasy, like he's regretting getting this real with me, so I blurt out, "I don't have a mom, either." The words hang between us like a spiderweb. His eyes widen in shock. Well, if he's sharing this much with me, the least I can do is match his honesty. "She died when I was little, too. I live with her best friend–slash–my guardian. Aya's really been there for me."

Suwa chews his lip before saying tentatively, "I noticed you kept saying 'guardian,' but I didn't, and don't, want to push it."

I shrug and drain my can. "I never knew my dad. There are roads I could go down if I wanted to learn more about either side of my family, but they pretty much cut all ties with Inay—that's my mom—when she had me. And I don't really wanna chase after people who've never wanted me, y'know? If they want me, they have to come to me." I run my finger against the edge of the table. "It also trips me out that we're having this convo, considering the way you blackballed me as soon as I got here."

Suwa groans. I start to apologize for bringing it up but he says, "You have every right to dunk on me. It's not an excuse, but . . ." His face darkens. "I've been going through some shit with my father. My sister used to mediate between us, but she got a job in New York after she graduated and without her, it's been . . . tense. But I shouldn't have taken it out on you."

He stops talking when a server sets down our orders. I honestly hadn't been that hungry, but as soon as I take a bite, it's like a gate opens in my stomach. I have to keep myself from licking the plate when I'm done. Aya cooks mostly Mexican, which is obviously sick, but I only regularly ate food like this when Inay was alive.

Someone's laughing. I swallow my bite and look up from my plate. It's Suwa. "Jesus, do you chew? You and my sister both eat like . . ." He mimics slurping noodles.

"What's her name?" The way he brings her up suggests they're close.

"Sayo. She's five years older, works in video production for this company that makes skate equipment. They're in New York now, but I think she's moving to Tokyo next year for their new project." His expression is so tender when he talks about her. "She's actually how I know about *Mugen Glider*."

A breeze ruffles the palms shading the patio, making the light in the space dance across the tabletop and Suwa's face. His lips part and reflexively I brace myself for the impact of whatever he's about to say.

"I don't remember too much about it, besides that quote. But you must be really into it. Anime, and not just the popular stuff."

Heat creeps up my neck. I rub my cheek with my hand and respond, my voice colored with embarrassment, "Real recognize real."

Suwa drums his fingers on the table and examines me. After a beat, he asks, "You have plans for the rest of the day?"

Nothing. "Not much. What's up?"

Suwa shrugs. "There's this place in Little Tokyo that I think you'd like. It's closed to the public on Sundays, but the owner pays me to restock. You could come hang out or whatever. If you help me, we can split the pay, or I can buy you dinner after." He's trying to sound nonchalant but I hear uncertainty in his voice.

"Yeah, sure." I grin broadly. Today's not going how I expected, but this is better. "Lead the way."

I drop Suwa off in front of a nondescript storefront near the Little Tokyo plaza so he can check in with his boss while I hunt for parking. After I find a spot, I walk up to and inspect the store's windows. Mostly gift-shop tchotchkes, sakura blossom–print face masks and stuff like that. The door clicks and a tiny old Asian woman opens it a crack, eyes me, and waves me in.

Ding. I step through the doorway. She returns to organizing a basket full of different stickers. I clear my throat. "Is Suwa in the back?" She ignores me. Does she only speak Japanese? Oh god, most of the Japanese cultural stuff I know is from anime. I bow awkwardly. "Um, sumimasen—"

"She's a little hard of hearing." Suwa's face appears over the landing to the second floor. He raises an eyebrow. "The hell are you bowing for?"

"I don't know!" I panic and bow again. Suwa laughs loudly enough that the owner looks over at me and frowns in confusion. My face burns as I make my way up the stairs.

On the ride over, Suwa had run me through some other details about his life. On the days we don't have practice, he works at a consignment store not too far from the school. The staff discount is how he can afford to dress like "the token baby gay in a teen drama." He stumbled into the Little Tokyo job when the owner caught him organizing some shelves during a regular visit, and he's been coming in weekly ever since.

There's another *ding* as I step into the second-floor space, and I freeze. "Holy shit!" I clutch my head between my hands. "Is this heaven?"

The upstairs room is papered over with anime posters and wall scrolls. There's a corkboard covered with Little Tokyo event flyers—karaoke contests, tanabata celebrations, public mochi making—from years past. But what makes my jaw drop is the labyrinth of shelves containing all sorts of anime DVDs, CDs, cassettes, and records of soundtracks and character song comps. There's a whole wall devoted to manga, mostly shojo: *Princess Jellyfish*, *Hana Yori Dango*, *Host Club*. When I see the crates of art books and storyboard comps, all in their original import packaging, I almost start drooling. Before we moved, Aya asked me not to work so I could focus on my grades, but I'm seriously tempted to get a job to cop some of this stuff.

A beautiful wooden sound system sits in the corner of the room, a little at odds with the rock music that's blasting out of its slatted speakers. From his perch on the ladder running up one of the wall-mounted bookshelves, Suwa says, "I figured you might be into this." He types something on his phone and starts descending the ladder. "Pass me stuff from that blue crate while I'm up here."

"Got it." We don't talk as we work, the music obliterating any chance of a real conversation. But at some point I can hear Suwa singing along with the track. He's got a good voice. For a moment, I think, *Ha-ha, what if—*

I shake my head. Suwa frowns and I clarify, "No, no, you're good. Of course you're a good singer. Don't tell me—you play guitar, too?"

"And bass. Ari and Lucía have their own stuff going on, but we usually jam all the time. It's tougher to schedule sessions in the fall, because of band. But I'll let you know when we get it together." Suwa hesitates before adding, "I . . . perform sometimes. My own music, at house shows. After I'm done with school I'm going to, I don't know, try to be a rock star." His tone is aloof but there's tension in the way he speaks, like he's still convincing himself that what he's saying is what he wants.

"Is there anything you can't do?"

I hadn't meant to sound so starstruck but Suwa smiles shyly, which is so out of character for him that I catch my breath. "I'm just another kid trying to make it in America. Tale as old as time."

"Yeah, right. You must be *good*, good." I reach into the crate for the last handoff, and freeze.

It's a CD of the *Mugen Glider* soundtrack. I pore over the jewel case. It's been forever since I rewatched the show. Of course the cover art is Marigold in their skimpiest outfit. Most of it appears to be instrumental score but the last track is the ending song. I've always wanted to listen to the whole thing instead of the ninety seconds that closed each episode, but I couldn't find it online.

Suwa reaches for the CD. Our fingers graze. I let out a panicked "Ah!" and fumble the case. Suwa catches it in the air but wobbles on the ladder. There's a tense second where he's almost okay, and then he falls into me, both of us toppling onto the floor.

Suwa quickly rolls off of me and inspects the case. I stutter, "Y-you should rewatch *Mugen Glider* sometime. It's definitely messed up, and the ending is really bittersweet."

"You don't say." He pockets the CD. I feign a gasp and he rolls his eyes. "If there's anything you're into, take it home. The owner doesn't care. A lot of this used to belong to the store that was here before, and sometimes people donate their personal collections. Most of it doesn't sell, except when a collector comes through and clears half the stock."

I pretend to look guilty about grabbing a Range Murata art book, then another by Yusuke Nakamura. Suwa raises an eyebrow. "You into art or something?"

"Or something." I pause. "I liked a couple of *Shonen Jump* series when I was a kid. But these days, anything with a really distinct style, that's my shit."

"But somehow, no Satoshi Kon." Suwa walks over to another wall of shelves and plucks a DVD out before handing it off to me. "This one's an incredible style showcase since the main character's an actress who . . . I'll stop there. It's totally underrated by Western canon because it's less violent and like, 'sexy' than some of his other stuff, but the heart of the film is . . . sorry, I'm actually done."

"Ha-ha. Thanks." I add it to the pile in my arms. Warmth spreads across my chest, and I look up from my bounty toward Suwa.

The late-afternoon light runs in ribbons across Suwa's face as he examines the shelf we just stocked. He's wearing a striped T-shirt, too, adding to the patterned effect. While he's not looking at me, I take a photo. And somehow, I know in my bones that this will be the first thing I paint in a long time.

We spend his pay on Japanese curry and rice from a restaurant around the corner. Nothing we talk about gets as deep as before, but Suwa's laugh comes easier and easier. I find myself cheesing to summon the sound. My heart hammers in my chest up until the moment I drop him off at a nondescript house on Rosewood. It's too dark to really see it, let alone get a look inside, but that doesn't stop me from lingering on the street before pulling away. Wondering if I should've stepped inside to . . . check in on him? We're only just talking. I smack my forehead with the heel of my palm.

When I get back home, Aya asks if I've eaten. I think I say something to her as I change my shoes for slippers before heading to my room, dropping the art books and DVD on my desk, and falling facedown on my bed.

My body is burning. I take out my phone and pull up the photo I'd taken of Suwa. And I whisper to nobody but myself, "I'm crushed."

Track 6

"Thank you all, have a great night!"

"Lucía, help us clean."

Lucía ignores Ariso and continues waving to an imaginary audience. "And thank you again to the Hollywood Bowl for inviting us!" Suwa snickers as he unplugs his amp and tucks his sky-blue bass into a soft case.

The night after the Sunshowers sweep our second competition, Suwa texts me that he, Lucía, and Ariso are finally gathering at Ariso's house to jam. When I tell Aya about it, she throws me her car keys. "I've got a gig tomorrow afternoon, so be back by then." I blast anime music the entire way over, riding the high of both Suwa's invitation and Aya's implied trust.

Even though the three of them mostly noodle around with effects and play a few impromptu covers, I can tell that they're really good. Mira fills me in: Ariso drums in their old section leader's band and once they graduate from De Longpre, they're going on tour. Lucía, who's a classically trained Spanish guitarist, is talking to people who are trying to put together a girl band for someone whose name she can't reveal because of an NDA, but that wouldn't happen until next summer.

Mira leans in conspiratorially. "And Suwa is auditioning to be Cola Carter's opener."

I mouth back, *For real?*

She nods. "She did an open casting call for her next tour. He sent a demo in June and took summer classes to graduate early just in case. They got back to him, actually right before band camp. The audition is New Year's Eve at the Shrine." She starts to say something else but Octavian cuts in, "Hey, he doesn't like it being brought up. It's a superstition thing."

"Y'all should stream these sessions." Feli raises his phone and takes a group selfie; no one but him is looking at the camera. As he types out a caption for a post, he continues, "You never know, right? Get on the right person's radar and then, poof. You're getting calls from labels."

Suwa frowns as he responds, "I'd rather focus on myself and share what I want, when I want, and only when it's as close to perfect as it's going to get."

Reva scoffs and elbows me. "What do you think of Mr. Perfect's manifesto, Baby?" Suwa flips her off.

I think of Memo, of people like them. The culture definitely rewards attention-seeking antics, but Suwa's so cautious and self-critical; he'd missed a note during his solo in the show and despite receiving his trophy with a wide smile, he'd barely looked at it on the bus ride back to De Longpre. I get the sense that as natural as Suwa is in the spotlight, he only enjoys it if he feels like he's earned it. And he'd never want to be in a situation he can't control.

"I think I'm the wrong person to ask."

"Oh, shit." Octavian taps on Feli's post. "Dude. Riley Ramirez liked your photo."

Everyone else but Suwa pulls it up on their phones. Mira scrunches her nose. "Grosssss. Supe, you don't have him blocked?"

"I didn't know he followed me! Done and done." Feli sighs. "The times, how they change."

I discreetly check my phone but can't make out an offending username. "Is this someone at De Longpre?"

Suwa gets up and says, "I'd rather not be here for this, but someone tell him." We all watch as he walks away.

The bathroom door clicks shut. Ariso takes a deep breath and clears their throat. "Uh, so. The summer before our freshman year, a documentary crew decided to film the Sunshowers, both the football team and the band, for a project on LA high schools."

"I heard about that."

"Yeah, it was set to be this big deal. They contacted all the incoming band freshmen about it. People were really hyped, but then—" Ariso's voice catches and they stop. "Sorry, it's just—"

"I gotchu, babe." Reva rubs Ariso's back with her hand. "De Longpre is like, definitely not as bad as some of the other schools around here in terms of homophobia and stuff. But the band's one of the only actually welcoming spaces.

"The production team found out and decided to reframe the documentary on *us*, like literally all of us here, and the other 'LGBTQ+ youth' in the Sunshowers." Reva twirls a finger in her hair tightly. "Which was totally fucked because not everyone was out to their families when the producers started going door-to-door for parental permission.

"Ari wasn't. Lucía wasn't. Supe—Feli wasn't. And Suwa wasn't. Like, they literally had their crew snooping on social media and interviewing kids like, 'Who are the gay ones?' It was such an invasion of privacy. Ari's parents are cool now, but it was weird for a while. Lucía's parents almost threw her out. Feli's dad still doesn't talk to him. Suwa's fam . . . god . . ."

Octavian picks up when Reva trails off. "It blew up. The film crew pulled out. A bunch of people at school got big mad. Riley was one of the football captains, and he and his goons really took it out on us. Some high-school-movie-villain shit. Cap obviously tried to protect us but there was only so much he could do. So we stuck together. Supe, didn't you punch Riley when he went after Suwa?"

"No, bro, I got punched *by* him. He fixed my nose, though; I broke it when I was a kid and he unbroke it." Feli taps the tip of it and says to me, "We're forged by fire, Baby, but we're also kinda intense because of what we went through."

Suwa walks out of the bathroom and takes the seat next to me. "Done?"

Feli calls back, "Wrapping up with a message about love and friendship!"

"Ugh. Gross." But he says this with a tenderness that lingers even when the conversation moves on. It's been a minute since I've felt this way, but I get hit with the sensation of being the odd man out. That I don't belong in the group, at least not in the way they belong to each other.

It's decided that we'll watch a movie before breaking for the night. Ariso sets up a projector and at Suwa's suggestion, we stream *Summer Wars* on the living room wall. Mira and Feli keep up animated commentary. Lucía lies across Octavian's lap and immediately falls asleep. Reva and Ariso curl around each other, Ariso running their hands absentmindedly through Reva's hair.

I barely pay attention to the movie. There's maybe an inch

between my skin and Suwa's. He's wearing a Sunshowers sweat-shirt and when he rearranges his body, the fabric brushes against my arm for a second. I almost, *almost* close the gap between us before he pulls away.

I keep looking at his face, the emotions that flicker across it as chaos unfolds onscreen. I've started laying down the lines for a painting based on the photo I took in Little Tokyo, but I make mental notes about his expression, the kinds of details that make a portrait real. He doesn't post any pictures of himself and he's also picky about his tagged photos, so these moments where he's actually close to me are my best shots at getting a figure refer-ence. His eyelashes are short but dark. When his face is resting, the corners of his mouth turn down. I try not to linger at the curve of his neck, instead focusing on the slope of his shoulders and the way he holds them high, tense, even when he's sitting. I think, in Aya's voice, *Boy needs a chiropractor.*

Aya would probably love this entire crew. They're the first friends I've made that I actually want her to meet.

I finally pay attention to the last third of the movie because Lucía wakes up and tucks herself between Suwa and Octavian, and they start talking about something band-related. As I'm watching, it hits me that the style of *Summer Wars* is similar to the *Digimon* movie. When I look it up, of course they're both by the same director.

Did Suwa pick Summer Wars *because of me? Or am I reading too much into it?*

When the movie's over, we all stay a little longer chatting be-fore leaving Reva and Ariso alone. Outside, Octavian and Suwa talk in low voices for a while before Octavian says, "I can grab Lucía, Mira, and Supe. Baby, you good giving Suwa a ride?"

"Yeah, sure." I wince as my voice cracks. And then it's just me and Suwa, who deadpans, "Shall we?" before walking his equipment over to Aya's car.

It doesn't start. I try turning the key again, bang the dash, even get up and pretend to know what I'm looking for as I raise the hood. After a while I get back in. So embarrassing. "Sorry. You should probably take the bus."

"Can I try?" Before I answer, he leans over the center console and says something quickly under his breath before taking the key out of the ignition, kissing it on the flat of the metal, placing it back in, and turning it. I let out a squawk of amazement as the car rumbles to life. Suwa shrugs. "It's something my father used to do. His car's a piece of sh—is older, too."

Now that we're burning gas, I should start driving. But I don't. "Reva said that a bunch of you have family stuff going on. You also mentioned it a while back and . . . I know there's probably not a lot I can, um, do for you but, if you need anything, or want someone to talk to about it. Besides your, uh, best friends in the world . . . I just, I get it. Even if it's not exactly the same."

I turn on the headlights and pull out into the street. We're about to get on the highway when Suwa says, "Can you actually take the other exit? For the ten west. And . . . drive."

"Yeah, sure." Of course I'm curious why, but the tank's mostly full, the moon's out, Aya didn't give me a curfew, and the boy I'm crushing on is asking me to take him for a drive.

There's barely any traffic on the road. After a few minutes of silence, Suwa turns on the radio and scans until he's happy with what's playing, which murmurs in the background. I keep my ears peeled for "when," but we keep gliding westward.

It's not until we start seeing signs for Santa Monica that Suwa navigates. We turn off after we pass the 405, then take Centinela to Sunset, where we turn west again. The road winds here, flanked by thick hedges and elaborate gates. This is a side of LA I've never seen before, and, after an open-top Benz honks at us before speeding past in the wrong lane, I don't think I'll be coming back.

But there must be a reason for this journey, and there is. We're still on Sunset when the road opens up. And then: The ocean glistens like a band of beaten silver on the horizon. I laugh in astonishment as I pull through the last bit of westward road. "Wow. So this is the Pacific."

Suwa makes a surprised sound. I turn toward him. He peers at me before asking, "Is this your first time seeing it?"

"I was gonna take a bus out here, or the train, when we first moved, but I've been busy, and the city's so big, and everyone lives eastside." I crack the front windows open and we both lean into the fragrant shore air.

Suwa laughs. The sound releases a warmth like sunlight into the car. He says, "Yeah, this is it. Um, turn right. We're almost there," and tilts forward in his seat, searching for something.

Our surroundings start to thin out. Beach parking and chain-restaurant plazas give way to empty stretches save for sporadic clusters of storefronts. Smears of forest loom in the distance. There aren't too many other cars on the road but as they pass us, their taillights glow like eyes in the rearview before being swallowed up by the blue night.

Eventually Suwa says, "Make a U-turn and park in that pull-out. You wearing shoes you can hike in? Nothing intense."

I make the turn, stop the car, and examine my tenis. They'll have to hold up. "I'm good."

"Cool." Suwa gets out of the car, walks to the edge of the road, and disappears.

I scramble out of the car and peer over the guardrail. There's a trail cut down the side of the road. I gingerly hop over the rail and scramble down, chanting a prayer in my head that I don't slip. But the path evens out into a grassy knoll, where I find Suwa.

He's surrounded by marigolds. The entire area's dotted with them, tall neon-orange blossoms that sway in the seashore wind. I cover up my surprise with a cough and take a seat next to him. "Whoa. How'd you find this spot?"

"My sister. Everything I know about Los Angeles is from her." Suwa keeps his eyes forward. "Santi, I'm going to tell you something that not even our friends know."

I turn my head toward him and ask, "Why me?"

"Because I was so mean to you when I first met you. Or, that's what I keep telling myself. But the truth is . . ." Suwa sighs. "I don't know. You remind me of her. Sayo. Not like, how you act; she's way louder and honestly kind of scary. But you both have this . . . openness. And instead of thinking that I could tell you about anything, I actually do." He covers his face with his hands. "Is this weird for you?"

"It's really not. But . . ." I turn around so I'm facing the road. "You look ahead. I'll just, be here."

The wind whistles around us for what feels like an eternity before Suwa says, "I can't go back to my house now."

A beat of silence, save for the sound of sand and grass rustling. I murmur, "What do you mean?"

I hear Suwa take a sharp breath. "My father basically kicked me out at the end of the summer. Because I want to pursue music.

Not play in a larger group, like in the band, but step out on my own and—and *own* it. Who I am. Everything that means.

"My family on his side is really old-school. His parents almost disowned him for marrying my mother, so he's spent most of his life trying to make up for it. When she died, he lost it. Drank a lot. Hit us some. And then I was outed, only to him, but that's when the rumors started. The whole neighborhood already knew that something was off with his youngest kid, and then it was like, oh, I wasn't just 'weird' but an actual freak."

"You're not a freak." I shouldn't interrupt him but I can't let that go.

Suwa laughs, the sound thick with emotion. "They made me feel like one. God, my grandmother and aunts came to the house and prayed over me, laying hands and everything. The things my uncles said, my grandfather did . . . On top of everything else going on, it got really, really dark." Suwa's voice hitches. "It felt like it would never end."

I don't register moving but suddenly my hand's on top of Suwa's. His fingers curl under my palm. I feel him take a deep breath. "I begged Sayo to let me live in her dorm, but then she found out that some of her marching-band friends have stayed with Cap before. If they were going through shit at home. She helped me pack and got me out of there. And then she told our father that if he didn't step in and step up for me, with his family and my transition, we'd both be out of his life forever. I'm not saying this for sympathy—back then, he wouldn't have lost too much sleep if it were only me running away from him. But not her. Never her.

"And a few months into freshman year, he cut his family out. I moved back. It wasn't great living with him, but Sayo visited almost every weekend while she was in college. And there were moments when things were actually kind of good. When it felt like we might actually be a family. And he could be proud of . . . his son. But when I told him about the audition, the extent of my dreams, he flipped out. It was like we went back in time, the way he spoke to me, and what he said."

I hear Suwa sniffle. "God, this is so melodramatic."

"No it's not. It's your life." I close my eyes. I remember what it felt like to armor myself every time I stepped into the world, unsure if I'd get through the day unscathed. I can't imagine what it would've been like if I hadn't had someone like Aya at home to support me, even when I pushed her away. "So you're living with Cap again now? That's where I dropped you off?"

"Yeah. Besides Sayo, I haven't told anyone else. Not because I don't trust our friends or whatever. But the last thing I want is for them to worry about me, again, when they all have their own stuff to deal with. None of us believe things really get easier after high school. But we also can't help who we are. I just . . . needed to share that with at least one other person here."

I look over my shoulder. Suwa's eyes reflect back the moon. I get up, instantly missing the warmth of his hand, slip my pocket knife out of my jeans, and cut down a few flowers.

I hope the moonlight blocks out the flush on my face as I present them to him. "Hey. You'll get your flowers one day. Even from him. But these can be yours now."

Suwa hesitates before taking them. Then he gets up, brushes himself off, and walks back toward the car. As we get to the bottom of the slope, he turns around and says, "You know, you're kind of smooth when you're not tripping over yourself, Baby." He continues up the trail while steam comes out of my ears.

When we're back in the car, Suwa plugs his phone in and puts on a song with a mournful melody that erases any chance for me to ask what he'd meant by that. But when it ends, Suwa says, "Thanks. For tonight. Any chance you could speed up a little?"

"You got it." The speedometer needle tips to the right. He rolls down his window and somehow, I know what he's about to do.

Suwa picks up the marigolds in his lap. He holds them out the window and they shudder before exploding, orange pom-poms falling apart into confetti. The petals seem to float before hurtling away and out of sight.

Then Suwa lets go of the stems and, against the roar of the wind, shouts, "Now we can go home."

Track 7

"Yeah, I know about Suwa. I didn't know he was one of your friends. Cap says he's a good kid. We've talked about him a little since he wants to do music." Aya tries the soup bubbling on the stovetop. "Mm. Un poco más limón."

Of course she knows that Suwa lives with Cap. They only talk all the time. I hand her half a lime. She squeezes it, pours something out of a Malher seasoning packet, tastes the soup again, and nods. "That's it."

As she portions out the servings into bright blue glazed bowls, I try to find the right words to describe how I feel about Suwa. "He's . . . not just a friend. I mean he is, but I kind of want him to be . . . more than that."

Aya raises her eyebrows but otherwise continues ladling soup, this time into a container she leaves on the counter to cool. After a beat of humiliating silence, she says, "So? Like a crush? You should ask him out, then."

I'm so embarrassed, I feel in pain. I've had versions of this conversation with myself for the weeks since I drove with Suwa to the Pacific, but everything sounds so much more childish when she says it. Still, I actually do want her advice.

"It kinda feels like he doesn't have time for, like, dating, but I don't know." I drop a handful of tortilla strips in each bowl and bring them to the kitchen table, taking care not to accidentally kick the wad of napkins propped under the short leg. "Like, he's good enough that he has a shot with Cola Carter. He'll probably leave school after this semester no matter what. There's no time. It'd make more sense to try to stay friends."

Aya shrugs. "Let's say he gets it. He'll still be around. There's rehearsals, he'll get label attention, he'll do press. Your last competition is the weekend after next? Cap will be freer after that; lemme invite them over. That'll make Suwa part of not only your school life, but your *life*."

I groan as I set the table. Aya pours two glasses of tepache and knocks me on the head with one of them. "You ask, I answer."

After dinner, I wash dishes as Aya preps more meals for the week, simmering chicken in mole sauce and checking on enchiladas in the oven.

She'd made Cap a part of her *life* a long time ago. The thought only occurs to me now. "Did you ever live with Cap?" He'd gone out of his way to help Aya with music since her parents were against it, but I wouldn't be surprised if he's been opening his door like this for his entire time teaching.

"Nah, but things were different back then. You had to keep your shit secret until you could get out, if you ever did." She wipes her eyes before tossing onions into another pan. "You got options now, but don't mistake that for freedom. Even in America. Even in LA."

CHOP. Aya cleaves a pig foot in half. "Anyway. Ask Suwa out. Or get one of your friends to set you up."

"Here you go, thanks for your patience!" Mira's smile slides off of her face as she walks over to where I'm sitting, throws her hat on the tabletop, and drops her forehead with a *THUNK*. I slurp down some more horchata before poking her elbow.

Mira lifts her head and rubs her eyes. "I need Prof to hook me up with that boba gig. He's making drinks, like, ten percent of the time, and the rest, he gets to chat up *the* hottest girls, not that he cares." She reaches across the table and takes a pull of my drink, then hollers toward the kitchen, "I'm on break!"

She turns back to me and raises an eyebrow. "What's up, Baby? Wanna move out of the sun?"

I tug at the collar of my shirt. That's not why I'm sweating. Out of the group, Mira's the one I spend the most time with because of our regular bus rides, and she's by far the easiest to talk to. But it still takes me a minute to summon enough courage to release the words burning in my mouth.

I stare down at my plate and focus on the cartoon cactus on my place mat. *Deep breath.* "Hey, so. Is . . . is Suwa—I know he's planning to be outta here soon but do you think he might, I don't know, wanna date someone seriously even, uh, despite that?"

The table rattles as Mira slams her fists down. "You don't know how long—" She catches herself. "He might, and, spoiler alert, y'all ain't slick. Suwa doesn't say much about them but we know all about your lil' dates—yeah, yeah, they're 'not dates.'" She scoffs as I protest halfheartedly. "The two of you just go off alone and talk about your feelings. Open your eyes, Baby, the game is *afoot*. Prof thinks he's gonna ask you out after the Festival of Music, but you should absolutely beat him to the punch and not because I've got money riding on this."

"How should I . . ." My mouth hangs open as I search for words. I feel relieved to have some confirmation that my feelings aren't one-sided, but I've watched enough movies to know that there's a long way to go between this admission and the moment when I finally put my lips—

I run a hand down my face and let out a soft "*Aaahhhhh.*"

Mira shakes her head. "So far gone. Well." She pulls out her phone and slides it over to me. "York High's throwing a Halloween wildfire relief fundraiser. The theme is 'Seven Minutes in Hell.' We can help you get ready. Prince Not-Really-Charming won't know what hit him. Say 'Thank you, Mira.'"

I mumble, "Thank you, Mira."

Who's we?

"Mira!" One of the other servers walks by and knocks sharply on the table. "You just took a break; stop flirting with your friend."

"Yes, ma'am." Mira puts her hat back on, gets up, mouths, *Capitalism*, then scoops my tray, cuffs my shoulder, and leaves me woozy.

"Turn around! Oh—oh my god." Aya can barely stand up straight, she's laughing so hard. "¡Está guapo! But don't let him pick anything off the ground."

My dignity is in the dumpster. Mira—Lucía and Octavian are here, too, but this is Mira's doing—dresses me like I'm . . . I never would've picked this outfit myself. Everything I'm wearing is Aya's, since she takes to my friends like lime to cilantro and opens up a box, ominously marked VINTAGE?, from the back of her closet. Mira adds a black feather boa to her cat costume; Octavian and Lucía deck their skeleton fits out with costume jewelry. And after trotting me out in everything from a sequined jumpsuit to a maid costume with a matching set of cat ears, Mira finally declares, "This is IT."

At the very least, no one will lose me in a crowd. I'm wearing a sheer red, mostly unbuttoned shirt embroidered with little silver stars and black leather pants with negative give. Mira'd slapped silver glitter randomly onto my face. Loose pieces sparkle next to the cross around my neck.

I take another minute in the bathroom to fiddle with my hair. Through the door, Octavian cracks a joke that has the rest of them howling with laughter. My reflection smiles; some glitter's caught in a dimple. I reach a hand up to brush it off, then decide to leave it.

Just this once, I flex a bicep and cock my head like a comic book pinup. Feli's lunchtime workouts are definitely working. My self-consciousness aside, I look like an Ai Yazawa character by way of Antonio Lopez: a little exposed, but kinda hot.

Before leaving for the party, we all pay our respects at Aya's ofrenda, which she always builds around Inay's memorial. Aya and Mira exchange phone numbers as we leave. Mira cues up her favorite album on our way to pick up Ariso, who squeezes in next to me, takes in my outfit, and deflates my ego: "You look like a gay space pirate."

The rest of them are singing along to "I Care." I clear my throat. Ariso's probably the person I have the toughest time talking to in the group, and I search for something chill to say. They're wearing a Siouxsie & the Banshees shirt and makeup that reminds me of visual kei bands. "You look scary." *Wait, not that.* "I mean, it's like classic Hell. Like you're homies with Satan." *Oh my god.*

Ariso narrows their eyes, then bursts out laughing. "That's what I was aiming for, so thanks." They clear their throat. "I don't mean 'gay space pirate' in a mean way. You'd pick up hella alien babes."

I pick at my shirt and say sheepishly, "It's not too much?"

"Oh, it definitely is." They tilt their head. "Suwa says you're into anime. You like Junji Ito?"

I read *Tomie* and couldn't sleep for a week. "It's . . . a little much for me. But I'm guessing you do?"

We're still talking about horror manga I'm never going to read when Octavian pulls up into a quiet, almost suburban cul-de-sac, save for the house that's been taken over by giant inflatable Halloween decorations. We line up on the porch and drop our donations into a cash-filled coffin guarded by a super-stoned La Llorona before stepping inside. I almost scream when an animatronic grim reaper shouts "Boo!" at the door. Mira and Lucía squeal and latch onto Octavian who, as the night's DD, sighs and turns down the sugary red "blood" that's being served out of a light-up fountain.

The inside of the house is actually hell, not because of anything evil but because it's already rank with body heat. All of the furniture has been covered up with black cloth. There's one lone light kept on by the bathroom but otherwise the house is only lit with spotlights that've been lined with paper cutouts so that giant ghost, bat, and jack-o'-lantern silhouettes project onto the walls.

As we struggle to find our way into the backyard, we bump into Reva, who's wearing a tight red strapless dress, sequined devil wings, and teetering heels. "I didn't expect you to be so fashion, Baby!" She dips her head to give me an obvious once-over, then shrugs out of the wings. "You deserve these."

After she slips them onto me, Reva claps her hands and cackles, "You're the devil's now!"

"As if." We turn our heads toward the familiar voice. "He's mine."

I turn around, and when I finally *see* him, it's like my brain's filled with bubble wrap and every single bubble is popping at once. Oh.

Suwa steps into a spotlight. He's wearing a cloud-print shirt under the jacket. Bleach-splattered black cutoffs, white knee-high tube socks, and worn white Docs. His eyes smolder behind thin slashes of silver eyeliner. There's gold glitter in his hair, some of which is tied up into a loose half-ponytail; the rest curls in effortless waves around his face. And of course, of course, he's wearing a gold spiked halo and a pair of plush angel wings.

"You are *so* welcome." Mira smacks her lips against my cheek and elbows me in the small of my back. I stumble forward and into Suwa, who catches me.

"Sorry. Hi." I step back to put some space between us.

But Suwa meets my gaze and closes the gap so he's right in front of me again. "Hi." And when he lifts a pair of devil horns off of someone too drunk to notice and slips them into my hair? T-K-O.

Feli emerges from another room in a priest costume so scandalous, Lucía and I discreetly cross ourselves. He takes one look at us and shouts over the din, "I get it, 'Watch *Euphoria*.' Let's get out of here, it smells like the band office after a game."

We follow him out into an equally packed but at least open-air backyard dotted with benches, folding chairs, and a few beat-up couches. The Sunshowers are popular in this crowd. Mira air-kisses a girl in a bloody cheerleader outfit, who then starts actually kissing her. Octavian gets tackled by a pair of boys in matching jumpsuits, who immediately take a photo with him and chirp, "We're sending this to Auntie!"

"Pleeease, don't."

One by one, our friends are picked off. Suwa waves to a few people and does a handshake-shoulder-bump with someone dressed as zombie Guy Fieri. But he stays by my side as we wind through the yard. We don't even talk to each other. Every few steps I take a sip and sneak a glance at him. Every few steps I don't see but feel him sneak a glance at me.

Eventually we find another drink fountain and refill our cups. And I finally let myself look at him the way I've wanted to this entire time. When my eyes make it back to his face, he meets them with his own; the air between us shimmers from the heat radiating out of dark-brown pools—I'm reminded of solar eclipses, the moon shading the sun, and, wow, that was some poetic shit—as his mouth pulls into an uneven, bemused line. *God.*

The yard's decorated with colored lanterns. When they sway and shift in a sudden breeze, Suwa's face glows with a dizzying array of colors, awash in lime, then gold, then white. He's indigo when he raises his cup. "Cheers."

The rims touch before tipping back. "Cheers."

"So." There's a faint flush on his cheeks. "You feel saved?"

I pretend to think about it. "Like here, or in eternity?"

"Like here." His finger pushes my cross into my chest. Now I can't think about anything else.

"What're you going to do with that photo of me?"

My eyes widen. "What photo?"

"The one you took in Little Tokyo. I'm pretty good at pretending not to notice things." Suwa leans forward. "Notice anything now?"

His lips are stained red. I swallow hard and respond, my tongue heavy in my mouth. "Yeah. This drink's stronger than I thought. What flavor is it?"

"Let's see if we can figure it out." Suwa hooks his pinky into my belt loop and pulls me in.

"*Wrooong theeeeeme.*"

It came from a group of guys sitting on a couch near us. Suwa glares at them. They're all wearing half-calavera masks with normal clothes. The one who'd shattered the moment—*so close*—slurs, "Hi, angel. Whatchu doing with"—he squints—"this maricón?" Under his mask, white with neon-orange highlights, he scowls.

Blue Mask shouts, "Man, that's a guy. Ay, love is love." They all burst into laughter.

I instinctively clench my fists.

"Wait a sec, wait a sec." White Mask barks, "Moon? ▮ Moon?"

Suwa hisses, "*Shit.*"

White Mask hops over the couch and jeers, "No way. You really did it. Hey, don't run from me. Didn't I tell you what would happen if I ever saw you again? Freak." He lunges for Suwa and grabs one of his wings; it rips off with a sickening sound, stuffing spilling out from the open tear.

The yard goes quiet except for rippling swells of whispers.

With a swiftness that startles both of us, I pull White Mask off Suwa and slam him into the chain-link fence surrounding the yard. My forearm's across his chest like a safety bar and I snarl, "Step off."

"Pretty boy can party." His eyes flicker between me and Suwa. "Do you make her screw you or do you fuck her like the lil' bitch she is?"

I could keep my cool and walk away with Suwa. I think of Aya, of all the times I've turned up with a black eye or bleeding knuckles or, once, a broken arm. In her voice, I think, *Fighting is the easiest way to defend yourself, but it ends up hurting you more than it hurts them.*

But I want to hurt him. My fist slams against his face. His mask clatters to the ground. Then someone behind me grabs my shoulder and twists me around. Knuckles smash into my mouth. High on the pain, I lick my lips—iron and salt. There are four of them. I spit a mouthful of blood onto the grass. Someone takes a photo with flash.

I don't dare look at Suwa.

Then, like a sign from above: From the edge of the crowd, someone yells, "Cops!" Seems like the massive speakers finally got on the neighbors' last nerves.

The warning ricochets through the yard. Everyone scatters. Through my blurry vision, the rush of bodies against the colored lights looks like something out of a Wong Kar-wai movie. Dazed, I search for someone, anyone—

"Let's roll." Feli pulls my arm around his back and shouts above the din, "How you feel?"

"Fine. Suwa." His name comes out as a plea.

Feli pulls out his phone after we hop the fence and cut through another yard. "He's heading to Prof's car with the rest of them. We're meeting at the Metro station. What happened back there?"

"He messed with Suwa. I couldn't, I didn't think—"

"As your friend, that was jacked-up. But as your bro . . ." He punches me in the shoulder. "Qué padre. Here, clean your face up." He takes off his shirt and hands it to me.

I wave it away; I don't think the mesh can handle blood. I wipe my mouth with the back of my hand. *Shit, will I be able to play at the last competition?* I laugh in amazement. When did I become the person who cared?

After I moved to LA. After I relearned how to care for myself and found people who openly, easily, cared about me. Including, somehow, Suwa, crash-landing in my life like a falling star.

But when I see him, a one-winged angel standing under a sputtering streetlight, the adrenaline in my body fades out.

"I'm gonna . . ." Feli jogs over to Octavian's car, which pulls away and makes a turn out of sight.

I point in their direction and start, "You should—"

"You shouldn't have done that." Suwa's trying to sound steely but his voice wavers. His back's against a fence laced with new-bloom moonflowers. That one-leg lean again.

I rock back and forth on my heels. "I didn't mean to white-knight you. And make everything worse. I'm sorry." My eyes flit between the dusty ground and the light-polluted sky and the boy my body instinctively moved to defend.

Suwa shoves off from the fence. When he closes his eyes, his lashes cut sharp slashes on his skin. The steel in his voice gives way to weariness. "I've been in and out of trouble with guys like him, but I don't want to pass my complications on to the person I'm . . . on a date with."

It's not the time, I *know*, but a broad smile spreads across my face. "So this *is* a date?"

Under his bangs, Suwa scowls. *Right, not the time.*

"Sorry, I'm . . ." *Hopeless.* I add weakly, "He insulted me, too."

"So that's what it was? A dick-measuring contest? Come on, Santi." Suwa tugs at a lock of hair. Glitter showers down around him. "Throwing hands? Really?"

Okay, I'd acted more on impulse than intention, but I knew Suwa probably didn't want or need the backup. Still, this mad? "He was going after you."

"He's a guy I went to middle school with, who had a crush on me, had a crisis of sexuality about that, and wanted to impotently yell about it. Supe was right by us. Ari and Reva were a few feet away. It would've ended there. I . . ." He covers his face with his hands. "That was *so* embarrassing."

"Suwa, I know you—"

"No, you don't." He says it loudly. A group of people in costumes walking toward the station suddenly turn around. On the street, Octavian's car pulls back, then pulls away again when someone (Feli? Ariso?) peeps us through an open window and shakes their head.

"This shit is so regular to me, I don't even register it. And I'm happier that way. It's not like anyone can tell me anything I haven't already thought about myself." Suwa's breath comes out in hot puffs. He sounds furious but his eyes are so, so sad.

And I do what my body tells me to.

Suwa lets out a gasp when I hug him, tight.

Old memories, of being pushed around in the hallways, running out of school as soon as the bell rang, resurface in my head. "Suwa, this isn't normal. This isn't 'regular.' He had a choice. You don't." I release him and take a step back. "I had a choice, too. I'm sorry I embarrassed you."

Suwa grits his teeth. "What is your *deal*?"

"I like you."

After it becomes clear he's not going to say anything back to me, I shrug and repeat myself, stronger now. "I like you. I think you're maybe the coolest person I've ever met, and I want to kiss you, but I'm not sure if you want to kiss me anymore, so we can call it."

I lower my eyes and start to walk past him to join the others. And everything else I'd felt tonight—anticipation, curiosity, desire—gives way to crushing loneliness. Game over. *How else did I think this would go?*

My eyes fly open when Suwa's hand grabs my arm to stop me. I watch him watch his own finger trail up my shoulder, slide over to my neck, and linger on the point where my pulse twitches wildly, then dip under my shirt to push me back until my body faces his. His finger turns into his hand; his palm sears the skin above my heart. His other hand blazes a path up my back along my spine. I let him lead me. My field of vision narrows to only his face.

His thumb runs over the cut on my lip and I act, as always, on pure instinct: I nip the pad. Suwa shudders when my teeth meet his skin and he bites back a soft gasp when I replace my teeth with the flat of my tongue.

He spits out a weak *"Fuck you."* Fangless. Then Suwa sighs like it's being ripped out of him. "Baby, stop me if this hurts."

I grin so hard that the cut on my lip splits open again. He draws a sharp breath through his teeth. We lock eyes before Suwa pulls my head down and we build a bloody, breathless bridge between his face and mine.

Track 8

"Five-minute warning." Suwa surveys the rest of the section and grumbles, "Where's Lucía?"

I rub my hand between his shoulders. "She just went into the bathroom. The line's really long."

He leans into me before saying, "Low-key, the best part of transitioning is using the men's." I'm not sure if I should laugh at the joke but Suwa feels me shake a little. The corners of his mouth turn up. "On that note. Watch my trumpet?"

Feli shakes his head at me as Suwa walks past him. "I need to get cuffed. Prof—"

Octavian stops his count of the trombones and replies coolly, "Even if I was down, I could smell the desperation. Shit, where's Raúl?"

As he walks away, Feli calls out, "That's not good bedside manner, bro!" Then he elbows me. "How goes, Baby?"

Instead of a real answer, I blush.

He snickers. "You've got it *baaad*."

It's true. The past few weeks have felt like one long swoon. When we're not in school or practice or at the skate park or working (only Suwa, but I hang around sometimes), we're on each other, fumbling in the back seat of Aya's car. On the roof of the parking garage by his Little Tokyo job. Under the cover of darkness on the Griffith Park trail. At a show that Ariso's band plays at a house party.

Once, we sneak into the band office on an off day. He brings his guitar to school and plays something for me, a rare treat since he prefers to practice alone as he counts the days down to his audition for Cola Carter. The song has no words yet but he sings the melody. I'm mesmerized by Suwa's fingers as they expertly glide across the strings, then mesmerized by them in a totally different way when they reach under the waistband of my jeans.

Aya finds one of his shirts in my laundry—"I know you don't know what Comme des Garçons is" (I do, because it's on *Endless*)—and sits me down for an excruciating convo on "talking about and initiating sexual intimacy using language and an understanding of gender that might be different from what you've been taught in school." She reads from a printout; we cringe the entire time.

"What're you boys talking about?" Mira slips between me and Feli, then sighs as she surveys the swarm of people gathered for the Festival of Music. "God. Last band competition of for-*ever*."

"You're not doing band in college?" I'd assumed that, because of the Sunshowers' rep, everyone continuing on with school would keep it up.

Mira shakes her head. "It wouldn't be the same. I love band because of . . . them." I follow her eyes: Octavian fixes a fresh-man's uniform. Lucía chats with one of the juniors as they refill their water bottles. Ariso watches Reva adoringly as she practices her routine one more time. And Suwa jogs over to Cap, who says something that makes both of them laugh.

"I'm jealous of them." Both Feli and I turn to her with puzzled expressions. "I mean, Prof's wanted to be a doctor since he was a little kid. Reva's got modeling. And Ari, Lucía, and Suwa know they want to go for music and have, like, real dreams. But I don't have anything like that. I mostly wanna chill and not mess up the planet anymore, but you can't put that on a college app or, like, a résumé. Band was something I actually wanted to work at, something real, and now it's . . ." She fiddles with one of her uniform tassels and frowns sharply, obviously trying not to cry.

"Aww, Mira. Come here. There's life after high school." Feli wraps his arms around her and I do the same, trying to comfort her even as her words lodge in my head. A few months ago, I would never have imagined that the people I met in marching band would become such a big part of my life. What happens when they're all gone? Where will I be—who will I be—in a year from now?

Mira wipes her face with her uniform sleeve. "Ugh, please, I'm not saying I don't have stuff I wanna do. It just gets to me sometimes. Blah, blah, blah. Okay, moment over." She practices smiling a few times and when the other sousa section leader calls for her, she skips off, turning back once to mouth, *Thank you*.

Feli gives her a thumbs-up but his face is thoughtful, too, a sharp contrast to the bravado he projects when he's directing the band on the field. And when he holds his fist out and says, "One last dance, Baby," I bump it and respond, "Shall we?" which makes him grin toothily. "Hell yeah. We shall."

It all still feels fresh to me. Lining up in the tunnel. Going through Cap's call-and-response routine and feeling my heart beat faster as the sound of over a hundred kids yelling obliterates everything except the routine that's become like second nature. After the announcer introduces the Sunshowers, I scan the Rose Bowl crowd and startle when I find Aya in the stands near us, wearing all yellow and stabbing an umbrella into the air to the amusement and annoyance of the people around her.

It only hits me after I've stepped into my starting mark that she's dressed as a sun-shower, in her own way. A wave of emotion crashes over me and I look around the field: Mira and Octavian on the far side of the formation. Out of the corner of my eye, Ariso, sticks poised over their snare. Reva, her flag fluttering around her, alert near the sideline. Lucía diagonal to her. Feli in front of all of us, mouth drawn into a stoic line.

Suwa by my side, where he's been this entire season. Where he'll be until . . . until what?

Before I have time to finish my thought, the whistle blows. I take my last first step.

After sweeping the Festival of Music, the Sunshowers are crowned this year's Southern California Band Association champions, with a special soloist award granted to one Suwa Moon. Right after the announcer calls out both honors, Feli straight-up carries Suwa to the center of the field. He looks at the mic like it's an unseasoned piece of chicken before leaning into the spotlight to mumble, "Thank you, Sunshowers forever," darting off while Feli delivers an actual speech.

The whole ride back to school, everyone roasts Suwa, including a group chant of "Sunshowers forever!" that unexpectedly leaves me with a tight knot of melancholy in my gut. Suwa's smiling and laughing, but—he and the rest of our friends must be feeling it, too—there's this sense of knowing you're living one of the best moments in your life, and it'll be over soon. As we swap seats on the bus, ribbing each other while we take photos and videos, I think: *Don't forget don't forget don't forget*, grasping on to every detail of this perfect day.

The sun's setting when we come back to De Longpre. After we're done unloading the bus, I spy Aya in the parking lot. She waits until almost everyone else has either decamped for the band office or left, before coming over to me.

Aya pinches my cheek. "Good job out there. Your count was off at the start but you got over it fast. And *you*. What a solo." She releases my face and holds her hand out to someone behind me.

I hold my breath as Aya and Suwa shake hands. "Thank you. You're the one who got him to do band? Santi talks a lot about you, always warmly. It's a privilege to meet you."

I snort at the polite tone Suwa uses but Aya melts. "Oh, you're as charming as Cap says. We'll see you later?"

"Yes, ma'am. I'm looking forward to it." Then he smiles sweetly at her before walking away to presumably go back to Cap's house, shower, and *see us later*?

Aya reads my confusion. "I've done most of the cooking, but you're gonna clean up the place and help with the finishing touches." When I don't immediately follow her to the car, Aya barks over her shoulder, "Season's over. Everyone's free. And I want to meet your boyfriend."

"He's not my—" The words leave my mouth automatically

but I catch myself. Suwa and I have only really been together for what, three weeks? But just because we haven't talked labels doesn't mean this one doesn't fit. I whisper to myself, "Boyfriend. He's my boyfriend."

Aya turns and raises an eyebrow. "You better practice. And pick it up, you still got boxers hanging up to dry."

An hour later, the entire apartment's been mopped, the warm peach tile gleaming from my labor. The clothes I didn't have time to fold and put away are shoved under my bed. All the counters have been wiped down and I've gone in with a toothbrush to clean the kitchen and bathroom sinks. Incense burns on the table holding Inay's memorial, with fresh flowers placed in a glass bottle next to the photo frame. Aya's in the middle of beating the kitchen rug out on the balcony when I hear knocking at the door.

I glance at the oven clock. They're not due for another fifteen so I open the door shirtless and sweaty, wearing my rattiest gym shorts and my chore slippers.

Of course they're early. Cap looks shocked, then clears his throat. "We can come back."

Suwa doesn't say a word, hopefully because he's staring at the sweat rolling down my chest and not because he's judging the off-model *DBZ* art printed on my slippers.

"Santi, where are your— Come in, come in, slippers are in the left closet, Santi, go shower! And put some clothes on!" Aya shoos me, then beams at Cap and Suwa. "This is long overdue. Suwa, would you like some wine with dinner?" Wow, she's really laying out the red carpet for him.

"I'd love that." I can feel him watching me as I dip into my room for clothes before popping into the bathroom.

Despite the awkward start, dinner is amazing. Aya serves a "not-not-Thanksgiving," since it's so close to the actual holiday: crunchy and deceptively spicy fresh rolls with sweet chili and peanut dipping sauces; mac 'n' cheese with a touch of coconut milk and a crispy panko crust; duck fat–roasted potatoes slathered with homemade yellow curry paste and cilantro and scallions from her balcony garden; and a whole five-spice-rubbed duck. So this is why our bag of plastic bags is full of ones from the Thai grocery. I fight down a burp at the table; we're going to have leftovers for days.

"Aya, my dear, you're a treasure in many ways but especially this. Suwa and I . . ." The two of them share a look. "We mostly order in."

Aya gets up and beckons Suwa toward the balcony. "Come over anytime, anytime. You two mind cleaning up? I wanna talk shop with Suwa."

Cap claps my back. "I wash, you dry, or do you prefer the other way?"

Aya glares at me before she and Suwa step outside. I can't let this old man do any real work. "Please pack some leftovers, sir. I'll take care of the dishes."

As I'm putting the last of the tableware away, Cap waves me over. We watch Aya and Suwa, backs facing us, talk. Her expression is serious and his is rapt, nodding along to every other thing she says. She shows him something on her phone; I see and hear his laugh.

"Kid's got dreams." Cap takes a long sip of coffee. "He reminds me a lot of her, when she was that age. Like a firework in human form, just waiting to find some stage big enough to . . ." He mimics the sound of an explosion.

Outside of school or festival grounds, Cap feels like a presence I haven't had much of in my life: someone who seems at
peace, like they've figured it all out. "Aya says things were really
different when she was a kid. And even the stuff my friends
went through before and, now, what you're doing for Suwa . . .
I know it probably doesn't mean much coming from someone
like me, but thank you. For the Sunshowers and, everything."

Cap scrutinizes me. I shift in my seat under his eagle-eyed
gaze. Then he laughs loudly and slaps his belly. "The way you
kids talk to me, put me in the ground already! Santi, I was lucky
enough to have people who opened their door for me when I was
young. That's the only real rule I follow: Be good to those who
open the door for you and those who knock on yours. And—oh,
I guess there are two—and forgive each other, and be open to
forgiveness, when things get hard. Which they will." His eyes
flicker to the balcony.

Aya steps through the door. "You talking about me?"

"Never, never." Cap turns to me and asks, "Like I was saying,
what'd you think of the Clippers draft picks?"

I stare blankly at him until I realize that he's joking. He
laughs again as he gets up, then says, "Suwa, Santi, why don't
you bring the leftovers to the truck? I'll be right down."

We walk two precariously balanced towers of Tupperware
down to Cap's truck together, then lean against the cab, shivering in the desert night chill. Suwa's only wearing a thin dress
shirt so I slide his hands under my sweatshirt.

"You should go back up." His breath comes out as a frosty
puff.

"I run hot. This feels great." I clench my jaw to keep my teeth
from chattering. "What'd you and Aya talk about?"

"Nothing I can explain quick and easy. But Aya's seen some crazy shit. She's badass."

My chest warms up. "Yeah. She is."

Suwa looks up at me with a serious expression. "Santi, I . . . have something to confess."

My eyes widen with worry. He continues, guilt coloring his voice. "I don't know how to tell you this, but . . . Aya sent me some baby photos that I *have* to share with the rest of the group chat. She's also been sending Mira pics; the one of you dressed as Sokka is—"

Suwa yelps as I yank his hands out of my sweater. "Nah, you can freeze your ass off after all." I pretend to walk away from him but he grabs the edge of my sleeve and reels me in, then presses himself against me and kisses me with a mouth that still tastes like wine and spice.

"Suwa! Shall we?" We break apart as Cap makes his way down the stairs. Before I walk past him, Cap wraps me up in a bone-crushing hug. From the door of our apartment, Aya and I watch the truck pull away, both of them waving. When they're out of sight, she closes the door, then leans against it and sighs.

I nudge her slipper with mine. "I would've helped you with the cooking if you'd asked, instead of springing this on me."

Aya cracks her thumbs. "You've been busy with band and your friends. And finals. I've seen the study guides in your bag." Her lips curve into a tired smile. "I knew this place would be good for you."

At first, her hand recoils when I reach out to hold it. Then she relaxes. "Santi. You happy?"

I murmur, "I'm happy. Aya, you could've given up on me a long time ago, and—"

Aya lightly smacks the side of my head. *Ow.* "Absolutely not." The firmness in her voice softens. "Like Mercedes wouldn't haunt my ass if I didn't give you everything I got. In the end, I just want you to make your own way. To take pride in what you do and who you are."

I rub the side of my head. I've always wanted to believe in this version of myself that Aya does. And for the first time in a long time, I think I do.

"Santi."

"Yeah?"

"You remember those art supplies I gave you? Back when you started painting."

"Yeah. I've actually started again. Or, I'm working on something, and want to keep it up."

Aya makes a surprised sound. "So that's why there's paint on the hallway floor."

Oops. I expect her to chew me out but instead she says, "Those were your mami's supplies. I held on to them for sentimental reasons but when you started drawing, I thought, *Of course.* You're her son in so many ways." Aya scoffs. "Down to the headaches you gave me. But we'd do it again, wouldn't we?" She directs this to Inay's photo, thinly wreathed in smoke as the incense burns to embers.

We give her a chance to respond. A light wind rattles the balcony door. Aya's eyes turn down.

I squeeze her hand. "I'm sorry. For making you worry. Thanks for letting me figure it out." In my head, I think, *I promise I'll make you proud.*

Aya still looks kinda sad so I continue, "And thanks for tonight. I'm . . . I'm glad the most important person in my life and my boyfriend like each other."

"Oh, mijo." Aya pulls me into a hug. I press my lips to her head and she sniffles.

"Mm, I gotta tuck in. Don't stay up too late." She musses my hair. "You're a good kid, Santi. Good things want to come your way, and stay."

Then, a small frown. "You need a haircut. The length makes you look young, and you're not a little boy anymore." I stay by the doorway and watch her walk away, shoulders fully down for the first time all night.

I walk over to Inay's memorial and wipe the glass frame clean before turning off the lights.

Track 9

Out of nowhere, winter arrives in LA. I don't realize how much I've missed rain until it crashes into the city, palm trees swaying as lightning flashes past our balcony window. The other kids at school wring water out of their shorts and run between classes with their backpacks over their heads while I'm unbothered, glad for my Florida-tested windbreaker and a pair of rubber boots I got for a song at Suwa's consignment job. Suwa wrinkles his nose the first time I shake my hair out in front of him— "You're such a . . . dog"—but he also immediately runs his hand through the curls before yanking it out. "Sorry, I shouldn't . . . touch it like that."

"No, it feels good. It's okay if it's you." I hold his wrist as he tentatively runs his fingers against my scalp. Despite a lifelong aversion to people touching my hair, I lean into his palm and this quickly becomes, rain or not, how we greet each other.

We still hang out with our friends outside of school a lot but more and more, we hole up on our own, playing video games and watching anime and finding new ways to make each other laugh and gasp. The apartment is brighter with Suwa in it, whether he's wrapped up in one of Inay's striped blankets reading manga on my bedroom floor or helping me measure out spices as I cook for him, mostly recipes from a bubbly Korean woman on YouTube.

My room, bare and sparsely furnished at the beginning of the school year, fills up with things that we experience together: ticket stubs from shows, Polaroids taken by Reva, art prints from his Little Tokyo job. But Suwa also brings me things, like pamphlets he picks up from street preachers, takeout menus from the restaurants and parking-lot pop-ups around us, and gaudy flyers from the billiards hall he and Cap live near. I tape everything up on my walls, sorting by color and style like a giant, undecipherable (except to us) collage of LA.

I haven't made much progress on my painting of Suwa but I vow to finish it before the semester ends. I keep the canvas, some old paintings, and my supplies tucked away when he comes over, to keep it a surprise.

Speaking of surprises.

The first time I enter Cap's house, which I'd only seen from the outside the night I dropped Suwa off after our beach ride, I stifle a laugh.

Suwa mutters, "I know, right?"

It's . . . disorientingly nautical, dark wood and brass everywhere. I've never seen so many barrels outside of a dock. Suwa's room is the exception. It actually reminds me of Aya's old studio bedroom back in Tennessee, a mix of music equipment on and leaning against folding tables, a pull-out couch, and one of those open-front school desks. It looks like a room that isn't meant to be lived in for too long.

But if Suwa really wants to pursue the musician life, that's how he's going to live. Passing through places, a comet with no destination except: farther.

It's how Aya used to live before Inay and I tied her down. And even though there are plenty of ways for me to distract myself from Suwa's upcoming audition and what it might mean for the future, I find myself thinking more and more, *Now what?*

This is where my head's at as Aya loads fried catfish and stewed pork onto my plate, telling me about her latest contract, a soundtrack for a VR installation. I half listen to her, chiming in with one-syllable answers. It's only when our waiter brings us our dessert, mango with sticky rice, that she snaps her fingers in my face.

"Santi. I know you don't like celebrating, but it's a big not-birthday. *Eighteen*." She sticks a candle in the rice and, to the bewilderment of the staff, lights it with one of the votives on the table. "I'm sure you feel it, too, but you've come so far in just a year. Less than that. Now make your wish, mijo."

I stare at the flame as it flickers and sputters. I'm sensitive about the fact that my legal "birthday" isn't my actual birthday. Inay had delivered me at home and, when her husband realized I probably wasn't his kid, he'd kicked her out. She'd spent an indeterminate amount of time on her own before she finally got a birth certificate; my "birthday" is the day she showed up at Aya's, eighteen years ago.

Still. Eighteen. What should I wish for? I close my eyes and, like a mirage, Suwa's face appears. I blow the candle out on my first try.

Aya's weirdly silent on the drive home, which only makes sense when she drops me off in front of the Echo instead. "I'll see you tomorrow."

I blink in confusion at her. This is a venue; is she working tonight? Then I read the marquee: SUNSHOWERS SHOWCASE.

Aya squeezes my shoulder—*ow*. "Please, like I was gonna let you go home early on your birthday." She unbuckles my seat belt for me and all but pushes me out of the car.

"There he is!" Feli jogs over, throws his arm around my shoulder, and fist-bumps the bouncer as we cut the line. "How was your birthday dinner, Baby?"

"I didn't know . . . you knew. But"—I slap my cheeks a few times to shake me out of my surprise-slash-food-coma daze— "please don't tell me everyone's gonna sing or something."

"Bro, give us more credit than that. We've got something *reeeal* nice planned for you."

The Echo's completely packed when we enter. We must be between bands because the stage is dark. Feli guides me through the crowd until we find Mira, Reva, and Octavian, who takes one look at my skeptical expression and says, "What part of 'Don't talk about it' did you not get?"

"Are you for real?" Mira lays into Feli. Thank god we're in a break between bands because my friends are many things but quiet ain't one of them.

I turn to Reva and ask, "What's going on?"

Reva bats her eyes dramatically. "Baby, let's say that *some of us* were curious about your and Suwa's sign compatibility, so Mira texted Aya and we learned all about your—no offense— tortured birthday history, and today happens to be a Sun-showers institution, though anyone can attend, so like, worlds collide."

Suddenly Reva grabs on to my arm. "Pretend we're straight. Those dudes over there are seriously skeeving me out."

I slide my arm around her shoulders. She giggles as she leans into me. We stay like that for a minute before she shrugs me off

and fixes me with a curious look, half concerned and half conspiratorial. "Has Suwa played you any of his music?"

I shrug. "A little bit, but not anything he's working on for
the audition."

The stage lights dim. Reva pulls me with her to the stage and
whispers, "Good luck."

A lone spotlight turns on to frame Lucía, guitar slung across
her back, who steps up to a mic. "What's good, Sunshowers! As
always, big love to Ames, who books this night every year for us."

Another spotlight focuses on Ariso, sitting behind a drum set.
I bite the inside of my cheek. *Where is this going?*

"Ari and I normally play with other bands but we're here to
do one of our best friends in the world a favor. You know him as
THEE best player in Sunshowers history. But tonight . . ."

What.

". . . Suwa Moon, take it away."

Time stops and I lay eyes on my boy, my boyfriend, my . . .
best friend, maybe. Looking like a *snack*, wearing a powder-blue
boiler suit with black combat boots. The top half of his face is
covered by a makeshift mask of black tulle but his eyes are visible
through the gauze. And his hair—

—it's been bleached, then dyed a bright bubblegum pink. My
jaw drops.

Is this why Lucía had asked me a few days ago about my
favorite anime hair? I'd thought she was going to dye her own.

Suwa clears his throat and adjusts the strap of his bass.
Through the tulle, his eyes peek downward. "Ames, you're a
real one. Lucía and Ari, thanks for letting me borrow your talent. This is a song that won't mean anything to anyone here
except . . ."

He lifts his eyes and scans the crowd until they land on mine. "You." A small, knowing smirk. "Happy birthday, Baby."

Someone else yells out, "Happy birthday, Baby!" and the whole venue chimes in. My chest tightens but not from panic; this *feeling* I don't recognize, a tidal wave of warmth, ripples through me.

Suwa turns to say something to Ariso, who tests the kick drum. Lucía strums chords. When she gives a thumbs-up, Ariso counts off with their sticks and opens with a quickly muted cymbal crash and stuttered beat.

I almost start laughing; I almost start crying. God, I've only dreamed about this melody for years—the ending-credits music of *Mugen Glider*.

And then Suwa starts to sing. Two verses in, I fidget, knowing what's to come, but it still bowls me over when the song tilts and pushes into the chorus. I see it so clearly, the visual sequence attached to the moment. Of Marigold free-falling, but the perspective of the camera is flipped so that it looks like she and the leaning clouds are scrolling across the screen instead. Streaks of gossamer glitches sliding down the frame, blooming into iridescent halftones.

I finally listened to the full song a few days ago, lying next to Suwa on his bed as we went through the *Mugen Glider* soundtrack. Of course Suwa chose it for this moment. He pays attention.

Lucía takes the spotlight for a guitar interlude. When he re-enters, Suwa's eyes are closed until he hits the final chorus. Afterward, he *beams*, his eyes crinkling like new butterfly wings. It feels so natural and so, so right to watch him onstage. He's cast a spell over the entire venue.

Suwa bows sharply, the way he always does after playing his solo in the marching show. I leap up onto the stage and hurl myself at him, sweeping him into a hug that leaves us both breathless. I hear my heartbeat pounding in my ears as Suwa does his hair thing, blowing his bangs out of his face and tugging the tulle down to his neck, before cautiously asking, "Did you like it?"

I lean in and lower my voice. "I loved it." A flash of indecision. We're still so new; there's no guarantee he feels the same way. But with my mouth against his ear, it tumbles out: "I love you. I love you, Suwa. Thank you."

I pull back. As the stage lights dim, Suwa still shines. The disco ball above the dance floor unleashes diamond rays that cut through the dark of the club, and my boy kisses me within the watery light.

We keep the celebration going with private-room karaoke. Ariso and Lucía sneak two cases of beer in their gig bags and for the rest of the night, our friends put on a spectacular postshow. Even I push past my self-consciousness and take a stab at a song, channeling my best Conejo Malo—it's worth it to watch Suwa visibly shiver when I bring my voice down until it gets husky. But Suwa gets me back when he sings "My loneliness is killing me" and crawls into my lap; my spirit leaves my body.

We somehow all pack into Octavian's car and, as our guardian angel, he drops us off one by one. He lets Suwa and me out a few blocks from my apartment building and after shouting our goodbyes, Suwa sprints toward my home, calling, "Keep up, Baby!" behind him. Maybe I don't run as fast as I can on purpose so I can watch him, laughing, always a little bit out of my reach.

"Shhh!" I try in vain to look serious as Suwa and I crash through my apartment door. *God, I hope that didn't wake Aya up.* But when I walk over to her room to check, it's empty. There's no one home. Oh, there's a Post-it note on her door. I peer at it through the buzzing fog in my head:

SANTI—CHAMPAGNE IN FRIDGE BUT
<u>STAY HYDRATED</u>. IF YOU HAVE A HEADACHE
ALCOLADO UNDER THE SINK. TE AMO. 18!

"What's that?" Suwa tries to perch his chin on my shoulder but he ends up leaning into my back. He scans the note. "Aya's so cool."

"She really is." I twist around to lean on the doorframe. "Let's get into some trouble."

As we walk over to the kitchen, Suwa mumbles something I don't catch under his breath. I pull my sweatshirt over my shoulders and ask, "What was that?"

Suwa's eyes linger on the hem of my shirt, which rode up. "Nothing. Feeling thirsty."

"Okay, jagi." We both freeze. I hear the endearment a lot in Aya's K-dramas and have been rolling it around in my head, too embarrassed to actually try it on Suwa. Until now. Before I can tell how he's reacted, I open the fridge and stick my face in, trying desperately to cool off my hot blush. "If you're thirsty, let's just have water." I close the door and pass Suwa two glasses off the dish rack.

Suwa fills them at the tap and hands one to me before draining half of his in a long gulp. A rivulet breaks over his lower lip and rolls down to his chin, where it collects into a perfect pearl, catching the light above the sink. I hold my breath, fixated as it swells and spills down his neck. When my eyes return to his face, he whispers, "Not that kind of thirsty."

I place my glass on the counter, dragging my finger along the rim. The movement releases a low drone that cuts through all of the background noise: One of the neighbors blasts music that's quickly lowered. Two dogs start barking at each other on the sidewalk. The apartment shakes a little as someone starts one of the building's washing machines, which clangs violently before settling into a rumble. Sounds of life. Sounds of intimacy.

I've only been in LA for a few months but this city feels more like a home than any other place I've ever lived. So much of that has to do with Suwa. I walk over to him and, after a beat of hesitation, unbutton one of the snaps on his suit. Another.

Suwa reaches a hand to the cross that hangs like a collar around my neck. "I've got another gift for you. If you want it now."

I shiver. We've covered a lot of ground already but not . . . this. The one thing we've talked about but haven't done. And something curls in my gut. Expectation. Understanding.

Hunger. It's my birthday, and I want him. I snap the button at his navel and slide the shoulders of his suit off. One hand reaches up to tug at my hair. The other cups my jaw to bring my face down to his.

I sigh into the first kiss, which makes him laugh. He's the one who eventually pulls away, circling my wrist with his fingers and guiding me through my suddenly unfamiliar home. The cloud of pink around his head bobs like a lure through shafts of light. The windows in my room are cracked open and I shudder so violently at the jolt of night air that my hand breaks free of Suwa's hold.

My involuntary reaction is a record-scratch and Suwa stops. "Santi, if you don't feel ready . . ." He looks at the ground. "You don't have to force yourself to—"

He's trying to cover it up, but I can hear the disappointment.

I take a seat on the edge of my bed and kick myself. "No, I— Suwa, I'm . . . I'm nervous. I don't know what I'm doing, and I don't want to . . . mess up."

What I mean is mess him up. Everything else has been so intuitive, but now? The words spill out in a rush. "I don't want to hurt you by saying or doing something that makes you feel weird about . . ."

"About me. My body." Suwa looks toward the window and tugs the shoulders of his suit back on before saying curtly, "Thanks for being honest."

The bed creaks when Suwa sits down next to me. I'm prepared for silence, so I whip my head up in surprise when he says, "That's not fair. I . . . I'm nervous, too. But I know you won't hurt me."

Our hands find each other. "I don't know how to explain it, but when I'm with you, I don't think about my body like that at all. You know how to treat me like . . . like a boy. But honestly, I feel like I could be whoever, whatever, and you'd . . . you'd like me. And now you . . ." He trails off.

I once shocked myself in shop class when I tried to pry a broken plug out of an outlet. A similar warm hum radiates throughout my body. I want to show him that he's wanted for who he is now. He's loved, for who he is.

My reflection stares back at me from Suwa's irises as I say, "Tell me what to do." I feel like a rotoscoped version of myself, hovering in some in-between space above and apart from my skin. "I just want to make you feel as good as I feel when I'm with you."

He openly gawks at me. I stammer, "Or, we can keep, um, talking about it—"

A thrill runs up my spine when he presses me onto my back, his hair a pink curtain framing my face. "No more talking."

And then the pressure in the room gives way. Suwa slides a hand up my shirt and helps me tug it off before running his hands across my bare chest. He lifts his arms so I can peel his binder off. My fingertips ghost through the trail of hair on his belly and trace the lean slope of waist into hip.

"Santi, I trust you. You trust me?"

I whisper, "I trust you."

And I let him take the lead.

Track 10

Mira's eyes widen when she sees me. "No way." She takes a candid and fires it off to the group chat, muttering her accompanying text out loud: "Baby's first formal."

I pull at the blazer. Aya'd insisted I wear a suit. "I look like an asshole."

"Uh, you look like the dreamy bad boy on a show about teenagers created by adults trying to work through their high school trauma. *Love* the earring." She points at the small stud; Aya'd pierced my ear at home a long time ago and it took nothing to re-pierce it. "I gotta keep checking people in, but your boy's holding down a table." She points me toward the courtyard where the Sunshowers Band Alumni Association holds their annual end-of-season banquet honoring the senior class. When I enter, Cap gives me a thumbs-up before continuing a conversation with someone who clearly went to high school a long time ago.

I've been to school dances before, so it's not too jarring to see my peers in ill-fitting suits and dresses. It takes me a moment to notice, but this year's seniors are also all wearing their band varsity jackets. But of course—of course—Suwa's wearing a black fringed shirt that's dotted with rhinestones, black jeans that *aren't* ripped, and pointed black boots. Aya's jacket is draped over the seat next to him. I grin as I approach the table and relocate the jacket to his seat back. "You saving this for someone?"

Suwa's face contorts into surprise for a moment before morphing into a smirk. "Yeah, but you're welcome to take it." He runs a hand through my hair and obviously checks me out. "The suit is hot. Who's it by?"

I check the tag on my blazer. "Prada?" I'm continually surprised by what Aya pulls out of her magic closet box.

Suwa raises an eyebrow before going back to surveying the scene.

I nudge his shoulder with mine. "How're you feeling?"

"Fine." He blows his bangs out of his eyes but his expression softens. "I don't know. All good things come to an end, but it's weird to actually think about this ending."

I watch him watch the room, his eyes reflecting the lights illuminating the courtyard. Neither of us misses the inflection of his voice, the way it catches as he says "ending." I slip my hand into his and we sit there, taking in the shared history of everyone else in the space.

Suwa perks up. "My old section leaders just got here. I'll be right back." He's already walked a few steps away when he whirls around and asks, "Do you want to meet them?"

I shake my head. "Nah, I'll hold on to the table. Go."

I watch him laugh and smile widely as he hugs his friends. My stomach twists with a weird, dark feeling. I don't think a single person from my other schools would greet me like that. The people in my life now are the closest friends I've ever had. But I only have another half a year with them before events like this become the easiest way to meet up. Even less time with Suwa, who I'm only finally getting to know the way I've wanted to this whole time. The heat of his body pressed flush against mine. The sound of his breathing steadying as he falls asleep. The wildness of his bed head, and the soft "See you" he says as a goodbye when I sneak out of his room in the mornings, crawling out his window to drop down onto the porch.

Reva plops into the seat on my other side. "Oh, perfect. I got way too much food, help me with this." She slides rice, macaroni salad, and part of her loco moco patty onto my plate. "The seniors are supposed to wear their varsity jackets to banquet but Suwa had to break tradition and wear yours."

Then she peers at me. "Baby, are you . . . okay? You've got this look on your face."

I shovel a bite of food into my mouth and respond between chews, "Nah, I'm good. Really."

Reva scoots closer to me. "It's okay, these 'end of the year' things are always emotional. And this one's, like, a real ending." I don't know how to tell her that it's more than that but then I notice that she's watching Ariso, who laughs at a joke told by people wearing jackets from last year's class.

"Ari showed me their touring schedule, and I know I'm supposed to be happy for them. But I just . . ." Reva's face is bright but her voice trembles. "We saw each other almost every day for over three years, and after next semester they're going to be away for months, and so will I, and Suwa will probably be long gone, and everyone else will start the next thing."

She waves away the napkin I hand her. "Sorry, I shouldn't— It's first love, right? Ari but also the rest of them. I know how this usually goes. But, I don't know, maybe for us, first love can last forever."

Reva quiets as the rest of our friends descend on the table. Lucía stumbles in her heels and almost drops her plate. Feli catches it but trips Ariso, who knocks into Octavian, who lands in Mira's lap.

"I can't believe I'm friends with these nerds." Then Suwa's next to me again, pressing his knee against mine. When he asks, "What were you and Reva talking about?" the lie comes easily: "How good the food is. Gotta learn how to make this."

Suwa smiles. "You better call me when you do." He tucks his hand into mine. I squeeze it and let my friends carry on around me, riding the current of their nostalgia and joy. All night, I repeat like a mantra in my head: *Don't forget don't forget don't forget*. We all found each other. That is the truly impossible part. And now that I know what home feels like, I'm never letting go of the feeling.

It's as we're leaving the school, heading toward the bus stop, that someone calls out, "Suwa!" He stiffens at the sound before muttering, "No way . . . she said she could only find flights on Christmas."

A tall woman with a buzz cut steps out of a car that makes Aya's whip look like a hot rod. Her boots sound like they're carved out of stone as they *CLUNK* against the parking-lot asphalt. "Hey, baby bro. I like your hair." Then she spots me and her mouth slices upward in an uneven smile. "I think I like *you*, too."

CLUNK CLUNK CLUNK. She walks over toward us. The stack of bracelets on her arm jingle in merry discord as she waves at me. "Santi, right? I'm Sayo. Suwa's sister."

My mouth opens but nothing comes out. Sayo cackles, but

then her tone turns serious. "You might as well come along with us. Suwa, we're going home."

"I don't want to do this."

Sayo weaves precariously through traffic. "Kid, I know you think it's done, but talk to him. I was just over there and it's so obvious that he misses you, even if he refuses to show it. Which, hmm, reminds me of someone else."

Suwa hisses, "He doesn't want to hear what I have to say. And I'm honestly shocked that you're taking his side."

I keep my eyes down and my body tucked as small as it'll get as the Moon siblings hash it out from the front seats. Aya texts me to ask if we're on the bus back home. I tell her we're on a late-night ramen run, then pull out my phone to disappear into the infinite scroll as Sayo tries to convince Suwa to meet up with their dad, this phantom I've only encountered in Suwa's scowls, silences, and tears.

Sayo laughs dryly. "We can't let Appa be alone. You know this time of year is the hardest." She throws a glance over her shoulder and grins wolfishly. "Are you the one who did Suwa's hair? It looks dope."

I get the feeling that Sayo's as rowdy as Suwa is reserved and that I probably shouldn't engage either of them right now. *Why'd I even get in the car?*

Because Suwa had looked like he was going to throw up and even if I might as well not be here, it still matters that I'm here, for him.

"Don't change the subject. Sayo," Suwa snaps, "I'm going to, what, walk in and say, 'I hope you've changed your mind about me, please accept me,' right when I'm about to take a running leap out of here? No fucking way. I don't want to stand before him and beg for my future, noona."

Sayo cuts in. "Aren't you exhausted being this hard on yourself all the time? And what's up, you transition and now you can't get upset without spiraling in self-loathing and repressed Asian-man anger?" She clicks her tongue. "This isn't how I raised you."

"You're not her." It's the quietest Suwa's spoken the entire ride but I wince at the sting in his words, and the specter of their mom. I've gotten so used to being around the version of Suwa who likes me that I'd forgotten how harsh he can be when he wants to be mean.

Sayo acts like the words roll over her. Or maybe she's heard them before. "Yeah, well, I'm the closest thing either of us got to a real parent growing up, so you're gonna have to deal." She somehow finds parking in K-Town in less than a minute and gets out of the car before walking over to the passenger door and holding it open for Suwa. "He's expecting you."

Suwa lets out a low laugh as he gets out. "He's going to toss me back onto the porch."

"You know that if he lays a hand on you, I'll knock his teeth out myself, and we can drop this forever. But he hasn't since he got sober. And he didn't throw you out this summer. You *left*." As if she suddenly remembers I'm also in the car, Sayo points at me. "C'mon, let's get to know each other."

"Leave him out of it." Suwa sticks his hands into Aya's jacket and, for the first time all night, he looks . . . really scared. "Please. He's not part of this."

"If you're as serious about him as you say you are, he'll get into it eventually. We'll be right here, okay?" She directs this to both of us.

I step out of the car and nod, then walk up to Suwa and wrap my arms around him.

Suwa had told me that he had no home to come back to. But the way Sayo had phrased it, it kinda sounds like this wasn't exactly how it went down. As much as I understand Suwa's reluctance to be here, I think, maybe, I get why Sayo would do whatever she could to bring her family back together. If I had the chance . . . I wish I had the chance.

Suwa's arms tighten around me. "Santi, I'm . . . I don't want you to see me like this." The admission comes out through clenched teeth.

I let him bury his face in my neck. Bubblegum pink clouds in my eyes.

"I'll be here for you. I'll always be here for you." I add, "Now and whenever." I'm talking about tonight, but also about everything that comes after the new year. Pouring all the fears I can't voice into those words instead.

When we finally pull apart, Suwa slowly turns and walks up to a faded two-story house with a blooming hibiscus bush in front. He looks back once, twice, before climbing up the porch steps and knocking on the iron gate door.

A light goes on. Suwa's swallowed up by a wash of incandescence as his dad opens the inside door, then slowly swings the gate open. He's smoking, the cigarette glowing like a firefly from the distance. When he turns in my and Sayo's direction, I'm startled by how much he and Suwa look alike. The same strong brow and jaw. But his dad's face is harder. I hold my breath until he breaks his gaze.

Suwa's dad says something to him, then steps aside. After a moment of hesitation, Suwa enters, throwing one last look at us before passing through the doorframe. His dad follows right behind; the gate clangs closed and then the light disappears.

"Are you sure this is a good idea?" I try to sound tougher than I feel.

"Suwa's told me a lot about you, Santiago Arboleda." Sayo leans against the car. She looks at ease, wearing fitted joggers and a baggy short-sleeve sweatshirt printed with the katakana for "sweatshirt." Under the glow of a streetlight, her smile looks impish.

"The way he describes you, I expected you to be Adonis in sweatpants." She sounds like she's trying not to laugh. "You seem very much just a boy to me."

I'm thinking that she straight-up ignored my comment when she says, "Suwa and I love hard. You have to, when you grow up in an environment where all you know is loss but no one ever talks about it. So the things you don't talk about sit in your chest and rot and rot and take over your heart. Until it becomes painful to even remember it exists, so in the moments when you actually *feel*, it's like you're being ripped apart. But I'm done living that way and I refuse to let him pretend he can, too. He and our dad have more in common than I do with either of them. They can still reach each other."

I'm reminded of all the people who've ever touched my arm and looked real sad into my eyes and said something like, *Tell us how you're* really *feeling*. "You can't force someone to, I don't know, heal. Let alone forgive and accept someone who hurt him the way your dad did."

Sayo stares hard at me. "If you could meet *your* dad, would you?"

My stomach lurches. Is it a Moon family trait to ask such pointed questions? "If you know my whole history, then which dad matters. And why he's showing up now."

She points at me. "But you're open to it, despite everything. Suwa—and our dad, too, now that I think of it—is so all-or-nothing." Her shoulders sag as she drops her hand. "For someone so hell-bent on repressing his emotions, Suwa's totally controlled by them. Like the thing about the frog and boiling water. But I refuse to let him sink into his emotional soup. The least I can do is throw him into some ice. Figuratively."

Damn. Siblings are scary.

"I don't really get what you're saying, but . . . I see why he loves you so much."

A flicker of surprise crosses Sayo's face. Then she says evenly, "I think I could say the same about you," which hits me like a kick to the chest. Suwa's never said "I love you," but I know it, I feel it, when he says my name, when he touches me, even when we're only around each other.

"Well, no one's come flying through the front door yet, so I must've done something right." Sayo picks a piece of lint off of her sweatshirt and flicks it off. "While we're here, you have any questions about Suwa? Don't be gross, obviously."

I make a face and she laughs. "You'd be shocked by what other people have asked me. There was this twerp in soph year who clearly had some kind of insane yellow fever and—it doesn't matter. What's Arboleda? Spanish, or Spanish by way of colonialism?"

"Ha. The second one. I have my Inay—mom's last name. Her family immigrated from Manila a couple gens ago. I know a lil' Spanish because my guardian's Mexican, but not really any Tagalog. I'm trying to learn Korean and Japanese but . . ." I stutter, "N-not because of Suwa, I watch a lot of anime and K-dramas"—*oh god*—"and I swear I'm into him for the right reasons"—*oh* god—"and I'm . . . gonna stop."

Sayo shakes her head. "Fascinating." I think she's making fun of me. "Seriously, though, ask me something, 'Baby.' I like you enough that I might tell you the truth."

Finally meeting the person Suwa was closest to growing up answers a lot of questions already. "I guess there's one thing." Sayo calling me "Baby" reminds me of one of my first convos with Suwa. I toe the curb and wince at the scuff this leaves on the shoes I borrowed from Feli. "What's his band name?"

Sayo hmms, then says, "You never asked him?"

"I did. He wouldn't tell me."

I'd honestly forgotten about it after initiation, but I don't really know what else to talk to her about off the top of my head. Suwa and I have already shared pretty much everything. Or so I thought before tonight.

She's quiet for a moment. When Sayo speaks, her voice is so soft I have to lean in a little. "I'm actually the one who gave it to his section leaders, since we were friends. Well. When we were little, our mom would take us to the beach all the time. I remember those days, but Suwa doesn't, not really. But the first time we went to the beach without her, he stared at the water, then tried to swim away. I followed him out and we both almost drowned. Thank god someone pointed us out to the lifeguard.

Our dad had been drinking and wandered off down the shore. It took them forever to find him.

"He yelled at us the entire bus ride home. When we got back, that might've been the first time he hit Suwa." I try to stop her, but she continues, "He kept saying, 'You can't leave me, too.' Over and over. Until finally Suwa screams: 'I am emotion!' But he still has like, that baby way of pronouncing things, so 'emotion' comes out as 'emo-oh-tion.'"

My heart drops into my stomach.

That sounds a lot like Memo's original username.

"After that, our dad got his act together. For a while. Until one of his brothers got married and the family banned us from going, even though our mom was gone, and that's when we all kinda knew like, oh, this was something that was gonna be held against us forever. As things got worse, it became this inside joke. Whenever we'd get mad at each other, we'd yell, like, 'You are emo-oh-tion!' and it'd usually cut the tension.

"I'm sure you know by now, but Suwa got outed right before high school. Our dad flipped out, but he would've kept quiet about it if word hadn't also gotten around the neighborhood." Sayo sucks in a breath through her teeth. "His family basically did their own version of conversion therapy on Suwa. They trapped him in his room—like, one of our uncles literally nailed the window shut. So I got Suwa out of there, and then I came home and threw the kitchen sink, figuratively, at our dad. His English slips when he's angry and out of nowhere, he screams, 'I am emo-oh-tion!' And I finally saw him, y'know? This big kid failing his kids in the way he'd been failed. And that's when I started wanting better for him. For us."

Sayo shudders. "Yeah, okay, this is why Suwa didn't tell you. But that's the story behind it. Emo Ocean. It's this . . . reminder of how far he's come." Her voice fades out over a sudden ringing in my ears.

```
Emo Ocean
@EmoOcean
@m-emo
```

When I first moved to LA, all I could think about was Memo. What it'd be like to finally meet them. Or, at least, find some kind of closure. I never, never even let myself imagine being friends again, let alone fall in . . .

My knees almost buckle. I touch my cross. Suddenly, the future collapses into the present into the past I was never going to escape from after all.

Track 11

Suwa leaves the house. Suwa and Sayo talk. They get in the car, so I do, too. Suwa's hand is in my hand. His face toward the window. I think I say goodbye before I leave but I'm not sure.

Aya asks me how the ramen was. I walk with my shoes on through the apartment, going straight into my closet to pull out one of my old canvases: the *Mugen Glider* painting I'd made for Memo—Suwa?—years ago, of Marigold emerging from their prison. When we were kids and I thought I was finally going to meet my best friend.

My heart beats like a hummingbird's wings. But now that I'm by myself, coming down from a night of almost Biblical revelation, doubt creeps into my thoughts. There's no way Suwa's Memo. I feel pretty lucky, but I'm not divinely favored; our reunion would be an act of God. It'd be impossible—

And yet.

I never got a good look at Suwa's phone background, figuring it was some random anime scenery. But when I examine one of Marigold's painted eyes, of course—of course—that's his wallpaper: a close crop of Marigold's sparkling anime iris. The same strokes, the same shades, just magnified.

Memo lives in Los Angeles. Memo has a bad relationship with their family. Memo makes their own music. Memo is trans. All these coincidences but I never dug deeper, never paid closer attention.

Suwa pays attention. He would've said something if he thought I was @bubblegum-crises/Canti, right? I sit on the floor and look up at the collage we made together of our world. Maybe Memo shared that photo of my art with other people. Maybe "emo ocean" came from somewhere, someone else. Maybe this is all coincidence, like the time Suwa whipped out that *Mugen Glider* quote out of nowhere—

He'd acted like he didn't really know the show. I rack my brain trying to remember what Suwa said but all I can think of is the way our hands had touched in Little Tokyo, when I passed him the soundtrack CD. If Suwa really is Memo, he hadn't exactly lied to me, but he'd glossed over his actual history with *Mugen Glider*.

Which is also what he did when he laid out the situation with his dad. I try to separate what I think I know about Suwa with what I remember about Memo. He doesn't sing like Memo . . . because his voice dropped and probably got stronger. He doesn't use "they/them" pronouns . . . but Memo had only said that "they/them" was what they were comfortable with back then.

How am I supposed to process all of this conflicting information?

And what do I do now?

My phone screen lights up. A string of messages from Suwa:

Sorry if that was really weird, and for Sayo's . . . everything

I don't know if you heard me in the car since we were both pretty checked out but

I think I'm actually going to spend Christmas with Sayo and my father

We still have a lot to hash out but

I don't know. It's complicated

Typing bubbles pop up, then disappear, then return:

Thanks for being there tonight. See you?

I put my phone down. The first sob surprises me; I hear the sound and wonder why I'm crying. Then the tears really start. I muffle myself with the sleeves of Aya's nice suit jacket and grit my teeth. I'm *not* going to cry. This is a good thing. I maybe found my best friend, after so many years.

So then why the fuck am I so sad? I clench my fists and slam them into the ground. Again. Again. A dull pounding that rattles the furniture and even shakes the weights I stack by my closet, which is now full of clothes Suwa thought would look good on me. My lungs burn.

Aya knocks on the door. "Santi? You okay?"

I take a deep breath and croak, "Late-night workout. I'm done now."

". . . Want me to bring you some water?"

Aya's no fool, but she knows better than to push it.

"Nah, I'm good. Thank you, though."

After a minute, her shadow disappears from under the door. I get up to turn the lights off, then crash into my bed, shrugging off the suit and wrapping myself up in a blanket. The one Suwa uses when he comes over. I breathe deeply to steady myself. There are only . . .

I count the days off on my fingers.

There are only eight days until the audition for Cola Carter. I can't spring this on him, not when he's already dealing with his dad and is about to put himself on the line for his dreams.

I look over at my finished portrait in the dark. It was—is—going to be my Christmas present for him. I crawl out of bed and with only moonlight as my guide, I add a title in the corner: *EMO OCEAN*, written in the style of the *Mugen Glider* logo. Slanting rainbow letters but instead of being bordered by a cloud, I draw a wave. If Suwa is Memo, he'll know what it means when he sees it. I'll give it to him after the audition, once he's knocked it out of the park.

I pack up my paints and tiptoe to the bathroom to wash my hands. In the mirror, I make eye contact with my reflection. *Eight days. I can keep this to myself for eight days.*

Eight days is forever.

Me, Aya, Cap, Sayo, and Suwa spend the night after Christmas together at Cap's house. Suwa gives me a gift, a supersoft hoodie printed as Unit 01. I lie and tell him that his gift is stuck in the mail, which makes his eye twitch even as he says that's fine. We're both radiating nervous energy, him because of the upcoming audition, me because of, well, him, and the question that screams in my throat—*Are you Memo?*—the entire time we're around each other.

During dinner, it's mostly Aya and Sayo talking. Cap's also

way quieter than normal and on the car ride home, Aya murmurs, "He wants to be supportive of those kids, but he doesn't trust that man." She looks at me during a red. "What's Suwa said about his dad?"

"Not a lot." I flick Agumon on the dash again and again. "They're talking, it's civil. He's spending most of his time practicing and shit, but he seems good, or at least it doesn't affect him. I don't know."

Aya cracks her thumbs. "What's wrong?"

"What do you mean?"

"You're brooding. I haven't seen 'brooding' in a long time." She parks by our building and turns the car off, clearly expecting me to defend myself or open up.

But I'm tired and there are still five days to go before I can finally release the ticking time bomb in my chest and get some kind of answer from Suwa, even if it's no, just cosmic coincidence. I get out of the car and walk up to the apartment alone.

The next day, Suwa and I do a video call. He invites me over but I pass, say I've got to help Aya. Instead I go on a run through what I now know is his dad's neighborhood. I'm not consciously trying to go to his house, but I end up there.

His dad's out on the porch smoking. We make eye contact, me panting and him with a thin line of smoke trailing out of the corner of his mouth. He frowns, takes the cigarette out, and stubs it against a post on the porch. One of the hibiscus flowers on the shrub shudders, then falls onto a scruffy lawn studded with wilted blossoms.

A flash. We both watch a rangy orange tabby hop up next to Suwa's dad, then jump over to an open window, sliding through the broken screen.

I can't get over how similar Suwa and his dad look. The similarity gets stronger when his dad glares, which he's doing now. Does he remember me from that night? My home training makes me want to walk up to him, introduce myself, and offer my hand for a shake. But based on the way he and some of the other people on the street are staring at me, he might not return it. And would I want him to, when these are the hands he's used to hit Suwa?

Still. He's actively trying to include Suwa in his life now. And clearly some part of Suwa wants to be in his dad's life, even though their reconciliation now is only possible because of the family who took him in when his own blood relations threw him out. Though he's supposedly changed, does his dad deserve another chance?

My throat tightens. You can't make those calls for another person, which doesn't stop me from wanting to. Mostly I wish I'd been able to do something for Suwa, even if he isn't Memo. But if he is, how much of Canti would he even remember? Because I remember everything, but if he doesn't . . . where does that leave me?

I jump a little and turn toward the road when a car, rap music blasting out of its windows so loudly that the ground seems to shake, roars down the narrow street before skidding into a turn. When I look back toward the porch, the inside door is just shutting.

"He deserves everything." I don't know why I shout it at the house, but I do. I run a few steps away, then twist my head over my shoulder to shout again, "He deserves it all. Don't get in his way." I take short sips of breath as I sprint up the hill. *Don't get in his way.*

"You're all packed and ready?"

"You sure you don't want us there?"

Cap and Sayo buzz around Suwa, who closes the trunk of Aya's car.

Suwa points at Cap. "For the last time, yes. You'll hover." He points at Sayo. "And you'll annoy the shit out of me."

"Make sure you deliver the package safely." Sayo slaps my back, hard, then calls out to Suwa, "If you totally blow it, the offer to go to Tokyo with me still stands!"

Suwa flips her off.

"Get there, check in, no nonsense." Cap slaps my back, harder, before wrapping his arm around Sayo. The two of them peek back at us before retreating into Cap's house.

Suwa gets into the car and slaps his cheeks a couple of times. "Okay. Let's go meet God." It takes me a moment to realize he's referring to Cola Carter, not that we're making a detour to some church.

The entire drive over, we listen to birdsong, like a stream of recorded birdsong, while Suwa lets the freeway wind tousle his hair. He pokes Agumon every now and then but is otherwise still and silent. I drive as carefully and quickly as I can and, in a truly amazing feat, find parking right around the Shrine Auditorium well before Suwa's audition time.

The Shrine is massive, an obvious relic from another era. There are . . . a lot of people here. We make camp in the middle of the lobby. The lights are already on but the sun's still not quite down, and the massive windows glow both indigo and radioactive orange.

Suwa checks in and gets a racing bib. "Eighty-seven. My birthday, lucky."

I frown. "Your birthday's July eighth."

"Nope." Suwa struggles to pin it on so I help him. "My mother never got into American dating, like, month first, days second. She wrote 'seven-slash-eight' on all of my paperwork. I'm a birthday fraud like you."

"What else do we have in common?" I hadn't meant to say that out loud. My mouth freezes in a panicked smile as I look down at him.

His eyes narrow. "I don't know? I'm going to the bathroom. Make sure nobody jacks my stuff."

When he's out of sight, I take a deep breath. There are only a few hours left until I show him the painting tucked away in the car. Until I finally know for sure who we are to each other. But until then, I gotta cool it. That was too close.

I text the group chat a selfie/confirmation we made it, then turn off my phone. Too nervous, and I'm not even the one about to play for internet icon and pop superstar Cola Carter, who walks through the lobby in a seafoam sweat suit, her signature two-tone hair tucked under a baseball cap and large sunglasses taking up half her face. *Hang on.* I look around the lobby. *Does no one else recognize that she's* here?

Cola catches me watching her and waves, puts a finger to her mouth, and winks before disappearing into a door marked STAFF ONLY. After I blink and rub my eyes, I notice Suwa staring with a dazed look on his face. *Shit, did seeing Cola freak him out?* And then his body tilts, sways like a leaf in a breeze, and he stumbles to keep himself upright.

I run over to steady him. He immediately tries to play it off.

"I should've eaten more, before." His teeth are chattering but he smiles wanly as he blows his bangs out of his eyes, putting on a show of being okay.

"Hey, what's going on?" There are only five minutes until his slot, but he looks pale. I press my palm to his face. His skin's a little clammy.

So even the untouchable Suwa Moon gets stage fright. "Suwa. Gimme your hands, we're gonna breathe. Like before. You're gonna crush the audition. You're—"

Suwa laughs sharply. "You want to know something fucked-up? I'm here because I want to play my music and have it stand alone, but also, at the heart of it, I want to be recognized for me, who I am, even if I try to frame it another way. Like I'm going to be the brave sucker who makes it easier for everyone after them. It's like, only just hitting me that if some people see me, like *see* me, I'm kind of terrified of what they might say or do. In theory that's not really enough to stop me from wanting what I want, but what if—what happens if I get it? Then it's not theory. Then it's my actual life. Can I handle that, that responsibility? Do I have this crisis every time I play, for the rest of my life? Fuck! I'm like a cat pretending it's a tiger, until I see wolves. What am I doing? What am I trying to prove?"

I hold his shoulders. *Jesus, he's deep into the spiral.* I ramble as I breathe deeply, "First of all. That cat thing. Doesn't make any sense. And there's nothing wrong. With wanting what you want. And Cola Carter already likes you. And you're not alone. I'm here. I've always been here. For you." The floodgates between my mind and my mouth buckle as the pressure in my chest strains for release, pushing me somewhere I don't actually wanna go. Like Odysseus's crew and the bag of wind.

Memo loved *The Odyssey*. Suwa helped me with my essay on Homer and nostalgia. The pain of homecoming. Of returning to something that will never be how you left it but is close enough for you to sense the echo, the slightly distorted reflection of what you really missed.

Suwa spits between breaths, "What is this? You keep dropping. Hints like a shitty crime show. Just say it. What're you talking about?"

The words ring hollowly in my head as they leave my lips: "Emo Ocean? Memo?"

A few weeks back, we all spent a day together in downtown LA. Reva's parents packed a feast and we hung around Olvera Street, people-watching and hanging out. Afterward, Mira insisted that I drive through this one specific tunnel, said something about it being used in movies. As we passed through, the light seemed choppy and distorted, like someone was animating my life but leaving out every other frame.

This strobing effect is playing across my eyes now.

Flash. Suwa's face, frozen.

Flash. Something dawns in his eyes. His mouth opens.

Flash. ". . . Canti?" And the rest of the world slides out of the frame except for two pillars of fire, one streak of crimson and another of thunderbolt-blue.

"Sayo told me your band name and—and everything fell into place. Initiation, quoting *Mugen Glider*; you pretended you didn't really know it, and I'm not gonna ask why, but we're here. I'm here." I release my hands from his shoulders. "You already have what it takes to impress Cola Carter. You made 'Exit Music.' This is the moment when everything happens."

For a moment, Suwa's face is eerily blank, a mask that tests a few impressions of emotions. But when it finally settles, I get goosebumps; there's an almost feral glint in his eyes. Lips curled into a snarl.

"You haven't changed at all."

I recoil from the cold snap in Suwa's voice.

He steps away from me and repeats, "You haven't changed at all. Oh my god."

"Eighty-seven. Eighty-seven." The voice, amplified by a megaphone, brings us back to our surroundings. Suwa stares down at his eighty-seven bib, grabs his gig bag, and walks away.

I push through the crowd after him. "Suwa, please, take a moment—"

"I . . . Is any of this real? Or was I just a—a mystery to solve?" Suwa laughs sharply. "And Santi, what the hell? How could you tell me this now?"

It finally hits me. The enormity of what I've said crashes through me like a wave. I'd kept this possible revelation at arm's length even from myself, because the reality is, Suwa being Memo would—does—complicate everything about our relationship.

I thought my burning question was, *Are you Memo?* But as the expression on Suwa's face becomes more and more crestfallen, I realize the actual question I'm asking is the one I've carried with me for years: *Can you forgive me?*

Suwa becomes animated with barely restrained fury. "I'm trying to imagine what you were thinking when, after realizing that you might've found the person who . . . Knowing everything, you decide the best way to reveal yourself is by dropping this bomb at the precisely worst possible moment. You're like whatever the opposite of Cassandra is. You make things happen when they don't need to happen."

Even when he's this mad, Suwa manages to point out how smart he is, dropping a reference to ancient Greek tragedy. That arrogant confidence from the beginning of the season, a smoke screen he dropped for me but that can go up anytime. I scoff; if he thinks I can't keep up, he's wrong. Of course he's gotten mad at me before, but this is—

No. He has every right to his reaction. But what I don't understand is why there isn't even a flash of joy.

Suwa heads for the person calling his number. I scramble to catch up. "What was I gonna do, let you shoot yourself in the foot? You're so close. The future is coming for you, Suwa. No matter what else came before." It's only after I take a ragged breath that I realize this is what I should've said to him from the start.

The people checking Suwa in politely pretend they aren't listening as he scrawls his signature on a final set of forms and snarls, "Wait, are you serious? You're the one who dragged 'what came before' into it, and also it obviously matters. But sure, pretend the timing wasn't astonishingly shitty. Did you ever stop to consider that there's a reason I don't touch that part of my life at all?"

I didn't. And I somehow become both light-headed and achingly heavy. "You were my best friend. You are my best friend, but you were back then, too. I never let you go."

"You should've."

I can't. "Suwa, I love you. I swear I wasn't holding out on you before and I'm so sorry I keep . . . I keep hurting you. I don't know what's wrong with me. But this, what we have, this was always real. This is the realest, truest thing."

A venue staffer clears her throat.

Suwa and I both turn toward her, and something about the way we look makes her rub her eyes, sigh, and mouth, *Thirty*, before pointedly ticking her arm like the second hand on a clock.

Suwa rubs his eyes. "Santi, what do you think is going on?"

I clench my fists. "Like here, or in eternity?"

Suwa's composure cracks and for the first time since the day I eavesdropped on him and his dad, he sobs, a sound that aches like an old wound.

"God, I can't believe I'm saying this." Suwa wipes tears away with the back of his sleeve and visibly gathers himself. "Santi, if you love *me*, why couldn't you have left Memo behind? And we could've been ordinary, but good. Instead of extraordinarily fucked."

He wipes his eyes with his sleeve again. "This is . . . This is a nightmare."

The staffer calls out, "Suwa Moon. Now or never."

"I don't want to see you when I'm done." And Suwa turns his back toward me, disappearing behind a door that hasn't even shut yet before a security guard gets in my space. "Performers and staff only past this point."

I can't really feel my body as I walk numbly toward an exit. There are so many people here, so many people who want what Suwa wants, so many people who'll be closer to their dreams if Suwa stumbles. Ugh, that's not fair. Who told me "all-or-nothing" recently? That's just it, nothing's ever that simple. Like, you can want to be recognized for being good at what you do, but also fear the heat of the spotlight. Like, you can love someone and want the world for them, but also hurt them because of how close you are, bodies and hearts so entwined together that every sudden movement leaves a bruise.

The air smells like oil and ash. I face the fading sky and fight the urge to yell. How else did I think this would go down? But what else could I have done?

I stare blankly ahead as I walk down Vermont; I definitely don't want to drive feeling like this. Okay. It's gonna be okay. Unlike before, Memo can't vanish. Suwa has to come back to somewhere and, sure, I'll stay far away until maybe, he's ready to talk. I'll text him tomorrow. Or maybe someone can pass on a message for me. Sayo seems like a great mediator.

No, I'm the one who screwed this up. The only person I can blame is myself, again. But unlike before, I know how to reach him. I'm going to show him how hard I can fight for something, someone I love.

Except . . . I can't get over the look in Suwa's eyes. I'd assumed that he felt the same way about Canti as I did Memo. And, of course, Canti had hurt him, but in a way that I'd hoped was forgivable. But I wasn't the one who had to bear that pain.

Would Suwa have accepted me from the start if he'd known the truth? Did I only get this close to him at all despite, not because of, the echoes of our past?

Would it actually be good for him if I'm in his life?

I wince when a roll of what sounds like thunder erupts up and down the block, followed by similar waves of distant crackling from the rest of the city. The sky fills with shimmering dawn—fireworks.

The noise obliterates my thoughts. My legs move like they're automated. I think I had a jacket in the car, which I'll have to come back for.

Another wall of sound. Some of the fireworks are so close, I can follow their whistling voyage from the street to the heavens, where they pin explosions to the cobalt sky. I hope Suwa can't hear them. He's gonna wipe the floor with everyone else auditioning. It's like Cap said. He just needs a stage big enough to *BOOM*.

A score of celebration sounds as I replay our conversation over and over in my head. I stop counting the blocks I pass. Sparks rain down at the end of a street. Kids in the road laugh and cheer as they get close enough to the face of danger to feel a thrill before running back to the safety of home.

Home. My phone's still off. When I turn it on, there are five missed calls from Aya. Right, we were supposed to all meet up after the audition. To celebrate the new year.

She picks up on the first ring. "Hi, Aya? I need you to come get me. Something's happened." I end the call before I even tell her where I am, or remember that I'm the one with her car.

I sit down on a curb and watch the "petals" of a giant orange flower curl and spin through the sky, then shatter into glitter that fades into smoke.

Now what?

The Moonflower Sessions

Track 12

"Wow. Sorry, I keep doing these double-takes like—if Sayo hadn't told me she had a baby brother, I totally would've thought you were a girl. Which honestly makes you perfect for this gig."

Edison pants and fans himself with his hand. "Doki Doki Dreamboy has a catch. Their whole thing is guys dressed as girls, so you'll have to cross-dress. Also, I can't pay you per se, but I've played the venue before and they actually have a tipping culture so you can rake it in that way. We'll give you, uh, twenty-five percent. Playful Cloudy would fill most of the hour but you could, I don't know, play your solo stuff in whatever time's left, if we have any."

All I'd done was go outside for some coffee, and now I'm being recruited as an emergency bassist for a band that's booked a set at a maid café–slash–gender theory minefield. I sip on my coffee and wait for Edison, one of my sister's work acquaintances and maybe the only straight guy I know in Tokyo, to continue groveling. I'm out to most of Sayo's crew but not him. As unselfconsciously as possible, I adjust my sweatshirt to make sure, even though I'm wearing a binder, the outline of my chest is fully obscured.

"We know we're not saving rock 'n' roll, we're just some guys. But this is our first gig in a while, and of course Joe, that's our bassist, gets into a day-drinking contest with a Russian so he's tanked, and when Mikio says, 'Hey, you know Sayo's brother, the one who played that crazy set at Heaven's Not Enough? He's been in the office all day and he's like, a musical genius, and so cute, we'll probably make twice as many tips than if we were playing with Joe's busted mug,' so I ran over here. You down? Put on a dress, make some money?" Edison smiles nervously.

There's no reason I can't. I've hit a wall of writer's block, and after three days of stewing in my "studio"—part of the room I share with Sayo that I've partitioned off with a screen—an outside excursion would be good for me.

Except: I'd be making the conscious choice to dress like a girl. A boy playing a girl, but who's to say the reflection of a reflection isn't the real thing, or something like that? I weigh my outward discomfort and inward irony against a possible payday.

I fight to keep my face neutral. "Make my cut thirty, and I'm in."

An hour later, I'm wearing a modest schoolgirl uniform and picking stock basslines as Edison and Mikio, two of the three members of Playful Cloudy—shoegaze lite, like a diluted-of-lushness Lush —croon at the giggling customers, who ask to take photos between songs. Gender swap aside, Doki Doki Dreamboy is a pretty upscale maid café in that all of the staffers look like late-round eliminations on an idol competition show. If I could work here, I'd probably make decent money. Even though my Japanese is terrible, it would definitely be a plus that I speak English, since most of the clientele are foreigners. But all of my documentation is under my dead name, for the wrong gender.

After we go through the Playful Cloudy songbook and Edison and Mikio tepidly jam, Edison clears his throat into the mic and says, in fake halting English, "Now, Suwa-kun plays solo!" Mostly polite clapping, except for a table of women in the back who'd obviously walked in drunk. I nod my head in their direction and one of them yells out, "Ganbatte, Suwa-kun!"

Everything is embarrassing. I wave at the audience and adjust my skirt, which keeps hitching up. Hmm. I didn't really think Edison would give me any time. I can't play anything I've been working on or anything I released last year, not without a real backing band or at least a track, but there's one song I'll always know how to play alone.

It feels a little cheap to debut it live like this, but fuck it, what does it matter? It's not like anyone outside this room is going to hear it anyway. "Hi. I'm Suwa, and I'm going to do a cover of a song that came out a long time ago. It's called 'Exit Music.' Thank you for letting me play for you." I stare down the barrel of the mic and try to ignore the sudden ache in my chest. And even though my performance doesn't matter, even though it barely sounds like the original, I find myself holding back tears when I bow curtly before leaving the stage.

A few weeks later, I'm on my way home from another mercenary gig, this time at a real venue for a real band, when Sayo calls me. "Suwa. Wanna meet at Famima? We finally wrapped up and I'm sooo hungrrry." Judging by her delivery, the Sleeping Forest team had all gone out drinking after their shoot.

I sigh and make my way into Ebisu Station. "I'll be at the stop in thirty, meet me there."

She's not at the stop. There are five Family Marts within walking distance, so I go in the direction of "home" and pop into the first one I pass.

Sayo's already checking out. The clerk at the counter waves shyly. I nod back at him, add a can of plum chuhai to Sayo's order, then take her shopping bags. "Where are the others?"

"They lugged all the stuff home. Gimme!"

She reaches into a bag and snatches a piece of karaage, which she shoves into her mouth. I wrinkle my nose as she wipes her fingers on her jacket, then starts ranting about some "film-festival bullshit" before she asks, in a much more subdued voice, "How was the gig?"

I crack open the can in my hand. "The guitarist couldn't decide whether or not he wanted to hit on me, so he kept missing his cues. Singer was cool, though. She said if they ever do a real Asia tour, they'll try to hire me. Which, you know." In the year I've been working these one-off shows with bands just passing through town, I've gotten a few offers like that. Nothing's ever come of them.

". . . Do you wanna talk about it?" Sayo rings the bell for our building, then yanks the gate open when the buzzer goes off. I shake my head no. We make our way up the stairs, and I kick open the busted front door to the cramped apartment that doubles as Sleeping Forest's "Asia HQ."

Sayo singsongs, "Tadaima," and closes the door gently behind us. I hold up the bags and deadpan, "The latest and greatest in konbini cuisine."

"Oh, yay." Erika ties her locs up into a ponytail and gets up from the kitchen table, which is covered in video equipment, errant skateboard parts, and a few whining laptops. She helps pass out food to the others, who are all either sprawled out on one of the many half-made futons or hanging around the kitchen. "How'd the gig go, Suwa? And hey, when're you gonna play an Emo Ocean show again? My friend at *i-D* keeps hitting me up to get an interview. About your music, but also"—Erika shrugs and smiles—"you know."

The summer after I moved to Tokyo with Sayo, I released an EP under the name Emo Ocean. I scrapped everything I'd written before and poured myself into a suite of blistering, still-bloody breakup songs. *The Moonflower Sessions*: a howl into the void, posted on Bandcamp with no fanfare. But since I'm friendly with a few bands, it got passed around the Tokyo underground, and after buzzy write-ups from a handful of Japanese blogs, *Moonflower* went international and grew a small but devoted following.

Including a particularly feverish community of fans who picked up some of the more personal stuff I'd coded in—about myself, about my body—and rallied around it. At one point, while poking around on the internet, I read a random blog's list of "queer musicians who'll make you cry on the bathroom floor" and found my own EP art, followed by a breathless write-up about longing and ambiguous identity. One particularly memorable bit: "As Emo Ocean, Suwa Moon takes you on an odyssey through heartbreak where he arrives, maybe, at himself—which might be the gayest thing I've ever written, but wouldn't even crack the top ten gayest lines on this EP. 'The shiver of heat masquerading as chill / But no love can be a suncatcher': HELLO? HELLO??? I'm screaming and crying into a pillow?!"

Flash forward another six months. Sayo's old college roommate's band, Magnetic Rose, asked me to open for their show at Heaven's Not Enough, this club in Shibuya. I accidentally took a train in the wrong direction and then got tripped up by transfers so instead of opening the night, I walked into the venue to see people already leaving. Not the best way to start your first real live show, but, I don't know, it was like some spirit possessed me. I leapt onto the stage and started playing, and I was still playing when the house lights went up, hundreds of people chanting for an encore: "EMO OCEAN EMO OCEAN EMO OCEAN."

Since then, I've gotten a few interview requests from the local press. A couple of scene bloggers, some fashion people, Erika's friend at *i-D* Japan. But the questions they want to ask me are a little too much about me, my nebulous "queerness"—their word—and not as much about my music. I haven't performed live as Emo Ocean since.

The gigging for other bands is how I make real money, but my side job is scoring films put out by Sleeping Forest. All those years of listening to anime soundtracks paid off, and I've started separately getting some buzz for that work. So that's my life these days, split between two personas. Emo Ocean: cult "queer" singer-songwriter. Suwa Moon: muscle for hire and budding composer.

One of the videographers, Damian, blows out a thin ribbon of smoke. "Can you blame them for trying? You"—he points at me before fake-swooning—"would be a wet dream of an interview. The elusive, mercurial Emo Ocean! A teenage prodigy, Asian, gay, trans, *and* a real firecracker. A diversity feature and a surefire sound bite. Who can resist a shot?"

Erika warns, "Knock it off." I pull the cigarette out of Damian's mouth and drop it in the trash. He stopped smoking when we started sleeping together, but once that ended, back to the fumes. I watch the cherry turn to ash, then crack open a bento and say, between chews, "No one's directly asked me if I'm trans, so don't go running your mouth about me. Please."

I stare fixedly at Damian, who rolls his eyes but goes, "I know, I know."

Sayo purses her lips. I narrow my eyes at her. She pitches her voice down. "'Sayo, I don't want to get into it.'"

I pitch my voice up to imitate hers. "'Suwa, don't you eventually want to talk about Emo Ocean?'" I bring my voice back down. "Not when there's nothing to talk about."

"'Nothing,' wow, dramatic." Sayo shushes me when I try to interject, then grabs my arm and drags me into an office/bedroom.

As soon as the door closes, she fixes me with a pointed look. "I let you crash with us because you said you couldn't be in LA anymore after . . ." Sayo pauses. She was going to say, *After you bombed your audition and dumped your boyfriend*, because that's what I'd told people had happened.

She pokes me in the chest. "That was over a year ago. Don't get me wrong, I appreciate your work. But is this really what you want to be doing?"

I bristle. "I'm good at it, and it keeps me busy."

Sayo crosses her arms. "Your level of 'busy' is literally superhuman. We're talking about your side job, which you do around your main job, which has you coming home at midnight on the reg. And yet. Do you know how many times I've woken up in the middle of the night to see you singing under your breath and plucking away on your bass, noodling around on Pro Tools?

You're making new stuff to what, keep it locked away? I don't buy it, and I'm not the only one. Don't be surprised that people want to know what you're doing next."

I sarcastically mumble, "Shit, me too."

Sayo squeezes her eyes shut and mutters something under her breath. When she opens them, she glares at me, but she sounds more tired than angry. "The last film in our series is coming out soon. In a month, Sleeping Forest's going to close this office. I don't know where they'll send me next, and I don't know if I can take you in. You coming along to Tokyo was really only possible because of Mom's background, but you won't be able to work or stay anywhere else without a visa, and I can't pay you to do this full-time. So you gotta find a way to move on, unless you want to stay here on your own. But once we're gone . . ."

She leans toward me. "Who will be your people, Suwa? Or will you just keep making your music alone, forever?"

The doorbell rings. I hear Erika sigh, "One moment," then the shuffling of her slippers against the floor.

The unspoken third option shimmers in the air: *Go back to Los Angeles. Home.* I pick at my nail polish. "I'll figure it out. I can't go back. Not yet." I try to sound defiant, but my voice comes out shaky. Betrayed by my body, as usual.

Our silent stare-off is getting uncomfortable, when Erika knocks. "Um, Suwa, there's someone here to see you." As Sayo opens the door, she mouths, *To be continued.* Then she lets out a yelp of surprise.

I turn toward where she's staring. There, standing in the kitchen and looking bemused, is Cola Carter.

———

When Cola purrs, "Hi, Suwa," I get goosebumps. She smiles winsomely. "Nice hair. You were pink the first time we met, too."

International pop star Cola Carter remembers me from that ten-minute audition? "Yeah, it's to warn predators I'm venomous."

Cola laughs at the joke, but I feel self-conscious under her scrutiny. She's immaculate, in incognito mode; all-black everything, including the hat that covers her signature black-and-blond split hair. Her skin's as perfect up close as it is in photos.

Meanwhile, there are dark circles under my eyes. My nail polish is chipped from picking at it. And my hair needs to be touched up, pink fading into more of a peach.

When Cola walks past us and back into the office, I quickly turn heel. Sayo does the same, shutting the door she'd just opened behind us.

Cola takes the seat on the far side of the desk, while Sayo and I settle into the guest chairs. I half expect Cola to put her feet up, but instead she keeps looking between me and Sayo, before my sister offers, "I'm Sayo, Suwa's sister. Would you like something to eat? Some water? Tea?"

"I'm good." Cola takes in the haphazard decor. Her street style's much more low-key than her stagewear. The only sign of her actual personality is her manicure, turquoise talons with tiny charms hanging off of the tips. I wonder how she plays guitar with them.

Cola catches me staring and does a quick spirit fingers. The charms jingle lightly from the motion. "They're for this trip. I'm scoping out Tokyo before I announce the dates for my next tour. I've got enough mana, in a sense, to pick my route now. This is the first time I'll play through Asia."

Sayo perks up. "Oh yeah? What venues are you looking at for Japan?"

Cola stretches her arms above her head. "We're trying to time it to Summer Sonic. The promoter keeps trying to sell me on an arena, but I think he's overcounting my Japanese fan base.

"But that's not why I'm here. Suwa." I bite the insides of my cheeks as I meet Cola's eyes. She tilts her head. "I've been a fan of yours for a while. Your *Moonflower* EP was, wow."

That wasn't what I expected at all. I shift in my seat, bewildered. "Um. Thank you." Those songs have *really* traveled.

Cola winces, which puzzles me. Then she says, "Emo Ocean. Great name. Memorable name. And yet, when I first searched it, I didn't get a single hit for artist social media or any press, except for a one-off show. Then I searched 'Suwa Moon,' but that only led to some local LA news mentions about a high school marching band. For all intents and purposes, a ghost released that music."

Cola leans forward. "So imagine my surprise when, a year later, I'm playing one of my favorite songs in the world, and the next track the algorithm picks up is a phone recording of someone doing a cover of 'Exit Music,' that's the name of the song, in of all places, a Tokyo maid café. And not just a cover, but an uncanny one. And when the video zooms in, I go, 'I know that face.'"

Cola pretends to examine her nails again. "So now I'm really curious, and I do more digging and start connecting some dots. The kid who played a fire audition for me but then withdrew his application dropped a red-hot EP six months after said audition, but has been in Tokyo exclusively playing for other people and making soundtracks for skate videos. Except for one set at Heaven's Not Enough and one song at Doki Doki Dreamboy, where he does, completely coincidentally, a pitch-perfect cover of 'Exit Music.'"

I hear Sayo suck her breath in. Sayo's one of three people in the world who know that I'm the person who made "Exit Music." Now, maybe four. I answer cautiously, "I'm a fan."

"A fan who has the exact same vocal cadences and style of playing as the original. The key's changed, but puberty comes for us all." Cola's mouth twitches into a smile. "Come on. Suwa Moon. Emo Ocean. You were Memo. I've been picking apart 'Exit Music' for years. I know I'm right."

I swallow dryly. Sayo lets out a sharp laugh. God, as much as I need her support in this situation, I wish she wasn't following my every move with hawk eyes; she's definitely going to grill me over Cola's comment about my audition. I shrug and steady myself. "Congrats. You found me. You should quit music and become a PI."

Cola lets my rudeness pass over her. "Will you ever bring Emo Ocean into the world and tour for *Moonflower*? Or, are you a maid café–only experience now?"

I deserved that. I pause before answering, "Sure. Probably. When it feels right." Sayo's radiating indignant-sibling anger grows hotter. This is all Cola Carter's fault. She shows up at our doorstep and both reveals that I lied about how I did on my audition and forces me to answer the questions I've been dodging for months.

Cola nods and murmurs, "Cool, very cool."

I drum my fingers against my thighs nervously. The idea that Cola Carter was so obsessed with a song I made when I was thirteen that she'd track me down in another country is freaky, but also kind of flattering?

Sayo nudges me with her knee angrily, and I ask, "What . . . are you doing here?"

Cola steeples her hands. "You know Gekkostate?" I nod; I'd gone to one of their shows a while back. She continues, "I originally wanted to make this offer to them, but on the DL, they're maybe going to break up soon. So I started putting out feelers about other bands, but I kept thinking about you. The kid who left his hit song unclaimed, then comes out of nowhere again with another hot streak of songs. Then immediately goes back into hiding."

Her eyes gleam. "Suwa. I want you to stake your claim to fame as a signee on my new imprint, Karma Demon, which I've built for people like us. Queer artists with total freedom and almost-major label budgets, with none of the major-label bullshit. And then I want you to step onto stages all over the world as the opener on my next tour."

My head fills with static as I take in what Cola said. I know these kinds of offers exist. Opening gigs for artists with little-to-no touring experience; record deals based on the strength of one song. My chest tightens, not with panic but with . . . want. I want to say yes.

Then Cola says, "I was thinking it'd be cute to use that maid-café footage as, like, your intro. I'm sure you know, but you're a really pretty boy, and—"

"You can't share that footage. And I'm sorry, but I have to turn down your offer." I start to get up, but Sayo grabs my wrist and forces me to sit back down.

I hiss, "Let go of me."

"No. This is your dream. I'd be the worst big sib in the world if I let you walk away." Sayo turns to Cola. "Can you show me that video?"

Cola pulls out her phone—no case, brave—and stabs at the screen with one finger before handing it over to Sayo, who immediately understands. Though my voice is low enough to pass, in my sailor suit, I'm a girl. I can only watch for a few seconds before turning away, a reaction honed from a lifetime spent glancing at mirrors and wincing.

". . . I'm sorry, what am I missing here?" Cola speaks soothingly, like someone trying to calm an animal stuck in a trap.

Sayo clears her throat. I glare sullenly at the desk, the grain of the fake wood blurring and morphing into EKG lines, mimicking the dull thudding of my heartbeat as I debate whether or not to tell Cola about myself.

I will never get a chance like this again. That's what I thought when "Exit Music" leaked, and again when Cola gave me a standing ovation at my audition, told me I'd passed to the next round, and asked me to call her manager in a few days to schedule a follow-up. But in my bones, I know Cola's offer now is the last lucky break the universe is going to give me. I've turned away from so many of the things I've wanted out of a combination of pride and fear. I was about to do that again.

What Sayo had said earlier in the night rings in my ears: *Will you just keep making your music alone, forever?*

That wasn't the dream that kept me alive; that got me out of bed even on the days when all I wanted was to melt into the mattress and disappear.

I pull the words out of my mouth: "I'm trans."

Cola blinks slowly.

I repeat, "I'm trans. As soon as I understood that gender was a thing, I knew I was a boy. But trying to assert that and, like, live as a boy has gotten me in trouble in the past, from people at school but especially my family. That's why I didn't claim 'Exit Music,' and it's at least part of the reason I didn't follow through with your audition. This video . . . it can't be my introduction. All I want people to see when I'm onstage is a boy."

I hold my breath. Cola's silent for a moment, but then she smirks, and for a second, I feel a stab of unease. She's going to take back her offer. Maybe she'll hold this admission against me.

"So. 'When I'm onstage,' huh?" She leans back in her seat and laughs. The tension in the room dissipates, and I feel a blush trickle down my face.

Cola stands up and leans so far over the desk that I can smell her perfume, something spicy. "Suwa, is that a yes?"

I jut my chin forward. "It's not a no."

Cola grins wolfishly as she sits back down. "Well, this is what I'm thinking. The Karma Demon summer showcase, where I'll debut all of my signees, is in the middle of July, so in three months. During that time, you'll re-release *The Moonflower Sessions* with new songs, and that'll be an album, with an appropriate budget. After the showcase, you and I will play that big New York festival, and then we'll hit the ground running. North America, Europe, back through the States, closing with a few stops in Asia. At least a year on the road."

She furrows her eyebrows. "There is kinda a catch. You'd have to get on the first flight to LA, tomorrow."

In my peripheral vision, Sayo's eyes grow wide, and my lips part into an incredulous smile. Of course. There's no give without take, and I owe my hometown blood, sweat, tears, and to my friends and family, the truth about why I left.

Cola, oblivious to the war in my mind, continues, "You're from there, right? Have you thought about who you'd want in a touring band? Otherwise we'll hold auditions."

I instantly think about Ari and Lucía. I'd always dreamed of bringing them into the band once I hit it big on my own and could promise them stability. But doubt immediately sets in. Will they even want to work with me now, a bandleader with less practical experience than either of them?

Cola pauses. "I know this is a lot to consider, and if you can't commit completely, I get it. But I don't think I can make this offer again." She reaches into her hoodie pocket and pulls out a printed plane ticket. "It's yours, if you want it."

After Cola leaves, the rest of Sleeping Forest goes out for karaoke, so it's just me and Sayo in the apartment. My sister wordlessly opens the fridge, cracks open two beers, and passes one to me before taking a seat on a couch. I sit down on the other end, twirling the bottle between my palms.

Sayo takes a swig, and then, *action*. "Suwa, what exactly happened at that audition?"

I take a sip. "Cola wanted to put me through. I withdrew. I lied to you, and everyone else."

"Does this have something to do with San—"

"Don't say his name." The words fly out of my mouth before I can stop them. I have the split-second thought, *So this is how he feels all the time.*

Sayo clicks her tongue. "Does this have something to do with . . . him?"

I run my finger over the opening of the bottle. "Sayo, do you remember the internet friend I had when I was a kid? The one who liked that anime *Mugen Glider* as much as I did?"

"*Mugen* . . . the one I fished out of the dumpster? Man, that was a weird show. And yeah, I remember your lil' friend. What about him?"

We're on our third beers by the time I finish talking. About *Mugen Glider*, @bubblegum-crises, Canti, and then the boy who'd appeared in my life like a geyser, obliterating everything and everyone that'd come before. I'm speaking sloppily by the time I finish, hiccupping between sentences. "So, that's the whole sad story. I met him, I pretended I found him but didn't actually think I'd found him, and then. Boom." I carefully place my bottle on the floor.

Sayo pinches the bridge of her nose. "Lemme get this straight. When he confirmed it, you dumped him, then ran as far as you could from him, even though it meant turning down Cola Carter?"

Why does everything sound so crude when she lays it out like that? "Sayo, it wasn't that simple." I close my eyes and immediately submerge into the memory of that New Year's Eve: the instant he spilled his secret, which I'd been keeping, too, in my own way, by denying the possibility of its existence. The uncertainty on his face that'd instantly given way to a hopefulness that shimmered like heat lines drifting up from sunbaked pavement. He'd acted like he'd been dealt a hand of Brights in a game of Go Stop. Like he'd looked up on a whim and caught a meteor shower on a cloudless night. Like he'd been waiting for this moment his entire life.

I hadn't been able to face it. "It" being his actual face and the idea that after all this time I'd spent reimagining and reshaping my body, my life, I'd actually been retracing my steps, returning to the version of myself I'd tried so desperately to erase and outgrow. And just like I did during our first breakup, I'd panicked and made what I prayed would be a clean cut, to finally leave who I was behind.

But my knife was dull and my hands shook. And a year and change later, an ocean away, despite all the ways I tried to blunt the pain—with retail therapy, with other bodies, with music, which worked the best and the worst—the wound still burns.

I open my eyes. I wish I could make how I'm feeling less obvious, but my face has slipped into the muscle memory of melancholy. But I don't deserve to mourn. I blow my bangs out of my eyes and rearrange my expression into indifference, even though I know my sister will see through it.

Sayo places her own empty bottle next to mine, then murmurs, "I know. It never is." She looks out over the living room, remembering something that makes her mouth twist.

Shit. The worst thing in the world is when Sayo's sad. I scoot over next to her, not close enough to touch but enough to let her know that I'm trying to be there for her or whatever. "I didn't know who else to turn to after that went down. It was easier to tell you I failed, and I needed your help."

"Suwa, I will literally always help you. That's like, big-sib code." Sayo sighs and runs her hands through her hair. "Does he know? About how you felt about your relationship before, because yeah, he shouldn't have dropped it like that, but it's not . . ." She trails off. "That's not the point. You're really going home, huh?"

I shrug. Sayo huffs. "Aight, then gimme your ticket." She

pretends to grab it, and I reflexively clutch it to my chest. She rolls her eyes. "If you weren't going to take Cola's offer, we'd be out at karaoke with the rest of them. But instead we're here, talking about the past and trying to see the future."

She turns to face me. Even before I transitioned, we didn't look that much alike. She took after our mother, while I took after our father.

We both think of our Los Angeles family at the same time. Sayo starts, "Y'know, Appa's been asking—"

"When we'll be back. He really only wants to know about you." My father and I had been talking semiregularly before I left Los Angeles, but once I got to Tokyo, our one-on-one communication ground to a halt.

Sayo picks at a loose thread on the couch. "That's not true. And you're the one who always suddenly has something to do when he calls. Anyway, even though you're going back home, you're a long way from K-Town, kid. No matter what, but especially since you'll be running with Cola, our family can't touch you anymore. If you want to like, capital C-O, Come Out, you're safe."

"You don't know that." But even as I say that, I know it's not totally true. Sayo basically saved me from drowning when I was a kid and probably saved my life again when she brought me to Cap, the summer before my freshman year. If she says I'm out of danger, then I am.

I flick her elbow. "What would you do? If you were me."

Sayo flicks me back. "If I were you, we wouldn't be having this conversation because I would've already linked up with a label or some big artist as soon as I could and made my mark on the world."

"Ha-ha." I pick at a scab on my knee. "Sayo, I mean it."

Sayo startles me when she laughs. "So do I. Suwa, you aren't the same kid you were when 'Exit Music' came out. You've changed. The world's changed, too. I'm not gonna pretend I know what it's like to be you, but you won't get anywhere by slamming every door someone else opens for you. Cola Carter wants you. She's *wanted* you."

My double-edged sword of a fairy godmother. Like clockwork, the voice in my head sneers, *Why do you think you deserve special treatment?* I know I shouldn't listen to it, but it raises a question I can't ignore. A lot of the artists I love are still on the fringes of the industry, fighting for the exact kind of chance that's being granted to me.

I don't realize I'm trembling until Sayo's hugging me. "I know it's a lot. But if you're at all leaning toward saying yes," she says as she releases me, "you gotta let Cap know. He'll for sure let you stay with him again. And your friends are in LA, yeah?"

I nod. "Everyone but Prof, but he visits pretty often to help with his sib's kids." It's gotten harder to keep up with each other, but we make it a point to do a group video call at least once a month.

Each time we chat, I catch myself listening for a voice that never materializes. Is he even still in Los Angeles? I've never asked, and no one else has ever brought him up.

Sayo sighs and holds a hand out to hoist me out of my chair. "Hey. I know I gave you a hard time this afternoon, but I'm so proud of you. You've grown into yourself here. Now the wake of your life is pulling you back." Then softly, "Let it happen, Suwa."

———

In the morning, Sayo sees me off to the subway station. We both cry, but neither of us does the other the indignity of acknowledging the tears. And when I get to the gate, I almost don't see Cola because she's still in her pedestrian disguise. Until she waves me over. "Suwa!" She dips her sunglasses low enough to shoot me a wink. "Glad you could make it. Now, let's talk about how you're gonna take over the world."

Track 13

Cola struggles to unwrap the onigiri I'd brought on board. Eventually I help her slide the plastic wings off. She beams. "This partnership's already working."

It'd better work, because we're stuck on this plane together for at least another ten hours. It's disorienting watching someone who's so poised in public obviously drop her guard and several grains of rice onto her lap. After she snacks, Cola sighs deeply and stretches her legs out. I do the same, less out of an actual need to stretch and more because I've never flown business class before. I look at my passport one more time before I tuck it away. Before I fly again, I want to finalize the changes to my legal name and the letter printed under "Sex."

Cola fiddles with her hoodie strings. "So, here's the deal with"—she puts her fingers into air quotes—"'modern music stardom.' You're gonna have to get used to giving yourself away. You'll essentially live on the road, because tour merch sales are the only way to make any kind of money." She continues speaking rapid-fire, words rolling into each other. I nod at what I think are the ends of sentences. *Should I pretend I'm taking notes?*

Cola pauses. "I'm not gonna push on this too much, but what

exactly is the deal with your family? Is your sister the only one you still talk to?"

"Mostly. My father . . . it's complicated." That doesn't even scratch the surface, but "complicated" is the only word that comes close to explaining the tangled knot of feelings I have about him. "My parents met in college, they had Sayo, they had me, and then . . . my mother died. But her family has been out of the picture for a long time. It's my father's side that I'm kind of worried about, even though I haven't been in contact with them in years."

"How so?"

"Everyone in my family, minus Sayo and my father, thinks, or more like insists . . ." My voice starts to shake, and I turn away from Cola. "That I'm 'still' a girl. Before I finally cut ties with them, they tried to beat it into me."

". . . Sorry about your mom. And, the rest." I almost laugh at the sudden somberness in Cola's voice, but I understand; what else can you say to that? I hear Cola smack her lips a few times before she settles on "Sayo seems like a gem."

I turn back toward Cola and say, with an intensity that startles both of us, "She's the only reason I'm alive."

Neither of us picks the conversation back up until a flight attendant offers us two flutes of champagne. Cola accepts both and passes me one, then holds hers up for a toast. "To Sayo, and everyone else who got you here."

As I drink, I mull over Cola's toast. I'm not overstating my debt to my sister. She showed me the world beyond the borders of our house, our extended family's homes, school, and church. She was the only person I told in my real life about my music dreams, and she tapped her high school friend group to source the laptop that became my original tether to the online world, then the other equipment and software I used to make "Exit Music."

When I think of Sayo, I hear the sound of my bedroom window opening and the branch outside it rocking as she let herself in. Eventually I learned to sneak out, too, but I was always paranoid. We'd touch down from the tree outside my window and I'd immediately run through what-ifs: *What if he checks our rooms, what if he goes out for a smoke, what if someone else in the neighborhood sees us.*

Sayo would ruffle my hair and tell me not to worry. We'd laugh and scream and skate through the streets under the cover of night. Whenever I cried, she'd tilt my chin up and crack jokes until I laughed, or sit with me and make me hum along to the songs our mother used to sing to her.

She even helped me get over my fear of the ocean, taking me to the beach to listen to the waves. Though I haven't gotten in any body of water since I almost drowned.

After my audition for Cola Carter, I called Sayo in the throes of a panic attack, overwhelmed by Cola's attention but also reeling from a sudden collision between my past and my present. She'd joked about bringing me to Tokyo, but as soon as I asked about actually joining her, she made it happen, taking my reasons at face value. And then she did what she always does: helped me up and told me to try again.

I show Cola some new music. I'm nervous at first, but eventually we hit a flow. I play a song, she gives notes, we discuss how it might fit into the *Moonflower* album. Eventually she says, "Here's the situation. It'll already be news that Emo Ocean is revealing himself to the world. But to be honest, I wasn't totally surprised when you told me you're trans. A lot of people online have speculated as much, so, well, how much do you want that to be a part of your story?"

I reflexively scowl before ironing out my expression. "My songs aren't about being trans."

"Right, they're 'about' a breakup. But people think you are something that, if confirmed, could mean a lot to them. And again, total honesty here, being a trans man of color is something that makes you stand out. I say this as someone who knows her fan base wouldn't be as devoted as it is if I weren't a Black woman, a lesbian, and smoking hot."

I start, "I make music for everyone who's ever—"

Cola immediately puts her hand up to stop me. She picks at her lunch—dinner? This flight feels like it's been going on forever—before saying, "Been through a big life change? Felt sadness? You've got aspirations beyond getting on the right Spotify playlist. Don't undersell the things that make you real. That make you different. And don't fall into the trap of thinking that your music will sell itself.

"You don't have to get into nitty-gritty details, but you're human, after all, Suwa. Try talking about yourself like you have a heartbeat. Believe it or not, people like that." Cola yawns, fishes a pill out of her purse and downs it, then slips on a sleeping mask. "Think about it. See you in a few hours."

I close my eyes and try to sleep, too, but instead I stew. I know she has a point: If I don't take control of my narrative, other people will write one for me. Still, even her light poke into my personal life instantly got under my skin.

I fidget as I remember what happened with the documentary

crew. That heavy breathing down my neck: *Tell us, tell everyone, everything*. Why do I have to tell anyone anything? Why is it only people "like me" who have to grapple with that kind of disclosure in the first place? Even though De Longpre let me change my name and gender in my school file early on, so all the Sunshowers news mentions identify me as a boy, my dead name and everything it implies are still on the record everywhere it counts. For as long as I'm in the spotlight but not explicitly out, I'll live under a sword of Damocles. There are plenty of people who negotiate this while living openly in the public eye. But there aren't too many people from my particular background who do so, something Cola didn't explicitly mention but that must be on her mind as much as it is on mine.

I eye the stack of paper sticking out of my backpack. My contract. Cola's mentorship and a deal with Karma Demon and releasing *The Moonflower Sessions* as an album only become real when I sign. But once I do, I hand over some control of my body of work and my literal body.

There's no reason I have to do any of this. So many trans people would be overjoyed to live ordinary lives. And shit, every other time I got close enough to feel the heat of the bright lights, I ended up running away. So what does it say about me now that I recognize the cycle, and return? What about me has changed? *Have* I changed, or will I find a way to fuck this up, too?

It's hard to think about anything seriously with Cola lightly snoring next to me, so I pull out my phone and open Instagram. I'd archived all of my posts except for one, a photo of the sky-blue Rickenbacker 4001 that's packed somewhere in the belly of the plane. I click on my chat with Cap—his response to my request to stay with him was, in true old-man texting style, YES !!! of course my boy !!! followed by a bizarre assortment of emojis—and laugh softly, then dip into my DM requests: offers to work with various producers, stylists, and photographers; people I kind of knew in high school but are reaching out now because they think I might be famous.

A new message from Sayo: Aren't you gonna miss this. A photo of a half-rotted sweet potato that'd been hiding in one of the kitchen cabinets. I wrinkle my nose and type back, Disgusting, but I'd be lying if I didn't feel an ambient sense of longing for my life in Tokyo. Between my father's issues and my mother's absence, Sayo was my de facto parent for so long. Tokyo was special for a lot of reasons, but at the top of the list, we got to live and act as equals.

I'd just turned ten when I came out to her. The first thing Sayo asked me was, "Do you want this to change us?" I think about her phrasing all the time, the implicit understanding that gender both did and didn't matter in how we acted toward each other.

Then I think back to the moment I told my internet best friend that I was going by "they/them," but what I'd wanted to tell him was that I was like "him." "He/him," with no reservations. As much of a boy as he was. As much of a man as he'd become.

Which means I also think back to the boys who teased me until I was crying, then when I cut my hair short and started wearing a binder, pushed me around until I cried. To the family members who already didn't accept me, then actively shunned me when they realized precisely how far I was from their idea of a "normal Korean girl." To my first therapist, who wouldn't sign off on hormones because I wasn't obviously depressed enough—whatever that means—to "need" them.

But I also think about my father, who, about a year after I started injecting testosterone, did a double-take in the kitchen and whispered, "I thought you were a reflection."

And then, I think about that night at Heaven's Not Enough. Running up to the mic and shouting, "My name is Suwa Moon, and this is Emo Ocean." I'd rehearsed with Magnetic Rose before and as they played backup, I tore through the *Moonflower* songs, leaving my bloody, beating heart onstage. Afterward, they'd taken me out for karaoke and, for one of the only times in my life, I felt like I was truly one of the *boys*, moving through the world with that boyhood cloaked over me like a blanket instead of as a shield.

I don't really want to explain my gender, the way it interacts with other parts of my identity and my art, to other people. But I also don't want to act like it's something I haven't worked to understand on my own: the pain of relearning how to sing, and the thrill of watching and feeling my body hew to a new form.

I refresh my feed. A new post from Ari pops up. A photo with the people they're currently gigging with, some jazz night in Hollywood that they'd complained was "artistically bankrupt but pays the rent."

I open up the group chat and type: Landing in Los Angeles soon. I'd rather explain IRL but Ari and Lucía, let's link and build ASAP. I add my flight number and send it out, then mute the group. Four hours to go.

———

"Mm-hmm, yup. Thank you. Yes, he's looking forward to it, too. Talk soon." Cola hangs up. "You have the rest of the week to lock your friends in for the summer. First impression, the team likes what you've got but before they put *Moonflower* on the release schedule, they want to vet you. And they have a few other questions."

She chews her lip before adding, "I have one, too. Would you put 'Exit Music' on the album?"

"No." My answer is immediate and curt. She seems taken aback. I add as an explanation, "I want to start fresh." I'll never forget how it felt to lose control of that song. Even now, remembering leaves a bitterness in my mouth that I still can't stomach.

"I only wonder—okay, never mind. Mm. Do you have a beauty, fitness routine or anything?"

"Not really? I take pretty good care of my skin, though." I'd had to; puberty hormones, round two. I take long walks to listen to my favorite albums, but I don't think that's what she means by "fitness." Early on in high school, Feli and Ari brought me to the gym to work out a few times, but I never got into it.

Cola scrutinizes me. "Maybe take up running or something. It's way easier to tour when you're in, like, fit and fighting shape." I grimace. I already know my body is going to be a pain point, even without dysphoria in the mix, but of course it hits differently when the critique is coming from outside myself.

Cola lists off a bunch of immediate appointments: media training; some design meetings to go over the album repackaging. Then she fidgets in her seat before blurting out, "Look, I would swear this is the last time I bring it up, but I can't promise that, so. How much are you willing to talk about your gender? Like, what it means to you now, but also what it means to transition? I'm sorry if my language isn't, like, right, but do you know what I mean?"

"Is that a condition before signing me?" I'd meant it as a joke, but my delivery betrays my worry.

Cola smiles cryptically, then answers, "Of course not. It's really up to you. But you know my take."

The night the documentary crew came to my father, I'd been out late with Sayo. We'd both snuck back into the house only to find him waiting in my room. He hadn't said anything at first, just walked out of the room to signal that we were to follow. The orange tabby kitten our father had scooped from a box on the street mewed at us as we went down the stairs. Later that night, Marigold would crawl under the covers and knead me, and I'd let him even though his paws pressed into the new bruises blooming across my back.

A few days later, "Exit Music" leaked.

The day after that, my grandparents came over and began their intervention to prove that, despite all the neighborhood rumors, the youngest Moon daughter wasn't actually trying to disgrace the entire family even more than she already inherently did.

And less than a month later, Sayo and I ripped out the nails sealing my bedroom window, and I promised myself I'd never step foot in that house again unless I was, at the very least, accepted back as a boy. As we ran away, Marigold followed us, a tangerine shadow who got as far as the block before turning back.

I know what Cola wants from me. To smile and wave at the audience and talk about how grateful and proud I am to be here, and how my being here is something to celebrate. To be the *T* in her diverse "queer" coalition. But I'm just a boy who's figuring out how to be a man. And I don't feel like I have the right to celebrate anything when I'm alive but so many of my would-be "siblings" aren't.

Still. It mattered to me when Marigold transformed in *Mugen Glider*. When people I followed online wrote or drew trans characters, or came out themselves. When the clerk at the strip mall cosplay store, an Asian guy, too, spotted me eyeing binders and went out of his way to share his and his friends' reviews of different ones.

Cola sips at her water before pushing some hair out of her face. She's waiting on my answer.

I think about my last conversation with my father in Los Angeles, the day before my audition for Cola. He'd barely been able to look me in the eyes as he brought out and unwrapped the hanbok he'd worn for his coming-of-age ceremony in Korea and told me, his voice solemn but shaky, "If you decide to join a celebration or hold your own, I'd be . . . I think it should fit you."

I'd left it behind, because I couldn't reconcile the sober, resigned man who grows flowers from seeds to lay at his late wife's grave with the erratic volcano of rage who once controlled every aspect of my life. Who, the summer before senior year, let some of that old rage out when I told him that I wanted to be not a face in a formation, but my own man.

I wonder if he feels like me and Sayo abandoned him anyway. I wonder how he'd react if I talked about him in an interview. But mostly, I wonder if it'll ever be possible for me to think about any of my oldest relationships without immediately being pulled back to the darkest time of my life.

"If you didn't feel like you had to share that part of your life, would you still have shared it?"

Cola blinks rapidly, startled. Then she plucks my contract out of my bag and folds through the pages. She sits with the question for a while before saying, "I started off as a personal vlogger, so I'll never know." She looks visibly uncomfortable as she continues, "You won't meet a lot of people who are like you, in the industry. I don't even mean in terms of your identity, but the idea that someone doesn't want to share everything about themselves . . . kind of goes against the conventional wisdom."

Cola laughs nervously. "Though, you've got fans who've already dug into your life. Including, um, me. Like, even when you were functionally anonymous, your art inspired that kind of intensity. I don't think you'll ever be able to get away from it, at least not if you keep making music like that.

"But the choice you have to make isn't really between sharing your personal life or not, which you can, and should, only open the door as much as you actually want to. It's between letting anyone believe they could be you, or reaching out for the mic and saying, 'Only *I* could've made this.' Neither is inherently better or worse than the other, but different artists have different needs, you feel me?"

Cola sometimes comes off as spacey in her interviews, but when she fixes her gaze steadily on me and asks, "So what do you need, Suwa Moon?" I'm reminded that she's been examining and switching between the roles of fan and performer, consumer and creator, for almost a decade now.

I lower my eyes and tune out the ambient hum of the lights, the deep drone of the engines, the scuffling of other people's movements, my own breaths. Inward, inward, until it's just me and my heartbeat. There've been moments in my life when I wanted it to stop. Music keeps me alive. Music has always been the beginning and the end of my dream. But I kept slipping deeper under the spell of the black hole, the white noise of the past.

Now, I need to wake up.

I open my eyes, take the contract out of Cola's hands, and sign.

After that, I swear I meet yet another version of Cola, fully relaxed and disarmingly open. She runs me through the other Karma Demon acts, and I lose track of time as we compare influences and go over favorite music videos, live shows, albums.

But then Cola says, breezily but with a conspiring overtone, "The person you wrote *Moonflower* about . . . have they listened to the songs they inspired? Like, 'Give me some contact / Not a splinter through a loveline.' Wow, but also, woof."

She'd talked about a few of her exes, so it's not like the question came out of nowhere. But that doesn't stop it from rendering me speechless. After absorbing so many appraisals of *Moonflower* as a coming-out story, it's almost a shock that she cuts straight to the broken heart of it.

I look at my phone. My lock screen's been the same for years: a close-up of a painting based off of a still from *Mugen Glider*. I barely hear my own voice when I whisper, "I hope not."

Cola makes a surprised sound, then offers, "That bad?"

I clear my throat in an attempt to keep my eyes dry and my voice steady. We're still not at a "crying together" level of comfort. "I was in love, but I didn't know what to do with it. So I let it take me higher and higher. But when I looked down, gravity kicked back in, and all I could do was fall. Even though he'd given me wings." Or something like that.

Cola raises an eyebrow, but pulls out a tissue from her bag and wordlessly hands it over. I press it to my face and laugh wetly. "Did you just interview me?"

She rolls her eyes and lets me sniffle for a while. I take a shuddering breath and slap my cheeks a few times.

"How do you feel?"

I nod and answer, "Okay. Not better, but okay."

Cola pats my back and whistles. "Attaboy. All right. Almost time. Flying into LAX is one of the best parts of the job. Well, not really LAX, but the view."

"I wouldn't know."

Cola all but shouts, "What? Suwa, you've never flown into LA before?"

I shake my head, and she motions to the window. I begrudgingly bring the shade up, and gasp.

It's all ocean. Up close it'd be completely terrifying but from a distance, whitecaps breaking up the seemingly endless expanse, it's a painting. Like a child, I press my face against the glass. Underneath a creamy, undulating cloudscape, the Pacific coastline cuts a rugged border, and my stomach drops as the plane begins its descent.

Cola pulls out a compact and touches up her makeup. I keep my eyes on the window as the Pacific cedes to beaches and freeways and mountains in the distance, and suddenly, I'm home.

Track 14

After we make it past customs, Cola's whisked away by a waiting entourage that mostly ignores me. Except for a guy who, between furious puffs on a vape, talks at me so quickly as to be mostly unintelligible, then slips his business card into one of my cases. Oh, I recognize his name; that's Cola's manager, whom Cola gleefully described on the plane as "the kind of person who does all the work for the group project." On the back of the card, he's written: *RADIOCLUB.KARMA. LOGIN "SWOON."* Swoon? No, his cursive *M* looks like a *W*.

I slip the card into my pocket before checking my watch. The flight landed early, but I still expected Cap to be here by now. I wouldn't be surprised if he'd camped in the parking lot overnight.

Just then, his truck approaches. I squint at the windshield. The silhouette is too short to be Cap. Aya? When I finally make out the driver, I drop my bags onto the curb. "Who let you get behind the wheel of Maui Wowie?"

Feli points and shouts, "¡Aquí, hermano!" then smashes into me. I wheeze. Damn, I'm definitely not in fit and fighting shape.

He snaps a candid before I can protest. His phone lets out a *whoosh*, and then both of our phones buzz rapidly. I pull mine out to text Sayo and check the photo, then peel Feli off of me. "Thanks for sharing that. I look constipated."

"You were flying for, what, twelve hours? I bet you haven't taken a good sh—"

I punch his arm. He shrugs it off and slings my bags into the bed. "Cap got caught up with some stuff, so you're stuck with me. Mira texted me a list of questions and wants you to record yourself answering them."

"Pass." And then I catch my breath. The cab of the truck is an instant nostalgia hit. The mellow-yellow leather seats. Cap's beat-up tea thermos left in his cupholder. I tuck my instruments in the space behind the seats, then run my finger along the wood paneling on the door.

We've only been on the road for five minutes, mostly commenting on Cap's "bachelor of a certain age" CD choices, when Feli pulls into the In-N-Out parking lot. Maybe he needs to pee.

"I'll wait in the car."

"Nah, this ain't how it goes." He opens the door for me and motions to follow him. And once we go around the building, there, assembled around one of the outdoor tables—

—my best fucking friends in the world.

"SUWA!!!" Mira bawls as she clutches me, followed by Reva and Lucía. Once they release me, Ari holds out their fist for a bump. "What's up, rock star?"

"One order of Suwa Moon!" Lucía holds up her phone, and Octavian's slightly pixelated face breaks out into a grin. "Hey, Suwa. Sorry I couldn't make it, I've got this huge presentation tomorrow. But I'll try to be down as soon as I can."

"*Sorry?*" I fight back a laugh. Feli and Mira are in school and working. Reva's modeling schedule has her flying all over the world. Ari and Lucía both have day jobs around their gigs. Octavian's hundreds of miles away in Berkeley. And yet, they're all here to welcome me back.

But as I emerge from the daze of the surprise, I notice that everyone seems a little . . . on edge. Big smiles but eyes a little too wide, or wary. Ari in particular is starting to fray, their mouth pulling tight at the corner.

Lucía clears her throat. "We got you some fries. We weren't sure if you'd be hungry." *We.*

"Thanks. I could eat." I take a seat. The rest of them settle down around me. Lucía props her phone up with a drink.

A wave of oppressive sound washes over us as a plane passes overhead. After it's clear that no one else is going to say anything, I say, "Sorry about the short notice."

Ari sucks in a breath through their teeth. "You leave with no warning, you come back with no warning. At least you're consistent, but I don't know if it's a virtue in this case."

I'd been expecting some remark about my sudden appearance, but nothing like that. "Uh, it's good to see you, too?"

"It is. Really." Reva touches Ari's arm. "Easy."

"Of course we're happy you're back." Octavian's walking, shadows and light playing behind his head. "But you said you'd explain IRL, and here we are. Unless you need me to actually drop everything and meet you in LA."

"That's a little dramatic."

Mira plucks one of my untouched fries and jabs it at me. "Oh, and spontaneously jetting off to Tokyo wasn't? Breaking up with—I'd definitely say he was one of us, and totally ignoring all of our questions about it, wasn't?"

"I told you, I failed my audition—" As I say that, I remember it's a lie.

Lucía shakes her head. "Those dots don't connect, Suwa."

I narrow my eyes. "Is this an intervention?"

Ari scowls. "No, because that would imply that you have a problem besides just being kind of a shitty friend. Suwa, we'll always be there for you. But you don't get to slip back into our lives after, what, almost a year and a half?"

"What happened, bro?" It's the first time Feli's spoken since we got out of the truck. He doesn't look at me as he asks, "Why'd you leave us?"

Shame floods through my body. I hadn't realized how badly I'd alienated my best friends. I hadn't meant to, which makes it worse, because that means they've spent this entire time letting me act like things were normal as they walked on eggshells, wondering what went wrong.

"It's not like we moped around. We figured, after the audition, you wanted to make a big change, dig into your own music, and then, boom, *Moonflower Sessions*! So it was worth it."

Reva's attempt to lift the mood is what breaks me. "Everyone, I am so, so sorry. I—I can't even properly apologize to you because even though I basically told you nothing, what I did tell you isn't true, either. All I can say is that it felt true; I *did* break down at the audition; I *did* break up with him for a reason that I still can't explain.

"The dream, but also the dream I didn't even let myself dream, they were right in front of me. And instead of being happy about this like a normal person . . . I was terrified. Because, if I got what I wanted and it didn't work out, I'd have nothing left to dream about."

The words flutter in the air in a diaphanous drift, then crystallize and fall back into me like hail. I've unlocked something I didn't even know I'd been keeping in my chest. My body trembles as I finally let myself feel the full weight of what I'd left behind, the possible futures I abandoned when I left Los Angeles.

Including the one where I was a good friend. I shut my eyes and grit my teeth. "My leaving didn't have anything to do with . . . You all deserved better." And for a moment, I wonder if my friends even missed me as much as I missed them.

But then Mira cups my face with her hand and squeezes. My eyes fly open. "Don't ever ditch us like that again, dummy. Do you know how weird it was to pick up a call on New Year's Day and it's your band director telling you that one of your best friends was peacing out of the country? And because he was so busy, he couldn't even be the one to say goodbye?"

I shake my head; I can't answer her with my mouth pushed into fish lips. Mira lets go of my face and crosses her arms. "I straight-up screamed. Anyway. Suwa, don't be a stranger. Even if you think we won't understand, at least give us the chance to say so to your face."

"Yeah, let your senpais talk some sense into you. You're missing out on twentysomething wisdom." Octavian snickers as I scoff—like he hadn't just turned twenty—but then we both relax into smiles. This is starting to feel familiar; being teased about "my youth" because I'm the only one with a summer birthday, the jostling and ribbing that underpin the affection we have for each other.

Lucía nudges me with her shoulder. "We've all seen each other at some pretty low points, so it's actually not fair if you don't let us help you."

"Okay, bring it in, bring it in." Feli grabs Lucía's phone and motions for everyone to get closer. "No escape!"

Reva chirps, "No escape!" And surrounded by my best friends, at the center of the world, I cry so hard, I start to laugh.

"Now that that's out of the way," Lucía looks at me curiously, "what do you need me and Ari for?"

I let out a gasp. "Too much." I'm talking about Cap's bruising hug, but it also describes how I feel laying eyes on my old home.

Cap had been privately planning his retirement for a while, and the winter after Sayo and I left for Tokyo, he finally stepped down from his band director role and made good on one of his lifelong dreams. With Aya's help, he turned his house into an informal music school, recruiting soon-to-be-former students of his to tutor younger kids in exchange for rooms to practice and record. The Woodshed: his next act once he officially passes the Sunshowers torch to Aya.

Someone's transformed the facade of the house. It's painted with a collage of instruments, their bodies and frames tinted with pearlescent highlights to mimic glass. The overlapping colors become their own patchwork design. Cap notices me looking and opens his mouth, then stops himself.

My best friend used to talk about doing murals.

I murmur, "It's amazing," and mean it, even as the high of homecoming begins to fade.

Cap releases me and waves Aya over. Another set of arms wraps around me, and Aya says, "Welcome home, Suwa."

I force myself to relax. Sayo and I aren't that physically affectionate with each other, and all of these cocoons of human contact are a little overwhelming. I step into the house and clear my throat. "Thanks, Aya. Where can I put my stuff that's out of the way?"

Aya grabs my bags and takes them up the stairs. "You have your old room here. We stored some equipment in it, but that'll be out by tonight."

Cap calls back, "I'll take care of it, you get ready," then explains, "Aya's hosting a workshop at the Feminist Center for Creative Work in a few hours. I don't suppose we'll see you there?"

I shake my head. "I have to hit the ground running. We're playing a private show in a week, and recording starts on Saturday."

Behind me, Ari sputters, "Saturday? Suwa, that's *tomorrow*." They step back outside while typing furiously on their phone. Lucía pulls out her own, dials a number, and follows them, saying, "Hey, Eduardo? Listen, I can't do that session with you after all . . ."

And then it's just Cap and me alone in the foyer. There's more salt than pepper in his hair these days. The crags on his face run a little deeper. But that warm, jolly energy is eternal.

He holds his fist out. "Welcome back, kid."

I bump it. "The place looks different. Less like a boat."

Cap had the interior-design taste of a veteran pirate who appreciated the finer things in life. When I lived with him, and then every time I visited him after I moved back into my father's house, I felt like a talking skeleton might appear at any moment and offer me rum straight out of the barrel, because he had multiple barrels as furniture.

There's still a giant GONE FISHING! plaque above the door to the backyard, but now everything is bright, like the smell of a freshly cracked citrus peel translated into a vibe. Warm, but not overbearing, orange painted on the walls. Botanical-themed accents everywhere, from the vines on the curtains to the pop-art flowers on the rug.

This must be Aya's doing, because this is what her place used to look like. It probably still looks like that.

"For the first time ever, I let a woman change the way I live." Cap laughs, then points at the shoe organizer hooked onto the coat closet door. "Yours are still there."

All of the plastic pockets are filled with slippers and labeled with a strip of masking tape. I once wondered aloud why he displayed them that way, especially since it seemed most of them hadn't been used in years, and he'd said with a misty voice, "Everybody wants to come home to home." I hadn't understood what Cap meant back then, but as I read through the names on the tape—all of my friends, Sayo, Aya—now I think I do.

I make a valiant effort to not look for his, but there they are. After all, this was—is—his home, too. Against my will, I smile: lavender slides, embossed with cartoon dogs and printed with looping Disney-font text, LOVE AND HOPE / RAIN AND SHINE. He's always had a soft spot for that kind of bootleg design.

His slippers look like they've been worn recently. For a moment, I let myself wonder if he's around, but quickly banish the thought. Someone would've warned me if there was any chance we'd bump into each other. Clearly he's been to the Woodshed, but if-when I see him again, I'll be prepared.

I take my shoes off, brush away the dust on my well-worn black plastic slides, and step into them.

Cap and Aya sit me down and feed me so many pastries, I feel like sugar's coming out of my pores. Then Lucía's voice comes from the doorway. "Suwa? Can we talk for a sec?"

She and Ari both sit on the porch railing. I lean against the side of the house. I've only asked them about re-recording the album with me and playing a couple shows, not even touring. But I'm clearly already uprooting their lives. "I totally get it if you've got other plans, or you can't make it work—"

"No, I'm just, I'm freaking out!" Lucía hops off the railing, crouches down to the ground, then pops up with her fists in the air. "Playing for Cola freakin' Carter! Recording with my best friends! Cola *freakin'* Carter!"

As Lucía repeats, "Cola freakin' Carter," under her breath to herself, Ari rolls their eyes but adds, "This is honestly the second-best possible way you could've come back to LA."

"What would've been the first best?"

"If you'd immediately turned around as soon as you got to Tokyo and apologized for leaving us in your dust." Ari's shoulders slump. They cut in before I can speak. "I don't mean that. I'm happy for you, and thanks. For thinking of us, bringing us in."

"Please don't talk like that." I drop my head and follow a line of ants marching past my foot. "I can't—I went to Tokyo and barely explored this whole other country, this part of my actual heritage. I ended up spinning in circles, doing what you two were doing but not as well, so caught up in my idea of my dream that I never made any real plans to get anywhere. Then Cola showed up and gave me a plan. I don't know if I'm ready for it."

"Suwa." Lucía flicks the center of my forehead. "In the nicest way possible, what's it like being this stressed all the time? You take care of the music. We'll take care of each other. We made it through high school together; we can make it through anything. On three, the motto."

She holds her hand out and looks at us expectantly. Ari mutters, "Seriously?" but places their hand over hers. I shake my head, but place my hand on top.

We exchange glances, counting down in our heads, and together, we whisper-shout, "Sunshowers forever!" as we pull our arms up, laughing at ourselves even as the phrase echoes in my head, repeating and fading out in someone else's voice.

"Thank you, you're so kind. Hit me up later, for real." Cola blows a kiss to someone who clearly wants to talk more with her. She turns to me and smiles widely. "Well look at you!" She loops her arm into mine and steers me toward a cluster of men laughing uproariously. She whispers out of the corner of her mouth, "We gotta say hi to the money people." My anxiety level ratchets upward as, one by one, the men assembled slowly fix their eyes on me.

The venue: Chateau Marmont, which I've only ever seen in paparazzi photos. The occasion: the spring party Cola's parent label's boss, who is now my big boss, puts on every year. The goal: to prove to these white guys in linen suits that I'm the future of music or whatever.

One of them, wearing a hat embroidered with FREE THEIR NIPS and sneakers that look nondescript but that I recognize as three-grand designer kicks, asks, "He's the one?" They all look me over in a way that makes me want to curl up and roll away, but only the asker's eyes drag up my legs, linger, roam over my chest, and settle on my face without seeming to actually see me. What Mira once called the "I expect 'customer service,' wink" gaze. I fight the nausea that ripples through me. It's been a while since someone openly leered at me like that, and I hate how easily my body responds to it.

"Gentlemen, Suwa Moon. I know you all listened to *The Moonflower Sessions* when it came out. So you know how great he is." Cola transforms as she talks to them, becoming pliant and giggly. "Play nice, okay?"

I smile rigidly. Cola wraps her arm around me, and I realize that she's purposely making herself a buffer. As we walk away, she sighs, "I know. But each one of them makes more in a month than I do in royalties for a year, and they control the artist budgets with an iron fist. The head of publicity, Eddie Engels— that's Nipple Hat—especially."

She pivots on her heel and puts her hands on my shoulders. "You ready?"

Right, I don't have time to get worked up. I jut my chin out. "I have to be."

Lucía, Ari, and I have spent the past week rehearsing the new songs I'm adding to *Moonflower* for the album. All tracks I cut from the EP because I didn't have the skill to put them together, but with them, I can. We used to jam together all the time in high school so that part isn't any different, but the stakes are considerably higher than any of the times we played before.

I look over at them; Ari, testing their kick drum, catches me and exaggeratingly mouths, *Cola freakin' Carter!*

They snap their mouth shut when Cola follows my gaze and says, "Your band is good."

"They're good. I'm lucky." I watch Ari and Lucía barter with the sound techs, doing their best to make this courtyard work as an open venue. I don't even really have the language to ask for what I want in terms of sound, but here they are, speaking for me in the way I need most.

When I see the rest of my friends, they wave at me. They're all here, even Octavian, who's immediately taking the train back north tomorrow morning for a track meet. I raise my hand and wave back.

Cola spots my cheer squad. "Mm, I think you're all lucky. Well! Showtime, Suwa. You're gonna blow them away." She steps back into the crowd, which parts for her.

I let out a puff of breath to get my bangs out of my eyes and pick up my gig bag from where it'd been leaning against one of the arched entryways. I have to get through this part. Once I start playing, I'll be fine.

And yet. Doubt seeps into my head. *Do I belong here? Can I live up to whatever promise Cola's sold them on?*

I feel her eyes on me as we set up. Ari's quiet, in their zen zone. "We're good to go when you are." Lucía squeezes my shoulder reassuringly. "This is *not* how I thought I'd be spending my summer. Playing for actual superstars."

It's technically not summer yet, but I can practically hear Sayo chide, *Don't be such a stickler, Suwa.* I smile to myself as I sling my bass over my shoulder and step up to the mic. Our friends jump and cheer from the back. I nod at them, then scan the courtyard. There's Cola in her unmissable pink vinyl skirt set. There's the leering guy, Eddie whatever. He's back at it; I catch myself before I scowl at him.

But his stare is enough to knock me off my balance. Numbness spreads like a stain through my body. Breaths short, too short. And just like when I auditioned for Cola a year and a half ago, I hear the taunting voice in my head. *How are you supposed to play for the world if this tiny crowd can rattle you? Who were you kidding, talking about your dreams like you deserve anything special?*

I'm spiraling, in front of people I need to impress. Cola coughs, and when I meet her eyes, she lifts an eyebrow, and I finally register the silence that's descended throughout the party. *She's waiting. They're all waiting.*

Then, another internal voice, cutting through the storm in my head like a whistling rocket: *Suwa! Breathe!*

The spell's released. I shake my head out and turn around to address Lucía and Ari. "Shall we?" A phrase lifted from Cap. Lucía grins. Ari gives me a thumbs-up. When I nod at them, they start counting off. I fix my eyes on the low sun glimmering through the cloud line, and I open my mouth to sing.

"I think I saw Cola cry. Way to go, man," Feli laughs, clapping me on the back. "The new stuff slaps. Not that the old stuff doesn't. . . . Anyway." He laughs again, nervously this time. I sip the drink I'd pulled off of a caterer's tray. If the rest of my friends also feel weird about the implicit subject of these songs, they're doing a great job of hiding it.

As for me, now that I've fully immersed myself back into

Los Angeles, the partition between the person who wrote those songs a year ago and the person performing them wavers. I keep looking around reflexively, listening for a laugh that used to give me butterflies. Then I remember why I'm here: standing on a platform built off the scaffolding of a broken heart.

I look down at my glass and tip most of it back.

Reva drapes herself around Lucía's shoulder. "Forget Cola, *I* cried. God, you're like a real band. That was so tight."

Now that the show's over, I feel relaxed enough to accept the praise. I polish my drink off, run my finger absentmindedly around the rim after I've set it down, and murmur, "It feels a little surreal." I'm talking both about the set and the entire party's atmosphere. Even though there are definitely people here younger than us, no one's being carded. Cola had warned me earlier in the night, "Free booze is still booze. I can't babysit you, so take it easy." But shit, I want to celebrate, or at least stop thinking about what I can't control. This is the first checkpoint to getting what I want, and I think I've passed with flying colors.

"There are actual famous people here. Like—" Mira points at one woman in the crowd. "I swear I saw her at that magazine stand on Fairfax. Like, on a cover." As my friends ogle her, I slip out of our circle to get another drink. I wander around, looking for a waiter, and in the process almost slam into the creep from before.

"Whoa." He holds onto my elbow to keep me from tripping. "Celebrating, huh?"

I try to pull my arm out of his hold, but his grip tightens. "Easy now." He walks forward, and I'm pushed back until I hit the wall. "Are you even old enough to drink, Suwa? Though I get why you'd ditch your chaperone." He leans in and continues before I can speak up. "Unless she's more than that. Cola says she's only into girls, but I mean . . . you *come* close, right?"

No way. A few passersby glance at us, but walk right past. The night's success sours, and through my haze, it hits me: The only friends I have here are the ones I walked in with.

The creep cages me in with his arms and sneers, "Cat got your tongue, baby?" But before I can spit in his face, he's being pulled back, and someone growls, "Leave him alone." The newcomer steps into the light of the hallway, and my head clears.

He's wearing a catering uniform, and his hair's buzzed, but it's him. *Santi.* The boy who has, twice now, broken my heart. Once by accident, and once—I swallow hard—with a jagged incision I can still feel in my chest.

But he wasn't the one who'd placed it there. I'd done it to myself. And now my karma's come to collect.

The creep eyes Santi scornfully. "We're busy."

Santi's eyes meet mine. Even though that guy keeps talking, I can't hear him. Being near Santi again is a sensory override. His lips almost pull into a smile but stop just short of one.

At some point, realizing he's not being heard, the creep stomps off. Maybe he's going to rat out Santi, who still acts first, thinks later. But once we're alone, Santi doesn't say anything, only jerks his head toward one of the staff-only doors and walks through it. Fuck. Why didn't anyone tell me he'd be here? I look at the door, which swings mockingly.

I follow him and step outside into an alcove that smells like ash. Santi's smoking, his face obscured by a low branch, the shadows across his face flickering with every sway of the wind. I watch him for a while. He finally looks back at me, smoke trailing from between his fingers, and I wonder if he's having trouble finding the right thing to say, too.

But when Santi speaks, it hits me. He's in control. "Did you hear they're remaking *Mugen Glider*?"

What. I laugh uncomfortably, then realize he's given me an opening. "I did. Maybe they'll give it a real ending this time." I thumb my phone in my pocket and, even though neither of us can see it, click a button so my lock screen flashes.

Santi drops the cigarette on the ground and stamps it out. He laughs, but the sound is flat. I had thought that if I ever saw him again, I'd have more to say, playing a bunch of scenarios in my head like a deranged dating sim. But this one—chance encounter turns into anime banter—never came up.

I clench and unclench my hands before blurting out, "What've you been up to?"

Santi murmurs, "What's it matter to you?" He scratches his head, and I instantly imagine what it'd be like to run my hand against his scalp and shiver. "They didn't tell you anything about me?" The way he said "they" makes me wonder how much he's talked to his—our—friends since I left.

He shoves his hands into his pockets and looks at the ground. "I finished up the school year. I got a job and saved enough to buy a shitty bike. Cap tried to talk me into staying, doing band again, but we both knew that was doomed. Someone I met through work told me about some seasonal stuff, and I took off. Worked, didn't work. Got my GED on the road. I came back here a few times, but this is the first I've stayed longer than a few days. One of Aya's friends hooked me up with this job.

"I thought I was just working another Hollywood party

tonight. And when I saw you onstage, I planned on laying low, but." He sucks a breath in through his teeth. "I guess I still can't leave you alone."

I want to scream.

"You sounded good tonight." Santi tilts his face back up, and my eyes start to tear, because now he's *smiling*. A warm, lopsided thing that brings out his infuriating dimples. "A bunch of people were hyping up your album. Emo Ocean's new-and-improved *Moonflower Sessions*. Cute. Everybody loves you." There's a teasing edge to his voice.

Before I can lean too far into the feeling gushing from the center of my chest, I ask the obvious question. "Do our friends know you're here?"

Santi shifts away from me. "We kinda grew apart after you left. I think it was hard for them to try to act like they knew what was going on—what happened between us. I don't blame them." He pulls out another cigarette and lights it. The glowing tip dances through the air like a firefly. "I text with Mira, sometimes. We got food the last time I passed through two, three months ago? For Aya's birthday."

Then Santi continues, his voice soft but sure, "I'm glad you're working with Cola. You *did it*, or you're doing it. Everything you dreamed of." He whistles, then takes a deep breath. His face darkens when he asks, "Was he part of it? Did I mess that up for you?"

I almost dry heave. And I let my anger carry me, move my body forward until we're breath to breath. I pull the cigarette out of his mouth and crush it in my hand. The ember burns me, and I tell myself that's why my body feels like it's on fire. "You think this is my game plan? Sucking up to someone like him?" My voice husky from dehydration and distress.

Santi breathes out. I feel the air lift and ruffle my bangs, and I steel myself for whatever he might say in response. But I couldn't have prepared for it: "I try not to think of you at all," said matter-of-factly.

I take a step backward. I know I heard him correctly, but I can't believe the Santi I knew would say that to me.

He shakes his head. "I should go. I . . . I have to go."

Just like that, he vanishes. His body disappears into the foliage around us, and I shudder at the sudden chill.

Track 15

Heavy. Every bone in my body has been replaced with lead. My friends ask me what's wrong, but only Octavian, our sweet, sober guardian angel, knows what I want without having to say it. He pulls me up with an arm around my shoulders, basically carrying me, and walks me to his rental car.

"My equipment—"

"Someone else can drop it off. You're going home. You feel sick?"

My palm's out in front of me, raw and gray with ash. At some point, I'd lost Santi's cigarette. "No. Yes. I don't know. I'm not going to throw up, if that's what you mean."

Octavian snorts and starts the engine. "I didn't want to be rude, but the cleaning deposit is no joke."

I groan.

He side-eyes me. "Suwa, what's going on?"

There's no way I can talk around it. "I saw him here."

Octavian makes a surprised sound before asking cautiously, "To clarify, when you say 'him'—"

"Santi. I saw Santi." His name tastes metallic in my mouth. "He was one of the caterers. We ran into each other, and we

talked, and everything is . . ." Weird. Wrong. I knew I'd probably see him again, but not so soon, and not like this. He seemed
like a fun-house mirror reflection of the person I'd once known.
Once loved.

"Oh." Octavian clearly stops himself from saying what he
was originally going to. When he speaks, it's with the deeply
serious tone of voice that'd originally earned him the "Professor"
part of his band name. "I didn't know he was back in town. I
don't think any of us did."

"What happened to him?" The words float out of my mouth
like bubbles, then pop limply.

Octavian snaps his fingers in front of my face. "Hey. Don't
chase the rabbit. For what it's worth, we did everything we could
to keep him in the group. Mira and Supe, especially. But . . . once
he started to drift, there was nothing we could do to bring him
back in. Though from what I hear, he's been doing fine, rolling
with some new people."

Is that supposed to make me feel better? And I shouldn't say
this, but I have to know. "Did he ask about me?"

"He did. At first. Then he stopped, and then he stopped
talking, period. You're annoyingly alike in that way." Octavian
pulls onto the freeway and, after some hesitation, says, "I don't
expect you to get into something that's clearly still a sore subject.
But this is what happens when you don't air a wound out."

"Thanks, Doc."

Octavian rolls his eyes. "Don't take it out on me. You're the
one who broke up with him. It shouldn't surprise you that he's
moved on, unless . . ."

He doesn't say it, but we both think it. *Unless you haven't.*

We spend the rest of the ride in an uneasy silence. But when he parks in front of Cap's house, Octavian takes off his glasses and rubs his eyes. "Clean the burn and wrap it until it scabs."

"I will." I clear my throat. "I'm sorry for being such a, you know."

Octavian scoffs, "No offense, but if I took the shit you sometimes say personally, we wouldn't be friends. Just, let them out sometimes, your feelings. I know, I know, it's weird. But nothing should faze you anymore." He turns to face me and gives me a quick hug. "Enjoy the wins, Suwa. You were amazing tonight."

I swallow hard and get out of the car. "I'll try. Thank you, again." Only when his taillights disappear around the corner do I sigh, fish my keys out of my pocket, and make my way into the house.

Cap waves from the kitchen. "Suwa! How was— What happened to your hand?" His face collapses into concern.

My hearing goes in and out as Cap worries. What Octavian said bothers me. He's right, I'm the one who broke up with Santi. What's done is done; I have to own it.

And yet. I've always been bad about picking scabs. And the one on my heart is beginning to itch.

"He called me." Aya comes down the stairs. Of course she's here. Cap's told me that they usually make dinner together. We both look up at her, but she was speaking only to him. "That job I got him through Ricky . . . They crossed paths at the party."

"Him . . . ? Oh. *Oh.*" Cap reaches for me, and I step into his embrace until my forehead hits his chest. He rubs my back with one hand and my head with the other. "Lemme make you some tea."

I nod numbly and slide my body into a chair around the living room table. A few minutes pass before Aya walks back into the room with a first aid kit. She takes the seat next to me. "Hand." I hold it out. As she wipes it down with an antiseptic, a welcome sting, she sighs. "Cigarette burn?"

"I did it to myself."

Aya looks tired. Her fingers tremble as she presses ointment cream onto the burn. "He told me what happened. With Memo and 'Exit Music' and everything that came after." She rips off a piece of gauze with more force than she needs before wrapping the cloth around my hand. "I know it might not mean anything now, but he wasn't the one who leaked your song. I was."

I slowly raise my head. Our eyes meet, but Aya looks away. One of the reasons I refused to believe Santi could be Canti was that Canti always talked about his mom. I of all people should've realized that you don't have to be blood-related to someone you consider a parent. So when Santi revealed himself to me, it didn't take me long to put two and two together.

Aya continues, "He left his phone in my room. I played his last listened-to song out of curiosity and the people I was working with . . ." She winces. "I should've told you all this before. But I didn't know how to bring it up, or if it would matter, once you stopped talking to each other."

I feel like I should be upset at her. And I am, but not about something that happened ages ago. It's the way Aya defends Santi, putting herself between him and me. The instinct to protect.

Growing up, I never got that from my father. Whenever someone came after me, he'd step aside.

"I already knew how the song got leaked." I clench and unclench my hand to stretch the gauze. "That's not why I broke up with him. And I don't hold anything against you. Really."

Aya tapes the gauze down. "I know it's selfish to want to set the record straight at this point, but I can't help it. You live long enough, you start to realize how rare it is for anyone to stay in your life, really. And a friendship like that . . ." Her voice catches.

I don't exactly know why, but I place my other hand over hers. She sniffles and gets up. "There are leftovers in the fridge, if you want any. By the time I'm done with him, Cap's gonna be a real chef."

"But I'll never be as good as my teacher! Drive safe, Aya." He waves as she leaves. And then Cap takes Aya's seat, mugs in hand. He places one on the table in front of me. I watch the steam rise out of his mug, my thoughts a swirling mess.

He speaks first. "Aya told me a while ago about how deep your and Santi's relationship goes. Sayo filled in some gaps, too." I smile wryly. He figured he couldn't ask me about it directly; always so considerate. Cap places his mug down and takes my hands in his. They're comfortably warm, and so is his voice when he says, "I will always have time and space for *you*. What's going through that busy head?"

"Even before I saw him, the night was . . . strange. We played well, though." I debate sharing more about the creep, but I don't want to make Cap worry. I slip my hands out of his to take a long drink of tea.

Honey ginger, with chrysanthemum blossoms half bloomed in the goldenrod murk. The first time I lived with him, he'd make me this every morning, hammily serving it up as a "cup of sunshine." Even though I rolled my eyes at it, it was one of the only things that'd reliably make me feel better. I've since made it just for myself, but it doesn't taste the same.

I stare into the mug. "Every single song on *Moonflower* is about him. The new songs will be, too. I memorialized all this pain without . . . but we were more than that. He was more than that. And I know it's too late to do anything about it, the record, I mean. But also what happened to 'us.' Maybe I'm making excuses now because, because I regret what I said to him. I regret . . ." I don't dare let myself finish the thought.

I've somehow stayed dry-eyed this entire evening, but Cap pulls a kerchief out of his back pocket and wipes his eyes, then honks into it. Once he's cleaned himself up a bit, he says, shakily but deliberately, placing his hand on my shoulder, "You made a decision, and it brought you to another path. I know me saying this won't cancel out everything you're thinking and feeling, but those songs are *yours*, and they're so special. It's hard to understand the impact when you're standing at the center."

Cap abruptly stands up. He leaves the kitchen and returns shortly with a plastic bin that rattles as it's placed down in front of me. "Open it."

I click open the lid. Oh. *Oh.*

There are letters, folded and crumpled from being pressed inside, revealing peeks of different handwriting. Some pieces of art, collages and portraits and comics. Everything in the box is addressed to, about, *me*. "To Suwa." "Dear Mr. Moon." "For Suwa Moon." "Mr. Emo Ocean."

I take out one of the letters:

Dear Suwa,

My name is Daly. It wasn't the name I was born with. I think you might know what that's about.

I'm fifteen, and exactly a year ago, Emo Ocean saved me.

Another one:

To Mr. Moon:
When my child was twelve, he told me that he was a boy,
which didn't really surprise me, and that the kids at school
were making life hell for him, which broke my heart. While
I was researching transition on the internet, I came across
a review of your EP, and it sounded like you might have
some experiences in common. I sent it to him, and I'm not
exaggerating when I say that your music changed his life.

I shuffle through more of the box's contents. There's a pencil sketch based off of the cover of the EP: a close-up of a tangle of blue-blond hair, into which a few half-furled white-petaled blossoms have been folded. There are photographs, Polaroids and glossy prints and ones clearly cut out of printer paper, of people dressed as the cover.

I'd made *Moonflower* for myself, to get over my high school heartbreak. But the songs have taken on a life of their own I hadn't realized before. I trace a finger over the folds of an origami flower. I'd felt so lonely in the world until I learned about *Mugen Glider*. Marigold had been a beacon of light for this kid who had to fight to grow up as a boy. My chest tightens as I try to process this feeling of responsibility. Cola knew from the start that what I represent goes beyond the music. Now, I have the chance to become that beacon.

Cap clears his throat. "I . . . may have talked about your music during last summer's band camp, and then when I did an orientation for the Woodshed. These are all from local kids and their parents. A few of the Woodshedders meet once a week for, well, they call it 'Gender Club,' I believe as a joke, but the name's stuck. They're the ones who dressed up as the cover last Halloween. Perhaps you could talk to them? Offer them some perspective about life after high school?"

I'm still too overwhelmed to answer, and also, what do I really know about life after high school? But when Cap continues, "Only if you have time. I know you're busy, and that a lot of this is painful to bring up," I put my own insecurity aside.

"I'll do it." I tuck what's in my hands back into the bin. "Tell me when, and I'll be here."

We both get up, and Cap pulls me into another tight hug. "I love you, Suwa."

"I love you, too." We finish drinking our tea, falling into familiar—familial—banter. When my head hits the pillow, the bitterness of the evening gives way to a restful, dreamless sleep.

It's easier to make a promise than to keep one.

Once recording and rehearsals start in earnest, I'm stuck in a tight social circle: Ari, Lucía, Cola, and a handful of label execs. Including the creep, who at least doesn't say anything during our meetings. But I learn about the Gender Club kids in passing. Not all of them are trans, but they do all ID outside of the gender they were assigned at birth. Shanice, Devin, and Nat attend De Longpre and are members of the Sunshowers. Roberto's in eighth grade, and Isobel's in sixth, Sunshowers-in-waiting referred to the Woodshed by their older siblings.

About a month after I landed in Los Angeles, I finally have a free afternoon on one of the days they meet. After an awkward introduction from Cap, their starry eyes wear off. The first thing Shanice asks me is, quite bluntly, "So are you trans or not?" Followed by, "I swear I won't post about it or anything. It just feels kinda obvious if you like, actually pay attention to the lyrics."

I'm preparing myself for some kind of tortured explanation about my music's origins when she places her palm on her heart, closes her eyes, and recites from memory: "All my faith has left my body / All my flowers bloom on graves / So maybe I can pass this body / On to someone who can still / Remember roses in the wild."

Damn. I blink quickly a few times to keep an upwelling of emotion from overflowing onto my face. I know what I thought I was writing about, but I really can't blame people for gleaning other meanings. And if even this subtext means that much, what would a confirmation feel like? So I simply answer, "Yes."

From there, the floodgates open. I find myself in the crossfire of questions I'm not in the least qualified to answer.

"How did you come out to your family?"

"Um, I haven't, at least not formally."

"What do you do about chasers?"

I wish I could tell them, *Don't worry about it.* "Don't let other people try to limit your identity, especially in that way. Definitely talk to older members of the community"—*besides me*—"to, uh, get a vibe check on someone if you're unsure."

Isobel, whose parents have drawn a line at letting her take blockers, starfishes on one of the blankets scattered across the yard. "Are you sure you can't act as, like, my guardian? I don't want to go through puberty twice."

I have to laugh; I remember my own days of desperately researching this exact train of thought. "There's more to changing guardianship than pointing at someone and saying, 'Guardian now.'"

"Okay, but couldn't I also"—she checks something on her phone—"get married, or join the army? I don't wanna shoot guns. Suwa, will you marry me?"

"No." I rest my forehead against my sweating iced coffee as they argue. It's so hot. Weirdly humid, too.

Shanice flicks her braids over her shoulder. "If he's marrying anyone, it's gonna be me."

Roberto snorts. "Uh, Suwa's only into guys."

I snap back to attention. "Huh?" None of my songs specify the pronouns of who I was writing about, which is why so many people thought I was writing to, and about, myself.

Five pairs of skeptical eyes focus on me. "I mean . . . I am. But what makes you say so?"

"Every single reference you make is about, like, dudes. I did learn a lot about Greek mythology, so thanks for that." I scoff, but he continues, "Also, you and Santi look pretty close in that photo."

My eye twitches. "What?"

Isobel chirps, "The one he has as his phone background," and I choke on my iced coffee.

"Santi hung out with us over the holidays, when he painted the house. And . . ." Devin shrugs. "I don't usually pay men any mind, but that man is *fiiiine*. You could do a lot worse. Wait, are you dating?"

There's no way I can get into my relationship with Santi right now. "Santi and I . . . hung out a lot when he moved to Los Angeles. Aya and Cap are basically family, so we're like . . . cousins."

"Uh," Shanice laughs, "y'all not posing like cousins. Wait. We had to reschedule prom for June because the gym was under construction. You should ask him out. *Wait.* Can Emo Ocean *play* prom?"

"I'll think about it." I check the time on my phone. "Don't you have lessons now?" I stand up and brush errant pollen dust and leaf litter off of my shoulders. The wind's picking up, and when I sniff the air, I get a heady whiff of ozone. Good timing.

"Just putting it out there, Suwa, if you need a personal stylist for some special occasion, like *prom*, call me." Shanice wrinkles her nose as raindrops visibly land on her face. It's really starting to come down now, so we scoop up the blankets before making a mad dash for the house.

One by one, Gender Club disperses. Except Nat, who obviously lingers, folding and unfolding a blanket until everyone else is out of earshot.

"... What do you wear?" Nat hasn't spoken outside of introducing himself, so it shocks me to hear the lilt of his voice. He clears his throat before pulling at his shirt and clarifying, "Your ... binder. I've been looking at different kinds, but I don't know anyone who wears one, except you."

His face is turning red, and he wrings his hands before blurting out, "If that's inappropriate, I'm sorry, I just—"

"It's not!" We both wince at the volume of my voice. I feel self-conscious in a way that I haven't in a while. "Mine are a no-name brand I got from, uh, a cosplay shop, but if you ever want to sit down and research some options, let me know, okay? I'll make time for you." I shouldn't make yet another promise I don't know if I can keep, but I recognize the half-hopeful, half-scared look he's giving me. The specific kind of longing that comes from seeing someone whose gender presentation validates your own desire to change.

He nods furiously before changing out his shoes and stuttering, "Th-Thanks, Suwa." His slippers tap quietly against the wood floors as he leaves. I let out a sigh, then a quiet laugh. I think I understand Cap a little better now.

The reminder on my phone going off snaps me back to attention: *post on socials / water plants if time (see fridge ref sheet) / rethink track 11 bridge / !!! COOK.*

The last point's the most important. It's my turn to bring dinner for Ari and Lucía, and I'd been roped into promising them something homemade, despite my warning that I've never even cooked for myself. I change my shoes and pad into the kitchen.

Wow. In sharp contrast to when it was just Cap and me in the house, Aya's stocked the kitchen up with *everything*. Farmers market produce in the crisper. Gochujang, black bean sauce, rice vinegar, black vinegar, palm vinegar, three different brands of fish sauce, a small army of seasoning packets in a smattering of different languages. I take a minute to think about something even I can make. How hard could fried rice be?

I run upstairs to change into a shirt I don't care about staining, then grab a pan from the hanging rack above the stove. This can be my mandated social media post for the day, a task that I've actually started to enjoy. Cola keeps asking me to post selfies, but I have more . . . I wouldn't call it fun, but it's more interesting for me to post random anime screencaps and slice-of-life snapshots. I do throw a few face photos in the mix, but only after I've scrutinized them from every angle.

I pour a selection of sauces into dipping dishes and lay out the garlic, ginger, eggs, and produce on a cutting board, then take a photo. My caption: *Shokugeki no Suwa*. I crack open a can of coffee. Showtime.

It's only after I've chopped up all the vegetables and the garlic's in the pan that it hits me. *Where's the rice.* The voice in my head takes on a gentler tone: *How can you forget the rice, Suwa. It's only the number-one ingredient.* I grab Aya's rice cooker and start a batch, but it's not going to be done before I have to leave for practice, so I start boiling some water and rice together in a pot.

I consider myself an organized person, but there's a difference between keeping a strict schedule and—*Why is the pan smoking?* The rice keeps sticking to the bottom of the pot. I add more water; no, that was a bad idea. I take a swig of coffee, but as I'm putting the can back on the counter, I brush the side of the metal pot and yelp. The can slips out of my hand and spills into the pan with the burned bits, and a plume of savory-sweet, distinctly coffee-ish steam hits my face.

What a disaster. I step away from the stove, hacking and half suffocating, and bump directly into someone. I turn on my heel and gasp, "Help me."

"Whoa."

Help me. I look up to find a bemused Santi, because, of course. He moves quickly and gracefully, turning off the burners, scraping out the coal in the pan, and poking at the tepid semi-porridge in the pot. He coughs. "What was this supposed to be?"

"Um." My cheeks flood with heat. "Fried rice? I'm supposed to make dinner for Ari and Lucía."

"Grab a pack of noodles, anything but the vermicelli. Should be in the right cabinet." Santi pours out everything in the pot and starts washing it. "Fill this with water, not all the way, and follow the package instructions. Please. I'll do the rest."

He opens up another cabinet and slides a wok out, before pausing to look at me, his head tilted. "Uh, nice shirt."

I look down. It's my sleep shirt, which Sayo had "won" from some street raffle in Akihabara. Looping cursive text printed above a chiseled airbrushed chest spells out, *Ask me about my waifu*, with "waifu" lettered into a bridal veil. I might as well embrace this. I say as dryly as I can, "Why don't you ask me."

Santi smirks as he swirls oil around in the wok. "Congrats. She's a lucky woman." He grabs an apron off of a hook on the fridge and puts it on. "Watch your water."

I'm hyperaware of how close we are, almost shoulder to shoulder. Santi cooks in silence. The quick work he makes of chopping up more produce and the practiced way he flips the ingredients in the pan suggest that one of his jobs this past year was working in a kitchen. But he's always been a good cook.

Once the noodles are done, I watch him stir-fry everything together while I thumb the burn scab on my palm. I've been so busy with work that I haven't had time to dwell on our last meeting, but I've also been repressing the memory. Details of that night—leaves rustling, smoke trailing—intrude into my line of sight.

When Santi rolls his sleeves up, I spot either dried paint or what could be tattoos on his forearms. He catches me looking and rolls his sleeves back down. I pretend to suddenly be interested in the mangoes piled up in a bowl on the kitchen island.

"Here." Santi steps away from the stove and puts the apron back on the fridge hook.

I clear my throat and try to sound casual. "Thanks for stepping in."

He shrugs. "I'm used to being the one who cooks, but . . . everyone tries." His lips twitch upward.

What does that *mean?* I grind my teeth and grab a container. It feels too awkward to try to keep talking, now that he's saved my dinner or whatever. *Just walk away. Again.*

Santi runs his hand over his head and sighs. "You can't feed other people something you haven't tasted." Someone, almost definitely Aya, put a bunch of cooking utensils in a vase. He pulls a pair of chopsticks out and grasps a bite of noodles and vegetables between them. Like a reflex, when he holds it up to my face, I open my mouth.

Goddammit. His cooking has only gotten better. Santi picks up his own bite and hesitates briefly before sliding the chopsticks that'd been in my mouth into his. I swallow and mutter, "It's, um, really good." He doesn't respond, and instead grabs one of the mangoes and pulls out his pocket knife.

I finish packing up the rest of the food and start washing dishes. I try to be savvy about it, but Santi can definitely tell that I'm watching him out of the corner of my eye. His knife flashes as he skives ribbons of skin off before slicing plump pieces around the core. He hums to himself as he snacks, fingers gleaming from the juice, which he unselfconsciously licks off. I'm soaking the first pan I'd used when he places his palms on the counter and starts talking.

"I'm sorry. About how I acted at your show. I'd been working double shifts and was running on fumes, but I was a jerk for leaving you there." Santi wipes his knife off on a kitchen towel and pauses before asking, "How is everybody?"

"They're okay. Everyone's pretty busy, so we mostly text, but Ari and Lucía are stuck with me because of work." I pick at a cuticle before mumbling, "And you weren't being a jerk. Except the jab about that guy. You really think I would do that? Sleep with someone to get ahead?"

"No!" A wave of relief washes over me when Santi responds immediately and emphatically, head snapping up. A faint flush climbs up his neck. "I know a creep when I see one but I . . ." He bites his lip. "I guess I wanted to see if you'd changed."

Santi's interrupted by the buzzing of his phone, which he picks up and unlocks. His eyes narrow, and he types for what feels like an eternity. I kick myself internally; I came back to Los Angeles to work. It's sheer coincidence that he's here, too. And once the initial hit of our reunion wears off, we'll go back to living separate lives. Right?

Except: I remember the first time Santi touched my face; the first time he touched my hand; the rush of blood out of my head when I saw him on Halloween, a split-lip devil with a wounded look, and the taste of his blood in my mouth; the taste of him in my mouth; the look on his face when I played our song, for him; a thousand chimes of laughter between us and our friends; and then the flash-fade of the fireworks that'd bloomed mockingly that fateful New Year's Eve.

Who am I trying to fool? There was no way I was ever going to see Santi again and avoid peeling back these layers of memories and history like mandarin skins. My friends and family have been protecting me from the consequences of my actions, but regardless of bad timing, our relationship would have always had to reach a turning point. He'd faced it bravely and completely, and me?

I'd turned away. I'm trying to turn away, again. I can say it's because there's too much else to do, which is true. If only that truth were enough to keep me from desperately wishing that he'd look at me the way he used to, the way I got used to. If only the foundation of my work wasn't built on, as I'd phrased it on a new *Moonflower* song, "A harmony that fell to pieces / From a fanfare to a whisper / Broken of and with devotion."

He's still typing. Now's my chance to go. But it couldn't hurt to know what Santi's up to now, if only so I can avoid him. Stifling my internal protests, I ask, "Do you come by the Woodshed often?"

Santi stops typing and puts his phone away. He seems startled by my question. "Huh? Oh. Not usually, but this Sunday, I'm doing a mural workshop. We're painting the side of a new brewery in Hollywood not too far from here. The, uh, the owners saw what I did with the outside of the house and reached out. I've been talking with Cap about doing something like this for a while. I came by to drop off some stencils."

He reaches up to touch his earlobe. He wears a hoop now, a small gold loop that might as well be taut around my neck, the way the sight of it makes me stop breathing.

Now I'm the one caught off guard when Santi keeps talking. "I started posting some of my art online. This creative agency in LA hit me up, offered to connect me to commissions for street installations, so I came back for that, too. I think I'll be able to drop the catering job soon, since mural work's been picking up. But the brewery commission is going to the kids. That's the goal, to make enough that I can pay it forward."

Santi scratches the back of his head and grins sheepishly. His cropped sweatshirt rides up.

He's not only making a living as an artist, but also nurturing a new generation of artists. This isn't a battle, but I'm losing.

Then he asks, "Have you met any of the Woodshedders? I've recruited Shanice and Nat to help organize the day, if you know them."

I answer unthinkingly, "Yeah, we met for Gender Club."

Santi laughs loudly. "They stuck with the name, huh?" He leans against the counter, and then, in an act of unbelievable cruelty, aims the full sun of his smile at me. "How about you join us? All skill levels welcome."

He's not playing fair. No, he's not playing at all. I'm the one instantly, hopelessly charmed by him, despite the distance and time we've been apart.

Santi reaches for the last slice of fruit and holds it up to his mouth. Some spirit takes possession of my body, and I step forward and intercept him, digging my teeth into the creamy flesh. I watch his pupils dilate in real time as I slurp it down, my lips just missing his fingertips. Heartbeat pounding in my ears.

"Suwa . . ." Santi blinks slowly. His fucking eyelashes. When I was a kid, I used to listen to girls complain about boys' eyelashes, *why are they so long, they don't need them*, a thousand facetious arguments about arbitrary gendered beauty standards. I get it now, though. How *dare* he.

He steps away from me. One foot becomes a canyon. Santi shakes his head. "Don't do this. Please don't do this."

"It looked good." What am I *doing*?

"No." My skin prickles. There's an edge of anger in Santi's voice. "I'm not playing this game. You—you don't get to pretend what happened didn't happen."

"No one's pretending anything. You're the one who came

in and stuck around. This time." I know I'm being petty. But I know he's aware of it, too, the charge in the air when we're near each other. The spark that'd started out as animosity before becoming—

Santi cuts into my fervent monologue. "'This time'? *This* time? When I moved to LA, for the first time in forever, I wanted to stay exactly where I was. Because of a lot of reasons, but at the top of the list was you. I would've stayed wherever you stayed and gone wherever you went. Because I loved you.

"I know I messed up before your audition. I own that. It was shitty, straight up. But there was room for us to have a conversation, to try to build our—our future, around the past. It would've had to happen eventually. And instead."

Santi slams his fist onto the kitchen counter. I recoil, the *THUD* both relaying his frustration and reminding me of a childhood spent dodging the sound. Then he takes a ragged breath and drags us back to New Year's Eve at the Shrine, the moment everything shattered: "Instead you dumped me and left the country. What the fuck, Suwa! 'I can't do this.' One text. No explanations to anyone else, and even though I could've told our friends the truth, I didn't. And I still won't, because even when I don't like you, I respect you and the relationship we had. But you left me with no one to talk to, again. And I thought, or I used to think, it's okay if you're done with me." Santi lowers his voice. "I realize now, for my own sanity, I gotta be done with you."

He washes his hands in the sink, head down. Barely audibly over the rustling of the towel as he dries them, he whispers, "This was a mistake. Aya told me you were coming back, and I should've treated that like a warning."

Santi pauses and meets my eyes. "I'm not gonna tell you you can't come to the workshop. But don't pull any stunts like that again. Good luck with everything, Suwa. I hope the next album is about something happier."

I can't cry. I won't cry. But something inside my body is gasping for air with a throat shredded and salted by unshed tears. What did he do to deserve the hollow look on his face besides love someone whose first instinct was to pin his pain down like a butterfly in a shadow box? He'd cared for me, and this is how I repay him.

I feel the words on the tip of my tongue: *I'm sorry. I was wrong. You shouldn't forgive me. Please forget me.*

But when I open my mouth, Santi shakes his head, and I watch a tear stroke the side of his face before he wipes it away.

His gaze flits down to my hand. When he speaks, Santi sounds like he's delivering a bad line reading. "I'm sorry about the burn. But everyone knows that's why you don't touch fire."

I don't move again until he's out the door. Then I follow the path he'd taken, stepping onto the porch in my house slippers. It's really pouring now, rain lashing the flowers loose from the full-bloom jacarandas that shade the sidewalks. I watch the street slowly change colors, pools of lavender spreading until it seems like I'm standing on an island in the middle of an ocean of sticky, sweet flowers.

I want to tell Santi everything. That even after I told him off in the bathroom that first day of band camp, I couldn't stop myself from noticing everything about him: his deep brown eyes and big dimples and sunlit laugh; the cross he touched as if to remind himself it was still there. I noticed when he got to practices and how quickly he left them. The way he'd walk away from a group if he saw me approaching. And then, how carefully he treated me when he caught me crying on the courtyard floor.

After one of the football games, I spotted a sketchbook that'd spilled out of his gig bag. I flipped through it, recognized the style of the drawings, and thought to myself, *What if*.

From there, it was easy. Of course Santi knew about *Mugen Glider*. Of course Santi used to live in the exact same places Canti used to live. Of course Santi loved the music I played him. He had to be a reincarnation of my first friend, my best friend. Even their names were so similar; a letter apart, destiny's typo. Not the real thing, but as close as I was ever going to get to it.

I used to dream about Canti all the time. We'd be floating, caught in a bubble. Because I didn't know what he looked like, all I saw was a form with a flickering face. Because I didn't know what he sounded like, we never spoke. I'd put my hand up to his hand, and our fingertips would never touch.

After I ghosted him the first time, I stopped having the dream.

Then I met Santi, and the dream came back.

Except now Canti's form had a face and a voice. When I put my hand up to his, I felt Santi's touch. And even though the only thing Canti ever said was, "Memo," my not-name, he said it in Santi's voice, and it'd be the last thing I heard before waking up in a cold sweat.

So on New Year's Eve, when Santi told me that he'd been Canti all along, the first thing I'd thought was, *Of course*.

And then, *Oh no*. All the things I'd noticed: How could I have been so willfully ignorant? Those flashes of the past weren't flashes. They were echoes, finally returning to their source. All the things I thought I'd escaped—the terror I'd felt when "Exit

Music" leaked, my guilt for abandoning Canti—had come back for me.

I knew if I ran from them, I'd be repeating the cycle, trapping both of us in a doomed feedback loop.

But I couldn't get over how impossible it was for us to meet again. To become friends. To become lovers. It felt like the universe was taunting me. I was getting what I wanted, but in the most bittersweet way possible. Because I knew that from now on, every time I looked at Santi, I'd be pulled back to that summer, that song. The nails in my window frame and my grandparents solemnly telling my father that if what they'd heard was true, I really should never have been born.

Maybe, I'd imagine, in another life, "Exit Music" stays between us, and Canti and I meet up. Maybe he helps me deal with my father, my family, and we stay in touch. Maybe he eventually moves to Los Angeles. Maybe we're in love for years, dancing around each other until some pivotal moment when everything comes together. Like the bridge into the final chorus of a song, like the moment in a performance where all you have to do is keep breathing, and you stop thinking, trusting completely in your body's divine machinery, and the crowd cheers as you take your final bow.

But in this life, we fall apart.

A thin streak of lightning stripes through the dull gray sky. And when the thunder arrives a heartbeat later, I open my mouth and scream.

Track 16

"This isn't working. The bass doesn't sound right in the play-back." I kick my water bottle to the other side of the studio and imagine how I look from the control room. An entitled brat, trashing the live room like it's his own tantrum chamber.

"Hey. HEY." Ari lobs a drum brush at me, and I snap my head in their direction. "You're working yourself up. Cool it." A pause. "Can . . . you give that back to me?"

"Yeah. Sorry. I'm sorry, I'm just." Thinking about love, and loss, and infinity. I unloop my bass from my body. When I reach down to pick up Ari's brush, I let the momentum bring me down until my face hits the floor. Maybe I should stay here forever. Surrender and let my body sink down to become one with the earth.

Lucía peers down at me. "Suwa. Are you okay?" Her tone suggests she already knows the answer.

I shrug as I peel myself off the ground. She and Ari exchange a look, and Ari clicks their tongue. "Fine, let's do this now."

They get up from the set as Lucía steps out of the nest of pedals around her and then they're both sitting on the floor with me. Lucía cocks her head to the side. "You wanna talk about it?

Well, I know you don't *want* to, but if we're really going to do this together, Ari and I should know what we're dealing with." She sighs. "That was a little harsh."

"Allow me." Ari picks their brush off the floor and spins it. "You've been showing up late to rehearsals all week. Reva used to joke that you never went anywhere in public without dressing like you might get papped, and you've been wearing the same stained sweatshirt three, four days in a row now? Spill."

I look up at the studio lights. As far as I can tell, Octavian's the only person who knows I ran into Santi at the Chateau Marmont show a month back. Or at least nobody's asked me about it. Unfortunately, I'm the kind of person who's apparently so fragile, people tiptoe around him so his feelings don't get hurt.

I could lie to them now and say that I'm frustrated with the songs. Which I am. But I'm also frustrated with the subject of the songs, whose face flashes behind my eyelids every time I blink. The one we're rehearsing now is a rework of an original *Moonflower* track, but the lines "It's never over with you / Just like a movie, but truer than true" hit differently now.

Change has to start with me, or something like that. So I tell them the truth. "I ran into Santi after the label show. Then I ran into him again at the Woodshed last week. I think he hates me. But he technically invited me to a mural workshop he's running this Sunday. Do I go and try to save our relationship, like, our friendship? Or am I the most masochistic person in the world?"

"I . . . think everyone should take a break." Ari turns around and faces the control room. Right, all of that was live. I laugh bitterly to myself. People work "for" me now. My bad behavior has an audience, and real consequences.

After a beat: "Do you want to be friends with Santi, or do you want his attention?" Ari's always been this blunt. I don't know how many situations they've deescalated on my behalf, simply by refusing to give in to the heat of the moment.

"Have you considered . . . talking to someone about this? I mean, like, professionally, since it seems so, um, present." Lucía tries to keep the worry out of her voice. She used to hide in the band office with me between classes when we thought we were going to get jumped in the halls.

"I don't know." I mean it as an answer to both of their questions.

"You should go."

I blink slowly. "What?"

Ari shrugs. "Back to therapy. And on Sunday. It's Santi's workshop but you're like, Cap's kid. You have every reason to go. And if you figure your shit out then, and it makes rehearsals actually productive, win-win."

I laugh dryly. "You don't think this is pathetic?"

"Honestly? I like Santi, but I love you and your music. Lucía and I aren't here just because we've played together before." Ari points the brush at me. "You have 'it,' Suwa. We've won trophies together, because of 'it.' I want to go where you're going. But that means you have to *go*."

Lucía shakes her head. "You're not pathetic. It's normal to miss people. But I don't want you to miss out on, like . . ." She throws her arms open. "Look at this space! Look at this equipment! This is for *you*. Own it."

Their words shake me out of my daze. Right. There's too much else on the line for me to get lost in my personal melodrama. "Thanks for the pep talk. Really. I love you both."

Ari smirks. "Leaving LA make you soft or something? I don't think I've ever heard you say you love . . . anyone."

Lucía smacks them on the shoulder, and they murmur, "Sorry."

"It's okay." I think I mean that. "Same track, from the top. Let's run through it once, then bring everybody back."

Ari takes a seat behind the set again. Lucía springs up and offers a hand to help me up. When she slings her guitar over her shoulder, she murmurs, "I wish we had a chance to play this live before the Karma Demon show. It's already almost June."

A light sputters on in my head. Yeah, maybe I should go back to therapy and unpack everything that's been going on. But I know that taking on more work will give me less time to mope. I point at Lucía. She raises an eyebrow and mouths, *What?* I summon the spirits of countless teen movie protagonists of yore, get down on one knee in front of her, and take one of her hands in mine. "Go to prom with me?"

"You want to play a high school dance." Cola does not sound enthused. "A month before you play what would've been your formal debut at Hollywood Forever, you'd like to instead blow your load on—" She raises her voice an octave. "—the De Longpre Sunshowers senior prom!"

Cola's house looks like it was entirely furnished by West Elm, which is disorienting. St. Vincent onstage, a wellness influencer at home. I shift my seat in a tasteful and extremely uncomfortable brass-and-wood kitchen stool. "Some marching-band people sent me fan mail. And I ended up liking my time in high school."

I do a double-take at my own words. I thought I was feeding Cola a line, but I . . . kind of do mean it. My years at De Longpre, especially the later ones, were largely defined by joy. I add, my voice softening with sincerity, "It'll be like a homecoming, but in the spring."

Cola looks pained, like she's caught between a laugh and a consolation. "You really don't have that much free time."

"It's only one day. It'd be a dry run for the summer showcase, and good publicity. 'Emo Ocean returns to his roots.'"

"That's very noble of you, Suwa." She smiles that ambiguous smile of hers. "Actually . . . you might be onto something. Would you come out there? As trans."

"*What?*"

I shouldn't be shocked by the question, but the way she'd asked, like my coming-out was another event to schedule on my calendar, shakes me.

"It's gotta—forgive the pun—come out at some point. Eddie's been breathing down my neck, wondering when the label can make that info public so the press team doesn't have to dance around the subject when people pitch us. The optics are perfect."

Eddie Engels. The creep from the party. "I don't care what Eddie wants."

"Mm, you better care. He's the final approval on all publicity."

I dig my nails into my palms and squeeze my eyes closed. "He came on to me at the party and tried to . . . If someone hadn't intervened, I don't know what would've happened. So, forgive me if I don't give a fuck what he has to say."

"I do. I have to." Cola takes a sip of her green juice and clicks her nails—natural, today—against the marble counter. "I don't like him, either, and now that you've told me that, I'll keep you the hell away from him. But he's besties with a ton of industry people, which, I know, says a lot about the industry, and I don't have the clout to topple him. At least not yet."

"So all I have the power to do is ignore him? What if he does it again?" My face is hot with a mixture of anger and shame and a demented variant of self-pity.

Cola stares at the recessed lights on her kitchen ceiling. "I don't know what to tell you. No one gets to this level without making compromises. I don't want to kill your idealism or, like, say you shouldn't have morals. But if you hold yourself and everyone you work with to such a high standard, you'll never get anywhere."

I've read enough blind items to know that the entertainment world is a cesspool, but now that I'm in it, the stakes feel different. Because I don't have a plan B if this doesn't work out, and right now Ari and Lucía are counting on me, too. "Is it worth it?"

I'm rattled when Cola cackles. "Fuck yeah. I pay my momma's bills now. I'm sending my nieces and nephews to college; I fund scholarships and charities. Anyone who says fame and money are overrated is either lying or doesn't have anyone relying on them."

Her phone buzzes. Cola stabs the screen with a ferocity that makes my knuckles ache in sympathy. Then just as abruptly, she looks up and points at me. "And I know you get it. I saw it when you played. You *crave* that moment of recognition, when you get up onstage and look out at all the people who've come to worship you."

Was that what she saw on my face? I've never questioned why I liked performing so much, only that once I start playing, the critical voice in my head shuts up. I discovered this when I started playing guitar for church, then confirmed it during my time in the Sunshowers. And that night at Heaven's Not Enough, I'd felt like ... like I had somehow left my body behind. Like the music I was playing was playing through me.

I thought that silencing that inner voice was the reason I'm drawn to the spotlight, but the idea that I might actually need its validation gives me chills.

Cola sighs and tosses her phone onto the counter. "All right. You're good to go for prom." When I don't answer her, eyes wide in a disbelieving stare, Cola smiles wryly. "Mm, there's a catch. As you know, my goal with Karma Demon is to carve a space in the big leagues by the gays, for the gays. And as part of this benevolent mission, you will get to know her."

I take Cola's phone when she slides it toward me. Her screen's open to the *BEATING HEART* byline page for Melissa Harper; I recognize the name because she writes a lot of the magazine's features. "What do you mean?"

Cola taps a nail on the screen. "You're going to make time for her in your schedule, from now until the Karma Demon show, for a cover story that'll drop right before tour starts. It's part of a special issue devoted to me and the other four acts on the imprint. You'll come out at prom, then go deep into the turbulent life and times of Suwa Moon, specifically focusing on *The Moonflower Sessions* and how your transition affects your music."

I bite back a smile. I used to collect *BEATING HEART* covers, ripping them off the stock copies in the library and lining my locker with them. But I protest, "That's not what *Moonflower*'s about. I told you before, it's a breakup album."

Cola props her chin on her hand. "No aspect of your breakup

was affected by the fact you're trans? Not one song is influenced by anything you went through before, during, after transitioning?"

What a way of simplifying the ongoing negotiation I have with my body. And my relationship with Santi wasn't a season-long special on *Live from Los Angeles: Suwa Moon's Transition Chronicles*.

"I'm sorry." My delivery drips with sarcasm. "Should I redo the cover, put a flower between my legs with an *X* over it? 'It's a metaphor for the feminine spirit, which makes crossing it out symbolic'—"

Cola snorts but replies, "I can't front, the execs would actually love that. It's so much simpler. But you're not simple. Nothing about you is."

"Is that a roundabout way of saying I'm difficult?"

"I can tell you that directly." Cola's face shifts into a thoughtful expression. "But like I said before, you can live with the projection that fans and the media cast on you, or you can get out in front of it. And . . ." She arches an eyebrow. "I know it matters to me when some baby gay tells me that my music helped them. That's not why I started making music, but it's what makes me keep doing it. Are you making music for yourself, really, or are you making music to be heard, maybe, by people like *you*?"

My stomach lurches, and I respond quietly, "I'm making music to be heard."

"So own it. Claim your identity and your community. Your history, your past, and your vision of the future." Cola taps her screen again. "Melissa's easy to talk to. She'll treat you and what you have to say well. Unless," Cola laughs breezily, "you'd like to save me the trouble and casually come out on social media or something. But that wouldn't be as dramatic, and for all of your posturing, you clearly have a flair for the dramatic."

I scoff. She shakes her head. "What, you're gonna tell me I'm wrong? Hm." Cola taps her chin with her finger. "You should have a more casual meet before prom. Next week she's with one of my other signees . . . What've you got going on this weekend? Anything that could be fun in a story?"

My head throbs. I can't do anything with my band; Ari's playing at a wedding and Lucía's pulling doubles at her day job. Should I take Melissa out on one of those obvious press dates? I instantly imagine a possible opening line for the story: *It takes me a second to find him amid the smoke and sizzle of one of LA Koreatown's famous BBQ restaurants. Suwa Moon's spent most of his public life just out of focus, a blur among many bodies, and he still retains the ability to slip in and out of a crowd. For now.*

But who knows when I'll get a chance like this again? I should shine a light on something I care about. And instantly, I think of the Woodshed, Gender Club, and the community Cap's been building his entire life.

Except: I know what's going on with the Woodshed this weekend. I bite the inside of my cheek to keep from laughing. Of course. How many birds can I take out with one stone? Maybe it'll be easier to face one fear when I have another to keep me distracted. Scylla, meet Charybdis. "I'm going to an event organized by . . . a friend. On Sunday. It's a mural workshop for some kids my old band director mentors."

She slaps the table and crows, "Perfect. Can you let your friend know the situation?"

I can try. "He might not say yes."

"He'll say yes. Everybody says yes." Cola keeps talking; I stop hearing what she's saying. In the back of my mind, I wonder if this is a wise idea. But even if it isn't, I think darkly to myself, at least it'll be a good story.

"He's giving me vintage Bruce Springsteen. He's a *Brokeback Mountain* Asian fan cast. He's serving twink on the range."

Shanice's assessment of my outfit—ochre canvas sneakers, tight dark blue jeans, dark red muscle tank, baby blue bandana wrapped around my head—is . . . not inaccurate. I pull my smock over my head and deadpan, "Yeehaw."

"Find me when the reporter gets here!" She skips away.

I pull out my phone and revisit my texts with Santi. I wiped our chat right before I left for Tokyo, so the only messages are:

I'm going on Sunday, to support the Woodshed
okay
Is it cool if there's a reporter?
sure intro her to one of the club kids

Between the lines: *Don't talk to me.* I put the phone away and scan the crowd. There are a lot of people here. Including . . . Who wears satin pants to a painting project?

"Suwa?" The flesh-and-blood version of Melissa Harper's byline photo blinks rapidly as we make eye contact. She types something on her phone before extending her hand. "Melissa Harper."

"Suwa. Obviously. Nice to meet you." We shake. She's smaller in person than I'd expected, and I relax my grip so I don't crush her hand.

Melissa gestures around her. "Cola's given me some background, but I'd like you to tell me what's going on today."

It's an ambitious project. Santi's mural is going up on the side of a new brewery on the bleeding border between Thai Town and Hollywood. The baseline image had been chosen by the owners: a diver cutting through the surface of a pool. But the execution is all Santi's vision. Every outline and shadow is getting a marbled treatment, on top of some sort of iridescent paint layering for the water itself. Palm tree reflections, loose hibiscus flowers casting pink-hued shadows. The bottom of the pool studded with opalescent "tiles." If the final product looks anything like the sketches Santi'd shown the group, it's going to be stunning.

When he saw me in the crowd, he unsubtly turned away from my direction. Neither of us acknowledged the other. And when Shanice approached me later and told me that I'd be working with her for the day, I knew definitively that I was being passed off.

I talk for what feels like an hour, but when I check my watch, it's only been a few minutes. Melissa nods and occasionally types on her phone. A few people mill around, clearly eavesdropping or otherwise checking out the stranger in the tight pants as she entertains a babbling cowboy imposter. Their presence makes me even more nervous, and by the end of my second answer, I'm already sweating, sounding shaky. I haven't even talked about anything real.

"Alejandro, Logan needs your help with the paint wash station. Everybody, leave 'em alone."

Melissa and I whip our heads in the direction of the voice. His voice.

Santi doesn't meet my eyes, but when he says, "Sorry about the flies. You got some space now," I know he's talking to me.

"Thank you." Melissa clears her throat. "Are you the organizer of today's event?"

Santi raises his eyebrows. "I guess I am."

Melissa nods thoughtfully, then says, "I'm Melissa Harper, with *BEATING HEART*. How do you know Emo Ocean, or rather, Suwa?"

For a second, I see it: a flash of wonder on Santi's face, his mouth lifted into that dimpled smile that makes me forget all of my petulant observations, and the fact that we're not in high school and he's not mine. Even though he was, at one point, open to being claimed.

But it's over quickly, and his face shifts into a neutral expression as he answers brusquely, "We went to high school together. Our . . . families are close."

"Is this your first mural workshop?" It seems Melissa's now interviewing Santi. This is a nightmare. I pinch myself.

"Yeah, it is. Uh, Suwa, I think Shanice is calling for you." Santi points at the other side of the mural, where Shanice motions frantically at me, then tells Melissa, "Good luck. He'll definitely be fun to write about."

He slings a pink-striped towel over his shoulder and jogs over to a group of girls flicking paint at each other, yelling, "Hey, cut that out."

Melissa turns back to me. Santi's intervention has weirdly given me a chance to regroup. "Actually, would it be all right if you asked me questions while I work? Shanice over there can fill you in on both the Woodshed's mission and what we're doing here today."

Shanice talks me through our part of the mural, then both

of us talk to Melissa. Nat's on my paint squad, too, and he quietly shades in flower shadows. It's counterintuitive to what I
would've imagined, but working while talking makes it easier to control my thoughts. I say a few things that make Melissa laugh, and I'm getting into the groove of the conversation
when, in the middle of an answer about staying true to the
spirit of the EP as I expand it into an album, I pour half a
bucket of blue paint down my arm and onto most of the left
side of my body.

"Suwa? Earth to Suwa?" Shanice waves her hand in front
of my face. Nat tries to brush some of the paint back into the
bucket, but all that does is increase its coverage.

Melissa clears her throat. "I'll get some cleaning supplies."
Blue dribbles off of my elbow, and out of the corner of my eye, I
notice someone take a photo. Goddammit.

"Who needs . . ." Then a laugh. *That* laugh.

Of course Melissa brings Santi over. I know I look pitiful because his eyes soften when he sees me, like I'm a fawn he found
wounded in the woods.

"Y'know, paint's supposed to go on the wall." For someone who
isn't speaking to me, he sure is saying a lot. I grunt in response.

Santi points into the distance. "There's a spot in the loading
zone back that way where you can scrub off with a towel."

"Right. I'll . . . go do that." I make my way there and strip off
my smock. Nothing can be done about my clothes so I keep them
on, but the paint on my skin's starting to dry and itch. As Santi
said, there's a cleaning station already set up in the area. I blow
my bangs out of my eyes and start scrubbing my arm.

A few minutes pass, when a voice too close to me reprimands,
"You're missing a bunch on your back." I nearly slip as I whirl

around, but callused hands steady me. Santi whistles. "And your front."

I should step away. I don't step away. "How bad is it?"

He makes a show of looking over my shoulder. He should let go. He doesn't let go. "It . . . looks like you tipped a bucket of paint on yourself." Santi lets go of me to take the towel out of my hand and circle around to my back. "Lemme get the parts you can't reach."

His breath is hot against my neck, and I fight the urge to run. This is too close. Goosebumps break out across my body when the cold cloth slips under the fabric of my shirt, and I feel the indentations of his fingertips against my skin.

"Hey. Are you . . . Are you planning to talk to Melissa about 'Exit Music'?" Santi's voice carries a tremor, and his hand stills. "Not that you should, or . . . It's your life. It's more, mm, it would be a chance to finally, I don't know."

His voice drops. "Sorry, it's none of my business. You can do whatever you want. You should never feel like you can't do what you want."

I close my eyes. What's *happening*? Can he feel the heat radiating off of my body? He told me I was bad for him. He told me he was done with me. But here we are, and I'm undone. And it'd be so easy to turn around, and. And what?

The towel lifts off my back, and Santi's uncovered palm torches my shoulder blade. I let out a gasp. My eyes are still closed. I can imagine it, though, the dazed, dreamy look on his face as he hovers at the cusp of action.

My ex–boy-/best friend is maybe about to do something. If he wants to. If I let him. When Melissa asks me about the heart of the album, and she *will* ask me, what am I going to tell her?

Should I go full trailblazer and, as Cola not unseriously suggested, frame the record around my body? In one sense, the record *is* about my body, as it processed the physical and psychic misery of losing not just a lover but a best friend: the nights I spent curled in a ball on my bed, shaking and crying; all the times I swore I saw Santi's face on the train or on the street or looking out from an ad and ran back to find him, only to gaze into a stranger's eyes; his phantom arm around my shoulders.

Santi's very real arm snakes around my waist. I take a deep breath. My shirt rides up. And slowly, shyly, his fingertips drag against the skin of my stomach.

"Suwa, how're you doing back there?" Melissa's voice, somehow both distant and too close, tips me back into the present. I shudder and take a step forward before pivoting around, and I look up at Santi's shaken expression.

The wound in my heart rips open. If I don't walk away right now, I'll do something I think we'll both instantly regret.

"I should get back. Thanks for your help with . . ." The towel's in his pocket, dripping blue down his leg. "With the paint."

I wipe my eyes with the back of my hand and start walking away, but Santi doesn't move. As I pass him, I hear him whisper something under his breath. I only catch the first part of what he says—"*I almost*," urgent as a prayer—but I don't stop to let myself hear the rest.

Track 17

"*Laaast* thing, I swear. You're sure you don't want to fly your outfits by anyone on the team?"

"We already picked them out. I'll grab them from the studio on my way to the gig. Sorry, I have to go. My sister's flight is coming in early."

Sayo's flying in this afternoon before she moves to Mexico City for her next film, and the Woodshed's buzzing with activity as we prepare for her welcome party. The house smells like heaven; Aya's been cooking all day. Outside, the jacarandas are starting to shed. My friends' shoes, placed in neat rows by the front door, are soled with lavender mush. Everybody's done with classes except for me, Ari, and Lucía: because De Longpre pushed their prom to after graduation, we're heading back to high school tomorrow.

I don't say it out loud, but I wish the rest of our friends could be there with us. But they all have conflicts, internships and work, so I'm savoring this chance to hang out. If only Cola would let me go.

Cola sighs. "Right, right, and you're doing a big celebration.

Okay, have fun. Make sure you get a good night's sleep before the big dance!" She hangs up before I can retort.

Then behind me, *CRASH*. I turn around to see Lucía, half slung over Feli's shoulder, yell and pummel his back as he laughs uproariously, phone raised to film them. Octavian, back in town for the summer, pats Mira on the shoulder as she holds what remains of the piñata—a now bisected cartoon mouse—and loudly fake cries. Ari and Reva walk into the room; Ari immediately turns around, while Reva puts down the streamers in her arms, grabs a roll of duct tape lying around, and screams at Octavian to begin surgery.

I head in Ari's direction. We meet by the back door, and when I lean on the other side of the open frame, they hand me a beer. "How'd your call go?"

More screaming and laughing behind us. I click the beer open; we bump cans, and after I take a sip, I say, "She still thinks it's a joke, but she's given her blessing."

Ari chews over something, then goes, "Can I say something that might fuck you up?"

I make a face. "Uh, no?" But curiosity gets the better of me. "What kind of fucked-up?"

"The kind you like in stories."

I mean, I have to let them share it now. After I nod, Ari takes a sip of their beer before saying, "You're going to senior prom after all."

My heart jolts. One particularly hard day freshman year, Ari and I were both sitting outside the principal's office, waiting for Cap to finish speaking to her. At Sayo's behest, I'd moved back home. Things were still rough, my father and I circling each other warily, two lost spirits forced to haunt the same house.

A bunch of seniors were in the reception area outside, chattering loudly about prom planning even though it was like eight months away. And mostly to myself, I'd said, "I'm never making it to senior prom."

Ari winks. "I told you you would."

"Really? You dropped that on me just to say, 'I told you so'?" I huff; my bangs fly out of my eyes. "You did. But tragedy could strike between today and tomorrow."

"Boy, you better knock on wood." Ari hears their name and sighs. "Reva's calling."

"Go get wifey."

They flip me off as they walk past me. I snicker, but a feeling I can't quite name passes through me as Reva runs up to Ari excitedly, eyes practically glittering as she says something that makes them beam.

We all knew the two of them were going to make it.

I have to look away.

"Suwa!" Cap comes through the door. "Help me with the A/V setup?"

I put my beer down and grab my shoes to change into. We work silently for a while, sorting out plugs and cords, then tracking the cables and testing the inputs. As we set up the projector we're using to screen some of the films Sayo's worked on, Cap asks, "Why the glum face?"

I immediately pull my mouth into a smile, but he shakes his head. "Lay it on me."

The first few days I lived with Cap were unbearably awkward.

He always checked in on me: "How's it going, Suwa?" "What're you thinking?" "You need anything?"

When Sayo came by from college to see me, I'd complain, and she'd flick my face or roll her eyes, talk about how ungrateful I was being.

I rub my eyes and mutter, "There's only like, a month, ish, until the Karma Demon showcase. And then I leave." I hesitate before adding, "I know I have some unfinished business here. But I don't know where to begin, or if I should."

Cap takes in the weight of my words. He clears his throat. "You know the thing about the frog and boiling water?"

I nod. Cap continues, "It's bull. Gotta be. A frog wouldn't sit there. But y'know what would? A human. People can get used to anything, even if they shouldn't."

I narrow my eyes. What's he trying to tell me? Then Cap hiccups. "Uh-oh!"

His breath smells like sangria. So that's what he's been doing in the kitchen, "helping" with the cooking. "How many pitchers have you and Aya cleared?"

"There's plenty left—oh, your sister's calling." Cap picks up the phone. "Sayo—slow down, slow . . . well, Suwa must not have his phone on him"—I pat my pockets and come up empty—"Uh-huh, do you need . . . oh. I see. Well, one of us can . . ."

I can't make out what Sayo's saying, but when Cap hangs up, his expression is serious. "Her rental broke down, and her phone's about to die, too. Ah, crap, all of us have been drinking."

"Not Prof. Where'd she say she was?" We step back inside and change our shoes while I scan for Octavian.

"Hmm . . . Somewhere in Larchmont. But, hold on, she

texted that she's getting a ride." Cap chuckles, "She's always been good at chatting up strangers."

My annoyance at Sayo sputters out. So effortlessly outgoing. She apparently got that from our mother. I sigh, say, "I'm going to look for my phone," and pad upstairs. Maybe I'd left it in my room.

"My" room. I close the door and walk slowly around the space. Even my bedroom isn't really mine anymore. Cap and Aya left it pretty much as it was when I left, so it doesn't take much for me to imagine Santi humming under his breath as we listen to records, or lying in my bed, making up fake constellations in the popcorn ceiling.

I can't escape him. I sit on the edge of my bed and hold my face in my hands as I try to remember what this room, my life, was like before I met him. Before he took me over.

"Suwa?" Aya's voice comes through my door. "You in there? Need to grab something I stashed in your closet." I take a deep breath and get up to open the door for her.

"You haven't had a day off since you got here, hm?" Aya digs around and pulls out a set of sheets, folding them in her hands. "Cola's really been working you to the bone."

"It's fine. I can work."

"You're meeting up with the reporter before the show?"

"Yeah, it's . . ." I sigh. Right, I can't forget about this. "I'm . . . supposed to come out tomorrow, too."

Aya laughs sharply. "What's 'supposed to' supposed to mean?"

"For the story. It's like, I'm back in the place where I transitioned. It's symbolic?" Even as I say it, I know it rings false. But I'd told Cola I would, and her guidance this far has been spot-on.

"But you have doubts."

After some hesitation, I nod. "I know it's probably nothing, but there's this part of me that wonders . . . what if word gets out to my family? They're definitely around, and I . . . I'll never be able to control what they say about me."

Aya takes a seat on my bed and taps the space next to her. I wrinkle my nose; a part of me bristles at this transparent attempt at mothering. Still, I take the seat.

"Fuck your family." My jaw drops. Aya shrugs. "Yeah, I said it. If they see you onstage, on fire, doing the thing you're meant to do, and they make a scene? We'll shut it down. You're blazing, Suwa. Nothing they ever say or do can put that out, you understand?"

I've always respected Aya as a person, but I'm beginning to understand why Cap handed his legacy off to her. "I think I do. Thanks, Aya." She gives me a quick hug, then gets up to go.

She stops halfway through the door. "One more thing. I know you kids think coming out is what you gotta do, but if you really want to, and I mean *want* to, at least do it on your exact terms. Not just because it's a neat story trick."

After the door clicks shut, I notice my phone resting on my laptop. Duh. As I walk back across the room, I hear something fall in my closet, so I investigate. And gasp.

It's the jacket. Santi's jacket. I never bothered to fully unpack my suitcase so I haven't rummaged around in here. I hadn't brought the jacket with me to Tokyo since, well, it wasn't mine. But if no one else has claimed it . . . I don't have a choice.

I stand in front of my mirror and slip it on. It'll always be roomy on me, but I want to believe I've grown into it a little. I slide my hands into the pockets and, just this once, smirk at my reflection. And just this once, how I want to look and how I actually look align perfectly.

Now I'm curious. What else is in here? For one, a box filled with sheet music. I flip through the pages; they're band scores, including some so faded and torn up that they must be from when Cap taught her. I also uncover a binder full of press clippings for one of her old bands, Horadorada.

And then—oh. Wow. A bin filled with school reports and pencil drawings. Sketches by . . . by Santi. Based on the dates, they're from our middle-school years. My fingers move on their own, sifting through this tender time capsule. And then they brush against something that static-shocks me.

I pull it out: a lightly crumpled manila envelope. When I flip it over, my breath hitches. It's labeled MEMO. I recognize Santi's handwriting, but it's blockier, messier.

Is there any way this could be something from when he—when we were talking about meeting up? I smooth it out and begin to undo the flap.

"Suwa!" Cap knocks on my door. "Sayo's here?" He sounds uneasy. I quickly shrug the jacket off, replacing it on the hanger, but fold the envelope and stick it into my back pocket.

"Baby bro!" Sayo rushes up and hugs me before I've even made it down the stairs. And into my ear, she whispers, "Please don't kill me."

"What? Why the hell . . ." The words die in my mouth as I spot her stranger savior.

Santi's taking off his helmet, and he's holding the one Sayo must've worn. I feel the floor begin to slide away from my feet as Cap overzealously invites him in. Santi switches his shoes out, puts the helmets down, and runs his hand through his hair, which is already growing into curls. And when he walks past me, his eyes catch on mine, but then he looks away, leaving me to tread water in the wake of his stride.

"Thank you, everyone, for turning it up. Especially Aya. When I die, I want her cooking buried inside my grave, ancient-Egypt style." Sayo raises her glass; the backyard breaks out into cheers. My sister nudges me with her elbow. "Our diet in Tokyo was, what, half instant ramen, half Famima snacks? No time or money to cook on the reg. This is such an upgrade."

Sayo leans across the table we've lit with candles to ask Aya, "Suwa's useless behind a stove. I tried to teach him when we were younger, but way too many close calls with knives. Any chance you can school him in the basics while he's here?" I scowl and reach for the last lettuce wrap. Sayo's no slouch in the kitchen, but between the two of us, I'm not the one who once set off the fire alarm while reheating frozen gyoza.

Aya, another goblet of sangria deep, wraps her arm around Santi's shoulders and plants a kiss on the side of his head. He scrunches his face up. "Sure. But Santi might be the better cook now. He's a magician in the kitchen these days."

Santi shrugs. And without turning toward me, he answers, "Only if he wants me." I choke on lettuce. If I die tonight, I'll use my last breath to accuse Sayo of murder.

Before we all sat down, I'd grabbed Sayo, pulled her into the pantry, and hissed, "*Explain*."

"I'm not messing with you. My car started smoking and sputtering, thank the gods for this, after I pulled off the ten, and I called you like fifty times, by the way. But right as I got off the phone with Cap, no shit, Santi pulls over." She'd raised her hand. "Scout's honor."

"You literally got kicked out of Brownies for lying— whatever. I told you about the last time . . . Santi and I crossed paths. I don't want to do this. I *can't*."

"You say his name now, huh? And yeah, it sounded like you were about to have a hot make-up kiss with— Did you peep those tattoos? You've totally been downplaying what's going on, because now that I see it for myself? Yeesh."

I'd scowled. "Are you on my side or not?"

Sayo had flicked my forehead. "Are *you* on your side, Suwa?" And: scene.

Aya takes a long drink of water before jumping into a conversation between Reva and Lucía. I'm trapped between Cap and Sayo, who keeps tilting past me to ask questions like, "Has my brother been pulling his weight around the Woodshed?" Judging by the color of her cheeks, she forgot to pop a Pepcid.

She's not the only person at the table who's a little rosy, a little buzzed. But the flush on Santi's face, faint but visible against the candlelight and the string lights strewn through the citrus trees, looks a lot like a blush. I keep sneaking glances at him, which would be a more effective scoping strategy if he weren't right across the table from me.

But it doesn't escape my notice that everyone else at the table chats with him like . . . things are normal. Even Ari's asking him about the mural he's working on now, something for a new horror movie coming out soon. In fact, at a table full of cross chatter, good food, and free-flowing wine, surrounded by almost everyone I love, I'm seemingly the only one with nothing to say to anybody.

When Santi takes his leave early, something about a work thing in the morning, he waves his goodbye to everyone but looks at me. I ignore the weight of Sayo's gaze as I halfheartedly lift my hand in return.

After he's gone, my brain works overtime to figure out *what* is in the air tonight. My friends have insisted on handling all of the dinner cleanup, and I join the assembly line, scraping plates before passing them off to Mira.

"So, Suwa . . ." Reva's got that conspiratorial tone in her voice. I'm going to get grilled about something. But I'm surprised when instead she says, "You were kinda quiet at dinner. Nerves?"

"Not really."

Reva bats her eyes. Here we go. But I'm not prepared for what she asks: "Then . . . is it because of what Santi did for you?"

When I don't respond, she tries again, "For his Friendship Redemption Tour?"

"Excuse me?" What am I missing here?

Mira turns the faucet off and fills in, "Santi tabled with me and Lucía at the zine fest last weekend and took Ari and Reva out to Moonlight Rollerway for their gay night. He got Feli and his date seats at that hot new Cambodian place, the one that opened right by De Longpre, yesterday. He's been hitting all of us up and, like, trying to reconnect? I kept up a little with him before, but he's doing some really cool shit these days."

Octavian realizes it first. "He was the one who picked me up at Union Station when I moved back after the semester, and you didn't know any of this."

In the two weeks since our mural encounter, I've buried my-self in work. Ari, Lucía, and I have finished recording, though we still meet up most days to rehearse. I've been spending more and more time alone with Cola and other label people debat-ing potential singles and my first-ever music video, or just plain alone, practicing and workshopping new material, including a few covers to mix things up on the road.

I told myself my increasing penchant for solitude was a last hurrah. We're getting closer and closer to *Moonflower*'s re-release date, less than a month away, and I have more press and pub-licity appointments coming up. But, as I sit with the waves of emotion breaking inside my chest, maybe I also burrowed into myself to avoid confronting the memory of Santi's hands, the nostalgic lance that'd carved a fresh canyon through my entire body. My heart had almost split open. And as I process what my friends just told me, it strains in my chest like a flower against a swooning wind.

"Suwa!" Ari calls out after me as I rush out of the kitchen. I stumble over my feet, quickly switching to my sneakers. Behind me, I faintly hear Sayo's voice, but I run down to the street, fol-lowing the lingering scent of smoke down the block, then an-other, only to suddenly lose the trail.

My heartbeat's pounding in my ears. Breaths coming in sharp and raw. Cola's right, I should take up running.

Wait. What am I doing? I slap my cheeks. Santi's probably long gone and, anyway, what would I even say if I caught up with him? That *almost* at the mural was a fluke. A moment of weakness on both of our parts.

And—a spike of bitterness shoots through me—if he really wanted to extend an olive branch, he would've reached out as part of his adorable "Friendship Redemption Tour." But he'd hit upon something true when he said that I was bad for him. That I'd be bad for him now. We're a record at the end of the side. I'm watching it spin and hoping to hear some secret track, but it's *over*.

Melissa, the *BEATING HEART* reporter, is going to be at prom tomorrow. I'm going to talk not just about the album, but about me. I laugh darkly. Compared to confronting my feelings for Santi, coming out genuinely seems like a much less daunting prospect. I take a seat on the curb and close my eyes against a cool night breeze.

I used to remember exactly what I said to Santi after he revealed himself to me, but I don't anymore. I'd spent so much time imagining my best friend, but when I finally met him, I realized I'd been idealizing a fantasy. My phantom in the clouds. When the real thing appeared, I wasn't prepared to actually know him. But how could I have been? What else could I have done?

I try to slow down my thoughts. For now: Answer the texts rolling in on my phone. For future Suwa: Stop running after a boy and go home; play prom; get real about going back to therapy. I clench my hands as my chest tightens and my vision begins to blur.

Then a pair of out-of-focus paint-splattered sneakers appear in front of me. My eyes climb up, and suddenly Santi's concerned face is level with mine. He opens his mouth, but I don't let him speak.

"Breathe. I know, I *know*." I wipe my face with the back of my hand, but I hadn't been crying. Until now. So I pull my shirt collar up to my eyes and will him to walk away.

But instead Santi puts his arms around me. And I let him, and I unhook my sweatshirt from my face, slide my arms against his, and lean into his hug.

Our bare knees brush. This can't be comfortable for him. This isn't comfortable for me, but neither of us lets go. Our bodies figuring out what our brains haven't. I try to form some sort of argument about why we shouldn't be holding each other like this, but everything I think I should say turns into breath, so instead I say the thing I wish I'd told him as soon as we saw each other again.

"I missed you." Santi's hold around me tightens as I pull the words out from between my teeth. "So much, I missed you." I hiccup, and he lets out a soft snort that tickles the back of my ear.

"I missed you, too."

Of course he's also crying now, which makes me laugh wetly. We sit there, trading tears, until I notice the smoke wreathed around us. When I pull away, a cigarette dangles between his fingers. And I almost laugh; one of my earliest memories of him is when he admonished me about the very same thing he's doing now. I can't resist the easy shot. "That's terrible for your regular lungs."

Santi hesitates in the middle of a pull and exhales away from me. He drops the cigarette onto the ground, where it rolls into gutter water, hisses, then disappears down a storm drain. And then we're both holding our breath, teetering on the edge of either a breakthrough or yet another breakdown.

I was always the one who initiated. "Your charm offensive with our friends is working. So you're staying in Los Angeles for good? Or at least you're not leaving soon."

A long beat of silence passes before Santi speaks. "Is . . . that why you came after me? You wanted to know when I'll be gone?"

He cracks his thumbs. He's nervous.

"You wanted me to come after you." I say this more confidently than I feel.

"I don't know what I want." Santi's mouth slices into something that's neither a smile nor a frown. "I keep telling myself every time I talk to you is the last time."

"Why?" I didn't feel my body move or register any movement from him, but we're somehow closer. His freckles have gotten darker. I only knew him at the end of summer, but here we are, at the start.

Santi laughs lowly. "Don't play, Suwa."

I want to hear him say my name over and over again. But as the person responsible for this mess, I have to do some cleaning-up. "I'm sorry. Santi, I'm so sorry. I didn't . . ."

I curl into myself and bury my head between my arms. "Everything I said about and to you back then was so completely misdirected. If I'd just dealt with my issues instead of constantly compressing them in, like, the accordion pleats of my heart—"

Santi laughs. I raise my head, both alarmed and embarrassed, but he says sheepishly, "Sorry, just—you really have a way with words." His voice softens. "Some of those *Moonflower* lyrics . . . 'The heir of Orion / Took me out hunting / But I was the game' . . . Ouch."

I let out a groan. He raises his eyebrows. "Oh, c'mon. Of course I listened to it."

I raise my face toward the sky, my cheeks burning. "I didn't mean it like that! I mean . . . I knew there was no turning back once the songs were out there. But I didn't have to make them. What we were, what we became to each other, didn't have to be so . . . like this."

I grind my teeth, frustrated with the way I keep failing to describe how I'm feeling. "Look, when you told me about our past, my fight-or-flight response kicked in. I chose flight, obviously. But I didn't move to Tokyo to write a breakup album. I never blocked your number. I kept everything up and checked, every day. I kept waiting for you."

But as I say that, I remember that he'd gone through this before. Sending messages into the void where I'd once been. No wonder he didn't want to do it again. So he'd taken me at my word and left me alone. Everything has been done before. The vicious cycle eats its own tail. I have no one but myself to blame for how we ended.

All for what? My pride?

I don't feel proud of myself.

Santi's quiet long enough that I look at him out of the corner of my eye. He's . . . crying again, but unlike before, the tears fall silently. His lips part like he wants to say something, but can't. Until: "A part of me knew that you'd leave LA eventually. And then you'd be traveling the world, meeting all kinds of people, for pretty much ever."

"So that would've been it?" The words scrape the sides of my throat. "It was always going to end?"

Santi chews his lip for a long beat before sighing. His breath smells like ginger. "Suwa, what do you want me to say?"

That you want me, like you used to. "That you were following your dreams, too." My thoughts unravel as soon as I voice them, but I push through. "I never asked you about your dreams.

I was always so fucking selfish. It looks like they're coming true anyway. And you did that on your own, but you shouldn't have had to."

Maybe we had to let each other go to get what we wanted. And maybe that's enough. Maybe this, a quiet acknowledgment and acceptance of mutual pain, is the only happy ending I can realistically hope for. I brush my palms off and move to stand.

Santi wraps his hand around mine. I'm so stunned that I sit back down. And he finishes what he'd started to tell me at the mural, before I walked away: "I almost thought I could live my life without you."

I shake my head, but he continues, "I guess I wanted to see if I could. That was part of it, me leaving. For . . . years, I looked for Memo in everyone I met, everywhere I lived. I only stopped when I met you. You took over. So realizing you were the same person . . . it was like a shock to me, too. But of course it was weirder, and harder, for you. Because . . . when I think about that time of my life . . ."

Santi's earring glints in the moonlight as he leans toward me. "All I wanted back then was for you to be happy. For you to get what you want. And that's still what I want. To see you happy, and free. Even if it means I can't be there as . . ." He squeezes his eyes shut, blinks quickly, and whispers, "Even if that means I have to get out of your way."

How can he say that about himself? Is that what he read into the breakup? My mouth opens to protest, clarify, refute, but all that comes out is a pant that lifts my bangs. Before I can find the right words, Santi's other hand reaches up, fingers grazing my scalp, and my mind goes blank. "That's one of the first things I noticed about you. Even when other people do it, I think, 'Oh, that's Suwa's hair thing.'"

No thoughts, only touch. "I might get a haircut. Before heading out on tour."

Santi hmms. "You need a trim? Touch-up color?"

"What, you do hair now?"

I'm joking, but Santi shrugs. "I've helped a few . . . friends out."

I ignore the loaded way he says "friends." "You cook, you cut and color hair. What else did you learn on your journey of self-enlightenment?" I immediately regret the tone I use, a combo of forced sincerity and real curiosity that comes out instead as mean and bitter.

Santi's eyes darken, but then he reaches behind his neck, tugs off his sweatshirt, and destroys me. He's wearing a half-buttoned Dodgers jersey underneath, and for the first time, I take in the tapestry he's made of his upper body. His cross peeks out behind the top button, and I bite back a sound that'll kill the momentum of whatever is happening right now.

"I spent a couple months in New York with some people who ran a shop. I was hired to help repaint and reinstall the space, but they taught me how to work a gun, like a tattoo gun, and I kinda got into it." He pulls down one of his sleeves—*god*—and adds, "I did a lot of trades. A couple were inspired by, um, anime, like this one."

Santi points at the flower that stretches up his ribs. It's a marigold, its petals suspended like asteroids gravitating around the slender stem. In my head, I run a finger down it.

He looks at me pointedly. "That was my first."

Despite having renounced religion years ago, I send a prayer heavenward: *Is this a sign?*

Then Santi clears his throat, slips his arm back into his sleeve, and pulls his sweatshirt back on. "I should get going. Early work and, yeah."

I try not to let my face fall. We both get up. I follow him, peeking at the outline of his face backlit by the moonlight. We don't talk again until we're almost back at the Woodshed.

His motorcycle's parked right in front of Cap's truck. This encounter doesn't scan. By the time I ran out of the house, he could've been miles away. But he'd stuck around.

I pick a scab on my elbow. A skateboarding accident from a few days ago. "Santi. Why'd you hang out here, after dinner?"

Santi tilts his head and asks, with a tone I can't register, "Why'd you try to find me after?"

One moment of honesty, and we're back to talking around each other. I ignore his question. "If you're free tomorrow or whatever, I'm playing the Sunshowers prom. I don't think anyone else is going, but . . ." I stop myself from finishing: *You're the reason I have anything to play.*

"Mira mentioned it. I wish I could but, again, work." Then he smiles and sends an arrow through my heart. "Hey. Someone else might be wearing the crown, but you're my pick for prom king, jagi."

We've both spent so much energy and time avoiding this exact scenario. But now that I'm here and he's here and I can see my reflection in his eyes, I'm weak.

I push him up against the side of the truck and kiss him. *Tastes like ginger.* Santi groans, and for a moment, I wonder if this is the last contact I'll ever get. But then he kisses back, hard, sliding a hand into my hair and another at the base of my skull. My hands grip on to his shirt to bring him closer, closer.

Every part of my body is on fire. I break away only to hiss, "Is this totally fucked?" As I say the words, I think to myself, *WHO CARES?*

Santi mutters, "Like here? Or in eternity," and presses his lips into the crook of my neck. I let out a gasp, which makes him smirk; he sighs as I shift my hips over his. We collapse into each other, teeth catching lips and lips catching sounds only he's ever made me make. But when he runs his hand up my thigh, we both hear a soft *crunch* that acts like a record scratch.

He reaches for what's in my pocket. The envelope I'd stashed there. When Santi unfolds it, his eyes widen. "Where did you find this?"

"In my closet. Aya put some of your old stuff there." I snatch it from him and put it back, and finally get my hands in his hair. "Do you want to keep going over the past, or do you want to do something with the present?"

His eyes flash. "You staying in your old room?"

I understand what he means immediately.

A few minutes later, we've snuck into the Woodshed, pulling ourselves onto the roof of the porch to get to my bedroom window. It's the route Santi had taken so many times in reverse to sneak out, both of us in agreement that we'd never live it down if Cap caught us together in the mornings. I feel delirious, retracing our steps like this. Body quivering with the same raw desire I'd felt back then.

But once we're in my bed, we can't seem to pick up where we'd left off. Santi's motions swing from too tentative to too aggressive. I never used to get self-conscious when I was with him, but now I feel hyperaware of every movement. I can tell he's

uneasy, too. Our desperate fumbling is the bridge we've put between us, but now that the haze of first contact is starting to clear,
every step we take across it is making me dizzy.

"Stop. Stop, stop."

I push Santi away from me and pull my knees up against
my chest while he swings his legs over to sit at the edge of the
bed.

We hadn't known anything else before, at least not in the
way we got to know each other. The way he touches me now is
different, changed by strangers I'll never meet. He's probably
processing the same thing.

"Have you . . . been with anyone, since coming back?" My
voice cracks.

Santi scratches his head, his voice dark when he asks, "You
think I move that fast, huh?" Then he sighs. "Since coming back,
no one, jagi— Sorry. I shouldn't call you that."

"You shouldn't. But . . . I like it." There's a steady humming
outside, only audible in the strained silence. Cicadas? I thought
there weren't cicadas in Los Angeles.

A much closer buzzing; I pry my phone out of my pocket. A
few recent missed calls from Sayo and a bunch of texts. Her latest one: so? I frown. As I'm checking my other messages, a new
one rolls in from . . . "BHB." I'd put that in as a placeholder the
fall of senior year, but never changed it.

are we in a tragic slice of life anime rn

Then:

sorry

I turn to Santi. He pretends he can't see me, engrossed in the glow of his phone. I stare at my screen and type back:

I'm sorry too

I pause before sending off my next message:

I shouldn't have tried to make this a Thing

I put my phone down and wait for his to buzz. But after it does, Santi scoots over and nudges my knee with his. I dip my head to look at his screen, where he's typed in:

i didn't do anything i didn't want to
but what i really want to know is

I watch him delete that message, then type out a new one:

suwa moon
do you believe in second chances?

Santi's contact name for me is a set of three emojis: crescent moon, black heart, wave. He clicks the button on the side of his phone, and his lock screen flashes.

It's us. I've got a huge scrape on the side of my leg, but I'm laughing, skateboard under my arm, head leaning into his. A curling lock of fresh pink sticking out of my backward hat. And Santi's got his arm around my waist. It's jarring, seeing him with longer hair. He's wearing my band jacket, and he's looking at me like he's in love.

When I look at him now, he has the same expression on his face. I move toward him at the same time he moves toward me, and we wrap our arms around each other and lie down together, twisting and shifting until we're entwined. The fire I'd felt earlier is still there, but burning as an ember. I poke Santi's side.

"Yeah?"

"Is this your stop for me? On your Friendship Redemption Tour?"

Santi's body shakes with laughter. "That was a joke. . . . Maybe. I don't know." His voice drops. "I think I owe you something better."

I whisper, my tongue loosened by this close contact, "Santi."

"Hmm?" His breaths are coming further apart. It must be late; my eyes flutter.

My finger slides lazily up his arm. "You know what I really want? For you to be in my future, in whatever way you want to be."

Santi makes a low noise in his chest. "That's something my best friend would say."

"Oh yeah?" We curl deeper into each other. "Tell me about them."

Santi's hand stills in my hair. Is he already asleep? Then he mumbles, "We had a huge fight a while ago. I think we're working through it, though. But don't tell him I told you all of that, if you happen to cross paths. He might think you're trying to take his place." His voice trails off.

"Lips are sealed. . . . Santi?"

"Yeah?" He yawns.

I press my face closer to his shoulder. "Stay for breakfast? I'll try to cook but if it's no good, I'll treat you." My finger traces a spiral into his skin. What I mean is, *Stay. Stay, knowing nothing's for certain. Choose to stay.*

Santi presses his lips to my head. "Sounds like a plan."

When I wake up the next morning to the sound of my phone ringing, everything aches. It's only as I shake and stretch myself out that I realize—

—he's gone.

Track 18

"Sorry, I slept through my alarm."

More like I'd never set one and I'd counted on the early riser to wake me with him. Over the phone, I listen to Lucía try not to sound anxious. She's the kind of person who has to be fifteen minutes early to everything. If I call a ride immediately, I might make sound check. "Yeah, I still have time to pick up our outfits." Probably not true; the studio's on the other side of town, and I'd be heading straight into traffic. "You and Ari focus on setup. I'm getting into a car right now. See you soon."

I walk through the kitchen on the off chance that Santi's there. No, but the dishes are all done thanks to my friends, who are always gracious guests. *Tch.* I was so fixated on my fucking feelings that I barely spent any time hanging out with everyone else, and now most of them are gone until the Karma Demon summer showcase six—no, five weeks away—and then tour starts three weeks after.

I go back upstairs and push on the bathroom door, but I knew it'd be empty. I can try every room in this house. He won't be here.

"If you're looking for Santi, he left a while ago." I startle, caught in the act by Sayo, who looks both like she just woke up and like she didn't sleep a wink as she leans against the hallway wall.

I walk over to her. Her eyes are puffy. "Jet lag was that bad?"

My sister walks into my room and takes a seat on the edge of the bed. "I was up when he came down. He told me how you spent the night."

What the hell did the two of them talk about while I was asleep and *alone*? "Love that for you." I pull clothes out of my suitcase. No, no, no. "I didn't sleep well, either, and it's going to be a long day." I switch over to the closet. Can I still fit into these jeans? I check my waistband for my current measurements, which makes me suddenly realize the MEMO envelope is no longer in my back pocket.

Did he take it with him when he left?

Why did he leave? When he'd promised to stay.

No. He'd never promised anything. I throw the clothes in my arms onto the floor, frustration making me feel light-headed and a little sick.

Sayo coughs hoarsely. "Suwa, I set you up last night."

I slowly turn around. She's looking at the Choo art I'd printed off the library LaserJet years ago as she continues, "After I talked to you, right when you got out of your audition, I called him."

Sayo's voice is even. Her eyes are still fixed on the prints. "I thought he'd said or done something that . . . I was so used to looking out for you, sussing out anyone who might mess with you. Who might hurt you the way . . . the way our father, our family, used to. But he told me that you were the one who called it off and, I quote, 'All I can do for him is hold him back.' I didn't know what he meant by that, so I didn't pass it on, and I figured you'd be mad at me for calling him. Then right before you left Tokyo, when you told me all about Memo and Canti . . . I finally understood."

At last, Sayo turns to me.

"I know you hate it when I meddle in your life. But you weren't giving me anything to work with. I reached out to Santi a while back and told him that if he wanted to make things right with you, he had a window of time to shoot his shot, but that it'd go fast. I—I never had a rental, he was always my ride to the Woodshed. And I hoped, I don't know, that you'd figure it out. But I got the impression that he's still scared to ask for what he needs from you, and judging by the look on your face right now, you didn't tell him everything you're feeling, either."

Sayo clears her throat. "You mad at me?"

I open and close my mouth like a guppy. Suddenly, Santi's comments from last night—*Even if that means I have to get out of your way*—make total sense. He didn't reach out because he thought he'd become a burden.

The feelings were always there. Santi was always there. And now I have to go to him. Except: I've got a show to play today, and I don't know when I'll see him again. But when I do, no more circling. No more missed connections. My hands curl into fists. The next time we talk, I'm going to speak straight from the heart.

Sayo coughs again. I turn to my sister. Nervous frown on her face. My original angel. God, I need to get better at treating the people I love.

Sayo lets out a squawk when I hug her. "I'm sorry for never telling you the truth about what I'm thinking, and how I'm feeling. For making you jump through all these hoops to figure out

what's going on in my head. I love you, noona. Thanks for med-
dling. I wouldn't be here without you. But first." I pull back and
sigh. "I need to get to band practice."

Sayo smiles faintly. "Damn kid. Look at you, all grown up.
What else do you need to do before—" She checks her watch.
"Uh, Suwa, your call time is like, now."

"I know, I'm screwed. And I've got nothing to wear." Wait. I
go back into my closet and pull out Santi's jacket. If only I could
magically figure out the rest of my fit, and also Ari's and Lucía's.

I scroll through my contacts to see if I know anyone who
might hook me up with some clothes on the fly and lives close
enough to meet me at De Longpre. When I see her name, I don't
hesitate to call.

Shanice picks up on the first ring: "No pressure but when I
read my horoscope it said, 'Prepare for an unexpected opportunity.' What's good, Suwa?"

"Yes. Yes! Oh my god, this is my birthday and Rihanna's birthday at the same time, yes." Shanice's excitement is contagious,
and when she tells me to "Twirl, boy," I do. Lucía whistles.
Devin puts their hand around their mouth and calls out, "He's
giving me confident elegance! He's giving me gender-bent Stevie
Nicks! He's giving me K-drama bad boy with a torrid past but a
heart of gold!" Nat flashes me a quick thumbs-up.

Through the power of Shanice's costume-designer mom's
closet, she's come up with an outfit that's almost as exciting as
what Devin's saying. I run a finger over the bright blue-and-
white lightning beading on the black silk shirt I'm wearing under
Santi's jacket. Slim black pants gently flare out over corset-lacing

boots. But the real "chef's kiss"—Shanice's phrasing—is what she's done with my hair. It's studded with flowers in an homage and semi-recreation of the *Moonflower* cover.

The blooms themselves are these incredibly fragrant white galaxies. Some kind of jasmine. I poke one of them, and Shanice scolds, "You're already gonna lose some, don't start now."

Ari comes back into the green room—a staff lounge with some couches, a card table, and a coffee machine—and lets out a low "Whoa."

Lucía chirps, "Yeah, right? That's our fearless leader."

All together, we look pretty great. Ari's dressed in a sequined black suit, which is easily the flashiest thing I've ever seen them wear, paired with beat-up black Vans. Lucía got the prom directive in the opposite direction with a pale pink silk spaghetti-strap dress over a white collared shirt and black suede boots.

I close my eyes and take a deep breath. After sound check, which I was somehow only a few minutes late for, I'd holed up chatting with Melissa. We'd talked about my time in the Sunshowers marching band and the friends I made there, including my band members. A bit about my relationship with Cap, a section of conversation that made her type furiously.

The entire time, I was thinking about coming out. I kept rolling words around in my mouth but everything I thought about saying was so . . . forced. The kind of quote I immediately side-eye when I see it in profiles: *It's important for me to be this thing because*, why?

And here I am, about to do the same damn thing. I look at my reflection in Shanice's makeup mirror and practice in my head, *It's important that I'm trans because . . .*

I can't finish that sentence.

"Presenting, the fabulous Emo Ocean!" Cola's voice turns every head in the room. She's leading an entourage of people I've never met while wearing a minidress that looks like it's made entirely out of silver streamers. They blind me when she shimmies over. "Suwa, ya clean up good." She waves at Ari and Lucía, who both do a terrible job of hiding their open awe. "Who got these threads?"

"She did." I walk up to Shanice and wrap my arm around her shoulders; she freezes. "Cola, this is Shanice." I point out Devin, whose jaw drops, and Nat. "They're the reason I'm here today. I was thinking, maybe Shanice could sit in on our *BEATING HEART* shoot, throw some ideas into the mix."

Cola nods at Shanice, who wears a mixed expression of delight and terror. "You sure have a knack for surrounding yourself with talent."

Then she smiles cryptically. "You . . . good on the thing we discussed?"

I pretend my ears aren't burning when I whisper, "Can I talk to you for a second?" Instead of answering, Cola raises an eyebrow and walks out into the hallway.

I clear my throat. "I'm not coming out today."

Cola blinks slowly. "Hmm?"

"This is their big dance. I'd be stealing their thunder. It isn't right." In my head, I add, *For me*.

Cola puckers her lips, then sighs. "I don't think I made myself clear before. After today, your gender is something people are going to explicitly ask you about."

"And if I want to answer them, I will. But I don't have to." I push my shoulders back to make my chest feel broader. "I know there's more to me than that. *You* know there's more to me than that. So if the issue is that the label doesn't trust me, they think I need a capital-*R* Reason to be interesting, I'll prove them wrong. I can present and perform my art without framing it as an exact mirror.

"And besides—" My voice drops, but doesn't waver. "A little mystery keeps 'em coming back."

Cola regards me. I lift my chin and meet her gaze. Eventually she breaks eye contact. "Fine. Okay. I trust your trust in yourself." Then she holds her hand out. "Good luck."

"Thanks." We shake, and as I open the door to return to the green room, Cola whispers, "Break a leg, Memo." She winks before calling over and leaving with her entourage.

I'm still riding high on our exchange as I walk back to Ari, and Lucía, who immediately asks, "Is everything okay?"

"Yeah, I, um." After this weird interruption, I should pull us together. Everything I want to say sounds corny in my head, so I try for something more aloof. "I hope this'll be the first of many shows we play together. Thanks for trusting me with your time."

Lucía turns to Ari. "This is why I gave all the leadership talks in band." She puts her hand in the middle of our circle. "Emo Ocean, assemble! Three, two, one."

When I first joined marching band, I hated its overly cheery rituals, which included a lot of actual cheering. It was something I only got over when I found other people to cheer with.

Ari and I place our hands on top of Lucía's, and at the end of her count, we yell, "Sunshowers forever!"

"Now kids, we've got a special surprise for you tonight. His album, *The Sunshow*—I'm sorry, *The Moonflower Sessions*, is coming out in a few weeks, but he's playing some new songs tonight for the first time ever. Please welcome to the stage . . ."

When we walk out, I shield my eyes from the lights with my hand to scan the gym floor as a tide of screaming floods over us. Toward the back, Cap and Aya jump and holler. Sayo waves. I smile and wave back. But it's hard to keep my smile from faltering. I know I shouldn't have expected anyone else here today—

Lucía pinches me and points toward the side of the hall. "Hey. Surprise!"

They're all here. All of our friends are here, including:

Santi, who's wearing a bright lilac suit and a pair of silver Docs that catch the beams shining out from the illuminated disco balls. We lock eyes across the room, and I'm sure mine are as wide as his.

There's a moment at the end of *Mugen Glider* that always makes me cry. Marigold, plummeting to their death, sees the clouds part for a split second. The silhouette of their lover flashes above and beyond them; it's the first and last time they actually see each other in the span of the show. Marigold speaks for a long time, and their lover calls out in response. The cold whistle of wind drowns them both out, but if you break down the scene and clean up the audio, you can piece together Marigold's second-to-last sentence: *The worst thing about music is that other people get to hear it*. Repeating their lover's only spoken line.

There's no canon source confirming it, but after scrutinizing the scene a million times in both the sub and the dub, then poring over decades-old threads on obscure internet forums, I think I've gotten as close as possible to transcribing Marigold's final words: *But I've always been listening for you.*

I watch Santi's lips move, but with the lights in my eyes, I can't read them. I want to jump off of the makeshift stage and ask him how it feels to be caught in a miracle with me. How even after all this time, all these changes, we've found our way back to each other. Again.

We always do. But we can't keep counting on fate to bring us together. This time, I'm leaving nothing to chance.

I tear my eyes away from him. Melissa's on one side of the gymnasium, against the wall. Her eyes keep flitting between me and where my friends are gathered. Cola's on the other side, staring at her phone. I clear my throat into the mic, and then all eyes are on me.

"I hope you're having a good prom." The fountain of cheering that erupts makes me laugh. "I'm jealous, you all look so *beautiful.*"

Someone shouts, "Boy, *you're* beautiful!" aaand I'm blushing. "Thank you. That's only because of Shanice Young, Devin Bennett, and Nat Quan. When you're all celebrating super responsibly afterward, give them a toast."

I pause and gaze out over the crowd. A knot forms in my stomach at the memory of my baby self, convinced he'd never make it to this moment. "I'm humbled to be a part of your moment. It makes me truly, indescribably happy that everyone gets to enjoy tonight, no matter who they're with."

I pause before adding, "On that note." I look at Ari and Lucía, then back out toward my friends in the audience. "Whoever you're here with, I want you to take a second to tell them how much they mean to you. How special this night is, not because it's prom, but because you're with *them.* That's the memory. Uh, okay." I cough awkwardly in an attempt to keep my blush from growing, "I'll shut up now. Except to sing."

I can't see Santi clearly through the mirrored light, but I swear I hear his laugh cut through every other sound in the room.

Aya crushes me in a hug, and when she finally releases me, there's glitter on her face and petals scattered on her shoulder. "Look at our boy, a star!" I let her cup my face with her hands and almost knock her over when Cap grabs me, and he is not picking me up, he *is not*—

My feet are off the ground. Cap shouts, "Sunshowers forever!" As he puts me down, he whispers, "I'm so proud of you, son," and I shake my head furiously. As though any of this would've been possible without his support and literal shelter. "It's all you . . . Dad." He tears up, and I repeat, "It's all you."

He releases me when my bandmates enter the room. Lucía's breathless when she slides her arms around my and Ari's waists. "Wow. We're getting good at this."

"You were both perfect." I wiggle out of her hold and, I can't help myself, I poke her arm. "I know I only asked about playing with me through the Karma Demon show, but what if we went on tour together?"

Lucía gasps, and Ari grins even as they tease, "What, like anyone else will know how to deal with you? Also, Cola's manager reached out to us months ago. Keep up, band leader."

"You were all amazing!" Mira leaps onto Lucía's back. Feli and Octavian are right behind, and while they pile on Lucía, Reva loops a lei around Ari's neck before bringing them in for a deep kiss.

Someone behind me coos, "Aww."

I spin on my heel to greet Cola, who's here alone. She scans the rest of the room, and for a moment, international superstar Cola Carter looks kind of awkward, twirling the streamers on her dress and taking in someone else's postshow afterglow.

Cap's busy talking to my friends, so I wave Aya over. "Cola, I'd like you to meet Aya Malandro. My . . . aunt, kind of." Aya raises an eyebrow.

They shake hands. Is it just me, or does the energy in the room crackle? Cola legitimately sounds awestruck when she says, "Suwa, you never said you're related to *the* drummer from Horadorada. I listen to your band *allll* the time. If you ever do a reunion tour, I'm there."

Aya makes a surprised noise. "I don't think so; most people have forgotten about us. But thank you for the ego boost, and the royalties."

"I'm gonna post about the set you did on *Unplugged*. Which . . ." Cola bats her eyelashes. "You don't look like you've aged a day since then."

The energy in this interaction is getting weird, so I cut in, "Hey, my next meeting with Melissa is in three weeks? Right after *Moonflower* comes out?" Timed to the summer solstice.

"Hm? Yeah." She refocuses on me. "Uh, I don't know what's going on in your personal life right now, but I think someone's waiting to talk to you outside."

Cola might've said something else afterward, but I take off, flinging the door to the hallway open.

I hadn't really had a chance to steep in the fact that I'm back in my old high school, having a true-blue senior prom moment, even if it's belated. Some of the ceiling panel lights have been covered with colored cellophane, giving everything—the marble laminate floors and chipped paint lockers and SUNSHOWER SPIRIT banners—a dreamy, kaleidoscopic cast. The muffled bass from whatever the DJ's playing pulses in the background. *Nostalgia, ultra.* I sigh and run my hand through my hair. When I bring it back down, flowers rain gently around me.

I bite back a private laugh as I walk toward the trophy case between the boys' and girls' locker rooms. My body has shape-shifted through these halls literally, as hormones changed it, but also figuratively as I learned how to carry myself without shame, without fear. Now, striding past these reminders of the person I used to be, I feel like an intruder in my own memories. This is where it all began.

Actually. That's not true. I stop in front of the case.

Next to me, Santi glows pink. He murmurs, "You're here."

The expression on his face isn't legible through his reflection. "Yeah."

"No, I mean." Santi points at something inside the case. "You're *here*." I bend toward the glass, to where he's pointing, and my breath catches.

It's a trophy for "Exceptional Solo Performance" from the Southern California Band Association. There, engraved on the plaque: SUWA MOON, DE LONGPRE HIGH SCHOOL. I press my finger to the glass.

Santi drops his hand. "I'm sorry I bounced, this morning. I didn't . . . I don't want to make things more complicated for you, today and—yeah." He pauses to clear his throat. "You were incredible."

"You believed in me from the start. More than I believed in myself." I turn to him without meeting his eyes. I don't want to lie to either of us and act like what's between us will ever be simple. Even if I lived a more normal life, we'd still be vulnerable to all the forces in the world we can't control. But those were also the things that brought us together in the first place.

I force myself to look up. "I don't want to leave again without telling you exactly how I feel. We've always been at our best together. And you were always the best for me. Don't ever doubt that. But I want to be more than friends. Santi, I want to be your best friend, and I'll do whatever it takes to win you back again."

Santi stares at me for a long, almost uncomfortable beat. Then he pulls something out of his pocket. The envelope. He opens it and hands me what's inside.

It's a drawing, done in colored pencil, of palm trees and, in the background, the Hollywood sign. Every outline, every fill, drawn out in multiple colors. The sky's shaded so that the negative space becomes clouds. At the center of the drawing is a kid with their back to the viewer. They're holding a bass in their hands, its strap crossing their back.

My own hands start to tremble. "Santi . . ."

"Flip it over." My body isn't obeying me, so he turns the paper over in my hands, and we hold on to it together.

Hey Memo. I let out a weak laugh. His handwriting's so wobbly, like he'd written this in a rush, cramped letters slanting and sliding into each other.

> *Hey Memo. Right now we're not really talking but by the time you read this letter I'll have already visited you. I'm gonna get to LA and hand-deliver this apology. I check your profile every day so get back online okay? If you still don't wanna talk when I give this to you at least wait until I'm*

gone before you rip it up. But you don't seem like the kind of person who'd do that.

You're an artist also, so you probably get inspired by random stuff like I do. I was walking home from school and saw these crazy clouds in the sky, and the light was nuts, too. So here's a mash-up of my world and yours, maybe not your LA but like the idea of LA.

I keep listening to Exit Music. I'm so sorry about the leak, and everything. I miss you.

Your friend forever, Canti (btw

my real name's Santiago)

P.S. I know the drawing's kinda bad but one day I'll make something as good as your music, for you.

The breath I take fills my chest like a river that's been un-dammed. I pluck the paper and the envelope out of his hands and fold them into my jacket pocket.

"Whoa!" Santi almost stumbles when I take his hand in mine and drag him down the hall. Blue, green, gold, red, purple, then through the double doors into the gymnasium, where the DJ's playing something slow and syrupy.

I look out over the swaying bodies on the dance floor. Everyone seems so fearless here, laughing with and holding and kissing each other without looking over their shoulders. It feels like so much has changed in just a few years, both at De Longpre but also the wider culture. What would it have been like to grow up in a more tender, accepting world? I spent most of my life afraid of who I was. Even now, I'm still scared sometimes. But I was never as alone as I felt. No one's ever as alone as they might feel.

I pull Santi onto the dance floor and ring my arms across his shoulders. After a beat of hesitation, he slips his hands around my back. His mouth by my ear. "Hey. I think this might be the first time we've danced together."

I hiccup, and he pulls me closer to whisper, "Canti and Memo didn't think they'd have any time at all. And I can speak for Canti. He'd be furious if Santi and Suwa didn't try to figure this out."

He pulls back and places his palm against my cheek. "One more time. One more chance."

I try to pull together an equally sappy response, when my stomach growls loudly enough that Santi snickers. We untangle ourselves, and I punch him lightly in the arm. "Jackass." My voice full of fondness. "I haven't eaten anything today."

Santi grins. "Let's go. Cooking lesson number one. You gotta make your own meal."

I pretend to wilt into his arms, which makes him laugh. "Damn. All right, you're in luck. I know a guy who runs a BBQ tent in the lot a few blocks from the Metro station, let's get some food into you. He's got ribs, wings, the works."

Sounds like heaven. "Text the group chat, see if anyone else is down."

"Done." Santi sweeps his arm out as he bows. "After you, *best friend*." I bump his hip with mine, and we leave prom laughing, just two guys holding hands as we dip into the young night.

Track 19

"Before we call it quits, I'm sure you know but the *Moonflower* reviews have been uniformly breathless. Congratulations."

"Thank you." I'm running on about two hours of sleep from a long rehearsal the night before, and adjust my sunglasses. The sunlight streaming in from the rooftop greenhouse where we've been talking for the past hour is eye-shatteringly bright. I should've pushed this interview back.

"I know the songs might not feel as fresh to you as they are for listeners. But while I'm here . . ." Melissa peers down at her phone. "Is there anything you'd like to correct or explain on the record, about the record?"

I laugh a little too loudly. Melissa stifles her reaction and says neutrally, "I'd just like to point out, compared to how you were the first time we met, the Suwa I'm speaking to now seems much more relaxed. Lighter."

I lean back in my seat. I feel it, too. Maybe it's because of all the time I've been spending with my friends, now that my schedule's cleared up a bit post—album drop. There are only two weeks to go until the Karma Demon show, but when we can, we get together like old times, skating and clowning around, hanging out for hours. It feels good but also bittersweet, now that we have to schedule time to be together. But it's also pretty fun watching groups of younger kids, surly middle schoolers and true babies who haven't even finished losing their teeth, doing the same things we did back then.

Most nights, I'll go for a run, then hang out with Santi in person or over a video call, watching anime, playing video games. I help him write grant proposals for new murals. More than anything, we talk. About Tokyo, about Los Angeles; long, spiraling conversations that only end when one of us has to be somewhere else or we're both on the cusp of passing out.

Lately, he's been texting about a dog. A stray that's started hanging around the Woodshed. She pays everyone else no mind but runs up to him. "I've been walking and feeding her, and I took her to the vet yesterday, but she's not like, mine or anything." Big, dopey eyes. Tan, save for her black snout. When I asked him if he'd named her, he'd flushed before rambling, "I've, uh, been calling her Clover. Cause she kinda looks like Norio's dog, from *Mugen Glider.*"

It's cute, how bad he is at hiding his affection. My face grows hot; he's not the only one having trouble with that. Nobody asks what's going on between us, but I don't think it's for lack of evidence or curiosity.

Melissa clears her throat and draws me back to the present. I swirl the ice in my water. "I think . . . I've made my peace with what I was going through, and who I was when I wrote the songs." Or, at least, I've done all I can to prepare myself for the cognitive dissonance of touring an album about the breakup of a relationship I'm currently rebuilding. "Like, of course I'm relieved that this thing I pulled out of my heart resonates with other people. But that's not why I made it. That's not why I make music."

"Why *do* you make music?"

I blink slowly. Has she really not asked me this question before? Then Melissa clarifies, "You mentioned that you played guitar in church and trumpet in concert band growing up. Then you did marching band in high school while making other music, Emo Ocean music, on the side. You've talked a lot about your old band director, but it just occurred to me that you haven't mentioned any influences like that from your childhood. Did you pick these things up yourself, or did someone encourage you?"

"Weren't you about to call it quits?"

Melissa's mouth twitches into a smile. "You don't have to answer me."

I don't. But I take my sunglasses off and study the beads of condensation sliding down the lenses. A thousand tiny Suwas, caught in the droplets, stare back at me. "Is it all right if we change venues? There's . . . someplace I should show you. It's not far."

Melissa nods, and I take a deep breath before getting up from my seat. I'm not really sure where I'm going with this, except that I'm as close as I've ever been to understanding myself. And there's only one obvious thing left to confront.

My heart's in my throat as we walk down Wilshire a few blocks before turning off. The storefronts give way to houses and apartment buildings. Chain-link fences and cracked high sidewalks, aunties chattering and waving large plastic fans printed with H Mart ads and coquettish celebrities. Melissa watches me take in these surroundings, and she stops a second after I do in front of a small two-story house with a sparse lawn and a thick hibiscus bush. A large tree encroaches on one of the windows.

I point at that window. "If you're brave, you can grab on to that branch there. It doesn't look sturdy, but it'll hold while you plant your feet on the V between those two branches. There's a foothold on the other side of the trunk, a knot." My hand drops. "This . . . is where I lived for most of my life."

Melissa stops typing on her phone. I close my eyes, and when I open them again, there they are. The shadows of my younger self, of Sayo's younger self, descending down the tree. Their contours glow faintly and leave glimmering residue behind them, marking the paths of their many escapes. Sometimes they go down to Wilshire. Sometimes they head east toward the bus stops and Metro stations. Sometimes they settle on the front porch steps, heads leaning toward each other as they confer over how they're going to get out of there.

"My father met my mother at choir practice. He played guitar, and she sang." I close my eyes again, but I can't summon any memories of her voice, only Sayo's echo. "After she died, he stopped playing. But when I was six, seven, he caught me messing around with his old guitar and got me some books. He never taught me, but he didn't stop me from teaching myself.

"My relationship with my father's side of my family is actively hostile, or it would be, but I haven't spoken to them in years. My relationship with my father isn't good, but I'll never forget, even when . . . even when his family members were picking through every part of my life, questioning every part of my personhood, my father made sure they never touched my music stuff. He'd hide my bass, my laptop, my recording equipment. It doesn't excuse everything else that he did, but—"

One of the front curtains ripples. My fight-or-flight response is about to kick in when a scowling orange tabby emerges through the broken window screen, leaps onto the porch, and saunters up to us.

"Hi, Marigold." I reach down to scratch him, but he swipes at me. So defensive, but so bold, seeking affection on his own terms. He'd been like that even when he was a kitten, a tiny ball of orange fluff that my father had placed on the kitchen table, how many years ago.

"My father . . ." I catch my breath. "We had a huge fight the summer before senior year started. I told him I was going to audition for Cola, and it got brutal, as far as verbal fights go. I started living somewhere else, but we'd begun reconciling, kind of, before I left for Tokyo. I . . . haven't picked that up, since returning to Los Angeles. But maybe he'll understand, once he hears the music. If he chooses to listen. That I haven't come back home empty-handed."

I didn't ever think I'd be able to say anything like that sincerely. But I did. And emboldened by my own admission, I continue, "He held on to me, or the idea of me that 'worked' for his family, for most of my life. Violently, sometimes. But eventually he released his hold on me, and released himself from his own past. These days, I have a 'new' family made up of people who love me for who I am, who make me want to be better." I laugh softly. "*Moonflower*'s a breakup album, but it feels like it's about a different kind of breakup, now. A message to the ones who loved me enough to let me go."

"Your exit music." I stiffen. It's not public knowledge that I'm Memo—Cola agreed to keep that secret for me—but before I can question Melissa, she continues, "Like the opposite of entrance music. The music that plays when you have to leave." She studies the look on my face. "Am I close?"

She is, but there's still something missing. Melissa had asked me about my gender obliquely at the beginning of our meeting today. Once I demurred, she'd backed off. I'm not going to fold it in at the last minute. So when I say, "Close enough," Melissa responds, "Okay," with the affect of someone who knows they're being gently let down.

Marigold lays his body down on my feet. "I suppose I'm stuck here forever now."

Melissa examines my father's cat for a long time. Then she murmurs, "I understand it's more complicated than this, but . . . I'm sorry. About your father, and his family, which was yours."

"Isn't this what it's all about?" I can practically hear Cola warn, *Don't*. But I continue, "I'm here to share my story, the pain that's shaped me into someone interesting, and you're here to witness and regurgitate it for listeners. 'I suffer, thus I'm relatable. I'm real. You can see yourself in me.' But I didn't get into music so other people would feel, I don't know, reflected. Because I made music despite my own reflection, to make myself believe that what I saw in the mirror wasn't all that I was or could become. Things are turning out okay for me now, but they were bad for a long time. All you see now is the shiny stuff, but it gilds a lot of darkness. And I don't want anyone to go through what I did. I don't want to draw a connection between my upbringing and my art. No one should have to justify their art with their suffering."

Tears build, but don't fall. I don't realize how deeply I mean the words until I start taking deep, shuddering breaths to get my emotions under control.

Melissa meets and holds my gaze. It startles me when she asks, "Are you happy, now? As Emo Ocean?" She makes a show of turning off her recorder and putting her phone away. This isn't off-the-record unless we both say it is, but it's an informal gesture and a question behind a question. *As yourself?*

There's no reason I should try to answer honestly, but she has me in her crosshairs. No, that's a cop-out. It's not Melissa's fault that this is how the industry works. And during all of our times chatting, she's revealed herself to be dryly funny and truly kind. Within the artifice and the bullshit, I can insist on keeping some things real.

"I don't know if I am . . . happy. It's never been that easy for me to actually be happy." I pick at a cuticle and unroll the words slowly. "For so much of my life, I pretended I could do everything on my own. I didn't realize that keeping to myself like that could also hurt the people I love. So, I'm working on it. Being happy." I slip my hands into my jeans pockets and look at Melissa. "I'm closer than I've ever been. So now I'm just . . . gliding. Waiting to see where the music takes me. Without forgetting the memory of feeling so alone, and dreaming about the day I would finally be seen, and heard, and . . ."

I don't think I have anything left to say.

Melissa puts her hand out. "Thank you, Suwa. Really."

I shake with her. "You'll be at the show?"

Melissa nods. "I'll be there as a fan, and the mother of a few smaller fans." She tucks a strand of hair behind her ear, then smiles faintly.

I grin, which visibly throws her. "Please say hi, after."

Melissa's smile grows. "Perhaps." She pauses, her expression softening before saying, "Off the record, I'm not an expert, but you're doing a damn good job of figuring out what makes you happy."

She checks her phone. "This is perfect timing. I've got another interview to get to. You need a ride anywhere?" I shake my head. Melissa turns to wave as she walks back to where she's parked.

I wave back, then look down at my feet, which are still anchored by Marigold. But then he bolts up and pads down the sidewalk.

There's only one person he greets like that.

"Suwa?" My father drops the groceries in his arms. "I—I was expecting Sayo later, but . . ."

He keeps searching for words as I pick up his grocery bags and walk up to the porch. I hear him come up behind me, then the sound of Marigold slipping through the window screen. Keys jingle; the gate, then the door opens, and my father says, "I got it from here."

But I step inside. I take my shoes off, put on glittery slippers that must be Sayo's, and walk the groceries into a kitchen as spotless as it is crammed to the gills with pots, pans, and condiment jars with labels I can technically read but mostly can't understand. This is new. "You cook now?"

"Why are you here?" My father looks at me like I'm a ghost. And it's not like I'm not. I can't imagine myself fully in this space. But when I run my hands down the butcher-block counter, I picture Sayo slicing up scallions, hands stained red from gochugaru. That one time she tried to teach me how to debone a chicken and almost lost a fingertip for her trouble.

But I also picture my father, three months in to my return, slamming the door on his screaming brother. My father, five months in, playing Korean folk songs—often spliced with, inexplicably, birdsong—off of YouTube on the Sunday mornings we normally would've gone to church as he watered the plants that, over the years, have taken over the house. He's since gone back, but to a new congregation.

My father, a year in, calling me "son" for the first time. He'd looked surprised at himself afterward; to this day, I can still count the number of times he's done this on one hand.

My father, three and a half years in, handing me his coming-of-age hanbok.

And then, I left.

I open up one of the grocery bags. "What're you making tonight?"

"Jjajangmyeon." He pauses. "Sayo . . . is still the best."

I check my watch. Reva's doing a housewarming for her new apartment tonight, but I don't think I have anything on my schedule until then. "Let's see if two half-Moons can make one meal." He lets out a startled sound that, I only realize a beat later, was a laugh.

We certainly try. Something doesn't taste quite right, but I remember a time he would've rather starved than do "a woman's work." I wash the dishes as he feeds Marigold, who won't eat unless he's in my father's lap.

I linger by the sink, and finally answer his question from before. "I was in the area, doing an interview. About Emo Ocean. I'm actually going on tour soon." I watch a drop of water drip off of a newly washed plate and lightly *plink* into the dish tray.

"Oh." My father doesn't speak for another minute. Then

he says, "When you return to Los Angeles, I might not be here."

I whirl around so quickly that I almost lose my balance. "What?"

He shakes his head. "I've been talking with Sayo about selling the house. I offered it to her first, but she had a reaction that I suspect you'd have, too, of not wanting to . . . be surrounded by some of the memories in this place."

"Where would you go?" Did his family finally drive him out? My heart skips a beat. I truly never thought I'd ever feel this . . . not protective, but concerned about him.

"Not far, still California." For the first time in my life, I think I watch my father blush. "You remember Mrs. Kim from church? Her daughter, Jaehee, was in Sayo's class."

I know she's a widow. He continues, "She runs a small farm in the Bay Area now. But last year, she hurt her hip. Jaehee was around, but she's going to grad school soon, moving to Chicago. I offer help, with accounting, but also my green thumb." He half smiles, and it hits me. We're both finally moving on.

Then: "Suwa." My father's face becomes very serious. "I'm . . . I wish your mother could see you now."

On their own, my legs cross the kitchen, and my arms wrap around his shoulders. "Take care, Appa."

My father is eerily still at first, but then he pats me once, twice on the back before stiffly pulling away. "Sayo says you have a big show coming up." He hesitates before raising a fist in the air like a cheer and calling out, in a voice that shakes just a little, "Fighting!"

My heart feels like it's breaking when I look at him. Imagining what our relationship could've been. "I'm going to grab some stuff from my room. Anything that's left there before I leave, you can toss." My parting conversation with Melissa lingers in my mind, and I whisper, "Thank you for making music a part of my life."

He whispers back something that makes my eyes instantly tear, and I turn to walk up the stairs.

Even after I moved back to this house, I kept most of my personal effects at Cap's. But a lot of baby Suwa's stuff is here. The cool white glow of my Blue Bear lamp fills the room. I pick up some errant trinkets as I search for what I'm really looking for. And then, I find it.

On my old desk chair: the box that contains my father's hanbok. I tuck it under my arm. Pause. I rap my knuckles twice on the window that's all but obscured by branches, run my hand over the ruined frame, then make my way down the stairs. My father's on the phone with someone; he nods from the living room, smoke rising from the cigarette in his other hand, and I nod back before putting on my shoes.

Marigold butts my hands as I tie the laces. I ask him, "Hey. Do you like me or not?" He purrs, and out of nowhere, I let out a sob, then another, wiping my eyes with the back of my hand as I pass through the doors of that house.

Do I even know anyone who lives around here anymore? I take in the narrow streets, the golden lawns, the palm trees pinning the city into not the earth but the low, hazy blue of the sky. The world was always bigger than my world. I was always bigger than the outline that people who didn't even know me drew for me. But now I'm stretching my arms out and letting the wind lift me higher.

My phone buzzes. Whoops. I was supposed to meet Ari at the

Korean bakery in . . . negative five minutes. I quickly check my transit app. I won't be too late if I run for the next 728.

I sprint down a boulevard lined with precariously slim palms. Farther down a side street, two kids pass a soccer ball between them. Someone's dog barks at a group of skateboarders screwing around on the corner. These were the streets where, when Sayo and I were younger, all the neighborhood kids would run around, screaming in delight. The purest kind of scream, where your chest and your lungs and your ribs seem to disappear and it's just energy blazing out of your heart. *I'm here. I'm alive.*

I'm here. I'm alive. I catch the rapid bus right before it pulls away, and leave the past behind.

Track 20

"I'm done. I'm finished." I rest my palms on my thighs and pant, sweat dripping into my eyes and down the back of my neck. "Carry me home."

"We're almost there." Santi grins and keeps lying. "You're doing great! What did that one review say?" He pulls out his phone and searches for ammunition. "Here we go. 'You really get the sense that Moon lives a life of quiet intensity until, brilliantly, he explodes.' Now's the time to go nitro."

I groan. Everybody keeps quoting *Moonflower* reviews to me like I haven't obsessively read all of them, a practice that Cola scoffs at—"Trust me, it'll get old." But for now, everything is strange and new. A few days ago at a coffee place around the Woodshed, some incoming De Longpre seniors asked me for a photo and an autograph. Interviews I did for zines and smaller magazines have been dropping, and I came off just the right amount of smart and fun. And yesterday, my first music video went live. It's a simple concept—just me singing to the camera, surrounded by some beautiful animation done by a friend of Sayo's—but the reception's been good enough that the label's promised me a way bigger budget for my next one.

There's less than a week to go until the Karma Demon show. I just got my amended passport back, and along with my name and sex, I finally changed my birthday. Shit. That's coming up soon. I'm in the final stretch of my true teenage years, though I suspect I won't feel like a real adult for a long time.

Santi kicks my foot, which makes Clover come over to me and lick my leg. I scratch behind her ears and grumble, "Do you want to carry me back? Can I ride you like a little horse?" She sits and barks sharply. Even the dog's telling me to get it together.

"You're already doing way better than when we first started. C'mon." Santi jogs in place, his cross dancing on the neckline of his T-shirt. "I'll make you dinner if you finish this last mile with me."

. . . That'll work. I take a few deep breaths and ignore the screaming in my lungs. When the crosswalk light turns green, we take off, Clover leading the pack.

Even just one month of running has already started to change me. My body still aches afterward, but my steps are lighter, bouncier. I like that moment when both feet are, however briefly, off the ground. During rehearsals, I have more energy and feel less drained afterward. It also doesn't hurt that I'm getting some real muscle definition on my legs, and not just because Santi's eyes have been lingering on them more.

"Make sure you keep this up. When you're on tour." Santi doesn't sound out of breath at all. "That way we don't have to start from zero when you come back."

I wheeze; how do people talk when they run? "What are you, my coach? I'm not going to make nationals this year, or ever."

"Ha." Santi abruptly stops. Both Clover and I keep running, then turn back toward him.

"Suwa." He hesitates before placing his hand on my arm. "It's easy to coast on beginner gains. But I know you know that. . . . The new doesn't stay new."

He's not talking about running anymore. I put my hand on top of his. "I know."

We haven't really talked about what happens next. It's not like, at least for my part, I'm actively avoiding the subject. My departure creeps closer and closer. All the time in the world still wouldn't be enough. But instead of scaring me, that fact soothes me. I'll always want to come home.

Santi clears his throat, but before he can say anything else, a group of skateboarders zooms past us on the street. One of them loudly calls out, "Gaaaay," but with a knowing wink.

"Um." Santi's bright red, and I don't think it's from the running. "If you can beat me home, I'll also let you pick what I make."

"You were going to let me do that anyway." I tap into my last reserves of energy and take off sprinting. Behind me, Clover barks and Santi yells in surprise; she probably started pulling him. I laugh even though my lungs are burning, and don't look back. I know that he'll catch up.

"Five-minute warning!" Sayo claps her hands. "Ready for it?"

I pace, listening to the screams die down at the end of a song. This roster's no joke. The group finishing up has, according to the backstage whispers, landed the opening gig for Halsey's next tour and a huge fashion campaign.

"Oooh, you look good, boy." Cola shoots me a thumbs-up as she walks by. Phone pressed to her face. "Yeah, I'm still here."

One of the marabou feathers on her jacket floats off and lands whimsically on Ari's collar. They turn to me and whisper, "She's shedding."

I bite back a laugh. Ari and Lucía have met Cola a few more times and no longer are so starstruck around her. We'll all have plenty of time to get to know each other better on tour.

There's a lot I have to do and not enough time before that begins. But I'll have to make do.

I sigh and pull at my pants. They're super cute, but I'm pretty sure someone's going to have to cut me out of them by the end of the night. Sayo notices my fidgeting but takes it for discomfort. "You're gonna be fine, kid. Hey—gimme your phone."

I act aloof as I pass it over, but I do want a shot to remember this. We look like—I snort as I think this through—anime Americans. Lucía's got her hair up in a high ponytail, wearing a deep-blue slip dress with white go-go boots. Ari's wearing a ruby-red suit and a bolo tie. Draping themselves over my shoulders, my bandmates put up peace signs, so I do, too.

"Wow, no smiles, huh?" Sayo sucks on her cheek as she taps the screen. "Caption ideas, go."

Ari deadpans, "Your best American teens," which makes Sayo gasp, "Perfect."

I check my watch. Here we go. I put my hand out and wait for Ari and Lucía to place their hands on top of mine for our now-regular preshow ritual. "We made it here. Let's see how much further we can go. Three, two"—I'm grinning so hard, my cheeks hurt—"one."

We chant at the same time, "Sunshowers forever!" as the band that went on before us files in. The singer grins and waves before calling out, "It's amazing energy out there. You're gonna kick ass."

I watch from stage left as Cola introduces us. It's such a Los Angeles thing, to have a venue in a famous cemetery. I shield my eyes. Sitting toward the front, Mira, Octavian, Feli, and Reva cup their hands around their mouths and scream something I can't understand.

Santi puts his fingers into his mouth to wolf-whistle. I slap my cheeks so I can blame my rapidly reddening face on that.

"—Emo Ocean!" Cola exits off the other side of the stage.

We'd passed on our specs to the setup team before, but our sound check was hours ago. I wiggle my limbs to get my blood flowing. Someone in the crowd screams, "Get it, boy!" and I laugh shyly before stepping up to the mic. "Uh, hello, Los Angeles." My delivery's shaky, but the cheering that erupts across the cemetery banishes my remaining nerves.

I laugh again, unselfconsciously this time, riding a giddy updraft of chaotic, fluttery emotion. The wind's at my back. *So this is how it starts.*

I look out over the living and the dead and take a deep breath. "My name is Suwa Moon, but you can call me Emo Ocean. I'd like to take a moment and say thank you to the city I call home. To the people who raised me and who've had my back through everything.

"That includes you." I smile and mean it. "All of you. Thanks for listening."

I bow curtly, then turn my body so I'm looking at my bandmates. "Thank you, too. Now"—I adjust the strap of my bass—"just like practice."

The songs seem to flow out of us. By the time we're at the end of the set, I barely remember having played at all. Every time I check in with my bandmates, they're lost in their own grooves, but we're synced perfectly. I can't stop laughing. As good as I think we sound now, I can't imagine how killer we're going to be once we've got real road-tested experience under our belts.

"Well. All good things come to an end." I take a swig of water. Some misses my mouth, and I wipe it off with the back of my hand. "We're going to close with a song you might already know, from years ago, but . . ."

I check in with myself. The timing's right. Everything's finally right. "I think, I'd like to share the story behind it now."

It takes me no time to find Santi in the crowd again. We lock eyes. My implied request hangs in the air, and when he nods, I clear my throat.

"When I was eleven, I met someone on the internet. We didn't know each other's names, faces. Anything 'real' about the other. But we liked the same things. We talked, all the time, and over time, we became friends. Best friends."

I look up toward the light-polluted sky. There's a perfect full moon out tonight. "I know things are so much more complicated now. But back then, it was . . . It felt like magic. We both knew we'd hit upon something true. Something real. And despite all the obvious barriers, I fell in love with him."

From behind me, I hear Ari go, "Whoa."

"My bandmates think this song is a cover. But . . . I'm Memo, and I wrote 'Exit Music' about this relationship. About coming out to him, as a boy, just like him, and both yearning for but also shying away from the chance to meet him in real life.

"A lot happened, between then and when we first met. Between when we first met and now, but . . . he's in the audience tonight."

I laugh. "Thanks for being here, Baby."

The gasps in the crowd soon turn into full-on applause. I can't keep my self-satisfied smile to myself. "This is our last song for the night. Thank you all, again." I studiously avoid looking at my friends in the crowd.

When we finish, I bow for the final time and leave the stage, and I know this is the beginning of the next, better but not best, chapter of my life.

"I cannot believe the *nerve* of you two."

"This is straight out of a Wattpad fic."

"You little shits, how could you not have told anybody?!"

Our friends swarm us backstage. My face hurts from being pinched and jabbed so much, and I pull away from Mira. "Why aren't you mobbing Santi? He knew, too."

Santi shakes his head furiously, which makes the strap of his overalls fall off his shoulder. He's not wearing a shirt under it, and I do my best not to stare at the plane of his bare chest. "I got my share already. It's your turn."

Lucía groans. "Why can't any of my internet friends be sensitive, artistic hunks or sexy, brooding geniuses?"

"Whoa, I'm not a hunk—"

"I don't *brood*—"

Everyone stops talking when Cola walks over. She's about to go on, and even I can't tear my eyes away from her in that outfit: a latex skirt, thigh-high lace-up boots, and a shirt that hasn't decided if it's a blouse or a bra. Her nails are natural save for a dab of gold glitter on her right index finger, which she points at me. "*That's* how you put on a show. Well done, Suwa. I'm looking forward to hearing that on the regular."

"I hope you don't expect me to come out every night."

Cola rolls her eyes. "Ha-ha. Oh, and nice jacket. What is that? Phoebe-era Céline?"

I laugh softly. "No, it's . . . it was my father's. He wore it when he became a man." I straighten my posture, like I'm on the field at the start of a marching show. It's a little big on me, but I'm sure I'll grow into it.

She observes me for a moment, her mouth pulled into that cryptic smile of hers. Only when her manager coughs loudly does Cola snap back into character. "Mm. This part never gets old." She daps my shoulder as she walks past me. "Enjoy the eye of the storm. I'll see you in New York."

I watch Cola's set from the side of the stage. I've watched live footage of her shows before, but I like to think that I set the bar high, so she went higher. But I have a long way to go before I can match her physicality, the effortless way she leaps, lunges, and prowls the stage that's been her second home for so long.

I wonder how she feels about creating the wave instead of riding it, like she did as a reporter. I wonder if I'll ever get used to the sensation of waves, the moment they crest right above you, hovering on the edge between the sea and the sky, reminding you how small you are compared to the big blue beyonds. Inspiring the kinds of feelings that used to strike mortal fear into my heart, and not just because I've almost drowned.

But I have a body that's capable of floating. That can hold a breath and break through the surface. To no one in particular, I mutter, "I need to learn how to swim."

"Want me to teach you?" Santi's hand reaches for mine. "I was a lifeguard for a couple weeks last summer." Seriously, what *didn't* he do?

We're still holding hands when we meet up with Cap, Aya, and Sayo at a restaurant a few blocks from the venue. Santi releases mine as Sayo slams into me.

"My baby brother!" She laughs against my ear. "I'm so fucking proud of you, Suwa."

"I'm pretty proud of me, too." I let out a sharp laugh at the enormous bouquet she's holding. "Jesus. Did you buy out the florist, or what?"

Sayo's smile softens. "They're from . . . Appa. I already sent him a few videos. I don't know if he actually watched them, but, well."

She passes me the bouquet. I cradle it in my arms. The flowers are intensely fragrant, and I press them to my face.

FLASH. Santi goes, "Shit," and laughs nervously. "Sorry, I didn't realize that was on."

Later that night, with the flowers arranged in a stock pot on my nightstand—the bouquet was too big for any of the vases—I scroll through reviews of the show, then eventually flip onto social media. Most of my friends have posted videos or photos of Emo Ocean onstage.

Except Santi. He's posted the photo of me with the flowers up to my face, my eyes closed but my lips curved into a smile that's equal parts exhausted and easy.

His caption: *did yall get the memo*.

Track 21

"And when he calls out, 'Thanks for being here, baby,' blushing under the hot lights, it would've been impossible not to root for him. Not just the man on the stage, but the boy who emerged from the darkness of his childhood into the radiance of love." Ari looks up from their copy of *BEATING HEART*, one of twenty stuffed into Mira's backpack, and begins to slow-clap. "Congrats, Suwa. This is great. She makes you sound like the boy Joan of Arc of the music industry. Johan of Arc?"

"Mm, but Joan of Arc is like, an OG genderfuck pioneer." Mira stops to cheer as Lucía lands a boardslide. "Freshman year, Suwa turned me on to, what's the guy's name again, who wrote about gay pagans and Christianity? Archibald Evans?"

"Arthur. Arthur Evans, *Witchcraft and the Gay Counterculture*." My phone buzzes. A text from Nat. We only got to hang out a handful of times, but he's opened up a lot since our first Gender Club meeting. We've been texting a lot about gender theory and trans history, fields of interest he hopes to intersect with studying law. He's so well-read and perceptive; I'd be fond of him just based on his personality, but I admit, I've started treating him almost like a little brother.

I text, You should read Arthur Evans to him, then sigh wearily at Ari. "Enough." Most of the piece went where I thought it would. A little more industry shit-talking than the label liked when we debriefed about it. Later Cola texted me a photo from the meeting of my obviously bored expression, followed by Gotta work on your poker face ^^;;.

What I'm still wrapping my head around are the details Melissa's written about my time in high school. She'd interviewed Ari and Lucía; and Sayo, Cap, and Aya copped to having answered some of her impromptu questions during the Karma Demon show. Yet I have a suspicion Melissa did a lot of legwork on her own. She only mentions Santi briefly, about that first Woodshed mural, but he—or rather, the specter of him—hovers over the story attached to my cover.

My cover. What none of us, Cola included, had expected was that *BEATING HEART* would release the issue with five different covers, instead of just her. I almost fainted when I opened up my comp copy and saw *my own face* under the logo of a magazine I've loved since I was a kid.

Each Karma Demon artist has their own epithet. COLA CARTER, THE MASTERMIND. MAUI COVENANT, THE NEW GUARD. And, splashed over a photo of me wearing a daisy-stitch, daisy-patterned sweater, winking in front of a trellis covered in morning glories that match my freshly dyed hair: EMO OCEAN, THE BABY. The only person who'd had a stronger reaction than I did was Santi, who'd laughed so hard he started crying.

"Ay." Feli pieces the five covers together in a pentagram formation and slaps the ground. "You got the Exodia treatment."

Lucía asks, "What's Exodia?"

Sitting next to me, Santi mutters, "Oh, this is gonna be good."

As much as I too want to hear Feli's take on the *Yu-Gi-Oh!* franchise, I get up and stretch as Reva calls for me at the other side of the skate park: "Suwa! Think you can beat that?"

Skateboarding is just like riding a bike, maybe. I push off and ollie onto the edge of one of the raised rails, but I don't have enough momentum to follow through. I brace myself for the fall, which doesn't make it hurt less, but that's what the wrist guards are for. A gift from Sayo, who'd said, "If you break any bones before you go on tour, I'll show Santi your old poetry blog," a threat that made my blood run cold.

I set a reminder on my phone: *reset PW to erase evidence of shame*.

"I know you're not going to listen to me, but I *reeeally* don't think you should be skating with this little light." Octavian checks his watch. "Uh, y'all know it's almost three?"

"Ah, c'mon, Prof. Who else is out this late?" Feli pulls his phone out. His flash briefly illuminates the skate park as he calls out, "Pose, bitches."

Of course, that's when a beam cuts through the darkness. "Hello?" A voice by the gate—what the hell is this, the neighborhood watch? "The park closed at sunset, hello?"

Reflexes honed by a combination of frequent trespassing and team sports, we scatter, climbing over the fence around the skate park before dropping down and splitting up. Santi and I crouch behind someone's car. We press together, skin sticking to skin in the thick summer night, for what feels like a thousand years or maybe only five minutes after the flashlight blinks off.

Once the coast seems clear, Santi nudges me with his elbow. "Hey. I'm hot."

I smirk. "Tell me how you really feel."

"No, I was thinking of cooling off." He leans closer to me. "Why don't we take a dip in the Stoner Park pool?"

I roll my eyes. "It's going to be freezing." The last syllable isn't out of my mouth yet when Santi gets up and scales the fence around the pool. It's only when he drops onto the other side that I give up and follow his lead.

When I touch down, he whistles quietly. "This place has a slide? Lucky-ass kids."

We walk over to the shallow end. I cross my arms and glare at the water.

Santi's reflection appears next to mine. "Is today the day Suwa Moon learns to swim?"

I frown sharply. "I don't have a suit."

Santi grabs a towel off of the lifeguard chair. "I know you don't shower with your clothes on." Before I can respond to him, he kicks off his shoes and strips off his clothes before walking over and dropping into the deep end.

"Santi!" He stays under for a beat, but when he pops back up, he shakes his head like a dog. With only the waning moon and a streetlight a block away for illumination, I can barely see him, but I can hear the grin in his voice when he calls out, "Your turn, jagi. It feels pretty good."

I look down at the slivers of silvery reflection. The reasonable part of my brain tells me not to get in: for starters, the pool will definitely be cold. And, I feel a little self-conscious about stripping naked in front of my ex-boyfriend for the first time in a while. And maybe there's a part of me that's just scared of the water.

But then I think about the fact that I'm leaving in less than a week. The day after my real birthday, in fact. One blink, I'll be gone again. So I shed layer after layer, grateful for the low light, then take a deep breath, walk up to the edge, and submerge.

It's fucking cold. I break the surface and gasp, limbs flailing even though my feet touch the floor. In between my gasps, I hear Santi laugh, and I hiss, "I hate you."

"No, you don't." He flips onto his back and slowly kicks his way across the pool. Show-off.

"Are you going to teach me, or what?" The question was meant to be sarcastic, but it comes out embarrassingly sincere.

Santi rights himself and swims up to me. When his hair's wet, it looks longer, and for a second we're in high school again, just two tall children splashing around in the shallow end.

"Okay. Lie down."

"What?"

"Try to lie down on your back. Don't worry about going under. I got you."

I take a deep breath, then push my feet off the bottom of the pool. After my body registers the lift, I let myself tilt backward. Water rushes around my face and for a moment, my chest tightens, but then Santi's hands are on my back, and I float.

"Remember this feeling." His face hovers an inch above mine. Then he steps away.

The instant his hands leave my body, I sink. I start thrashing, and then his hands are back. "Y'know that episode of *Adventure Time*, when PB and Marcy have to find the witch who stole Marcy's stuffie? It's that trap. You can't fight to float. You have to free your fear and trust yourself."

I mutter, "Wow, deep." Santi shakes his head, then releases me again. I briefly panic as water laps up to the edge of my vision, but right before the fear sets in, I have an epiphany. Imagine the water is wind. I'm a kite, and I have to let the invisible current carry me.

I stop actively fighting that sinking feeling, and let it happen. Santi whispers, "You're floating."

I whisper back, "No, I'm flying."

A few minutes later, I'm breathing raggedly. My strokes are rough and choppy compared to Santi's, but I'm swimming after all. One lap across the pool. Then the adrenaline leaves my body, and I suddenly find myself colder than ever. "I—I think I need to get out, n-now."

After we're both toweled off and back in our clothes, I remember, "Shit. Prof was my ride over here."

"You gotta be up early or anything?"

I stare at Santi's revised outfit—he's tucked his tank top into his shorts pocket, so he's just wearing a leather jacket over his bare chest—and he drawls, "It's a new look, for the culture."

I pinch myself and answer him. "I . . . don't have anything planned for tomorrow. Besides sleeping in as long as I can."

"Do you want a change of scenery?" Santi looks away from me as he asks the question.

My pulse quickens. "Oh?"

He tilts his head toward the street. "You trust me?"

"You know I do."

We hop the fence again. I trail Santi for a few blocks, then catch the helmet he tosses at me before sliding it on and slipping onto his motorcycle behind him. He's stuck the Agumon bobblehead that used to live in Aya's car onto his dashboard. Adorable.

Santi turns his key in the ignition. It doesn't work. He tries again, then again. "What the hell? This has never happened before."

I take the key out of his hands and under my breath, sing part of the first *Cardcaptor Sakura* opening theme song. Then I kiss the flat of the metal and hand it back to him. Santi fixes me with a look that teeters between bemused and something that makes the corners of his mouth turn down, before he says, "Let's see if we still got the magic."

The bike starts. I tighten my arms around him, and then every other sensation is drowned out by my ride rumbling to life between my legs.

Santi blazes his way through west LA. Even though I dried off, I'm freezing by the time he pulls to the side of the road. It's only as I'm dismounting that I realize I have no idea where I am. But the deft way Santi undoes the padlock on the door of whatever he's so eager to show me signals that he comes here often.

The door creaks, sheet metal rubbing against the wheel tracks. "Long story short . . ." He steps in, and I scurry into the noticeably warmer space. "A friend of Aya's got a job up north and left her studio to me. I should've cleaned, watch your step." He pulls on a chain, and a single bare lightbulb sputters to life.

When he said studio, he meant *studio*. It's a pretty small room already, but it feels extra crowded because of the tubes of paint and stencils littering the floor and the cramped shelves. Paper, everywhere; I recognize what look like mural sketches scattered throughout. There's a pillow and a blanket thrown onto a beat-up futon. Above that, an open window with a speaker and a lighter resting on the sill.

But the main occupants of the room are canvases, stacked

against the walls and propped against the shelves. Some of them are in a style I don't recognize, and the others are unmistakably Santi's. An apron drapes over an easel in the center.

Santi immediately strips off his clothes again, save his boxers. "I don't know about you, but my clothes are still pretty wet. You should let them air out overnight." He turns around, hands out in front of him, his eyes wide. "If you wanna crash. No pressure, really." High summer freckles so bold against his blush.

For the second time tonight, I strip down. Under real light, I keep my binder and briefs on. It feels weird to walk around with bare feet and no slippers, until Santi tosses me a pair. I study the printed design; it's the *King of the Hill* cast drawn as Sailor Scouts. Where does he find this stuff?

Santi reaches over for the pack of cigarettes resting on the easel. I'm genuinely surprised when he throws them into the trash can.

He rubs the back of his head with hand. "I've been trying to quit. Well, it's more like . . . I don't remember why I started." Santi chews over what he says next. "I know it's not your birthday yet, but . . . would you like your gift?"

I take a seat on the futon and rest my heels on the metal frame. "Um. Sure. Do you want me to . . ." I close my eyes.

"Yeah, that's good. Just, hold on." Loud clattering. Santi curses under his breath, then the sound of wood shuffling against the concrete floor. When he says, "Open them," I do.

It's me. It's me, and I'm laughing, doubled over at a joke lost to time. But I'm also holding a marigold in my hands, watching it dissolve into the wind. And I'm also standing with my back toward Santi, slanting light intersecting with the stripes on my shirt. And I'm also playing my bass, mouth frozen in a shout as

I leap, forever suspended above the stage—a shot from when I played Heaven's Not Enough.

Santi's painted an impossible portrait. An assemblage of Su-was, caught and pinned to the canvas, stacked and filtered and warped on top of each other until it's difficult to tell where parts of me begin and end. It's unsettling and then overwhelmingly stirring.

"I know you're kinda picky about photos of yourself. Which is totally—I get it, I just thought . . ." Santi's voice wavers.

I walk up to the canvas and reach a finger out. Its point hovers right above the rugged landscape of paint layers. I don't dare touch. I don't dare laugh, but it's so sweet and funny and well-meaning, the disparity between his low-key demeanor, down-playing his style and skill, and the dramatic, delirious scope of his work.

My voice cracks. "Thank you."

Santi shifts from foot to foot, hands behind his back. There's shyness, and something else I can't place, in his voice when he says, "This was going to be your Christmas present. Back then." He turns his body so now we're both facing the painting. "But I never got the chance to give it to you, so I held on to it. Kept adding to it. This part in the corner, I haven't actually finished yet. After it's signed sealed delivered, it's yours."

Santi adds softly, "When I saw the footage from your show at Heaven's Not Enough, that's when I knew. That you were gonna make it."

Our hands reach for each other's at the same time.

I examine the painting closer as the reality of the next year and more sets in. "Santi, I'm leaving again. My life is going to be me, leaving. Over and over."

His hold tightens. "I know. But something's different, Suwa." He turns his head toward me, and I meet his eyes. "I think you feel it, too."

I think I do. "It's not a promise."

His other hand reaches up to stroke my cheek. "Not a promise."

"But not *not* a promise." I don't let myself turn the sentence into a question. We'll either work it out, or we won't. But it's not all-or-nothing. Like he said, it's something different.

Santi nods, then releases me and reaches under his futon. When he shows me the joint, I scoff, "Seriously?"

"Uh, I saw you do like, a ten-second bong rip at Reva's party." He grabs the lighter off the sill and sparks the end, then takes a seat on the edge of the frame. Santi's face flickers into focus as he pulls from the joint and then he crooks his finger at me. "C'mon, best lungs in the band."

"That still doesn't make any sense." But I close the gap between our faces and part my lips. Eyes closed as he places his mouth just over mine and breathes out, letting the damp heat of the smoke, of him, flood over me.

He takes another drag. This time, when he breathes out, I meet his lips with mine.

Santi's not my boyfriend. He's my boy best friend. That's what I repeat to myself as we kiss, passing smoke until our lips are parting with every breath, every gasp, every moan as he pulls me into his lap, then flips us over so he's straddling me.

When he turns on the window speaker and fiddles with his phone—something both coy and heady drifts down over us—I tease, "Wow, really setting the mood."

He murmurs, "Would've been too on the nose to play one of

your songs," and I vacillate between pushing him off of me or burying my face into the futon. In the end, I do both, and Santi laughs so loudly that the walls ring with the echo.

Even though we were just naked around each other, we're both visibly nervous as we skim off our final layers. I chew my lip before pulling my binder up and over my shoulders. I've only done this for—with—him. So why am I blushing? I've been here before. Santi's been here before.

My body sure remembers him. But the disaster of our last attempt at this kind of intimacy is fresh in my mind. I try not to let my impatience for a rewrite show as he takes forever and a half to drink me in. Maybe he's applying his artist's eye to the contours of my body and his body and the new forms they make when they meet, which have changed in the time we've been apart and will continue to change.

I finally get to run my finger down the marigold on his ribs. Santi touches his cross and shudders, "God."

Then he reaches for me, and I surrender.

Track 22

"Sorry we're late!"

Sunlight spills through the doorway as Aya drops a small mountain of groceries at her feet. I start to pick up a few bags to bring them into the kitchen, but she shoos me. "Go, go. We'll see you tonight."

I step out into the afternoon glare, and there he is. Santi holds on to Clover as she whines to greet me. "Yo. Lead the way, Baby." I groan, and he laughs as he slips his free hand around my waist. "What? That's your official *BEATING HEART* nickname, I don't make the rules."

It's almost time. I'm leaving early tomorrow morning for New York, and then tour starts in earnest. But before tonight's preemptive birthday and farewell dinner, I'm checking something off of my Los Angeles bucket list: walking east through the city down Sunset's strange slide.

Luckily, I've got someone along for the ride. I look up at Santi, singing one of the many songs he's made up for Clover. He's planning on formally adopting her once he finds his own place, but I've caught Cap feeding her fruit in the Woodshed kitchen.

We start and immediately make a series of detours. Steamed
sticky rice wraps at that one Thai dessert shop. A pit stop at
Skylight to browse the magazine section, where Santi places my
BEATING HEART issues in front of the other ones. As we continue on, Santi points out tags and murals he likes. He takes a
picture of the marquee on the Echo; Aya's started working with
a few bands as a producer, and one of them is playing there next
weekend.

We make several more stops for food. Tacos from a truck that
brings out a plate for Clover. Gushing slices of mango covered in
Tajín and lime juice from a sidewalk vendor. We go up Alameda
Street to get aguas frescas, then set a course for our destination as
the sun's light begins to wane.

At this point, our phones start buzzing. The new fam
chat—me, Santi, Sayo, Aya, and Cap—comes alive as the other
three members coordinate tonight's logistics. The friend chat
starts popping off, too; Octavian's driving all the way over from
Palms with Reva in tow, and she's live-texting his frustration with
traffic. By the time we make our way to the night's venue, an
open courtyard in a building one of Aya's friends lives in, the sun's
not quite set, hanging over the horizon like a runny yolk.

I'd insisted on something low-key, and somehow, the version
of how I want something to go in my head matches up with the
vision in front of me. There's a long table covered in Daiso table-
cloths and mismatched silverware purloined from the building's
communal kitchen. Aya insists I don't lift a finger, so I focus my
energy on putting together a playlist. Yellow Magic Orchestra,
Shin Hae-chul, Faye Wong—it just so happens that these are all
artists on the vision board for LP 2.

Around me, the people I love move with the natural choreography of camaraderie. Mira nearly trips Octavian while they're hanging up lanterns. Feli, Lucía, and Reva dart in and out of the kitchen to grab last-minute things for the food and bring finished dishes out. Ari and Cap set up chairs, and Sayo and Santi help Aya finish up the cooking.

When we sit down to eat, Aya says grace in Spanish. I don't want to incite waterworks, so I've forbidden toasts. Naturally, everyone ignores my directive. At some point, Cap has to leave the table, he's crying so hard. But once we start eating, the mood is bright.

Boiled fish and creamy tofu swimming in a blistering pool of chiles and Sichuan peppercorns. Obscenely lustrous honey and gochujang-glazed wings. Whole roasted corn drenched in scallion butter and crema and drizzled with El Chilerito. Aya's "special fusion" sopa de fideo, made with cumin-spiced lamb and moringa leaves and moqua. Japchae laced with slivers of pickled vegetables and mushrooms, and, of course, bowls of glistening white rice and hijiki rice, grains studded with seaweed and edamame.

I swear I don't have room for dessert until Aya brings it out. Crispy fish-shaped pastries filled with (she talks through the options) red bean, taro, or egg-custard paste. Santi somehow eats five on his own—he's always had a sweet tooth, and based on the way she scarfs down the scraps he passes her, Clover does, too. Afterward, there's a round of coffee and tea, along with fried dough puffs served with ube jam and pandan-flavored coconut butter.

"I. Am. Going. To. Explode!" Mira holds her plate up reverently. "That's it, I'm dropping out and going to culinary school." She, Octavian, Feli, and Reva rank local restaurants while they clear dishes. Ari, Lucía, and Sayo split a bottle of wine as they take down lights and take care of the trash; I can tell Ari's being nice, listening to the other two complain about dating, but when I mouth, *Need help?* they shake their head and mouth back, *I'll live.*

I get up to help Aya bring some platters into the kitchen, but she actually slaps my hand away. "No. Santi." She points at him. "Go do your thing. Cap picked up that dog bed you pointed out at Echo Bark, we'll bring la perrita home." Santi's face lights up, and he sweeps her into a hug. She whispers something in his ear; they both look at me before picking up their conversation in low tones.

Cap steps up next to me. "One more night." He ruffles my hair. "I know you'll be back, but I'm gonna miss you, kid."

"You won't even notice that I'm gone." The lie hangs in the air.

"I'm not saying I'll be counting down to your LA dates, but . . . make sure you eat enough, and good stuff, okay? Don't try to tough it out, if the difference is a couple of bucks. I haven't forgotten what I used to eat in the service, but I wasn't a *rock star* on the road." Cap pauses before continuing, "Take it easy. Aya's been regaling me with stories."

I nudge him with my elbow. "I was up to no good even when I stayed with you. I'll be okay."

Cap frowns. "Is that so? Well, Suwa, I'm serious. You have a lot of people waiting for you to come home."

"I know." I rest my head against his shoulder. "I love you, Dad."

"I love you, too." Cap lets out an "Oh!" when Aya waves at him. He points toward the doorway. "This is the part where I let you go."

Santi's put on a sweatshirt, which I recognize as one of Cap's,

printed with the cover of Nick Drake's *Pink Moon*. He slings a
fanny pack over his shoulder so it hangs across his chest, then
tosses me another sweatshirt; it's the EVA one I'd gifted him for
Christmas years ago. I try not to obviously breathe in his smell
as I pull it on and then I hug everyone goodbye for the night,
and beyond.

We walk through Little Tokyo on our way to wherever we're
going. Nostalgia washes over me in waves. The place I used
to work is closed for the night. Whoever's singing the Utada
Hikaru cover at the open plaza karaoke is killing it. By the time
we reach the Seventh Street Metro Center station, I'm panting.
"We really had to walk all the way here?"

"DASH still doesn't run at night, and the buses, with wait
time, would've taken twice as long." Santi unzips his bag, pulls
out two TAP cards, and hands one to me. "When's the last time
you went to the beach?" Oh. *Oh,* I finally get where he's going
with this, and I follow him through the turnstile.

We wait in silence for our train to pull into the station. He
murmurs, "After you," as we board. I take a window seat, and
he sidles up next to me. We place our hands next to each other
on the seat, pinkies overlapping. It still doesn't always feel safe
to hold hands in public, and it's late.

Santi pulls out his phone and a pair of earbuds. "Sorry if it's
corny, but I made a playlist for the ride."

It's pretty good. I try to turn off the part of my brain that
constantly analyzes music as the train creaks, then emerges
aboveground. Parallel to Figueroa, where I once had to rescue
Mira after a Kehlani show at the Novo. West down Exposition
past Sayo's alma mater. Then the train takes flight, and we gaze
out over the shimmering lattice of artificial lights that link the

city together. Farther, farther out, and my eyelids flutter before closing shut.

When I wake up, it's to Santi shaking me by the shoulder. "Rise and shine, jagi." We're the only ones left in our car, and he presses his lips to my cheek.

He all but carries me outside, and I immediately shiver. I always forget how much colder the Westside is, and I'm thankful for both my sweatshirt and his arm around me.

Before long, the concrete and asphalt under our feet becomes slippery with sand, then gives way to it completely. Santi steers us away from the pier. We seek out the darkest, most solitary patch of shore and stare out at the waves.

"I'm gonna miss you." He lets the wind carry his words.

I stare at the line where the sky cedes to ocean. "I'm going to miss you, too."

Neither of us says anything for a few minutes. We just listen to the waves beat against the shore. Until Santi asks, "Suwa, when was the last time you actually hung out in Venice?"

"Maybe a couple of years ago. Why?"

Santi starts walking. I trail him. Our footfalls make no sound and leave no trace in the sand, every step quickly erased by the blustering wind.

Half an hour's passed before he turns toward land. We walk past the boardwalk and the storefronts, deeper into the neighborhood. Right when I'm about to ask him where we're headed, Santi takes a sharp turn, and we emerge into a street gallery of murals.

Most of them are of familiar subjects. Cute girls and grimacing men. Abstract patterns and natural mimicries. Except:

Two bodies back-to-back, hands entwined. Waterfalls spilling out of the hollows where their faces should be. All set against a chaotic backdrop, snippets of text and images stitched together into a brilliant patchwork. Even though I haven't seen these pieces in years, I know what they make up: the collage of all the offerings I brought Santi in high school. The version of Los Angeles only we knew.

Written along the bottom, a lyric from "Exit Music": *I dream beside you / My friend in the mirror*.

There's a tag in the corner: #TheMoonflowerSessions, and . . . *EMO OCEAN* written within a rainbow wave. Just like the logo for *Mugen Glider*.

I open my mouth. No words come out. But in that instant, I have an epiphany for a new song. About falling, and failing, and forgiveness, and fate. About releasing the past, and believing in the future.

It goes something like this:

Coda

"The worst thing about music is that other people get to hear it."

—Mitski / Stern Grove / July 14, 2019

There's no reason Suwa should be nervous. Still, he takes a deep breath as he moves through the maze of the library. It doesn't take long for the people around him to start doing obvious double-takes—"Is *that*," "No way," "Oh my god, wait, doesn't his best friend go here"—as he crosses the room and taps Santi on the shoulder. When Santi turns around from his seat, his jaw drops.

Suwa puts his finger up to his lips. He smiles in the reflection of Santi's glasses. "Mira let me in." They're both at the same school, though she's a first-year grad student while he's, as he'd put it over text to Suwa when he broke the news, *a freshman again*, studying art and education. Suwa told Mira his plan to surprise Santi a few days ago, and this afternoon, she'd picked Suwa up from the airport, crushing him in a long hug before driving them to her apartment.

They'd grabbed coffee, running through everything their friends have been up to over the past four years. Emo Ocean's just wrapped up their second headlining tour; their sophomore album, *The Sunshower Sessions*, catapulted them into a whole new level of exposure. Before they prepare to record their third record, Suwa's ordered his bandmates, and himself, to take a monthlong sabbatical.

Sayo's home, but she's heading to Lagos within the week. (As he chats with Mira, Suwa makes a note on his phone to lock down a time for the Moon siblings to visit their mother's grave.) Reva and Ari left for their belated honeymoon. Lucía's introducing her girlfriend, one of the Emo Ocean roadies, to her family. Feli's up north for his sister's graduation. Octavian's busy with med school. After catching each other up, they made a date to meet again over the weekend as Mira had texted Santi to track him down.

Suwa whispers, "You free to hang? I know you're in the middle of finals," but Santi's already packing up his books. They cut across the quad hand in hand; Suwa pulls his hat lower over his eyes, but he wouldn't be surprised if Santi was drawing attention on his own. He looks good in a college sweatshirt.

It's not until they're in a more secluded section of campus that Santi abruptly stops and turns. Suwa almost crashes into him as Santi slips his arms around Suwa's shoulders. "Welcome back, jagi."

Suwa leans into his hug. They take in the smell and feel of each other's bodies. Santi tugs the sleeve of Suwa's jacket. "I don't know if I ever told you, but this is actually Aya's."

Suwa pulls it tighter around his shoulders. "If she wants it back, she can ask for it."

Santi shakes his head. "I don't think anyone else can wear it as well as you can." He pauses before smirking and saying, "But out of all your outfits, the one from the maid café—hello." Someone on Reddit had discovered the first live performance of "Exit Music" and now everyone was running the video.

Suwa scowls and rolls his eyes. Santi's smirk disappears. "Sorry, sore spot?"

"Not really anymore. I'd honestly forgotten about the whole thing, but I suppose nothing ever truly disappears on the internet." Suwa purses his lips. "I still spent an entire therapy session talking about it. Mostly, I wish the sound quality was better. Since it's a part of music history now."

Santi shakes his head, laughing, then asks, "You hungry?"

A pause. "I could eat."

They take the bus to Sawtelle, where they polish off some tsukemen. At one point, Santi puts his phone on the table and Suwa sees the background: it's him, wearing a Sleeping Forest hoodie and holding a bouquet of flowers, grinning widely as he winks and throws a peace sign to the Seoul crowd at Rolling Hall. The tattoo on his arm, his first and only so far, stands out brilliantly because of the photographer's flash: an angel blowing a trumpet, its bell filled with a bouquet of bright orange blossoms.

Santi's clock is off. He goes, "Oh, gotta fix that," and looks at his watch, and that's when Suwa realizes that Santi's phone was set to the last time zone he was in. A warm, tender feeling flutters in his chest.

They leave Sawtelle and walk westward. Past the pool, past the skate park, eventually approaching an apartment building wrapped by a lush wisteria trellis. Suwa breaks the easy silence by asking, "Did you watch the finale?"

Santi nods. "Yeah. I'll always love the original, but," he says, smiling, "I like how they wrote Norio more. And the new ending is, at least to me, better."

All those Sleeping Forest scores caught the ear of the music supervisor for the *Mugen Glider* reboot, and she asked Suwa to contribute to the new soundtrack. He wrote and recorded most of the instrumentals on the road, but he spent a few days in Tokyo adapting some of his own songs for the show.

Unlike the original, the reboot ends more ambiguously. Marigold still crashes their glider and falls. The viewer still only catches a glimpse of their lover in the sky. But as Emo Ocean's cover of the original theme song kicks in, a thermal counteracts Marigold's descent, and their body levitates within the cloud line. The camera pans until it's right above Marigold, zooming and focusing on their face until they make an expression that's neither a smile nor a frown.

Instead, something like wonder.

"Also, the music this time around." Santi whistles. "So good." Suwa elbows him, and he laughs before slowing to a stop. "Well. Here it is."

They walk down a path to the back of the building, then go up a flight of narrow stairs. Once Santi opens the door, they're greeted by Clover, who rams her head into Suwa's leg and whines. An orange tabby cat, lanky in the way not-a-kitten, not-quite-an-adult cats are, mews angrily from his perch on the windowsill before hopping down to slink around Suwa's ankles.

"I know, it's been a while. Wow, Paprika's really grown." The humans switch their shoes out for slippers. Suwa continues, "I'm glad you two seem to be getting along."

Santi shifts from foot to foot, humming to cover up his impatience. When he holds his hand out, Suwa takes it and lets Santi lead him into the studio apartment. It looks like a typical "first time living alone" space, all furniture that can break apart and dishes piled on narrow counters and stacked in the sink.

Except for the art on the walls. A framed poster for Emo Ocean's first Los Angeles headlining tour stop from two summers ago. Random mementos of cities, venues really, from around the world, tacked and taped up. Above the easel draped with a color-splattered apron: a painting of overlapping Suwa portraits, long since finished and signed, in the corner of the canvas, with *EMO OCEAN* written in a rainbow wave.

Santi's been talking, something about a party a friend of his from volunteering is hosting in Frogtown. Suwa mumbles, "Sure, let's go."

Santi squeezes his hand. "Hey. Are you . . . How do you feel, about this?"

They both scan the room. There's an Ardneks print floating above a standing mirror. Clover's dog bed is next to a low bookshelf straining to contain volumes upon volumes of manga; Suwa's eyes linger on the copies of *Our Dreams at Dusk* Yuhki Kamatani had personally gifted him. There's another tall bookshelf filled with art books and records.

A photo on Santi's nightstand also catches Suwa's eye. From Mira's Halloween party last year, which she'd held at a karaoke bar. Suwa's normally banned from singing because that's his "actual job," but she'd made an exception that night, and he'd killed the club with a string of increasingly rowdy covers. In the photo, he's holding the microphone, one hand cupping a blushing Santi's face.

A week later, Emo Ocean had left again to do a mini tour in southeast Asia—Suwa had had to fight the label, hard, for the opportunity. Cola Carter helped him make his case by playing the "his Asian heritage endears him to a hyperpassionate fan base in the region" card. The night of Santi's birthday, Emo

Ocean played a club in Jakarta and got the audience to sing for him. Ari reported, via Reva, that Santi started sobbing when he watched the footage.

Another photo. Their entire friend group, wearing their band varsity jackets, snapped at an alumni banquet by Sayo, whose blurry finger made it into the frame. Standing behind them, Cap and Aya—wearing her Sunshowers marching band director blazer—beam. It'll be another year, at least, before they can all be together again. Santi catches Suwa staring at the picture, and gives his hand another squeeze before letting it go.

There'll be more of those moments. Missing moments. The years will pass; the people they love will move in and out of their lives, and they'll dip in and out of their own life together. But they're here now. Jacarandas shading the sidewalks and nights that barely seem to slip into dawns. Sun days, everybody already on summer time, though it hasn't hit the solstice yet.

As they walk back through the apartment, Suwa pauses in the golden light streaming through the plants that have taken over the sitting area. They'd been gifted by their previous owner. Leaves and flowers cut their silhouettes into the sunbeam that illuminates the mural Santi's painted on the living room wall: a trompe l'oeil field of rolling clouds.

Suwa takes out his phone and snaps a photo to post. His caption for the shot is *mugen*. Depending on what kanji you use, it can mean "infinite," or it can mean "dream."

When they go back outside, the ceiling of the city's been painted through with deep indigo, though the horizon burns with a lemon glow. Santi stops at the foot of the building's stairs. He closes his eyes and takes a deep breath, letting it out as a long sigh. "Another summer. This is our season. Not that the other ones aren't good, with you." His voice is wistful when he says, "Anything's good, with you."

Suwa nudges Santi with his shoulder. "So sentimental." He tilts his head toward the sky, but it's so bright he squints. "And, it's not . . ."

"Not what?"

Suwa shrugs and blows his bangs out of his eyes. "It's technically not summer yet. But it always feels like it."

"Like here? Or in eternity."

Suwa studies Santi for a beat. Then he murmurs, "You know what I mean."

Santi laughs and folds a piece of Suwa's bangs back into place. A breeze ripples down the street, and the jacarandas shudder before dropping some of their brilliant flowers. Obscured behind the floral flurry, their faces tilt together.

And suddenly, summer begins.

Acknowledgments

Thank you, thank you, thank you, to—
(imagine each entry as a kiss on the cheek)

[FROM THE HEAD:]
- The good people at Flatiron who devoted time, energy, and thought to the care and keeping of this book, but with particular gratitude, Andrea and Sydney
- The editors and writers who've inspired and challenged me throughout my "media" "career," but especially Susan, Eva, Nicole, Jenn, Gina, Tasbeeh, Rawiya, and Jenny
- The line cooks, boba slingers, photographers, janitorial staff, summer camp teachers, cool teen girl cashiers, animal caretakers, call center translators, delivery drivers, security guards, and worker bees who've looked after and out for me "on the job"
- The wildly talented artists I've interviewed over the years, including Japanese Breakfast, Caroline Polachek, Rina Sawayama, MUNA, and Mitski
    - and singularly: Speedy Ortiz/Sad13/Sadie, who both instigated this whole publishing odyssey and introduced me to the tarot, whose Major Arcana makes up the spine of this book

- Everyone who kept me from figuratively and literally stepping in the hole during my three years in the [redacted] Marching Band
- R & P, the two grad student editors at my college writing job, for turning the entirety of the outlet's Los Angeles live music coverage to a freshman without a car
- The music instructors, band directors, and English teachers who helped keep the flame alive

[FROM THE HEART:]

- Anyone with whom I've ever broken bread, cooked, gone to a show, gossiped, watched anime, yelled about anime, cried, discussed literature/theory/fan fic, ran down an empty street at midnight, watched stars, taken shots, crashed a party, and performed
- Sarah, for taking my fluttering heart into her hands, understanding my mission from the get-go, and coaxing me out of the nest and into the air (Big Bird couldn't have asked for a better editor, truly)
- Dana, an agent of/from God, for instantly realizing what that first draft *could* be and teaching me how to teach myself how to write a book (I meant it when I said that this is the most loving working relationship I've ever had)
- April, for being *thee* blueprint and bringing me into your orbit, which has launched me into so many others (you're my ult)
- Emery, my senpai (sorry), for keeping me sane at w*rk and bearing witness as I wrote [redacted] number of drafts in our windowless room (let's go fill Moomin Valley with crime)
- Sulagna, for holding my hand into and throughout adulthood with openness and generosity (and introducing me to the head/heart/guts split, which has clearly! left! a deep! impression!)
- Amar, for being such an enabler and down for everything in a way

that's made me bolder, and always offering the right different perspective to make the world seem bigger (Daniel x Daniel)

- Aly, my lady of YA horror, for waking me up to the world of book writing and gleefully teaching me how to navigate it (let's X the "internet" from our internet friendship soon, please)
- *American Boyfriend* by Kevin Abstract, *Puberty 2* by Mitski, *Twin Fantasy* by Car Seat Headrest, *FLCL Original Soundtrack, Vol. 1: Addict* by the pillows, and *Blond/e* by Frank Ocean
- Anyone who's ever made a playlist for me, or gotten one made by me

[FROM THE GUT:]

- My best friends in the world, for making Los Angeles my favorite place to be and entwining me in your lives as we've grown up together like new shoots in a forest; how close the sky looks from the canopy, now :^)
- Terry and Gerard, for making it easy to come home
- Cam, Vicky, and Richard, for inviting me into your family and trusting me with your hearts and his
- Steff, for being my berry best neighbor forever and my second lil' sis through the years (and, uh, introducing me to anime) (dattebayo)
- Diane, my froggy friend :} the Smile to my Peco and the strangest/sickest artist I know, for "merrily" joining me in the "hole" since eighth grade geometry and being my favorite person to unwind and unpack thoughts about art, life, and dreams with
- Mimi, my original angel, for being the first person to believe in me and the best person I know; I love you, 妹妹, and will say it more often
- My parents, for giving me my big imagination, my love of music,

and a tenacity that's brought me somewhere miraculous; one day, I'll find the language to tell you all about it, and you might be proud

- & Colin, to whom I turn like a leaf reaching toward the light; the best moment of every day is when you wrap your arms around me and I get to eavesdrop on your big, beautiful, blushing melon heart. I love our world, our creature comforts, and you. All we want is four walls and adobe slats for our girls.

P.S. To you, reading—here's the rest of what Mitski had to say at Stern Grove:

> "Thanks for letting me do my favorite, favorite, favorite thing. Thank you for connecting. Thank you for saving my life. Thank you so much."

P.P.S. liomin.com/BEATINGHEARTBEATS

About the Author

Lio Min has listened to, played and performed, and written about music for most of their life. Their debut novel, *Beating Heart Baby*, is about boys, bands, and Los Angeles. They've profiled and interviewed acts including Japanese Breakfast, Rina Sawayama, MUNA, Caroline Polachek, Christine and the Queens, Raveena, Tei Shi, Speedy Ortiz, and Mitski.